M000295767

ALL I EVER WANTED

OF LOVE AND MADNESS, BOOK THREE

KAREN CIMMS

LONE SPARROW PRESS

All I Ever Wanted
© 2017 by Karen Cimms

Cover Designer: Garrett Cimms
Cover Photographer: Garrett Cimms
Cover Model: Olka Cimms
Interior Designer: The Write Assistants
Line editing: Lisa Poisso

ISBN: 978-0-9974867-4-2

FOREWORD

All I Ever Wanted is the third book in the *Of Love and Madness Series.* It is not a standalone and it is strongly recommended that you read *At This Moment* and *We All Fall Down* before reading this book to fully understand and appreciate these characters.

This series is not a typical romance, but it is a love story. It is at times dark, and it can be gritty. I hope you'll trust me to see you through to the end.

To the victims and the survivors and those who love them.

She fought·on
Because fighting meant
She hadn't yet lost.
— n.a. denmon

CHAPTER ONE

NOVEMBER 30, 2012

The green ironwork bridge rose up before them, the only real color on this steel-gray day. It had been years since that bridge had carried Kate Donaldson over the Piscataqua River into Maine on her yearly summer vacations, but it looked exactly the same as it had then. A tiny shiver ran through her. Excitement? Perhaps. Or maybe it was fear.

She was a 42-year-old woman running away from home.

Tom's Lexus rumbled over the bridge. Her attorney and friend—her only friend—seemed unaware she had woken, which was fine. He'd probably try to engage her in conversation, and she wasn't up for that. She'd left her life, her children, her husband, everything but Charlie, her dog. It was time to make a new start. To heal. To somehow come to terms with the past six months, learn how to move forward and forge a new life for herself.

This sudden move, this disappearing act, was rash, but having almost taken her own life, she needed to take control of it now. As crazy as it seemed, especially just a day after being released from the hospital, it made her feel determined, empowered. It was as if she'd completed the outline of a difficult jigsaw puzzle without the picture on the box to guide her. Fitting in the rest of the pieces wouldn't be any easier, but if she wanted to put herself back together after the worst year of her life, she didn't have a choice.

The question was, would she still recognize herself once the puzzle was complete?

"Hey, sleepyhead. You finally awake?"

"Yeah. How much longer?" The muscles in her ass were cramped and she needed to stretch, but she didn't want to ask him to stop. She didn't want to be more of a burden than she'd already become.

"Less than an hour, but I have to stop for gas. There's a service plaza a few miles ahead. Hungry?"

At the power of his suggestion, her stomach grumbled noisily. "I guess I am." Must be the meds. She couldn't remember the last time she'd felt hunger.

"There's a Burger King if you're desperate, or we can get to the house, unload, and then head to Yarmouth or Freeport. Do you like lobster?"

She made a face.

"You love Maine but not lobster?" He seemed genuinely surprised.

"Yes to Maine, no to lobster." Thoughts of Joey filled her head. Her best friend, Tom's secret love, tragically gone from them both. "Joey loved Maine just as much as I do."

"He did. That's why he bought the house for you." Despite the pain in his eyes, he smirked. "But unlike you, he loved lobster."

"Not when we were kids." The overwhelming sadness she already carried grew heavier at the memory of all those summers in Maine when her parents had allowed her to bring her dearest friend. Now that Joey was dead, memories were all she had. Memories and a house he had bought her, but had never told her about. And then there was the corporation he'd left her as well.

That she refused to think about. Thanks to Tom, at least for now, she didn't have to.

She leaned against the headrest and stared out the window as they sped past tall evergreens and a tidal creek until she could trust her voice not to crack.

"My parents would buy lobsters a couple of times a week for themselves and a package of red snappers for me and Joey. I guess he eventually developed a taste for the real thing. Not me."

"Are snappers those bright red hot dogs?" Tom asked. "I can't bring myself to eat a hot dog that color, but I love lobster. It was the only thing Joey ever cooked. Whenever we could get away together, I did all the cooking. But when we came up here, he'd buy a few lobsters and cook them himself."

Sadness tinged his voice. Joey's death five months earlier had gutted him, but since his and Joey's relationship had been a secret—even Kate hadn't known until the night Joey died—he hadn't even been able to grieve properly.

"But he still loved those red hot dogs." He smiled, but she could see it took some effort.

They pulled into a service plaza near Kennebunkport. While Tom filled up the Lexus and dashed into the service plaza in search of food, Kate took Charlie for a walk.

"You're a good boy," she said, giving him a scratch behind his ear after he'd marked several tree trunks and the leg of a picnic table. She sat on a bench waiting for Tom as dusk settled in around her, Charlie's head resting on her knee.

"I just hope you aren't disappointed that I'm dragging you away from your home, but I can't do this by myself. I'm going to need someone to talk to, to help me feel safe. Like it or not buddy, you're it."

IT WAS dark by the time they got to Cumberland. There was little Kate could make out other than lights from the houses they passed. Now and then she'd catch a glimpse of an evergreen wreath hanging on a door or Christmas lights twinkling in a window. The weight in her chest grew heavier.

Tom turned off the main road onto a narrow street lined with large homes of various styles. At the end of the street, he banked into a short driveway. A motion sensor light flickered on, displaying a charming, cedar-shingled cottage. A window box hung in front of a double window.

Kate stepped from the car, and before she could stop him, Charlie bounded over the seat, ran to a large tree at the edge of the driveway, and promptly lifted his leg. When he had finished sniffing the trees and the bushes, he ran several laps around the car. Too bad she didn't find the prospect of their arrival as exciting.

The air, which held only the promise of a chill earlier, had grown colder. She shivered and filled her lungs.

"I smell the ocean."

"You should. It's right there." Tom pointed to the right, where the nearly full moon threw a path across the water. "It looks even better in the daylight." They each grabbed a suitcase, and she followed him up a brick walk to the front of the house. He unlocked the door, and Charlie bolted in ahead of them. He skidded along the hardwood floor and slid into a small table. A vase teetered dangerously but managed to right itself before it could crash onto the floor.

"Charlie!" Grudgingly, he returned to her side, head down. He wasn't used to her scolding him, and even when she did, he usually ignored her.

She grabbed his collar. "I'm sorry."

"No need to apologize," Tom said. "This is your house."

It was her house, but the circumstances were difficult to digest. She pressed her lips together and nodded, pushing away the weight of sadness and grief that she carried everywhere with her these days.

Tom set down her suitcase and slipped his arm around her shoulder. "I know it's a lot for you to take in, but Joey bought it for you. He loved it here as much as you did, and his memories of the two of you growing up were his fondest. He also wanted you to have a place you could call your own. Here it is." He waved his hand like Vanna White introducing a new puzzle board. "Let me show you around."

He began the tour with the garage, leading her through the laundry room, which included a state-of-the-art washer and dryer and a large pantry.

In the garage was an older model Saab convertible. "The keys are in the kitchen drawer. The car's in excellent condition, but I'll take it to a garage tomorrow and have it looked over. We'll get snow tires put on as well."

She thought of her own red Saab, which had been riddled with bullets back in August when an irate landowner had burst into a township meeting she was covering for the newspaper and killed seven people, including her dear friend Eileen, before he was shot and killed by one of the officers responding to the scene. At some point during his rampage, while she'd been hiding in a bathroom stall, Sedge Stevens had also turned the gun on her car, a sign that she had been one of his targets.

Icy fingers ran down her spine. She pressed her fingers against the wall, steadying herself, as she swallowed back the dizzying sense of panic that gripped her whenever she thought about that night. "I don't plan on doing much driving."

"You can't sit here and shut out the world, Kate. You promised to see the psychiatrist. That's non-negotiable. We'll also go pick up a new cell phone for you, and you'll check in with me every day. Understand?"

"Tom, I'm perfectly capab—"

He raised his hand. "Stop right there. This is how it's going to work. You check in with me every day and see the psychiatrist every week, or I tell Billy where you are."

"Tom!" She wasn't a child to be scolded or threatened.

"I told you, the only way I'm going along with this is if you give your recovery a hundred percent. Do I have your word, or do I have to drag you and your suitcases back to the car?"

"Fine." She shrugged. "You're right. I promised you, and I promised Joey."

His jaw tightened at the mention of the dream in which she'd promised Joey she would seek help. Tom could believe it or not; it made no difference to her. That vision—or dream, as he called it— was what had convinced her not to take her own life.

He assessed her expression carefully, and when he seemed satisfied, he continued the tour, although with much less forced enthusiasm.

In the kitchen, she ran her hands along the cool granite countertops. The appliances were stainless steel, and the stove was a professional-grade model with five burners. Not that she would be doing much cooking or entertaining. She would have loved this kitchen at home.

This is home, Kate. Right.

Beyond the breakfast bar was the dining room, with a large wooden table that would have been perfect for hosting holiday dinners. Running the length of the dining room and adjacent living room, was an entire wall of windows, including patio doors that led to a deck. Tom flipped on the outdoor lights, and she could see that they were actually on the second floor, due to the slope of the property. There was an in-ground pool, and beyond that, a garden in hibernation.

"I always wanted a pool," she murmured.

"Now you have one."

In the living room, two large white couches formed an L, with one facing a white brick fireplace. Atop the mantel were dozens of books and two elaborately framed oil paintings. On the wall opposite the windows were two massive bookcases.

"I can't get over all these books." Her fingers traced the colorful spines.

"Joey insisted the house be filled with bookshelves and books. He said you love to read."

If hearing his name didn't hurt so much, she might have laughed.

"How ironic. Joey wouldn't have picked up a book unless it was in his way."

"True, but this is what he wanted for you."

Two large rattan chairs and a rattan coffee table snuggled in the corner, facing the wall of windows. On the table were a pair of binoculars and a field guide to northeastern birds. She picked up the book and thumbed through several pages.

"There are bird feeders on the deck right outside the window. You can put food in them if you wish, and the birds will come to you." He was beginning to sound like a Realtor desperate to make a sale.

"It's wonderful, really." She put the book back where she'd found it, feeling very much as if she were in some stranger's home. "I just don't understand why he never told me. It doesn't make sense."

"He would have, eventually. He only bought it two years ago. There were renovations to be completed, landscaping, decorating. Plus I don't think he expected you to be too receptive to the idea that he bought this place for you. He was certain you would've tried to talk him out of it, if not downright refuse to accept it. He was going to tell you he bought it and have you visit a few times. And when you fell in love with it, as he was sure you would, he would've told you then. Look around, Kate. This place was designed for you. The books, the gourmet kitchen, the garden—it's all you."

A fat tear rolled down her cheek, and she wiped it away. If Tom noticed, he pretended not to.

"C'mon." He slipped an arm around her shoulders. "We aren't even halfway finished."

"You're kidding! I could be happy right here for the rest of my life." She gave him the illusion of a smile, but it was a lie. She didn't believe she'd ever be happy again.

Tom led her down the hallway. The first door on the right led to a guest room with its own bathroom. It was cozy and decorated like the rest of the house, in a casual, Frank-Lloyd-Wright-meets-Pottery-Barn kind of way. Comfy quilts with matching pillow shams covered the bed.

The windows here, like the others she'd seen, were uncovered.

"How come there aren't any curtains?" The sight of her reflection staring back at her made her feel exposed and vulnerable.

"You don't need them. You'll see. There isn't any traffic passing the house the way it's situated. But it's your house. If you want curtains, that's up to you."

At the end of the hall was a large bathroom, a small dressing room, another guest room, and the master bedroom. The second guest room was larger than the first, although it didn't have a bathroom. But it faced the driveway and would allow her to see anyone coming to the front door. This would be her room.

When he opened the door to the master bedroom, she was even more certain of that. What she'd seen so far reflected her tastes, but the master bedroom was all Joey. It was sleek and modern, in cool tones of gray and plum. A king-sized bed with a black lacquered headboard was situated on the far wall, and over the bed was a stunning composite of black-and-white photographs in matching silver frames. The photos were close-ups of a man's body.

"That's you, isn't it?"

Tom gave her a weak smile.

"They're beautiful." She slipped her arm around his waist.

"I still can't believe he's gone." His voice broke on the last word, and he clamped a hand over his eyes as she guided him to the side of the bed. She rocked him gently, swallowing her own tears and the guilt she felt for allowing him to tend her needs when his own went unmet.

"I'm sorry," he said after he pulled himself together.

"Don't be. Tommy, I haven't been much help to you these past few months, but please don't ever feel bad being yourself or showing your feelings around me. Please. Comforting you is the very least I can do."

He gave her a quick peck on the top of her head, and wiped his eyes. "C'mon." He pulled her to her feet. "There's a lot more house to see."

He wasn't kidding.

The upstairs had been all blond hardwoods, but the downstairs was carpeted in oatmeal Berber. There was a home office, a large family room with another fireplace, comfortable leather sofas, and an enormous television. The back of the house featured another wall of windows looking out onto the pool and patio. Off the family room was another guest room, a small kitchen, another bathroom, and a large, empty storage area.

"What's this for?"

Tom pressed his hand to the back of his neck. "It could be a gym."

Yes, she could see that, although there had been an elliptical exerciser in the dressing room upstairs.

He stepped inside the room. "This was left empty for a reason. The walls aren't finished, but they've been soundproofed."

A giggle slipped out. "Tommy! Really? What were you guys planning to do down here?"

A flush of pink crept up his cheeks. "Nothing like that. Remember, this house wasn't about me and Joey. It was bought and remodeled for you."

"What in the world would I need a soundproof room for?" No sooner had she asked the question, she had her answer: Billy

"Joey thought he could create a studio—practice, record, whatever. He left it for Billy to finish himself."

The whole idea unnerved her. This room brought Billy into this new space where she'd gone to hide. She backed away abruptly.

"Could you lock that up? Throw away the key, for all I care."

She stalked down the hall and across the family room, opened the patio doors, and stepped outside. Shivering, she stood at the foot of the dormant garden, her eyes focused on a halo of light in the distance. No matter how far she ran, would Billy always hold her heart in his hands, even if he no longer wanted it?

Tom came up behind her. He stood in silence. Could he feel her grieving?

"The narrow band of light beyond that island on the horizon is the city of Portland," he said finally. "You can't really see much more than the glow of lights at night, and only if it's clear, but there it is."

"It's like another world, isn't it? I feel like I've traveled a million miles since yesterday."

"It's like stepping into another lifetime."

She nodded. "I have one foot in my past and another in my future. I just have to come to terms with all that stuff in the middle."

"That's one way to look at it, but I don't recommend doing that on an empty stomach. And I don't care what you say, I hear yours rumbling."

The thought of going to a restaurant was uncomfortable. He must have sensed her hesitation, because he put his arm around her shoulder and led her back toward the house.

"Go get changed. I'm going to take you to my favorite place. It's quiet and peaceful—you might even say romantic. No one will bother us. I promise you'll like it."

"Tommy, I can't—"

"Sure you can. Besides, I drove." He winked. "You can pay."

CHAPTER TWO

The first few days were damp and dreary. Not cold enough for snow, but cold enough for a chill to settle deep in her very core. Kate woke early the morning after Tom left. Gray light filtered through the barren branches outside her window. Pale strands of pink stained the horizon.

She dressed quickly. Together, she and Charlie descended the steep hill down to the water. She shoved her hands into the pockets of her lined jacket and stood at the edge of the steps that led to the dock. Her breath floated in tiny clouds about her face, mimicking the mist atop the water. A cormorant skittered across the glassy surface, then lifted out of the water with a great disturbance of air and headed toward the open sea. The expanse of ocean that lay before her was deserted. Empty docks lined the cove. The boats harbored there had long been removed for the winter.

A forest of dense pine ringed the inlet. At high tide, the water seemed more like a lake than a finger of the Atlantic. The rising sun illuminated a thin band of white clouds hovering above the tree line, still black against the fading darkness. Shades of orange, from palest apricot to deepest tangerine, streaked the horizon until Kate was finally forced to shield her eyes as the sun burst above the trees in a neon ball of butterscotch, blinding in its brilliance.

The imprint of the fireball was seared upon her closed lids, and despite the cold, she felt the memory of its warmth upon her face. Her senses awakened. Her lungs held the tang of the salty ocean and marshy shoreline. She heard the haunting cry of sea birds springing to life as darkness surrendered to day.

It took her by surprise, but there it was—a fleeting hint of promise. No more than a flutter, really. Her heart was heavy, and it was nearly impossible to see beyond the sadness, but somewhere deep inside, an errant ray of light squeezed its way through a tiny crack and called her name. It was gone in a blink, but she recognized it all the same: hope.

It was time to move forward. She pulled her old cell phone from her pocket and turned it on. Forty missed calls and messages—almost all of them from Billy. She hadn't listened to or read any of them. The pain was still too raw. She shouldn't look at the pictures, either, but she couldn't stop herself.

Determined to ignore pictures of Billy, she doted over pictures of her children and her grandchildren, but she couldn't stay away from his face. The last image was from May. She was smiling at the camera, and Billy was smiling at her. She'd meant to have it printed for her desk at work, but life had fallen apart not long after it was taken, and she had forgotten about it.

She ran her finger over his face and felt her heart break a little more. She shoved the phone back into her pocket. Careful of her footing on the slick, frost-covered boards, she picked her way to the end of the dock, sending gentle ripples into the cove.

When she reached the end, she pulled out her phone. She closed her eyes and gripped it tightly in her hands and said a silent goodbye to the memories it held. Then she opened her eyes, pulled back, and hurled the phone as hard as she could. It traveled less than twenty feet before dropping into the frigid water with a soft plop. A lifeline to her past, it bobbed to the surface, spun once, and then disappeared into the murky stillness.

CHAPTER THREE

K ate avoided going anywhere for nearly two weeks. The
psychiatrist had a sudden emergency and canceled their
appointment, and Tom had left the pantry and refrigerator so well-
stocked she hadn't needed to venture out once.

But the cupboard was looking pretty bare, and the economy-sized
bag of dog food was almost empty.

The thought of just one trip was scary, so she might as well do
everything at once. She hadn't been prepared for a Maine winter on
the coast. Walks with Charlie had become downright painful as she
struggled to withstand the wind whipping off the cove. She needed
mittens, a scarf, and a hat. A heavy-duty parka and warmer boots and
socks wouldn't hurt, either. She could have shopped online using the
debit card Tom had secured for her, but she'd lost so much weight she
had no idea what size she was anymore. She wasn't up for the hassle
of returning things if they didn't fit. It would be easier to combine a
trip to L.L. Bean in Freeport with a visit to the grocery store in
Yarmouth. And to reward Charlie for being the perfect companion
and protector, if Bean's had any dog sweaters, she'd buy him one
while she was at it.

As if he knew she was thinking about him, Charlie thumped his tail against her leg as he lay curled at her feet. He'd not only been her sole companion, he was the only living creature she conversed with beyond her daily calls from Tom. She didn't even have a plant to talk to. She added "plant" to the two-page list she'd been working on for the better part of the afternoon.

It was Saturday. She waited until almost eight, then loaded Charlie into the back of the Saab. He panted in her ear as she backed out of the garage. After she scolded him for trying to lick the side of her face, he settled himself onto the narrow back seat for the remainder of the short ride.

The streets of Freeport were lined with shoppers, and painful reminders of the season were everywhere. Christmas had been her favorite holiday, and she had successfully put it out of her mind. But the giant tree in the square outside Bean's and the decorations all through town were another kick in the stomach.

The store was more crowded than she'd expected at that hour. She tugged off her scarf and jammed it into her pocket. It was too hot and there were too many people. Instead of trying on things like she'd planned, she raced through the store grabbing sweaters and flannel pajamas a size smaller than she normally wore, then suffered through a long line in order to pay for her purchases. If she had to wait one more second before stepping out into the frosty night air, she would have passed out.

If she wasn't so low on supplies, she would have driven straight home.

At the grocery store, she loaded her cart with several days' worth of fruit and enough fresh vegetables to make several batches of soups and stews to freeze. She picked up bags of flour and sugar and a supply of canned goods and loaded up on paper products, cleaning supplies, and dog food. She tossed in a couple of rawhide bones, although Charlie deserved a T-bone steak at this point.

It was almost eleven when she pushed her cart to the front of Hannaford's. One cashier was checking customers while the other closed out her register. There were two people ahead of her, both with full baskets. She reached up on her toes, trying to see into the parking lot. Charlie had been alone in the car for over a half hour. It wasn't bitterly cold, but he wasn't used to being outside this long.

The line moved forward, and her eye fell on a lone copy of *The Boston Globe* on a rack near the register. In all caps, the bold two-deck head proclaimed the unthinkable. Beneath it, a picture of a woman shepherding at least a dozen children stretched across six columns.

Kate's hands shook as she reached for the newspaper to read the caption.

"Police told children to close their eyes so they would not see blood and broken glass as they were led from the Sandy Hook Elementary School after a gunman opened fire Friday."

The sudden weight on her chest expanded, cutting off most of her airway. She was thrown back to a voice she had tried not to think of for the last several months: *Mrs. Donaldson. I'm going to ask you to close your eyes and just trust me.*

Had these children done as they were told? She hadn't. The horrific images burned into her brain snapped to life.

"Awful, isn't it?"

She startled. A tall man with a long gray ponytail and a beard stood behind her. The floor beneath her feet turned rubbery, and she grabbed the handle of the cart to steady herself. The paper fell to the floor.

The man moved toward her. She stepped back.

He bent to pick up the newspaper, which had opened as it fell, the pages scattered across the floor. "Are you all right?" he asked.

She grabbed her purse from the cart and started to back away as the line moved forward.

"Ma'am?" the cashier called.

There was no air anywhere. She had to find the exit.

"Ma'am!"

The first door she came to wouldn't open. She pounded her fists against it, but it did no good. She backed up, and this time, it swung open automatically. She ran until she was safely inside her car.

At home, with the door locked and bolted and her legs no longer able to hold her, she collapsed onto the floor and cried for a world she wanted no part of.

CHAPTER FOUR

K ate didn't leave the house for three days, not even to take Charlie out. Instead, she let him loose in the fenced-in pool area and watched as he trotted to the end of the stone pavers and into the overgrown garden to do his business.

On the fourth and fifth days, it snowed.

She disconnected the lines for the television and computer. The world was dangerous and frightening. The less she knew, the better. Completely cutting herself off from the world, however, wasn't an option. She needed food and other supplies, especially for Charlie. But still, she couldn't bring herself to go out.

From her dining room window, Kate watched a young man visit the home across from her. He came several times a week. He would stop at the bottom of the driveway and collect the mail, then carry several bags and boxes into the house. He would stay for about a half hour, then leave. Once she watched him guide an older woman into his car, and the two of them drove away. A few hours later they returned, and just as carefully, he led her back inside.

On the sixth day, she sat near the window, thumbing absentmind-edly through the pages of an old Danielle Steele novel, when she saw him pull up. Spurred by a gnawing hunger in her belly and fear that she would soon have nothing to feed Charlie, she grabbed her coat from a peg in the mudroom and pulled on her boots, then returned to her seat by the window. After about twenty minutes, she tugged a knit cap firmly over her shorn head and hooked the leash onto Charlie's collar.

She stepped outside and shivered. It was cold, but far more unsettling was the feeling of being exposed after locking herself away for days. But she had no choice. It was either this, or go to the store herself, and one stranger seemed a far lesser evil than a store full of them.

The thick snow cover amplified the sound of voices coming from her neighbor's home. Kate waited at the edge of her driveway, and as the young man backed onto the street, she flagged him down.

Surprise marked his face as he rolled down his window. "Where'd you come from?"

"Over there." She pointed. Her smile felt stiff and unnatural. "I moved in a couple of weeks ago. I have a favor to ask. I need someone to do some errands for me. I can't do them myself. I see you come here several times a week, and I was hoping maybe you—or if you know someone trustworthy—might be able to help me."

He was young, maybe Devin's age. He wore his long, dark hair in dreads. A bullnose ring protruded from his nostrils. A tattoo of a shooting star was barely visible above his scarf, inked below his pierced ear.

"I don't know." He eyed her curiously. "I just pick up some groceries for my grandmother." He motioned toward the large contemporary house at the top of the driveway. "She had a stroke last summer, so I do some of her shopping and check in on her a couple of times a week. I don't have a lot of extra time . . ."

"I'll pay you. And it won't even be that often. I have a list." She pulled out the crumpled paper, still in her pocket from the previous week. "It's a lot of stuff, I understand, but I won't need anything else for a couple of weeks, maybe longer. I just can't do it myself." Desperation choked her last few words.

He narrowed his eyes. "You look like you can do your own grocery shopping."

"I can't though. Not right now. I'm . . . I'm not well." She had to convince him. "I'll give you a hundred dollars to shop for me. Plus a tank of gas." She pulled several hundred-dollar bills, wadded up in a ball, from her pocket. "I have money. See?"

He looked at her as if she were crazy, which was the way most people had come to look at her, and reached for the money. Was he agreeing or just trying to keep it from falling onto the driveway? Since he'd touched it, she wanted to shout, "No backsies," which would only confirm that she had a loose grip on her sanity.

"I guess I could use the money. Grandma just gives me five bucks." He snorted. "Okay. When do you need this stuff?"

"I'm out of dog food and toilet paper. I don't care about me so much, but the dog—"

His eyes crinkled when he laughed. "Yeah, and toilet paper. I hear you. Look, I have a class in about an hour. I can go after that. I'll be back around six. How's that?"

She was so relieved she almost wept. "That would be perfect. Thank you."

He scanned the list. "A plant? What kind?"

"Huh?" *The plant, remember? To talk to.*

"Never mind. I was just—it's not important."

RIGHT AT SIX, Kate opened the door to find the young man standing on her porch with a Christmas cactus in full bloom. She brought it into the kitchen while he returned to his car and began carrying her groceries inside.

When he finished, he handed her a receipt and her change.

"I'm Shane, by the way." He smiled and stuck out his hand.

"Kate," she answered, recalling too late that she hadn't wanted to use her real name. He was wearing fingerless gray knit gloves, and when she accepted his hand, the contrast between the warmth of the wool and his icy fingers was startling. It was a sharp reminder that she hadn't touched another person in almost three weeks.

"Nice to meet you, Kate."

She pulled one of the hundred-dollar bills from the handful of money he had handed back to her and held it out to him. "Thank you."

"I feel guilty taking this. Not that I can't use it, but a hundred dollars is a lot of money just to go grocery shopping. It didn't even take me two hours, and fifty dollars an hour is highway robbery."

That was true, but it was worth it. She would have given him two hundred dollars if he wanted. She pushed the bill into his hand. "Please. I insist."

He shrugged and stuffed the money into his coat pocket. "Do you want me to help you put all of this away?"

"No, that's fine, but thank you."

"I don't mind, really. I mean, if you're sick or something, it's no big deal. If you want to sit, you can just tell me where things go."

"I'm sorry?"

He pointed to the knit cap she'd tugged on before answering the door. "My mom had breast cancer, so . . ." He gave her a knowing smile.

Her hand flew to her head. "Oh. No, I'm not sick." *That's a lie, Kate, and you know it.* "Not like that. But thank you. I'm sorry about your mother."

He didn't look like he believed her but assured her that his mother was fine now.

"Are you handy, Shane?"

"Kinda."

"I need some work done around here. I want dead bolts on all the doors, and I need more motion detectors outside too. Can you do that?"

"Yeah, I guess." He drew out the words. "This is a real safe neighborhood, if you're worried."

"I know. It would just make me feel better."

He tugged off his gloves. "Okay then. Tell me what you want, and I'll pick up the stuff. I probably can't get to it until Monday, though—oh, wait. Monday's Christmas Eve. That probably won't work for you."

Christmas Eve. It might have hurt less if he'd just punched her in the stomach. She took a second to steady herself.

"That's fine. I'll be here."

She led him through the house, pointing out the doors that were to get extra dead bolts. He gave her a curious look when she explained she also wanted one on her bedroom door, but he wrote everything down on the back of her grocery list.

"Are you okay?"

"Excuse me?"

"It's just—all these locks. Are you afraid of something? I mean, if you're so scared of a break-in, maybe you should just get a gun."

She shook her head vehemently. "I don't want a gun in my house."

"Hey." He lifted his hand to touch her but pulled back when she flinched. "Hey, I'm sorry. I don't like them either. It's cool. I didn't mean to upset you."

She shook her head again, almost dizzy at the mere mention of a gun.

"You're right. Let's get these dead bolts up." He followed her into the foyer. "You know, I can probably get this stuff at the hardware store in the morning and do the work tomorrow, if that's okay."

Relief washed over her like a warm hug. "Tomorrow's good. Tomorrow would be very good."

Shane stepped out onto the porch she'd shoveled just before he'd returned from the store. He smiled hesitantly.

"By the way, the plant was from me. I hope you feel better. Or whatever."

SHANE WAS BACK the next morning with his father. They worked for several hours, securing all the doors and setting up motion detectors outside, one on every corner of the house and on the barn.

When they had finished, she practically had to force him to take the two hundred dollars she offered. "If I called someone out of the phone book, I would've paid at least twice that, so please take it. I'll feel bad if you don't."

He agreed, reluctantly, then dug around in his pocket and pulled out a scrap of paper with his home number and his cell number. "Just call if you need anything or when you want me to go to the store again."

"Thank you." She plucked a magnet in the shape of a lobster off the side of the refrigerator and secured the slip of paper beneath it.

"You know, Tuesday's Christmas. I have to pick up my grand-mother anyway, so if you aren't doing anything, you're welcome to join us. My mom said it won't be any trouble or anything."

"Thank you," she said. "That's very kind, but I can't. Please thank your mother, but I won't be celebrating the holiday."

"Oh, sorry. So you're Jewish?"

"Something like that."

CHAPTER FIVE

S now fell Christmas Eve, but by morning, the air was clear and crisp. Sunlight glittered on the newly fallen crust as if great handfuls of mica had been scattered in every direction. Kate stood on the porch, wrapped in the silence. It was so quiet she could almost believe that the rest of the world was too busy making merry to pose a threat. The air was cold but intoxicating. She filled her lungs, shaking off the cobwebs of the past several weeks.

Charlie ran circles about the yard, glad to be outdoors and not tethered to a leash, while she shoveled the front steps and the short brick path to the driveway. A good eight inches of snow had fallen. She considered shoveling part of the driveway for the exercise if nothing more, but why bother? She wasn't going anywhere, and no one was coming to visit.

Damn, it was cold. She called to Charlie, who had wandered beyond a tall copse of conifers that separated her yard from the neighbor's.

"C'mon, boy!" A dusting of snow covered his snout. He wagged his tail, but he didn't budge. As she moved toward him, he took off, intent on playing. She felt guilty. He needed way more exercise than he was getting. He darted behind the trees, and she ended up flailing about in nearly a foot of snow before she caught up with him near the next-door neighbor's gazebo. The home, a two-story colonial with a wide back deck and a magnificent view of the cove, was currently unoccupied, which was fine as far as she was concerned.

She dragged Charlie home and dried him off. After a long, hot shower, she slipped into a warm pair of pajamas, and poured the container of Italian wedding soup she had defrosted earlier into a pot. While it simmered, she built a fire in the fireplace.

She eyed the rustic iron wine rack in the dining room. Nearly a dozen bottles of Joey's favorites, hand-picked by him most likely, tempted her. She selected a bottle of his favorite shiraz, opened it, and set it on the coffee table in front of the fireplace. When her soup was ready, she filled Charlie's bowl with dry dog food, ladled a scoop of the broth over his food, and brought it into the living room so they could eat together.

"Merry Christmas, buddy," she said, ruffling the top of his head as he noisily dove into his holiday dinner.

She settled onto the couch and pulled a quilt she'd made for Joey several years earlier around her like a hug. Although she wasn't hungry, she forced herself to finish half the soup. She set the bowl on the floor for Charlie and picked up her wine glass.

The logs crackled. The clock above the mantel struck three. She'd successfully spent the day not thinking about her family, but the chime tore away the veil. The awful fight she and Rhiannon had at Thanksgiving, when she'd asked her daughter to hold Christmas at her house, came tumbling back. Like it or not, Rhiannon was probably hosting everyone right now. Of course, they could have gone to her in-laws, and Devin might have spent the day with his new girlfriend, Danielle, and her family. It had only been a few weeks and already they were scattered to the winds, no longer a family. In her mind, at least.

The shiraz dulled her senses as forty years of watery Christmas memories washed over her like a slideshow. Like a stake of holly through her heart, recalling how happy she'd been last year was painful.

She pulled the quilt around her tighter.

Her marriage in shambles, her best friend dead, and here she was, holding onto her sanity by the thinnest thread, hiding away, trying to figure out how to survive.

How could her life have changed so much over the course of just one year?

When the memories threatened to overwhelm her, and the fire was little more than embers in a bed of black ash, Kate tossed back the dregs in her glass and headed for bed as the last of the day's light faded in the west.

Tomorrow, Christmas would be over. Then maybe, hopefully, the darkness surrounding her might fade as well.

CHAPTER SIX

Days passed in a haze made foggier by medication and amplified by nightly glasses of wine. When her supply began to dwindle, Kate cut herself back to a glass a day. Besides, one glass was plenty. Combined with the antidepressants she was taking, it doubled or tripled its potency. She wasn't less depressed, but at least she was sleeping.

But a promise was a promise, so although she hadn't wanted to, she followed up with the psychiatrist. It turned out she wasn't available over the holidays, and then she wasn't available because she was going away for a week after her son went back to college.

They scheduled an appointment for the third week in January, but Kate canceled after another heavy snowfall. She didn't need much in the way of excuses, anyway. It had been almost two months since her incident. She wasn't suicidal. She just didn't want to be bothered. Besides, she'd never believed a psychiatrist would help.

"How's it going?" Tom tried to sound chipper during his daily phone calls.

"Fine."

"What's new?"

"Clint Bunsen just put up his storm windows, and the Tollefson boy is miffed because his father thinks they should put theirs up too, since the mayor did."

Several beats of silence followed.

"What?" he asked.

"And although Father Emil's hay fever is winding down, he's still hoping to avoid the blessing of the animals this year . . ."

More silence.

"And Charlie says to say hello."

"Who the hell is Clint Bunsen?" Tom demanded. "Wait a minute. Are you reading *Lake Wobegon Days?*"

She laughed.

"Jeez, Kate. You had me worried there for a minute."

"Sorry. There's nothing going on around here. I sleep. I eat. It snows. And I let Charlie in and out several times a day."

"Did you see Dr. Marsh?"

"Not yet. The weather's been bad."

"Kate—"

"I have to run. I have something on the stove, and Charlie's dancing around by the door. I'll talk to you soon. I'll see her this week, promise. Love you! Bye!"

At the sound of his name, Charlie opened his eyes and swished his tail, but he didn't bother getting up. Kate stood at the window, looking out over the cove. It was cold and gray. The icy rain that had begun to fall earlier had turned to sleet. Ice pellets pinged against the windows and accumulated on the deck. A fire would be nice, but she didn't have the energy. She pulled on another sweater, put the kettle on for tea, and made cinnamon toast for dinner.

TOM CALLED THE NEXT DAY, and she let it go to voice mail. She did the same the next day, and the day after that. On the third day, when he sounded frantic, she called him right back.

"I'm sorry," she apologized as soon as he answered. "I was outside with Charlie."

Hearing the word *outside*, Charlie moved to the door, looking hopeful.

"Kate." Tom sounded relieved but frustrated. "You can't do this. I promised I'd make sure you were okay, and if you don't answer the phone . . ."

Who had he promised? Her children? Billy? No, not Billy. The man who had captured her heart had broken it into pieces so small it might never be put back together.

Don't think about it, Kate. Let it go.

She pinched the bridge of her nose. "I'm fine. I met with Dr. Marsh. I think we're off to a good start."

"Thank goodness."

"I don't want you to worry."

"Too bad. I fully intend to worry. So what else is new?"

"Johnny Tollefson just published two poems in a literary maga-zine, but while home from college, he drove over old Mrs. Mueller's rock garden and took out her ornamental windmill."

"Funny," he said dryly.

"Mrs. Mueller didn't think so."

AFTER A WHILE, it was easier not to answer the phone. She told Tom she was seeing the psychiatrist. And she would.

Eventually.

Maybe.

She had her reasons for not going. For one, she didn't feel like it. And the weather was always so iffy. But she knew she wasn't getting any better sitting alone day after day or locked in her room night after night. With no medication and no wine, she hardly slept. And when she did, she dreamed. That was the worst part.

There were two different kinds of dreams now. The first had

started soon after the shooting last August and was usually variations of the same theme: She was being hunted by a man with a gun. He would find her and take aim. But she would always wake at the click of the trigger, sweating, her heart beating as if it were trying to escape her chest.

The second type of dream started soon after she'd arrived in Maine. These were even more realistic and sometimes almost as upsetting, but for a different reason. These dreams felt dark and warm, womb-like. She was alone, moving as if looking for someone. She would feel him before she could see him. From behind, he'd wrap his arms around her, and the scent of lemongrass would fill her nostrils. Billy. He'd press his lips to the curve of her neck. The touch and feel of those kisses burned in her memory. He would lift her up, then carry her to bed, where their lovemaking was slow and tender. They never spoke. When it was over, he would kiss her eyelids and the tip of her nose like he always did, and finally her lips, where he would linger. He would draw a finger along the side of her face and look into her eyes, searching. When she blinked, he was gone.

And just like after the other dreams, she woke up sweating, her heart pounding. Only instead of fear, she was awash in grief.

CHAPTER SEVEN

The pounding woke her. Kate jerked upright, her book crashing to the floor. Charlie scrambled from his spot beside the sofa. He barked and skidded his way across the hardwood floors, down the hall, and into the foyer.

It was midday; sunlight streamed through the windows; but her heart pounded almost as loudly as the incessant knocking. Gathering the quilt around her, she made her way to the kitchen and peeked out the front window. She couldn't see who stood on her steps, nor did she recognize the car.

"Kate!" The muffled voice on the other side of the door was definitely male. "I'm going to use my key!"

She scooted into the foyer. The dead bolt was on. No one could get in, even with a key.

"Who is it?" Her voice grated from lack of use.

"Me. Tommy!"

She turned the knobs, unlocked the dead bolts, and opened the door. He stood in more than a foot of snow on her unshoveled porch. The tips of his ears were bright pink, and the jacket he wore seemed ill-equipped to ward off the bitter cold wind sweeping off the water.

"What are you doing here?" she asked, stunned.

His eyes were wild. "What am I doing here? What the hell are you doing here?"

She didn't like being scolded, even though she probably deserved it. She stepped back to let him enter, but he didn't. He was too set on reprimanding her.

"We had an agreement," he shouted. "You promised you'd go to therapy, and you haven't. You promised you'd work on getting better, and you haven't. You aren't even answering my phone calls."

There was nothing she could say to defend herself, so she didn't.

"Kate, I made a promise to make sure you were okay, and I don't feel like I'm keeping up my end of the bargain. And you promised me —and clearly, you're not keeping up your end of the bargain either."

The look he gave her made her cringe.

"I'm sorry," she said, embarrassed for worrying him. "Would you like to come in and yell at me, or would you prefer to stand out there and do it?"

He stomped snow from his feet and stepped into the foyer.

"How long are you staying?" she asked, eyeing the large suitcase he'd carried in.

"As long as I have to," he answered, untying his boots. "You have an appointment with a new therapist Friday. I'll be driving you myself."

When she opened her mouth to protest, he held up his hand. "Don't even start. I'm in charge now."

His face was the color of a hothouse tomato, and when he tore off his hat, static caused his hair to stand on end. He tossed his hat and scarf over the jacket he had just hung in the laundry room, then spun around and glared at her. He was so uncharacteristically disheveled and irritated, she couldn't help but laugh and hug him.

"I'm sorry I scared you, but I'm happy to see you."

His chest gave way as he exhaled. He returned the hug, tentatively, and then with more feeling.

"You are an exasperating woman."

She tightened her squeeze. "So I've been told."

DR. ELIZABETH CRANE—OR Liz, as she insisted on being called —saw patients in her home, a large Victorian near Fogg Point with expansive views of the cove from her first-floor office. She was a pretty woman, maybe ten or fifteen years older than Kate, with dark, gentle eyes, and a deep dimple when she smiled, which was often. She wore a heavy sweater over a denim skirt, tights and clogs. Long silver earrings tinkled when she tilted her head.

The office was more like a den or sitting room, with deep, cushy chairs and a sofa, and a fire crackling cheerfully in a large stone fire-place. It felt more like visiting an old friend than a mental health professional, and despite her earlier misgivings, Kate could feel some of her nervousness slipping away.

"Tom's told me a little about what you've been through." Liz tucked a strand of silver-streaked chestnut hair behind her ear. Her nails, Kate noticed, were painted a dark, navy blue, an edgy contra-diction to her earth-mother characteristics.

"Just a little?" Kate didn't mean to be confrontational, but she was sure Tom had said more than *a little*.

"I'd like to hear what you have say."

How was this supposed to work? There was everything to talk about and nothing. And dragging it all out into the open would just make everything worse.

"I don't really know what to say." At least she was being honest.

Liz nodded thoughtfully. "I think in this case, we shouldn't start at the beginning but with some of the most recent events."

Recent? For the past few weeks, Kate had done little more than lie in a ball on the couch every day, then get up and go to bed to sleep for a few more hours, after which she would wake up shaking or in tears.

"I understand you were hospitalized recently."

Right for the jugular.

"Tell me about that."

What could she say? It was hazy at best. The clearest memory of that weekend was the dream when Joey had come to her and convinced her not to walk off the edge of the cliff. The rest was pea soup.

"My daughter had me committed against my will." She surprised herself with how angry she sounded.

"Did she have a reason?" Liz asked gently.

Kate crossed and uncrossed her legs. "No. Maybe. I don't know." She clenched a handful of loose denim in her fists. When she realized what she was doing and that the doctor was watching, she flattened her palms against her thighs, but before long they returned to their mindless clutching and unclutching. "I guess she thought so. My husband—my ex-husband . . ."

God, that hurt. She pressed her lips together until she could be sure her voice wouldn't break. She tugged on her knit cap.

Breathe in. Breathe out.

"My soon-to-be-ex-husband had made an appointment for me to see a psychiatrist because he didn't like the way I was acting. He wanted me to get better so he wouldn't feel guilty for leaving me." She gripped her jeans again. "They've always been close."

"Who?"

"My husband and my daughter. She'll do whatever he wants. It was probably his idea."

"Has he done anything like that in the past?"

"Have me committed?"

"No. Did he do anything to make you feel like you were unstable for no apparent reason?"

Kate shook her head. After the shooting, Billy sometimes lost his temper, but for the most part, it seemed as if he were trying to be understanding. Then again, the sooner she got better, the sooner he could be free of her.

"Tell me about the day you were committed. What happened?"

"I don't remember that day, but the day before, I'd been drinking. I don't normally drink a lot." That was exactly what someone who drank too much would say. "Anyway, I'd had too much to drink, and I guess Rhiannon freaked out when she found me. I woke up in the psych ward."

The doctor scribbled a few notes on the yellow legal pad in her lap. "You sound pretty angry."

"Wouldn't you be angry?"

"Of course. If that was all there was to it, it seems pretty high-handed to have you committed for overindulging. Was that all it was?"

Kate picked at a loose thread on the inner seam of her jeans and shrugged. "I might have scared her," she said quietly.

"How so?"

"Like I said, I had too much to drink. I was drinking whiskey. I never drink whiskey. I only took it because my hus—because Billy left it out and I was feeling stressed and . . ." She felt defensive. "I don't know why I drank it. I just did. And I got drunk, and I was looking for a dress to wear to—"

She couldn't say it out loud: *I was looking for a dress to be buried in.* She spun her wedding band around her finger. If it got any looser, it would fall off; although why would it matter?

"I went into the attic and took down my wedding dress. I put it on, and at some point—I don't remember when or even why—I cut my hair. All of it." A tear dripped onto her wrist.

Liz set the legal pad on the table beside her and leaned forward.

"Would you remove your hat, Kate?"

She shook her head.

"Please?" Her voice was soft and warm. "Help me understand what you did."

She hadn't even let Tommy see her with her head uncovered, and to show a total stranger what she'd done? It was humiliating. She toyed with the silver hoop in her ear. But if this was a step she needed to take to get well, then maybe it was a small price to pay. With a steadying breath,

Kate reached up and dragged the cap off. Her hair had grown over the past nine weeks. In some spots it was little more than an inch long, and in others, a bit longer. At least the bald spots were now covered.

"Thank you. That was very brave."

As ridiculous as it sounded, she was right. It would have been easier to stand up in the room naked than to expose this thing that clearly demonstrated she had lost her mind.

"Would you like to get your hair fixed?"

Kate shook her head. "I can't. I don't like to go out, and I don't want anyone to see me—not like this." She tugged the cap back on.

"I understand, but I have a friend who could fix it for you if you'd like. She works from her home. No one would see you. When you're ready, I can call her."

Liz's expression was friendly, but it still made Kate feel uncomfortable. If she started pushing her to do things, go out and face her fears, this would never work. She just wasn't ready.

"I'll think about it."

The urge to curl into herself was strong. She shifted until she was almost facing the window. A large black bird—a razorbill, most likely —caught a current on the far side of the cove and soared over a glittering sea of whitecaps. The rocky shoreline was edged in a forest of pine trees so deep and green, one might have been fooled into believing it was summer rather than the dead of winter.

The last time Kate had been to the beach was last spring. Cape May. She and Billy had shared a picnic at sunset. The beach had been empty, and they positioned themselves to watch the moon rise over the ocean. She closed her eyes and recalled sitting between his legs, her back against his chest as he twirled strands of her hair around his fingers.

Her heart weighed a thousand pounds.

"I had long hair," she blurted. "Almost to my waist. I guess it's silly for a woman my age, but it's who I was." She stared at the toe of her boot. "I don't recognize myself now."

"Do you remember why you cut it?"

Why? No. The sound? That, she might never forget. It raised the hair on her arms to think of it. The scissors had been dull, and the blades had tugged and sawed, chewing their way through her hair like rats. She shivered and attempted to tuck a strand of hair behind her ear, a habit that hadn't disappeared with her hair. She cringed when her chilly fingers brushed her neck.

"I guess when I looked in the mirror, I no longer saw me. It was my body and my face, but it wasn't. Inside, I felt ugly and dead, and I thought . . . I think I thought that the outside should match the inside."

The room was warm, but she pulled her sweater closer.

"And maybe I did it to spite my husband."

The realization was both enlightening and exhausting.

"I'm tired. Can we stop now?"

"Just a few more questions."

Not feeling that she had a choice, she nodded.

"Do you feel at this time that you're a danger to yourself or anyone else?"

"I could never be a danger to someone else." Kate smiled sadly. "Never. And no, I'm not a danger to myself. I've seen the bottom. I want to get as far away from there as possible."

"If I give you another prescription, will you promise no drinking for now?"

She didn't think she had a problem, but clearly, the doctor thought the potential for one was strong. She nodded.

"I'm going to write you a prescription for an antidepressant. We're only going to use these for a little while, just to get you over the rough spots. I depend on active therapy to heal. Let's get to the bottom of what's going on and figure out how to deal with it. I'd like to see you again in a couple of days. Let's get off to a good start, then we can drop to once a week."

Liz seemed so sincere and confident in her ability that Kate felt it too. She pushed herself off the chair, her body feeling much heavier than it should.

She snugged the knit cap lower and had almost reached the door before she stopped. "So. Your friend. Do you really think she could fix my hair?"

CHAPTER EIGHT

"It's cute," Tom said. "You look like a little fairy."

"Not exactly what a girl wants to hear, but I guess it's better than being called a freak."

"You know what I mean. A pixie, that's it. Like Tinkerbell."

Kate touched her hair. It was so short, but at least it was even, and the front had been spiked up with some kind of gel. It was cute, although it wasn't a cut she would ever have had done had she not chopped her hair off first with a pair of utility shears.

"You think I should go blond too? Like Michelle Williams?"

They were sitting at a light in downtown Portland. Tom scrunched his face as if trying to picture her as a blonde.

"I don't know. Red, maybe, especially with those green eyes. Although seriously, you're beautiful just the way you are. I wouldn't do a thing."

Beautiful? She snorted. "Joey gave me an ultramarine-blue streak back in high school. I was grounded until it washed out."

His face softened, but still he chuckled. "Did he get in trouble?"

"No, but I did. After that, he wasn't allowed in my bedroom unless my parents were home, and the door had to remain open."

"Probably what my parents would've said too, if they'd only known."

Laughing, she reached across the console and wrapped her mittened fingers around Tom's leather-gloved hand. "I'm glad you're here, Tommy, although I'm sorry to have interrupted your life again."

"I needed to do this." He gave her a quick glance before taking the ramp onto the interstate. "I had to get away. Stephanie's in Florida with Lian for a month. I told my dad I needed some time off. He knows something's up. We have a new associate who's picking up some of my cases—not that I do much litigating anyway. Anything else, they can reach me on my phone. Plus I have my laptop if I need to do any work."

She grimaced.

"What's the face for?"

"I had the internet and cable turned off. I'm sorry, but I don't want to connect with the outside world right now. I don't want to see the news or watch TV."

"No TV?" he asked in mock horror. "What do you do all day?"

"Sometimes I'll watch a DVD, but usually I read. When I get a delivery from the grocery store, I'll cook and freeze stuff."

"What do you mean 'delivery'?"

"Shane—jeez, I don't even know his last name." Had he told her his last name? "Anyway, Shane's grandmother lives across the street. He comes a few times a week to bring her things and visit. I flagged him down and asked him to shop for me. He's the one who put in all the dead bolts and the motion detectors. He thinks I'm Jewish and I have cancer."

"What?" The look on his face was almost comical.

"The hat, for one thing. I told him I didn't have cancer, but I don't think he believes me."

"Makes sense. How did you become Jewish?"

"He invited me for Christmas. When I told him I wasn't cele-brating—"

"He assumed you were Jewish."

"Pretty much."

He cleared his throat, and she readied herself for a lecture. "I'm worried about you hiding out from the world."

"The world is an evil place, Tommy. I don't want any part of it. You can't blame me, can you?"

"Maybe not, but that's no way to live. Think of what you're missing."

"What? Kids being murdered in their classrooms or gunned down in a movie theater? Terrorists? Child molesters? I'm not interested in what's going on in the world." She shook her head. "All I can think about is getting through today. Tomorrow, I'll worry about tomorrow. I can't do more than that."

She thought the subject had been dropped, but he continued as the trees flashed past on either side. "I understand, but promise me you'll talk about this with Dr. Crane?"

Her fingers curled into a tight fist inside her mitten. "I promise."

TOM STAYED FOR TWO WEEKS. The night before he left, he talked Kate into going to dinner at The Channel Grill, his and Joey's favorite restaurant. After everything he'd done for her, she found it difficult to refuse.

"You're such a good cook." He sopped up Madeira wine sauce from his mussels with a chunk of crusty bread. "I'm surprised you're such a finicky eater. You don't like seafood, lamb, duck."

She scraped the goat cheese off her salad, then speared a piece of pear and a bit of arugula onto her fork. "Maybe it's because my parents made me eat things I didn't like even if they made me gag. Maybe I'm still rebelling after all these years. It's my body. I should say what I put into it."

He pushed the last chunk of bread around the bowl until it was practically clean. "I'm surprised you're not anorexic."

"Give me time," she teased. "Good thing I'm in therapy."

"Might be worth a mention."

"My parents have been gone a long time. It would be silly to start blaming my problems on them now, wouldn't it?"

"I don't know. Damage from our past stays with us forever if we don't find a way to deal with it. I had both your parents in high school. Your mother was downright scary."

"You thought she was scary in school? You should've lived with her."

A memory of sitting alone at the kitchen table, staring at a cold lamb chop, materialized. Just thinking of its pungent aroma turned her stomach.

"You were pretty young when you ran off with Billy. Maybe if they were different, you wouldn't have done that."

A fire crackled in the hearth nearby, its orange glow flickering across the white linen tablecloth. She considered Tom's words.

"If I hadn't discovered my parents hadn't wanted me, I probably wouldn't have run off when I did, even though they forbade me from seeing Billy. But as far as he and I were concerned, I don't think things between us would've changed. Of course, if I hadn't moved in with him when I did, I might not have become pregnant. Then we wouldn't have had Rhiannon, and you know . . ." Becoming mired in her loss, she blinked a few times to ease the prickly feeling at the backs of her eyes. "I was head over heels. Nothing could've changed that. I can't speak for him, though. I thought it was what he wanted." Something had lodged in her throat. "He's the one who changed his mind."

Tom wiped his mouth and returned his napkin to his lap. "I don't think so, Kate. He's—"

She held up her hand. No way was she having an in-depth conversation about Billy. "We were talking about my parents. You're right. They screwed me up, and I will tell the doctor. Okay?"

He frowned but nodded.

She set down her fork. "Although I don't really want to discuss

Billy, there is something I do want to ask of you. Not that you haven't done enough already."

"I'd do anything for you."

Tom was a wonderful friend. For the first time in a very long time, she realized she still had blessings to count.

"Around Thanksgiving, I found a box in the attic. It was filled with canceled checks from Billy's checking account, hundreds of them going back as far as 1991, all made out to someone named Jessie Jones. The first were for a few hundred dollars, but the most recent were as much as $1,500. They were all dated the fifteenth of the month."

Just talking about it was making her stomach cramp.

"We never had a joint checking account. Billy took care of everything, and I never had a clue how much money we had or didn't have, but we lived pretty frugally considering what he does for a living."

"Did you ask him about the checks?"

"No. And he knew I never went in the attic. He could've hidden anything up there."

The look on Tom's face confirmed he was probably thinking what she had been thinking. She reached into her purse. "I kept one. Judging by the stamp on the back, it was cashed at a bank in Houston." She handed it to Tom. "I want to know who Jessie Jones is and why Billy's sending her money. I have a pretty good idea, but I want to know for sure."

Tom looked skeptical. "Are you sure that's what you want?"

What she had to say would be difficult, so she said it quickly, getting it all out at once. "That box was the final blow. It's what pushed me to do what I did, as foolish as it was. It's when I decided I'd rather be dead than face any more heartache."

Even in the dim light of the restaurant, she could see how pale he'd become. "Kate—"

She held up a hand. "I'm okay. Really. I think we both can assume Billy has another child somewhere. We already know he was unfaithful. I just need to know."

"You want me to hire a private investigator?"

It was going to hurt like hell, but what difference would that make at this point? It was over. She nodded.

"I don't know about this. How are you going to feel if you're right?"

"I don't think it's possible to hurt more than I already do, but not knowing is eating away at me."

"A detective could get expensive. Who knows how long it will take?"

She stared into the fire. Thanks to Joey, she had more money than she knew what to do with. "This is important, Tommy. I need to know who this woman is and why she's been in my husband's life all these years. I deserve the truth."

The hum of conversation from nearby tables, the tinkle of flatware on china, and the dulcet tones of a piano in the lounge filled the restaurant. She and Tommy sat in silence.

He tucked the check into his wallet.

"I was asked to give you a message."

She raised her hand to stop him. "Please don't."

It didn't matter who the message was from. She wasn't ready. One day, maybe she could hear it.

Today was not that day.

CHAPTER NINE

February turned into March and March into April. The days grew longer and warmer, at least for Maine, and Kate found it harder to stay inside. Locked behind the walls of her garden with nothing but the view of the ocean, she had found a small oasis of peace.

She'd spent the morning clearing away dead leaves and rotted mulch from the base of the beach roses and the flower beds. Resting on her rake, she filled her lungs with the organic scent of soil and the marshy ocean air. It was definitely there. A flutter. Not quite happiness, but a hint of its possibility. The sun warmed her upturned face. She might have even smiled as she went about her task, reveling in the stretch of unused muscles and the gentle ache in the back of her legs.

Charlie, too, had taken to his new home. After spending the earlier part of the day chasing squirrels and chipmunks, he'd stretched out over the warm pavers near the pool for a well-deserved nap.

Over the scratching of her rake, she heard a car door slam. Charlie's head popped up. He flew up the stairs to the upper deck, where he jumped and barked and spun in circles, ignoring Kate's commands. Another door slammed, followed by the thud of a trunk closing.

"Come here," she demanded. He didn't even glance in her direction.

Typical.

She dropped her rake and slipped into the house, locking the patio doors behind her, and sped upstairs and into the kitchen. She slid open the door from the dining room, reached out, and yanked Charlie inside by the scruff of his neck.

From the mudroom, she could see two cars and two men in the driveway next door unloading items from the first car. Tom had said someone lived there part-time, and the men were taking items from the car, not loading them into it.

She slumped against the wall. The neighbor. Someone who had every right to be there.

The rest of the neighborhood had ignored her thus far. Hopefully the new arrival would do the same.

THE NEIGHBOR SEEMED in no hurry to meet her, and since Kate remained barricaded in the house or within the fenced yard most of the time, she didn't run into him accidentally either.

She was in the laundry room, about to turn on the dryer, when someone knocked on the front door.

"C'mon Kate." She scolded her pounding heart. "It's ten o'clock. Murderers don't usually knock."

Sure they could.

Barking and carrying on as if he knew for certain a murderer was standing on the porch, Charlie came flying through the hall. He slid across the slate foyer and slammed full force into the front door with a thud. So much for making believe she wasn't home.

Another knock, harder this time.

She grabbed Charlie by the collar and pushed him into the laundry room, then pulled the door shut. Frantic, he jumped and clawed at the door from the inside. His nails, which should have been trimmed a long time ago, were probably doing a number on the woodwork. He needed a visit to the vet. And maybe a shock collar.

The knocking continued. Relentless, whoever it was.

"Yes?" she called through the door.

"Hello?" The voice belonged to a man. She stepped back and stared at the door as if she'd suddenly developed X-ray vision.

"Can I help you?" She double-checked the dead bolts.

"Anybody home?"

Was he deaf or trying to be funny? "Can I help you?" she asked, louder in case it was the former.

"Hello!" he called again.

"Good grief," she said out loud, although not loud enough for anyone to hear, and certainly not the deaf man on the other side of her door.

"Who is it?" she yelled.

"Harold!"

She made a face at the door. "Harold who?"

"Why are we yelling?"

"Harold who?" she yelled again.

"Your neighbor!"

She figured that, but still wasn't about to open the door.

"I'm sorry." She lowered her voice a bit, although with the racket coming from the laundry room, he might not hear her after all. "I just got out of the shower. I can't open the door right now."

"Sorry. Just wanted to apologize for not coming sooner and introducing myself."

"That's okay. Thank you." The yelling was hurting her head and her throat.

"I'm Harold!"

"Nice to meet you, Harold."

"And?"

"Excuse me?"

"You are?"

Wanting to be left alone. There was no way out of this. She would be polite, then, but that didn't mean she had to be social.

"Kate. It's nice to meet you, Harold. I have to get ready to go out. I have an appointment. Thanks for stopping by!"

Nothing. She pressed her ear against the door.

"Hello?" she called.

"Hello?" he answered.

Oh, for crying out loud. "I have to get ready."

"See you later."

Not if I can help it.

"DID YOU FEEL THREATENED?" Liz asked after Kate shared her encounter with Harold.

"I know it sounds crazy, but it was unexpected and . . ." Kate toyed with the hem of her sweater. "Yeah, I did. It's like I've made no progress whatsoever."

"I wouldn't say that." Liz leaned back in her chair. Kate liked when they spoke like this. It was more like a conversation and less like she was being picked apart to see how she ticked. "But let's talk about next time."

"Next time?" Of course there would be a next time. "Muzzle the dog?"

She was only half joking.

"We're all hard-wired with a fight or flight response to dangerous situations. It's how the species has survived. Because you have post-traumatic stress disorder, you're having a difficult time determining the difference between a real life-threatening event and what you perceive to be life-threatening. When someone experiences the type of trauma or traumas you have, it isn't always possible to look at the whole picture and use all of your resources to determine what to do next. It's like tunnel vision. Something is happening, and you aren't able to depend on usual logic to guide you. We have to work on getting past that so you can make an informed decision as to whether or not your life is in danger."

It sounded simple, but in practice, it was anything but.

"When you heard that knock on the door, what could you have done differently?"

Kate snorted.

"What?" Liz asked.

"It's ridiculous. Who thinks their life is threatened by a knock on the door unless they live in a crack house or something?" She stared at the grain of the dark mahogany coffee table in front of her. "I'm crazy." Her voice was so low she was surprised that Liz answered.

"You're not crazy. You're trying to heal from a traumatic event. You'll get there."

She swung her foot so frantically her entire body vibrated. Would she? Would she ever feel normal again? She absentmindedly traced a pattern on the upholstery of her chair.

"I guess I could've looked out the window."

"And if the person didn't appear threatening?"

"Ask who it is?"

"And?"

Her gut said go hide, but logic had a different answer. "I guess if the person didn't seem threatening, which in my case seems like a long shot, I could open the door."

This was where Liz was leading her, but her mind went in another direction. The next time she saw Shane, she would ask him to install a storm door with a lock. That way, even if she did open the door, there would be a locked door between her and whoever was on the other side.

"Kate?"

Her head snapped up. "I'm sorry?"

"Then what?"

"Honestly?" She shrugged. "I don't know. I'd be polite, but I'm not ready to engage. I'm not ready, and I don't want to."

A small frown registered on Liz's face. "That's honest. We'll work on that."

That, and about a million other things.

CHAPTER TEN

The way she startled, anyone might have thought Kate had heard a gunshot. It was only a knock on the door, but it set her heart—and Charlie—racing. The clock on the mantel was about to strike five o'clock.

She closed her book and stood.

Ask who it is.

She made her way to the front door.

Look through the window. If they don't appear threatening, open the door.

"You're a certified nut job," she muttered aloud. She grabbed Charlie by the collar and cuffed him affectionately on his head.

"Who is it?"

"Harold. Your neighbor. I have something for you."

She rested her forehead against the heavy wooden door. With a shaky hand, she flipped the two dead bolts and gripped the doorknob tightly. Opening the door would be taking a giant step toward normalcy.

Let's not get ahead of ourselves.

She cracked the door open a few inches. The man standing on her porch had to be well into his seventies, but his tanned skin was almost as smooth as her own. His hair was more salt than pepper, and a bead of white was visible along his forehead and temples, indicating a recent haircut. He wasn't tall, just a couple of inches taller than her perhaps. He looked as if he had stepped out of an L.L. Bean catalog: woodsy brown barn jacket, khakis, and the iconic rubber boots. She had the same pair sitting in the mudroom. She even had the same jacket, only hers was a deep pine.

Swell. She was now dressing like a seventy-some-year-old man.

"Yes?"

"Hey there," Harold said, only it sounded like *they-ya*. "I brought you some lobster." *Lob-stah.*

"Thank you, but I don't eat lobster. I don't like fish."

"This isn't fish." He flashed a wry smile. "It's lobstah. That's seafood."

"I don't like fish or *seafood*."

"Have you ever tried it?"

"No, but—"

"Here you go, then." He shoved a doubled plastic grocery bag in her direction. "You can't live in Maine and not eat lobster."

What was that? The state motto?

He held the bag aloft and although she kept shaking her head, he didn't back down. They could either stand there all afternoon, or she could take the bag. Between Charlie trying to knock her out of the way and wanting her neighbor to disappear, she had no choice but to accept it.

With a wink, he spun around and headed back across the lawn.

"Wait!" she cried, holding the bag in one hand and Charlie's collar in the other.

He raised his hand above his head and gave her a little wave. She had been dismissed.

What the hell was she supposed to do with a lobster?

She yanked Charlie inside and closed the door. It was at that moment that whatever was in the bag announced it was still very much alive and in a hurry to get out.

"Oh, dear god."

She rushed into the kitchen, dropped the bag into the sink, and took a step backward. Rising onto her toes, she gingerly pulled the bag open with a pair of kitchen tongs.

"Oh, shit."

There were two creatures inside, writhing and stepping over each other, each determined to climb out. The only thing slowing them down was the seaweed tangled in their enormous claws and the thick blue rubber bands that kept them from snapping at each other. Or her. They glared up at her with beady, stalk-like eyes, their antennae waving angrily.

Ugh.

She'd seen lobsters before. They were bright red and came on a plate with a ramekin of melted butter on the side. Or they were swimming in a large tank at Red Lobster. They didn't show up at your front door, uninvited, in a plastic bag from Hannaford's. The smell of steamed lobster had always turned her stomach, and it seems they smelled no better when they were fresh, either. And the longer they languished in her kitchen sink, the worse that smell was going to get.

Being out of the water hadn't slowed them down much. Too bad she couldn't just sneak back over to Harold's and leave them on his front porch—or better yet, send them back where they came from.

The bag shifted ominously.

Why couldn't she send them back?

She slipped on her jacket and tugged on her boots. From the living room, she grabbed the large fireplace tongs. Carefully, she threaded the bag handles over the end of the tongs. She stuck a pair of poultry shears in her pocket, then carefully headed down the path to the water, mindful of the pulsing, gyrating bag.

Dusk had fallen, and although it was growing darker, she was afraid to move too quickly. She descended the ramp and stepped out onto the dock. It swayed gently. She waited for it to steady, set the bag down, and pulled it open with the tongs.

Nothing happened.

She peered into the bag. It was safe to pick them up with the bands on. People did it all the time. Still, the thought of touching a lobster's cold, hard body gave her the heebie-jeebies.

She used the tongs to pull the bag open wider. Again, nothing.

"You guys couldn't wait to get out back there in my kitchen. C'mon. Shoo!"

They were no longer in a hurry.

She planted her feet, opened the tongs, and tried to grasp the lobster nearest her around the middle. It stretched its large claw toward her, and she jumped. The dock bobbed up and down. When it stilled, she tried again, standing behind the bag this time against the unlikely event the creature decided to charge her.

"Better safe than sorry," she mumbled.

This time, she was successful. Gripping the lobster with the fireplace tongs, she held it only high enough to remove it from the bag. She reached into her pocket and pulled out the shears, then carefully snipped the first rubber band. The thing twisted and lurched toward her, waving its claw. At the same moment, the other decided to make a break for it.

Kate stumbled backwards and accidentally flipped the first lobster into the water. It sank like a rock.

She peered over the edge of the dock. Returning the lobsters to the water had been her goal, but not with the bands still on. What if the thing couldn't defend itself with just one good claw?

His partner appeared bound to reenter the water on his own terms. She sidled around behind it, grasped it firmly with the tongs, and moved closer to the edge of the dock, where she carefully snipped the rubber bands on each claw. Once freed, it opened and closed them as if stretching luxuriously. She held it out and dropped it into the rippling tide.

"Look after your handicapped friend," she said. "Seems I've left him just as half-assed as everything else I touch."

CHAPTER ELEVEN

I t had been weeks since Kate had awakened sweating and shaking from one of her dreams. While the details of this one slipped away as soon as she opened her eyes, she couldn't shake the pervasive sense of impending doom. She shivered, not sure if it was from the sudden chill of the cool spring air against her damp skin or the fear that washed over her.

Pale strips of dusky light peeked from beyond the curtains she'd hung and into the darkened room. She glanced at the clock. It wasn't quite five thirty.

She pulled on her robe and stumbled to the kitchen. She didn't feel threatened. There had been no noises or thumps in the night. There was nothing wrong as far as she could see, but what if something was wrong elsewhere? Like at home?

There would be no falling back to sleep, that much was clear. While the coffee brewed, she stood at the wall of windows and watched the sun climb above the trees, turning the sky different shades of pink and orange. Despite its beauty, the unsettled feeling remained.

At the stroke of eight, she called Tom.

"You're lucky you caught me. I was just about to step into the shower. Everything okay?"

She gnawed on the pad of her thumb. "I had a bad dream."

He was quiet.

"Not just a bad dream. Sorry. I have lots of those. This was different."

"How?"

"I don't know. I woke up with a bad feeling, and . . . Is everything okay?"

"I guess. What do you mean?"

"Is everyone okay? The kids? Are they okay?"

"As far as I know."

Poor Tom. What a burden she'd become. But even though she realized it, she couldn't help asking him for more. "Could you check? Please? I know I told you not to tell me anything unless it's an emergency, but I woke up with this feeling—"

"How about I give Devin and Rhiannon a call later? Just check in and see how they're doing. Would that help?"

"Yes," she said softly. "Thank you."

"No problem. I'll call after I get to the office."

"And Tom?"

"Yes?"

As much as she hated to bring it up, she couldn't help it. She had to know he was okay. "Billy, too."

BY THE TIME Tom called back, it was late afternoon. Kate answered on the first ring.

"I'm sorry it took so long," Tom said. "Rhiannon never ans—"

"No specifics, please. Are they all right?"

After a few beats of silence, he answered. "Yes. Fine."

She felt like shit. "Tommy, I'm sorry. That was rude. I just don't think I'm ready to hear any details. My head is still firmly lodged in the sand, and I'm not ready to pull it out. Just knowing everyone is okay is enough. For now."

"You know what's best."

"I don't. But I'm getting there."

THERE WAS a small market in Falmouth, Gehring's, where Kate went when she needed anything between Shane's shopping trips. The prices were high, but it was never crowded.

Hearing from Tom that her family was fine had settled her spirit. And for the first time in a long while, she was hungry. Really hungry. Soup just wouldn't cut it. So she donned her sunglasses and a baseball cap and headed to Falmouth.

She selected a small steak and some fresh asparagus, then dallied over a bottle of Sancerre. She was no longer on medication. There was no reason she couldn't have a little wine. How else would she know if she could drink responsibly? She tucked the wine in her basket, along with some coffee creamer and butter.

She unloaded her items onto the worn, wooden counter and waited for the clerk to finish with the customer before her. A display of handmade soap wrapped in fancy cream vellum and fixed with a seal of colorful washi tape was artfully arranged near the register. She plucked several from the basket and sniffed. The first had a spicy orange scent, and she set it on the counter with her other purchases. The next smelled like bayberry—too Christmasy. The last one took her breath away, although it shouldn't have. Lemongrass was common.

It was also Billy. It was as if he'd walked up behind her. And for a second, she wanted to turn and find him there.

She set the soap back on the display and brushed a strand of hair from her eyes. The faint scent of lemongrass lingered on her fingers.

"Did you want the soap?" the clerk asked.

"Just that one." She pointed at the orange-scented soap.

She'd been able to keep Tom from sharing even one detail about her family, yet just an innocent whiff of Billy's signature scent had set memories flying at her like bats from a cave.

She paid for her groceries, climbed into the car, and sat in the parking lot, her fingertips pressed to her nose. The lights inside the store began to flicker off. The scent was barely noticeable. It might even fade before she got home. If not, she could just wash it off.

She unbuckled her seat belt and bolted across the street. The bell above the door clanged.

"I changed my mind." She grabbed the bar of lemongrass soap and set it in front of the register.

"I've already begun closing out—"

"Please?" She swept up the remaining three bars.

It was crazy. Stupid. She was trying to escape the memories, not crawl inside them. *Walk away, Kate. Get back in the car and get the hell out of here.*

But no. She pushed the soap forward. "All of them."

KATE UNWRAPPED a bar of soap and put it in a fancy dish in the bathroom. She did the same with a second one, setting it on the nightstand next to her bed. The other two she wrapped carefully in tissue paper and tucked them away in the linen closet.

Later that night, she lay awake, faint traces of lemongrass wafting up from the nightstand. She reached out in the darkness for the soap and held it beneath her nose, then she rubbed the corner of it on her pillow. She dropped the soap back into the dish, cradled the pillow in her arms, and drifted off to sleep on a cloud of painful, sweet-scented memories.

CHAPTER TWELVE

That afternoon's session with Liz had been one of the harder ones. Kate had talked about growing up with Joey and how difficult it was to lose him. And then, with everything that happened so soon after his death, she had shut down and never gave herself the time to grieve him properly.

They had also spoken about why she no longer listened to music. That was simple. It was too painful. Music stirred up far too many memories. Silence was infinitely preferable. Silence let her hear the sounds of the birds gathered at her feeder or nestled in the thick hedge of rosa rugosa lining her patio. She could hear the patter of the rain on the roof and the lapping of the ocean on the cove.

And of course there was Charlie. So silence? Not so much.

After a dinner of cold fried chicken and pasta salad, she poured herself a glass of wine. It was only the second glass from the bottle she'd bought a few days earlier, proof that despite those last few months in Belleville and her first few weeks in Maine, she hadn't turned into a raging alcoholic. She sat on the deck, rocking and watching the tide come in as the sun set behind her and evening nestled into place.

She sipped and rocked, distracted only by the distant rumble of a motorcycle as it grew closer. Too close, in fact. The usual fears galloped back, along with a gnawing sense of frustration at her weakness. She darted inside and peeked through the dining room window. There was indeed a motorcycle in her driveway.

Charlie went ballistic with the first knock.

"Who is it?" she called, swallowing the fear in her voice.

"Shane."

The tension unfurled as she unbolted the door and pulled it open.

"That's new." She tipped her chin toward the neon-green crotch rocket in her driveway.

"It's my dad's. Want to go for a ride?"

He had to be kidding! "Thanks, but no thanks. Those things scare the daylights out of me."

"C'mon. You don't know what you're missing."

"Pass."

He grinned at the bike and then at her. "I came to pick up your list. I'll do your shopping tomorrow after class."

He followed her into the kitchen, where he handed her a plastic grocery sack.

"What's this?" She opened the bag and jumped. "Jesus Christ!"

Startled, he took a peek. "Cool. Lobsters."

"You handed them to me!"

"It was hanging on your doorknob."

She set the bag in the sink and hooked a thumb toward Harold's house. "My neighbor."

"So the old curmudgeon's back."

"That would be him." She handed Shane the shopping list. "I have another job for you when you can get to it. I'd like a storm door put on the front. A good solid one with a heavy lock."

"No problem. Pick one out online and order from Home Depot. They'll deliver it, since I don't have any way to get it here, and then I'll put it on for you."

"Can't. I don't have internet."

He looked gobsmacked. "You're kidding. How do you check email and stuff?"

"I don't have email and stuff."

"Seriously? Even my grandmother has internet."

"Seriously." She grimaced as the bag thumped against the inside of her stainless steel sink. "So, my door? Find something good and solid, and let me know how much. I'll give you the cash, and you can order it and have it delivered. Please?"

He stretched out his hands and mimicked riding the bike. "Maybe I'll head over now—vroom, vroom—and check 'em out." He tucked the list into his back pocket. "I'll call you later and let you know how much."

Before he left, he gave her one last chance to go for a ride. "You don't even need a helmet," he added, as if that would sell her on risking her life.

"Thanks, but no."

She closed the door and turned the dead bolts. Then she stowed the lobsters in the refrigerator. First thing in the morning, they were going for a swim.

A FEW DAYS LATER, Kate heard a muffled knock on the new storm door. She peeked out the kitchen window. Harold stood on the front steps, holding another bag.

She opened the door and unlocked the storm door. As taciturn as ever, he shoved the bag into her hand.

"Thank you," she said with abundant patience, "but like I told you, I don't eat lobster."

"Who said it's a lobster?" He turned neatly and headed down the steps.

"Oh. I'm sorry." She carefully opened the bag. Sure enough, there were two lobsters inside. This was getting ridiculous. "Harold!"

He marched back, reached into the front pocket of his checked shirt, and pulled out a small index card. "Here's my grandmother's recipe for lobster bisque. It's an award winner." He handed her the card and stomped down the steps.

Before she could remind him again that she didn't eat lobster, he stopped and faced her, squinting against the morning sun. "Funniest thing happened. I pulled a lobster from my trap this morning, and he was already wearing one of my bands. Fancy that! I assume he's an old friend of yours?"

He gave a little wave as he left, laughing all the way.

What were the odds? She stared after him until the movement of the bag demanded her attention. Her "friends" were getting antsy. She carried the bag into the kitchen and set it in the sink. The recipe Harold had given her seemed easy enough, other than cooking the lobster.

"How does that go again? Stick them in head first so you don't hear them scream?"

The thought alone was enough to make her march down to the dock and let them go, except the tide was out, and it would be hours before she could set them free.

"When in Rome," she muttered as she pulled out Joey's lobster pot, filled it with water, and set it on the stove to boil. If he could boil a lobster, she sure as hell could. She imagined him looking down at her, laughing, and enjoying her discomfort. Or maybe he was cheering her on, reveling in her pushing herself beyond her comfort level, which was exactly what she was about to do.

Later that day, she stood nervously on Harold's front steps, holding a large plastic container of lobster bisque. She knocked. When he didn't answer, she rang the bell. It took everything she had to not run back to her house. She waited a few moments, then rang it again.

A gruff voice called from deep inside. "Coming!"

When Harold opened the door, he didn't seem surprised, although he was a bit disheveled.

"I'm sorry. Did I wake you?"

He scrunched his face as his hand rose to smooth the ruffled hair at the back of his head. "No."

She didn't believe him. What was she doing here bothering this man, anyway? It's not like she wanted to encourage any sort of relationship. This was a stupid idea. Just give him the soup and go already!

"I, um, I made your mother's bisque." She handed him the container. "I added a few touches of my own. I hope you don't mind."

"Why would I mind? My mother was a terrible cook. I gave you my grandmother's recipe."

She resisted rolling her eyes. Was he always this cantankerous? "Right. Sorry. Anyway. Thank you."

"You're welcome."

The door closed with a snap.

"Well," she said. "Alrighty then."

HAROLD WAS BACK a couple of days later with the empty container and another bag. He was making it difficult to live as a hermit.

"I told you," she said, trying not to sound rude, although maybe that's what was needed, "I don't eat lobster."

"You ate the soup."

"I tasted it, that's all."

"Your loss." He thrust the bag at her.

"Harold, really. This is very nice, but I don't eat lobster."

"Who said it's lobster?" His pale blue eyes sparkled.

"I'm not falling for that again."

"Suit yourself." He pulled a folded slip of paper from his shirt pocket, handed it to her, and stalked across the lawn.

She peeked in the bag. Clams. And a recipe for clam chowder.

A few hours and one trip to Gehring's later, she had a large pot of clam chowder simmering on the stove. The initial stink the clams created in the kitchen had evaporated into a rich, heady aroma, but she still wasn't inclined to taste more than what she collected on the tip of her pinky. Still, like the bisque, it was pretty tasty. When it cooled, she ladled it into plastic containers and stashed one in the freezer for when Tom came to visit. The rest she took to Harold.

"Here you go," she said when he opened his front door. "Again, thank you."

"Is it as good as the lobster bisque?"

She tried to look stern, not wanting to encourage him in any way, but she smiled anyway. "I guess. I only tried a little. Thank you again for your generosity, but it's a waste of money. I don't eat clams either."

He chuckled. "I didn't buy them. I rake my own. Those clams in there come from your own back yard."

"Really?" It was a novel concept to her, but it didn't make eating them any more enticing.

"Want to come in?"

She shook her head. "No, thanks. I have to get back."

"Why?"

She gave him a blank stare. Why? She couldn't think of a logical thing to say. She just shook her head again. "Thanks, but I have to go."

Back at home, she locked and bolted the door behind her. Even though some days, it was difficult to remember exactly why.

CHAPTER THIRTEEN

E arly morning. The forest dressed in shades of brown and gray,
dense with scrub oak and mountain laurel. The leaves curled in
on themselves against the frost. The cold air burned her lungs. Mist
hung from the trees and each branch. Each blade of dead grass was
encrusted with crystals, the icy beauty melting at the softest touch.

Silence, save for the crunch of leaves and branches along the
narrow path. Birds kept to their nests, stealing a few precious moments
of predawn slumber.

She was not dressed for hiking. Bony fingers of the dormant forest
snagged and tore at her wedding gown. Shivering against the cold, she
pulled her cloak tighter and pushed forward, her vision hampered by a
fog so thick she could feel it, until she came to a clearing.

In the gloomy distance lay a field, rough and rugged, yet starkly
beautiful. She made her way toward a cluster of boulders, dotted with
lichens and surrounded by brush, and sat on the smallest of the great
rocks. Her ankles were scratched and bloodied from the narrow path.
Her feet were bare and dirty. She smoothed the dress beneath her
fingers, gingerly touching the puckers and snags. Dirt stained the
frayed and tattered hem.

The forest began to wake. Squirrels and field mice skittered among the dead leaves. Birds chirped in the wood. Their vocalizations grew louder, and the topmost branches swayed.

The mist shifted, and a stark, dark mass of crows became visible. Their cacophony swelled. A murder of crows, they swarmed the clearing, picking at the ground, anxious to see what the earth offered up for their morning meal.

There was a rush of movement on the far side of the clearing. Frightened, she slipped from her perch and hid behind a tall boulder. Two figures approached, shrouded in the swirling mist, and stood at the far edge of the clearing. The crows lifted from the field. Moving as one, they settled in the trees. Branches came alive, swaying and writhing, black as night.

A fierce roar shook the ground, and she grasped the cold, rough stone to keep from falling. A foul stench filled her nostrils. The roar came again. The tang of burning hair and flesh hung in the air. She covered her nose with her cloak, fighting waves of nausea.

She crouched behind the rock and peered around it. A monstrous creature moved toward her, breathing great plumes of fire. Its body was blackened and scorched. Blood seeped from open sores. Its face was terrifying, with great, sharp teeth and eyes like burning embers. The dried grasses around the field burst into small fires as it moved, and the clearing, so peaceful moments before, was nearly aflame.

"Grendel!" a voice boomed. The monster turned.

Three riders sat on horseback. The one who had called to the creature rode into the clearing on a great black steed. Dressed in medieval armor of chain mail and leather, he wore a breastplate of molded metal and on his head, a helmet of beaten gold. His hair, golden as well, hung long past his shoulders.

The monster swung its great head and stalked toward the rider, who leaped from his mount, pulling out a great longsword.

Grendel? She peeked out from behind the boulder. Beowulf?

The grunts and sounds of mayhem shook her. She winced at the dull thud of metal hitting bone. The monster screamed and lunged.

The fighter moved from its path and struck again, driving his sword deep.

She should run. Back to the woods and away. But she was frozen with fear, powerless. She closed her eyes and prayed, until with a great, loud grunt, the fighting stopped. She drew tighter into herself, her head buried in her knees, her arms wrapped around her legs.

The beat of hooves grew nearer. The rider dismounted.

"Come."

She lifted her head and opened her eyes. He towered over her, and the sun hanging behind him cast his face in shadow. He reached for her hand. Believing she had no choice but to go, she raised her hand, unsure if she could stand on her own. He clasped his large hand around hers and led her to the horse. Then he lifted her into the saddle with ease and swung up behind her. He slipped off the helmet, handed it to her, and closed his arms around her, holding her in place. He made a clucking nose, and the horse began to move. She tried to see his face but saw nothing but golden strands of hair lifted by the breeze.

"Billy?"

"Shh."

They rode from the clearing, passing his two companions. They, too, seemed familiar, but when she looked, they had disappeared. On the far edge of the clearing, the two figures were also gone. As was the monster.

"Is it dead?"

"No," he answered. "Not yet."

KATE STIRRED, lost in that place between sleep and wakefulness. She fought opening her eyes. Despite what had begun as a nightmare, she felt safe as she slipped from one plane to the next. The feeling of strong arms still surrounded her. If she opened her eyes and pulled back the veil, he would disappear.

She buried her face in her pillow and let the familiar scent of lemongrass carry her safely back to sleep.

CHAPTER FOURTEEN

"I blame *Beowulf.*"

Kate sat in Liz's office. She'd had the same dream several times, enough that it was clear it was time to dissect it and figure out if there was a message in there somewhere. *Beowulf* had to be the key.

"I had to read it in college, and I'd been struggling with it. I think I was just so unhappy at the time that it was difficult to concentrate. It was the weekend I met Billy, and I had a test on the book that Monday. I did okay, I think. I can't really remember. But I had mentioned the book to him, and he raved about it. My parents were upset that I hadn't gotten a better grade, so I promised to reread it. I dropped out soon after, so it didn't matter."

Liz appeared to be confused by her ramblings.

"I came across *Beowulf* on a shelf a couple of weeks ago and figured I'd give it another try. I had begun reading it the first night I had that dream. When I pictured the characters in my head, I saw Billy as Beowulf." Might as well fess up. "And if you must know, he's also been Mr. Darcy in *Pride and Prejudice,* Heathcliff in *Wuthering Heights,* Edward Rochester in *Jane Eyre,* and a blond Jamie Fraser in

"*Outlander.*" She ticked off the list of book boyfriends on her fingers. "You get the picture."

"He's very much on your mind, isn't he?"

She couldn't help but sigh. "I try not to think about him, but I can't control my dreams."

"Perhaps not, but there can be messages in your dreams, especially in the instance of recurring dreams. When you have these dreams, try and write them down as soon as you wake, and we can try to determine what those messages might be." Liz crossed her legs and gave her an encouraging look. "Can you think of anything right now?"

Her mind went blank as if she'd been presented with a pop quiz on a topic she'd failed to study. She shook her head.

Liz offered a gentle nudge. "There's one thing that happens in every dream that's the same: Billy fights the monster and rescues you. And each time, you ask him if the monster is dead, and he says 'not yet.' Right?"

She nodded reluctantly.

"Perhaps he can't kill your monster."

"My monster?"

"You said each time the monster comes toward you, Billy arrives and stops it. Perhaps you need to kill your own monster."

Her throat felt thick, and she struggled to swallow. She didn't kill monsters; she kept the lights on to keep them away. She bolted her doors against them, hoping the more locks she had, the safer she'd be. She hid from them in attics where they couldn't reach her. Or in bathroom stalls while they shot and killed innocent people. Or in other states four hundred miles away, where their words or actions could no longer hurt her.

It was only a dream, yet the thought of facing the monster of her imagination terrified her all the same.

"I don't think that's possible." Her throat was so dry she had to force the words past her lips.

Liz looked determined. "Yes, Kate. It is."

CHAPTER FIFTEEN

Kate loved to cook, and Harold, it seemed, loved to eat. He showed up almost daily now, bringing her lobsters and clams. For her part, it was easier to give in and accept them, although she still cringed when cooking the lobsters. She tried out new recipes and froze what she could. She gave some to Liz or to Shane, but the bulk of her culinary creations went back to Harold, who was enjoying a steady diet of chowders, bisques, and the occasional lobster roll.

She didn't feel put upon or taken advantage of. She assumed Harold missed having someone to cook for him. And if she were being honest, she missed having someone to cook for.

On a particularly sunny afternoon near the middle of May, she gathered up that morning's efforts—two containers of Manhattan clam chowder, a tray of cinnamon rolls, and half a roast chicken; the other half would feed her for the rest of the week—and headed across the lawn.

She transferred everything into one arm, rapped on the door, and waited. His Cadillac was parked in the driveway, so she knocked again. She was about to walk around back to see if he might be in the gazebo or working in one of his many flower beds, when the door creaked open.

He was still in his pajamas, pale under his tan, and his skin was covered with a light sheen of sweat. His hair stood up as if he'd just climbed out of bed.

"What's wrong?"

"I'm just feeling a little peaked."

"Peaked? You look awful."

She stepped past him into the front hall and set the food on a table in the foyer. Slipping into mom mode, she planted her palm on his forehead. No fever, but his skin was cold and clammy.

He began to wave off her ministrations, but his hand dropped to his chest.

"Are you having chest pains?" Her own chest tightened at the thought.

His right hand gripped his left bicep. "Kind of."

Shit.

She guided him to a chair in the foyer. "Where's the phone?"

"Kitchen. On the wall leading into the dining room."

It was easy enough to find. Chinese red, it hung on the wall in all its 1970s glory, with push buttons and an extra-long cord. She dialed 911, then stretched the cord until she could see Harold. He was leaning to the side, his elbow resting on a Queen Anne console and his head in his hand. What she knew about him could have been inscribed on the head of a pin, but she couldn't imagine he was one to give in to illness easily.

"Could you tell them to hurry," she whispered into the phone.

She hung up, knelt beside him, and took his hand in hers. "They're on their way. It won't be long."

Other than that, she didn't know what to say, so she said nothing.

The sound of sirens interrupted the stillness. She let the paramedics in, then stood in the formal living room off the front hall and watched helplessly.

"Come with me," Harold said, pulling off the oxygen mask and reaching for her from the stretcher.

She let him take her hand and curled her fingers over his.

"We're sorry, Mr. Larsen," the paramedic said. "There's no room in the ambulance."

She made a split-second decision. "I'll meet you there. I promise."

HAROLD'S HEART WAS FINE. It was his pigheadedness that nearly did him in.

Kate was sitting beside him in the emergency room when the doctor entered. She stood to leave, but Harold insisted she stay.

"This is my daughter-in-law."

A bit dumbfounded, she mumbled a hello and sat back down.

The doctor folded his arms across his chest and gave Harold a hard look. "The good news is you didn't have a heart attack. The bad news, as you've probably already figured out, is that we spoke to your doctor, who told us you have pancreatitis. Dr. Ingraham tells me you were given a special diet several months ago, and it would be his guess that you haven't been following it."

Harold's eyes narrowed, and his mouth set in a thin, hard line. He wasn't about to volunteer any details.

The doctor glanced at Kate. "What's he been eating lately?"

More guilt—just what she needed. She prepared to rat him out on the cream soups and the more recent addition of homemade cookies and pies, but Harold cut her off before she even opened her mouth.

"She doesn't speak much English," he said. "Barely a word. My son met her during the war."

War? What war?

The doctor looked confused but didn't pursue it. Kate, on the other hand, was too stunned to answer.

When the doctor raised his voice, as if speaking more loudly would somehow bridge the language barrier with her, she had to press a finger against her lips to keep from laughing.

"We're going to keep you overnight just as a precaution. If everything checks out in the morning, we'll send you home." He finished his professional scolding of Harold and shouted his goodbye at her.

As soon as the doctor left, Kate folded her arms and glared at Harold. "Daughter-in-law?"

He shrugged. "They wouldn't let you stay, otherwise," he pointed out matter-of-factly.

"Perhaps not, but—"

"Shh!" He interrupted her as a nurse came in to prepare him for the move upstairs.

Feeling more than a little foolish, Kate smiled blandly and watched as the nurse took his pulse and checked his blood pressure.

"So what do I speak?" she whispered when the nurse had stepped out and pulled the curtain.

"How the hell should I know?" he answered, as if it was the most ridiculous question he'd ever heard. "And before you ask, I watched a movie last night about Germany during World War II, and it was the first thing I could think of. I'm not exactly myself today." He waved a hand over his hospital gown, as if she could have forgotten where they were and how they'd gotten there.

"Now listen." He motioned for her to come closer. "I assume you locked up the house. There's a key under the flowerpot near the front door. You might as well keep it. You need to bring me a change of clothes, my toothbrush, and my book. It's on the nightstand. I was just getting to the good part when you interrupted me."

Interrupted him? "You're something else, you know that?"

Despite his sickly appearance and general grumpiness, there was still a spark of mischief in his eyes.

"Tell me something I haven't heard before."

BY THE TIME Kate reached Harold's house, the gnawing pang of guilt that had begun in the hospital had blossomed into a full-on onslaught. She tried to convince herself that it wasn't her fault—how was she to know he had pancreatitis?—but guilt was an old friend and not one willing to easily abandon her.

The soup and chicken were still sitting on the table by the door. She tossed it into the trash. The cinnamon buns would have been fine, but not for someone on a restricted diet. No wonder he had stifled her by telling the doctor and nurses she didn't speak English. He'd made sure to keep her from asking pertinent questions about his follow-up care.

"Well played, Harold," she murmured.

Other than earlier that day, she had never been inside Harold's house, and she felt uncomfortable being there now by herself. The rooms were large and spacious, but the décor was dated. It probably hadn't been changed since his wife died, which judging by the floral wallpaper and brass fixtures could have been the early nineties. Framed photos lined the mantel in the living room, including four eight-by-ten high school senior portraits. All boys.

Everything in the house was neat and in its place except for the bed in the master bedroom, which was rumpled and unmade. She smoothed the covers and tucked the pillows under the dated chenille bedspread, giving it a final pat before grabbing his book, *The Hard Way*. She collected the trash bag she'd left in the kitchen, made sure the house was locked up tight, and ran home to walk Charlie again before she returned to the hospital.

WHEN KATE ENTERED Harold's room a short time later, he wasn't alone.

"Is this your daughter-in-law?" the nurse asked.

Harold nodded, and the nurse smiled at Kate. "Hello!"

Given the volume of her voice, Kate assumed this nurse was also under the impression she spoke no English and therefore shouting would improve her comprehension. She nodded and rolled her eyes at Harold.

After the nurse left, she unpacked Harold's things.

"So you like Jack Reacher?" She set the book on his tray table, next to what looked to be his untouched dinner. "Ironic."

"How is that ironic?"

She tapped her finger on the cover. "*The Hard Way.* In your case, it should be *The Hardhead.*"

Despite the dismissive sound he made deep in his throat, she caught the flicker of a smile.

Hiding a smile of her own, she poked around at his untouched dinner. Filet of flounder that appeared to be seasoned with little more than a few grains of pepper, some steamed broccoli, and a scoop of parslied potatoes.

"Yuck," she said, replacing the lid.

"Exactly."

"What about the soup?" There was a small bowl of what may have been chicken broth.

"Fat-free, sodium-free? No, thanks."

"Jell-O?" She held up the cup, wiggling it to entice him as if it were homemade chocolate mousse.

He made a face but accepted the offering, tore off the foil lid, and stabbed his spoon in angrily. He took a mouthful, then tossed it onto the tray.

"I'll starve to death if I'm here much longer."

"A little dramatic, don't you think? Speaking of your death, why did you keep eating the soup I gave you? You should've told me you couldn't have it. I'm dealing with enough guilt right now, I don't need something else hanging—"

She snapped her mouth shut and directed her attention to the items she'd just unpacked.

"You need to eat something," she said finally. "Even if it's just

Jell-O. Do you want me to ask if they have any other flavors, if you don't like orange?"

"You don't speak English, remember?"

"I forgot." She frowned. "So what's the plan? How long are you staying?"

"It was a mild flare-up." He pointed to the bag of IV fluids running into his veins. "If my enzymes and electrolyte levels return to normal by morning, you can pick me up around eleven."

"Oh, I can, can I?"

"It's the least you can do after almost killing me."

She felt the blood drain from her face and the beat of her heart quicken.

The smug smile that had formed on Harold's face faded just as quickly. "Sorry. That wasn't funny. It's not your fault. And it certainly wasn't the soup. It's my fault. I'm supposed to stick to a bland diet. I find that cruel and unusual punishment. Especially since you're such a good cook."

"Thank you." She struggled to steady her voice. "But you should've told me. I would've cut back on the fat and still made it taste good."

"It's not the same."

"Maybe not, but what's most important?"

A young man came to collect the tray. Kate waited silently.

"You didn't eat," the man said. "Do you want me to leave it?"

"Blech." Harold pushed it away. "Could you bring me a different flavor Jell-O? Like cherry or strawberry?" He glanced at Kate and scowled. "And maybe reheat the soup. I'll try it again."

After the orderly left, Harold settled back against the pillows. He looked tired, but the color had returned to his cheeks. "So. What's your story? Why are you hiding out up here?"

Kate lifted her hands in the international gesture of ignorance. "*Je ne parle pas l'anglais.*"

He broke out into a wide smile and laughed. "Touché."

CHAPTER SIXTEEN

It rained for days. April showers were a month behind in Maine since spring had arrived so late. Outside Kate's windows, the ocean matched the gray sky, but otherwise the world was a wet, vibrant green studded with a brilliant array of color. Daffodils bloomed along the base of the pines. Azaleas cozied up to the house in a riot of deep pinks and purples. Leaves sprouted on the dense beach rose hedge that lined the fence by the pool.

Rain didn't bother her. It made her nostalgic for the sound of a foghorn and filled her with memories of summer vacations, scampering over rocky ledges at Two Lights in Cape Elizabeth on rainy afternoons with Joey, searching for sea glass.

The whitecaps dancing over the water in her cove called to her like a long-lost friend. Without giving herself time to think, Kate snuggled into a warm sweater, slipped into a raincoat and a pair of rubber boots, and headed for Portland. It was drizzling when she pulled up near Dyer Cove. The little lobster restaurant was still there, its parking lot all but empty on a rainy Tuesday afternoon. The beach was empty as well. Fog rolled off the ocean, blanketing the small cove.

She locked the car and jammed the keys into the pocket of her jeans. A broken-down concrete abutment and a large piece of driftwood separated the parking lot from the beach. She climbed over the log and stepped onto the wet sand. The air was thick with mist. The foghorn was doing its job—two long, low blasts every half minute or so. It was loud but reassuring. Life should come equipped with a similar warning that would sound before you found yourself smashed and broken against the rocks.

Thick fog swirled around her. The end of the rock ledge that separated the cove from open ocean had disappeared into the mist. The surf pounded the shore. The deserted beach was anything but quiet.

Kate inched closer to the water, sidestepping the churning foam as it licked her boots. She bent her head against the light drizzle and scanned the shore for sea glass. A large piece of frosted white caught her eye. She snatched it up and squeezed it in her clenched fist. It made her think of the pink sea glass heart Joey had given her in a dream, the dream in which he'd convinced her it wasn't her time to die and she should do exactly what she had done—come to Maine. It had only been a dream, or perhaps the result of her drunken excess, but it had seemed so real—so real that the memory was as sharp as the glass pressed in her hand now.

She spied another piece of frosted glass, pale green and almost as large as the first. Every time she tucked a piece into her pocket, she saw another and another. The rough seas of the past few days were making for a good haul. She was reaching for a piece of dark cobalt blue when a loud bark caused her to stumble and nearly land on her bottom in the wet sand.

A baby seal lay partially in the water just a few feet away. It pushed up on its flippers. Each time the water rushed in, it shimmied further away.

"Hey there, little fellow," she said, loud enough to be heard over the crash of the waves but not enough to sound threatening. It had a sweet face, a cross between a walrus and a puppy.

The seal kept its eyes on her and worked its way back into the water with the help of the incoming tide. Once it was buoyant again, it swam out from the shore. It stopped, gave her a look, then dove and came up a few feet farther away. Each time, it looked back to where she was standing.

"You're being coy, aren't you? You're a little flirt."

The seal dove and resurfaced farther away. It spotted her and barked. It floated for a while, watching her, then dived and resurfaced. It seemed as fascinated with her as she was with it.

Even after it got far enough from shore to be swallowed up in the fog, Kate waited. When it didn't come back, she made her way to the parking lot. Her jeans clung to her legs, and a fine layer of moisture seeped into her jacket. She was soaked through and felt the beginning of a chill, but her heart was lighter, thanks to the blessing of the little seal pup.

The sky opened up just as she reached her car. She lifted her face. Rain washed over her, into her eyes and ears and down the back of her shirt, mingling with tears that had sprung from nowhere. How long she stood there, she wasn't quite sure, but when she finally looked down, her heart had made a decision.

She had touched the very bottom. It was time to rise up.

THE TRIP HOME WAS UNCOMFORTABLE, but she didn't mind. She felt new. Clean. Chilled to the bone yet energized.

She stopped at the grocery store in Falmouth, where she pushed past the desire to cut and run. She white-knuckled her cart through the store, focused on her task, and trying to remember what other items she would need. Coconut, chili peppers, fresh ginger, cabbage, and peanuts. A simple recipe, but a monumental undertaking—for her at least.

Even though her jeans rubbed her calves and her coat was soaked through, she stopped at Harold's. He answered on the second knock.

"You look like a drowned rat."

"Nice to see you too." She smiled. "I'd like to invite you to dinner tomorrow. I'll make something healthy."

He looked skeptical. "Healthy?"

"And delicious, I promise."

"I guess I could come for dinner. What time?"

"Six thirty?"

"Red or white?"

"Surprise me." With a wave, she bounded down the steps.

At home, she took a hot shower, lit a fire in the fireplace, and made herself a cup of tea. Then she curled up on the sofa and picked up *Beowulf*.

"Okay, you big Geat. Time to figure out why you keep invading my dreams."

CHAPTER SEVENTEEN

"That was excellent." Harold pushed his plate away and rubbed his hands over his trim belly. "You sure all that was healthy?"

"Absolutely. I mixed panko bread crumbs with coconut for the chicken and used cooking spray instead of oil. The Thai salad had a little olive oil in the dressing and just enough peanuts to give it flavor. And for dessert, we have oatmeal-chocolate-chip cookies, and while those aren't low-cal or low-fat, they're healthier than the regular version."

"I'm stuffed. Maybe I'll have room a little later." He topped off her wine glass, added a healthy splash to his own, and raised his glass. "To a wonderful cook."

They clicked rims lightly.

"I'm glad you enjoyed it. I love to cook. I haven't done much at all lately. No point cooking only for me."

"I guess not." He swirled the wine around the bowl of his glass before taking a sip.

"Grüner." She read the label on the bottle. "It's light and crisp. I like it."

"It's Austrian. A new favorite of mine."

"Very nice."

"My wife was a decent cook. She didn't care for wine, though. Actually, she wasn't much of a drinker. Maybe a glass of champagne on New Year's, but that's about it."

She shrugged off a twinge of regret. "That's preferable to raising a few glasses every day."

He nodded and set down his glass. "So what's the deal?"

"Deal?"

"What's your story? You still haven't told me why you're here."

"I live here," she said a bit shortly. "You haven't told me your story either."

"Not much to tell. I was married. My wife's name was Pat. I'm a retired marine biologist. We had four kids, all boys. Pat died about ten years ago. The boys are all grown with lives of their own. I live here from April through October. The rest of the year, I live in Boston near my son Steven."

He pointed a finger at her. "Your turn."

"Let's just say I can't sum up my life in one neat little paragraph. I've been through the worst year you could imagine, but I'm beginning to think that I might actually survive." She raised her glass. "And that's all I care to say on the subject."

He nodded and then promptly ignored her last statement. "You a widow?" He lifted his chin to point toward her left hand, where she still wore her engagement ring and the narrow gold band Billy put there on their wedding day.

She dropped her hand into her lap, protecting it from further scrutiny. "A widow? God, no." The thought was like a punch in the stomach.

"Your husband in the military?"

At that she laughed. "Definitely not." She nervously twirled the rings around on her finger. "We're, um, separated."

Harold didn't look satisfied but had the good manners to table the conversation.

"Hey, I almost forgot," he said suddenly, as if he truly had forgotten and wasn't just trying to change the subject. "Next weekend is Memorial Day. My boys come up with their families. They help get the big boat out in the water, and we go fishing, put the lobster pots out, and dig clams. Then we have a huge blowout on Sunday to celebrate the holiday and my birthday. The neighbors all come. It'll be a great chance for you to meet everyone. I happen to know that no one on this street besides me has a clue who you are."

And I'd like to keep it that way. "I can't. But thanks for including me."

"What do you mean, you can't?" He looked at her as if she were crazy. "What the hell else could you be doing?"

She began to clear the table. "I can't. I'm not comfortable around people, if you must know. To have you come here tonight was a big deal for me."

"Don't be ridiculous. You came to the hospital last week. There were lots of people there."

"Yes, and that was hard. In fact, it was a big step for me, so thanks for getting sick." She flashed a big fake smile at him, and he laughed.

"Kate, you have nothing to feel uncomfortable about with my family or any of the neighbors. If there were anything wrong with any of them, I sure as hell wouldn't invite them to my house."

"I can't, but thank you." She brushed some imaginary crumbs off the table. "So when is your birthday?" Not exactly a smooth segue, but she wasn't discussing this further.

"Was."

"Excuse me?"

"Was. My birthday was Sunday."

"Oh, no! Were you alone for your birthday?" It disturbed her to think of anyone being alone on their birthday. That she had already missed Devin and Billy's birthdays gnawed at her.

"Who cares, at my age?"

"Still. You shouldn't spend your birthday alone."

"When's your birthday?"

She was tempted to tell him it had passed, but she hated lying, especially when there was no good reason for it. "July 19."

Hopefully, he'd forget. She had no intention of celebrating her birthday, that was for damn sure.

"So about Sunday," he began.

Like a dog with a bone. "So," she responded. "How about dessert?"

CHAPTER EIGHTEEN

"The dream is essentially the same?" Liz asked.

"For the most part, only it's not as foggy." Kate thought for a moment. "In fact, I can almost make out the people who come to the circle before the monster."

Liz lifted an eyebrow. "Oh?"

"One is a woman. I think it might be my mother."

"Why do you think that?"

She closed her eyes and pictured the figure from her dreams. "She's tall and thin, all sharp angles. Hard edges. Even her hair, cut right at her jawline. And the way she stands. Perfect posture, arms folded, legs straight. I can't see her face, but I sense that it's my mother."

"And the other person."

"It's not my dad. He was taller than my mother, but he was loose, gangly, kinda like the scarecrow from *The Wizard of Oz*. Always a bit rumbled, a little bumbling. Not quite as kind." Her voice trailed off. "But not unkind." It was difficult to explain her father, especially when she'd never really understood him herself. "His students usually liked him. If they'd had a contest for most unpopular teacher, my mother would've won hands down. That might be why I didn't have more friends in high school. No one wanted to hang out with me if it meant they had to come to my house."

"That must've been hard."

"Not really. I had Joey. Being his friend was a full-time job." The memory warmed her. "I wouldn't have had it any other way."

"You were lucky to have a friend like that."

Blessed too.

"The other person? I think it might be Sedge Stevens, the man who shot and killed all those people at the meeting I was covering. The one who probably wanted to kill me too."

"Why do you think it's him?"

"He's kind of stocky like Stevens. And even from a distance, I can tell he has long white hair and a beard." She shrugged. "It's just a feeling."

"Can you think of anything else different about the dream?"

She thought for a moment. "The battle ends the same, only this time, I didn't hide. I was still scared, but it's like I knew Beowulf or Billy or whoever he is was going to stop the monster. When it was over, I waited near the boulder. The man vanished like before, but this time, the woman stepped into the clearing like she was daring me to come closer. But then the warrior climbed onto his horse and rode toward me like before. When I looked back, she was gone."

"Did he speak to you?"

"I asked who he was, but he just said 'You know who I am.' Then I woke up. It must mean something, but I'll be damned if I know what."

Liz jotted a few notes and set the legal pad on the table beside her. "Do you think you deserve to be happy?"

"What?"

"Do you think you have the right to be happy?"

The question was unsettling. Her knee-jerk answer would be that she didn't deserve happiness, but why wouldn't she? If she could accept that she wasn't responsible for the shooting and the deaths of all those people, didn't that free her to be happy someday?

"I guess everyone deserves some happiness."

"What about you?"

"Do I deserve it?"

"Yes, do you deserve to be happy?"

"I don't know. Maybe?"

"You're not sure?"

Kate squirmed against the cushions. "I was loved. Once. Twice, I guess."

"But not anymore?"

She shrugged.

"When you say twice, to whom are you referring?"

"Joey, of course. And Billy. I know he loved me once."

"But you don't believe he still does."

It was still difficult to discuss Billy. If she had a choice, she would table this conversation indefinitely. Saying his name felt like opening the door to all the pain and heartache simmering just below the surface. It was necessary, but that didn't mean she had to like it.

She shook her head. "He may still care about me, but after leaving like I did, maybe not even that anymore."

"Why do you think he stopped loving you?"

The look she gave Liz was probably rude, but it was a dumb question. "For starters, he cheated on me."

"People cheat for lots of different reasons. Not loving their spouse isn't necessarily one of them. That in and of itself isn't proof that he doesn't love you."

"Well, it's a pretty crappy way to show you care."

"I agree, but it's not necessarily black and white. You said you don't know all the details, and when he tried to tell you, you stopped him."

Kate dragged a pillow onto her lap and wrapped her arms around it. "I didn't think there was any point."

"People are flawed, Kate. You're overly aware of yours. Your self-esteem is so low you don't believe you're worthy of happiness. But I don't believe that has anything to do with recent events. I think your feelings of being worthless and undeserving go back to your childhood. Your parents are gone, but even if they were still alive, there would be nothing you could do to change the way they treat you. You would just have to learn not to let their criticism and negative thinking affect you."

Liz picked up her pad and flipped to a fresh page. She drew a line down the center and began to write.

"Here's some homework." She tore the page out and handed it to Kate. "On one side, I wrote *Strengths*, and on the other, *Weaknesses*. I want you to think about this over the next few days, and I want you to write ten of each under each column."

"Ten strengths?" Twenty weaknesses would be much easier.

"Let's think about it right now and get a head start," Liz said. "Go ahead."

Kate didn't like this at all. "This feels like bragging."

"It's not. It's identifying for yourself what you're good at. I have something: you're kind."

Okay, that she could accept. But kindness had its own problems. "Kindness often gets you hurt."

Liz handed her a pen. "True. Write 'kind' under *Strengths* and 'overly sensitive' under *Weaknesses*."

She didn't like it, but did as she was told.

"When I see you next week, I'd like to see the list complete. Just ten of each. I think you'll be surprised to see all your strengths laid out before you. Also, once you've identified your weaknesses, you'll be better able to tackle them head on."

It sounded simple, but it would be difficult to dig deep enough to find the positives. Still, it was a step forward, and she pondered some of the possibilities as she drove home. She was honest, trustworthy, loyal. Even though she sounded like a Girl Scout, she felt a flicker of empowerment, as if she might be closer to getting a grip on her own life.

CHAPTER NINETEEN

Sunday was sunny and warm. The windows were open, and by late morning, Kate could hear cars arriving next door. Voices multiplied and grew louder. A stereo played music from the fifties and sixties—the first music she'd heard in months. At least Harold wasn't a fan of grunge or alternative rock, because her heart wouldn't have been able to take it.

The aroma of hamburgers and hot dogs cooking on a charcoal grill wafted through the kitchen window, and her stomach growled. She poked around in the refrigerator. The best she could find was a container of yogurt and a slippery red hot dog, which she tossed in the trash. She closed the windows on the front of the house to deaden the sound and the smells and escaped with her book downstairs, where the goings-on next door were somewhat muted.

She'd barely read a page when she heard a knock on the front door. Charlie was up the stairs and skidding across the hardwood before she could even get herself off the couch. The knocking grew louder.

She wrapped her fingers around Charlie's collar and yanked him off the door. "Knock it off!"

She opened the door, expecting Harold, only to find a man who looked a lot like him. He was about her age, attractive despite a nose that had probably once been broken. He had close-cut, sand-colored hair, Harold's light blue eyes, and a crooked smile to go with his crooked nose. He held a plate covered with a cloth napkin.

His smile deepened. "Kate, right? I'm Jeff. My dad sent me. I'm to invite you again on his behalf, and if you insist on being stubborn —his words, not mine—I'm to give you this plate of food." He dramatically removed the napkin, bending low and presenting it as if she were Cinderella and he had the glass slipper on a velvet pillow.

She also couldn't help but notice Harold had sent the care package over on good china, meaning she'd be expected to return it. She'd bet anything the crowd at his house right now was eating off paper or Styrofoam.

"It's nice to meet you, Jeff, but as I told your father, I can't come over."

Charlie wouldn't stop barking and trying to pull away. She pushed him behind her and stepped out onto the porch, closing the door partway.

"Are you sure?" Jeff shared his father's Boston accent. "Dad had the party catered, other than the lobsters and clams, which I under-stand you don't eat." He frowned as he said this.

"Look, Jeff, I'm sorry, but I was kind of in the middle of something—"

He handed her the plate. "By all means. Here you go. It was nice meeting you, Kate. I hope to see you again soon."

Doubtful. In her haste to get back inside, Charlie zipped past her and practically launched himself at Jeff.

"Charlie! Stop!" She reached out to grab him and almost dropped the plate. "Goddamn it!"

Jeff seemed to be enjoying the lavish affection from her traitorous dog. She stepped into the kitchen and set the plate on the countertop for safekeeping. Jeff trailed behind her, leading Charlie by the collar.

"Here you go, buddy," he said, scratching Charlie's ears and throat.

"He's such an attention whore. I hope he wasn't slobbering all over you. I think he's sick of me."

He smiled a charming, crooked smile. "I can't imagine that at all."

A total stranger was standing in her kitchen, and while it made her uncomfortable, she was more annoyed than frightened. Of course this was Harold's son. Pushy must run in the family.

She moved toward the door. "Thank you again."

"This is really nice." He ignored her completely and walked through the kitchen into the dining room to check out the view. "I haven't been in here since the Cunninghams owned it years ago. I never met your friend. My dad said he was a nice man—a little out there, but funny."

Why would he leave? She didn't want to talk to him about Joey or anything else.

"I'm sure you miss him."

"I do."

"It must be hard for you, being alone all the time."

She wasn't sure where he was headed with this conversation, but she wished he would go back to where he came from.

"If you need someone to talk to, I'm a good listener. I'll be here all week." He rested his hip against the counter and folded his arms. "My dad says you need a friend."

If Harold were standing in her kitchen right now, she'd throttle him. "I had a friend," she said, a bit churlishly, "and he's gone. I had a lot of things that are gone. Thank you again for the food and your kind offer, but I'm fine. Please remind your father of that."

She should have been embarrassed for lashing out, but she was too annoyed. First with Harold for talking about her, and second with his son for his presumptions. Exactly what kind of friend did he think she needed?

In spite of her little outburst, Jeff's eyes remained warm. They also held the same hint of mischief his father's usually possessed.

"Like I said, I'm a good listener." He put his hand on her shoulder and gave it a light squeeze.

She stepped back. It had been a long time since she'd been touched, and she didn't like it. He was invading her home and now her personal space.

"If you change your mind or if you want seconds," he continued, "you know where to find us. Just follow the sound of the band."

Band? Sure enough, she heard the familiar sound of guitars tuning up.

"Good thing my dad invites the whole neighborhood, or someone would be calling the cops. I hope you like rock 'n' roll, because whether you join us or not, you're going to hear it."

Her heart plummeted, and her throat went dry. "Your dad likes rock?"

Jeff laughed. "Hardly. It's all hippie music to him. It's a local rock band. They're good. They played my brother's wedding a few years ago. Since then, Dad hires them for the picnic. Come over, you'll see."

She shook her head. "I, um—the phone."

Lame, Kate.

It was obvious no phone was ringing, but Jeff said nothing as she ushered him to the door and locked it behind him.

A band? She toyed with the idea of going out to get away from it, but even if she could think of someplace to go, she couldn't stay out all day and half the night. She'd been facing her fears, hadn't she? Maybe it was time to confront some emotions.

Downstairs, she tried to focus on her book, but the sound of the lead guitar beckoned like a siren on the rocks. Who was she kidding? She may not have been born with music in her blood, but it lived there now. She slipped out onto the patio and curled up on the daybed.

Almost every song Harold's band played triggered a memory. Most made her sad, but they didn't kill her. Only one made her cry, "Sweet Child O' Mine." It was the song Billy had asked her to dance to the night they met. She closed her eyes, eighteen again in her high-heeled boots, swaying in the arms of a beautiful stranger. She could feel the beat of his heart against her cheek and the press of his large, warm hand against her back, pulling her so close the metal of his belt buckle had made her shiver.

When the song was over, she opened her eyes. Charlie's head rested in her lap as she absentmindedly stroked behind his ear. The darkness before her was watery, distorting the beam from the nearly full moon into a jagged path across the cove, but the music—and the memories—hadn't destroyed her.

———

KATE FELL ASLEEP EASILY that night and woke early. She dreamed of Billy, but the memory evaporated as soon as she opened her eyes.

She took Charlie for a walk down at the water's edge, and by the time they returned, the coffee had finished brewing. She poured herself a large cup and stepped out onto the deck, relishing the feel of the smooth boards, warm beneath her bare feet. The sun hung high above the trees, and the birds were already in full voice. Another beautiful day. She settled into the rocker, pressed her toes against the railing, and rocked gently.

The tranquility was short-lived.

At just a few minutes past nine, a knock at the door engaged Charlie's frantic barking. Harold, most likely, coming to scold her for not attending his party.

Wrong again.

"Morning," Jeff said with a big smile. "Did you enjoy your dinner?"

He seemed rather energetic, considering the party had gone on pretty late.

"I did, thank you. I would've brought the dish back, but I see you still have company. I didn't want to intrude." Could he tell she was lying? She had no intention of going anywhere near the place until everyone was gone, him included.

"No intrusion, just my brothers and their families. They're getting ready to head back to Boston. I'm staying until next Saturday."

"Yes, you said that. Let me get your dish."

This time, he waited on the porch. When she handed him the clean plate, he tucked it under his arm.

"Dad wanted me to ask if you'd like to join us for a boat ride this afternoon. We haven't been out together since last summer, and I miss it. It's a beautiful day."

And it was. It was perfect, actually.

"We're going to sail up toward Cape Elizabeth and maybe out to Two Lights. You can't appreciate Maine fully unless you've seen the coast from the water."

Tempting, but she couldn't. Or wouldn't. "No, thank you. I can't."

His face darkened slightly. "Would you at least think about it? I promised Dad I'd convince you to join us. You don't want me to disappoint him, do you?"

"Really, I c—"

"Look, Kate." Those blue eyes and good looks weren't the only thing he inherited from his father, who was also stubborn as a mule. "We're heading to church soon. We'll be back in about two hours. If you change your mind, just come over. No strings. You don't even have to talk to us. You can sit on one end, and we'll sit on the other and ignore you. But I promise you'll enjoy it. I can't think of a better way to enjoy God's handiwork on such a beautiful day than getting on the water."

He pouted and gave her what was clearly meant to be puppy-dog eyes. She recognized it for exactly what it was: flirting. She wanted to march across the lawn and set Harold straight before this went any further. This was the last thing she needed. It was nice to think she could attract someone if she wanted—but she didn't.

"I'll think about it." Her answer surprised her.

"That's all we ask." He was smiling again. "See you later."

He jogged across the lawn.

"I said I'll think about it!"

He raised his arm dismissively, exactly like his father.

She leaned against the heavy oak door after she closed it and sighed. It was tempting. The Portland Head Light had always been one of her favorite places. Being out on the water would be like breaking free, shaking off the grip of the shadows that still had a hold on her. Then again, if Harold had some designs of hooking her up with his son, she didn't want to encourage that in the least. She'd told him she was separated, not available.

She poured herself a fresh cup of coffee and returned to her rocking chair outside. A cormorant stood on a large boulder, strutting and preening, and spreading its wings to dry in the sun. It lifted into the air and flew lazy circles over the incoming tide. It dipped and rose, soaring up and over her house, then back again. Each circle grew wider until it eventually disappeared from view.

Kate rose and stretched her arms up and out. She wasn't ready to soar, but maybe she could stretch her wings.

NERVES GOT the better of her as she crossed into Harold's yard. Maybe this wasn't such a good idea. She was turning back when he called out to her.

"You're coming! Wonderful!" Harold stood on the top step of his deck, beaming.

She didn't see Jeff, which was perfect. If she was going to do this, Harold needed to know that his plan to fix her up with his son wasn't going to fly. No matter how nice he was or how good-looking or charming, it wasn't happening. After all, she'd been charmed by the best, and look how that had turned out.

"Look, Harold." Kate kept her voice low since the windows were open. "About Jeff. He seems very nice, but I'm not interested in getting involved with anyone right—"

The sliding door opened and Jeff stepped out.

"You changed your mind!" He sounded pleased. "This will be just what the doctor ordered. I promise."

Kate felt the smile freeze on her face as Jeff unfastened the top button of his black shirt and slipped the white clerical collar out from the bands that held it in place. He looked as if he were trying not to laugh.

"Give me a minute to change, and then we can get going," he said. "That okay with you, Dad?"

"Whatever you say, Father."

Jeff gave her a wink before heading inside.

Her throat had gone dry. "Your son's a priest?"

"Yup." He was grinning now. "What did you think? I was trying to fix you up?"

As embarrassed as she was, she couldn't help but laugh.

"You know what they say about assumptions," he said.

She made a face. "Yes, but why am I the only one who feels like an ass?"

"Good question."

CHAPTER TWENTY

T hey made their way down the steep, narrow steps to Harold's dock and boarded a small Zodiac that took them out to a boat so big it had its own bathroom, galley kitchen, and a bed. They set sail with Harold at the helm, heading out of Broad Cove and south toward Portland.

"On the left is Peak's Island," Harold called over his shoulder. He pointed to a two-story building with a large, wraparound deck. "See that white building there? That's where my son Steven and his wife, Susan, got married, right out there on the dock."

That was surprising. "Not in church?"

Jeff shrugged and smiled.

"And here on the right is Bug Light and just beyond that, Spring Point. In just a minute or so, you should be able to see the Portland Head Light."

She shielded her eyes and stared into the distance. Sure enough, there it was. Spotting the familiar silhouette gave her the same sense of excitement she'd had as a child. This had always been a magical place for her. All the memories tied up in this sliver of coastline were still there.

They made their way closer to the iconic lighthouse, which was just as beautiful from Casco Bay as it was from land. Harold throttled down the engine as they neared the promontory and she stared up at the monolith, squinting into the sun.

Jeff stood beside her, his hand shielding his eyes. "*A new Prometheus, chained upon the rock,*" he said, reciting a piece from her favorite poem, "*Still grasping in his hand the fire of Jove. It does not hear the cry, nor heed the shock, But hails the mariner with words of love.*"

"'*Sail on!' it says, 'sail on, ye stately ships! And with your floating bridge the ocean span,*'" Kate answered. "'*Be mine to guard this light from all eclipse. Be yours to bring man nearer unto man!*'"

A smile spread across his face. "Another Longfellow fan."

"I am."

"They say he used to walk from his house on Congress Street a couple of times a week to visit the lightkeeper."

"I remember reading that and also that this lighthouse was the inspiration for the poem."

"She knows her Maine history, Dad," Jeff called back to Harold.

"I wouldn't go that far, but I always loved this lighthouse and Longfellow." She almost added that her mother had made her read Longfellow's poems one summer during their vacation, but while it was one of her better memories, she didn't want to introduce the darkness that usually accompanied thoughts of her mother into such a beautiful day.

Kate gripped the rails as a passing boat caused them to rock in its wake.

"Want to see Two Lights?" Harold asked.

"Love to." She resumed her seat in the stern.

The breeze picked up and the temperature dropped as they motored out of the harbor and into open water. She slipped on her jacket and zipped it up, then moved up into the bow to watch the seals swimming nearby or sunning themselves on the rocky shoreline.

Maybe that flirty little seal she'd met a couple of weeks ago was watching her again.

They sailed past Two Lights and a bit farther out. It was unnerving to be so far from land, but it was also thrilling. Part of her wanted to keep going, maybe all the way to Nova Scotia. But before long, Harold swung around and headed back to land. They picked up speed, and the roar of the engine and the rush of the water against the sides of the boat discouraged conversation. With the wind in her hair, the salt spray on her face, and the warmth of the sun on her back, Kate settled in, her mind untethered to the past, and let herself absorb the experience.

"It's been a while since I've had such a nice day," she said later, as Jeff helped her from the Zodiac onto the dock. "Thank you. And Jeff —Father Jeff. Thanks for being so persistent."

"Jeff, please. You don't need to call me Father. You'll make me feel old."

"I was raised a good Catholic girl. I'd be punished if my mother heard me call you by your given name."

"Not acceptable," he insisted. "Jeff is fine."

She led the way up the steep stairs into Harold's lush back yard. It was time to go home. Charlie needed to go out, but she couldn't seem to move from the yard. She didn't want the day to end. She didn't want another night of sitting alone, staring out at the ocean and feeling sorry for herself.

"I understand if you already have plans." The words poured out before she could change her mind. "But I'd love to take you to dinner tonight. Today was wonderful. I needed this more than you could imagine."

Father and son exchanged glances.

"Nothing but leftovers here," Harold answered.

"That would be nice," Jeff said. "We have no plans."

"But you're not paying!" Harold's gruff façade returned. "I'm not into these women's libbers. No woman should ever pay for dinner."

"I insist."

He turned abruptly. "Insist all you want," he called over his shoulder. "You're not paying. We'll pick you up at eight."

Jeff gave her a lopsided grin. "You have to learn to pick your battles. This isn't one you're likely to win."

JEFF PULLED into Kate's driveway exactly at eight. Harold stepped out and offered her the front seat.

"Don't be silly. I'll sit in the back."

Of course he ignored her.

"Fine." She rolled her eyes and slid in beside Jeff.

Harold opened the back door but stopped before climbing in. "Damn it. Just remembered, I was supposed to make a call at eight. Business. You two go ahead. The reservation is for eight fifteen. Don't be late. I'll be there as soon as I'm done." He slammed the door shut and started back across the lawn.

"We can wait," she called after him, but as he so often did, he dismissed her with a wave of his hand.

"That's silly for him to take his car."

"Battles, Kate. Remember?"

A few minutes later, they pulled up to The Channel Grill.

"This is beautiful," she told Jeff as the hostess led them to a table on the deck overlooking the water. The staff had dropped screens around the outdoor area to keep the mosquitoes out, a courtesy she appreciated, as no-see-ums found her quite tasty. "I've been here before with my friend Tommy, but only during the winter."

Jeff told the waiter there would be three for dinner, but after a half hour, Kate knew Harold wasn't coming.

"Did he plan this too?"

"Probably, although he didn't say anything to me about it. I think his intentions are good."

"Obviously it's not a fix-up." She toyed with a breadstick. "At least I hope not. I haven't been to church lately, but I'm pretty sure priests still can't marry. Dating is probably frowned upon as well."

Jeff laughed. "My dad thinks you need a friend. Since you won't talk to him—and even if you did—there isn't much he feels he can say to help you. He's convinced I'd be a good friend. I think he looks at you almost like a daughter."

"Or a daughter-in-law."

Judging by his expression, Jeff hadn't heard what Harold had told the staff about Kate when he was admitted to the hospital, so she explained.

"That bugger," he said, whistling under his breath. "When was this?"

"You didn't know he was in the hospital?"

He shook his head, so she told him everything, from the steady diet of creamed soups to the foreign daughter-in-law.

"No wonder he adopted you and then took your voice away." He shook his head. "That sonofa—"

She pressed her palm against her chest in mock horror. "Father Jeff!"

He took a sip of his Manhattan, then continued to sell himself as her new best friend. "Dad likes you, and he's worried about you. I'm a great listener, Kate. And a good counselor. Not only does it come with the territory as a spiritual adviser, but I did graduate work in psychology before I decided to go into the priesthood. Caring for people is my greatest joy. I believe it's God's plan for me."

Her fingers gripped the napkin in her lap. All she'd wanted was a nice dinner out in gratitude for a special day. She wasn't in the mood to be psychoanalyzed.

"I'm happy for you, and I'm glad you think God has a plan for you. Unfortunately, I don't think he has one for me. To be honest, I think he's forgotten who I am."

Jeff folded his hands and looked at her intently. "I'm sure it feels that way, but God always has a plan. Sometimes you just need to listen and let him guide you to it."

If God had a plan for her, she wanted no part of it, considering how it had gone so far. The world was filled with evil people and she'd never done anything to hurt anyone, yet she'd been through hell. Now here she was, alone, fighting to survive.

"Look." She lowered her voice. "You don't have a clue what my life is like, what I've been through, what I've seen, or what I've lost. There's no fu—there's no way you could know how to help me, even if I wanted your help." She set her napkin on the table and pushed aside her avocado salad. "Could you please take me home?"

His hand stretched across the table and settled on her arm. "Kate, please. I didn't mean to upset you. I promised my father I'd talk with you. Yes, he's a meddling old man, but he means well. He doesn't know what happened to you, but he knows it's something big. It isn't healthy to keep to yourself like you do, and I agree with him. And since he had no luck getting you to talk, he called in the big guns."

She twisted her lips to keep from smiling. "You're the big guns?"

"Afraid so." He removed his hand. "I wasn't planning to take vacation until autumn, when I usually come up and help him close the house. He begged me to come now. It wasn't easy. Church is hopping this time of year with all the tourists."

"Hopping, huh?"

"Absolutely hopping."

She poked at her salad and thought about what he said. He didn't prod her to talk. After a while, the silence felt strangely comfortable.

When the waiter returned, Jeff apologized and asked him to clear the third place setting. They talked all through dinner and dessert, and by the time they had finished their coffee, they were the only ones left on the deck. When Jeff motioned for the check, the waiter informed them it had already been paid.

"He's a piece of work, isn't he?" she asked, shaking her head.

He grinned. "That's my dad."

"You're lucky. You know that, don't you?"

"Yeah. I do."

"My father grudgingly accepted the role but never embraced it.

My mother, in her own special way, made me rue the day I was conceived."

She was touched by the honesty of his grimace.

"And my husband, whose parents were far worse than mine, did his best, but he had no idea how to be a father. He spoiled the first one and often treated the second like some alien life form." She folded her napkin and rested it alongside her empty coffee cup. "Then there's me. I tried so hard not to be my parents that I hovered over my kids until I drove them both crazy. My daughter probably hates me, and my son most likely hates his father because of me. It's such a mess—and that, believe it or not, is the least of it. I'm not getting any Mother of the Year awards for having disappeared without telling anyone where I was going or even that I was going."

To his credit, Jeff just listened. He didn't offer advice, and he didn't try to fix anything.

When they got back to the house, she invited him in for coffee. They sat on the deck overlooking the cove. The moon, high in the sky now, cast a beam of yellow across the water. It had been a beautiful day and other than a few bumps, a beautiful evening. She felt uncharacteristically unburdened. Her work with Liz was going well, but that was different. It was work. It was hard, soul-searching, gut-wrenching, let's-get-to-the-bottom-of-this-and-fix-it work. But tonight felt as if her heart had been a piece of furniture in a closed-up house, and Jeff had come along, thrown open the windows, pulled off the dust cover, and exposed her to the light.

CHAPTER TWENTY-ONE

K ate was growing stronger. Not only was Liz helping her get a
handle on her post-traumatic stress disorder, but they were
tackling the pain of her childhood. She wasn't responsible for her
mother's unhappiness and disappointment. It was an unfair burden,
and she was trying let it go. She was even learning to let go of the
guilt she carried from the shooting.

To believe that she was a valuable person worthy of love no
longer seemed a concept out of her reach. Figuring out how to fix her
relationship with her children still loomed, but she had to believe
she'd get there eventually. Tackling what Billy had done? Despite
what Liz said, that might be something she would never be able to
deal with.

In the meantime, her new family, as she had come to think of Jeff
and Harold, was making her feel at home and more settled than she'd
felt in the months before Harold showed up on her doorstep. Jeff
would often come up from his parish in Ogunquit on Tuesdays, his
day off. He would call the evening before, and they'd make plans to
go out on the boat if the weather was nice.

Even though being out in public places still caused her palms to sweat and her pulse to quicken, at least at first, they'd sometimes go shopping at the Maine Mall or in the Old Port. It was difficult, but she was learning coping mechanisms for high-anxiety situations. Jeff even talked her into going to the movies. It was almost like dating but without the awkward good night at the door—or the danger of having to get her heart back from the man who still possessed it.

Baby steps.

Despite that improvement, she wasn't so sure she was ready when Tom called to tell her he'd heard back from the private investigator. She gripped the phone tightly, prepared for the worst.

"Well?"

"It's not what you thought. Not even close."

"So you're about to tell me Billy's been donating fifteen hundred dollars a month for the past twenty years to an orphanage in Houston?"

"Not exactly. He doesn't have another kid. And it's not going to an old girlfriend, either."

"A new girlfriend?" She was being glib, when what she really wanted to do was throw up.

"No, but you still won't like it." She heard him shifting restlessly on the other end. "Jessie Jones is his mother."

She slumped against the kitchen counter. "What?"

"Jessie Jones is his mother."

"No, she's not! What the hell kind of detective did you hire? His mother's name is Janet Donaldson. Or at least it was." Despair washed over her. This detective had gone on a wild goose chase and come back with a duck.

"No, Kate. It's her. She's been blackmailing Billy all this time."

"What the hell? How did he—"

"Jessie Jones is her stage name. She claims to be a singer. The detective tracked her down at a bar not far from the address where Billy's been sending the checks for the past few years. All it cost him was a few drinks, and she sang like a canary."

If the topic hadn't been so serious, she would have laughed at him for adopting the lingo of a mobster. Instead, she told him to go on.

"The more she drank, the more she talked. Turns out Billy has been paying her so she and his father would stay away from you and the kids."

Her jaw unhinged. "What?"

"That's right. Blackmail. What our guy was able to piece together was that Janet showed up not long after Billy won his Grammy. Said she even met you once. Do you remember?"

Of course she remembered. A couple of months after Devin was born, Janet had approached Kate at a park near their apartment, although she'd lied about who she was. Billy had shown up a few minutes later and, visibly shaken, had whisked Kate and the kids away. At home, he'd told her who the stranger was, and later that night, he'd told her how she had abandoned him after his father had been run off by his grandfather. She'd chosen her husband over her son. The last time he'd seen her, she'd conned him out of his college money and the small inheritance he'd received from his grandparents.

"I do remember. But after that day, we never heard from her again."

"*You* never heard from her. That's because Billy told her to stay away. She agreed, for a price. She told the detective all she wanted was the money, anyway—she's not the grandma type, she told him. She said whenever Billy tried to cut back or weasel out of paying, she'd offer to fly north with his father and pay you all a visit the next time he was on the road."

This was unbelievable.

"You still there?"

"Yeah, but it doesn't make sense. Was he afraid she was going to tell me something he didn't want me to know?"

"I don't think so. It sounds like he just didn't want her or his father in his life, and he was willing to pay to keep them away."

"Why not just tell me? Good lord. I did everything else he asked of me for twenty-four years. Why was this different?"

"As hard as this might be to believe, Janet told the detective Billy is afraid of his father—still. That's why he's been willing to send checks every month since 1991. They started at five hundred dollars and went up from there."

She couldn't wrap her head around any of it. "Billy isn't afraid of anyone, Tommy." The more she tried to work it through, the more confusing it became. "Maybe he's just trying to help her out. She's his mother, after all. Maybe he just didn't want me to know, although I'd never begrudge him helping his family. But to lie about it? Okay, not a lie—but an omission is almost a lie."

Most of her fights with Billy had been about money. For someone who often made good money, he had been extremely frugal. Not to mention secretive. Kate had no access to their checking account and no idea how much money he made. It had been an issue throughout their marriage.

"I wonder if this is why we never took fancy vacations or bought expensive things," she mused, "because he always had to make sure he had money to give to her."

"Without asking him, you may never know."

Kate's eyes roamed across the blue summer sky outside the window, unfocused. Actually, that wasn't true. Maybe there was another way.

CHAPTER TWENTY-TWO

K ate stuck the scrap of paper on the refrigerator with a magnet from a sandwich shop in Yarmouth: JESSIE JONES, 1955 BEECHNUT STREET, HOUSTON, TEXAS

According to her calculations, Billy had easily given his mother over $180,000 over the years. It was mind-boggling. The more she thought about it, the angrier she got. She thought of all the fights, especially the ones about money.

One particularly ugly fight came to mind from about eight years ago. Billy had quit touring to focus on his own band again, but there was no money coming in. Nothing was going his way, and naturally, Kate had been getting the brunt of it.

It all escalated when she came back from the grocery store one afternoon empty-handed because her debit card had been declined.

"Do you know how humiliating that was?" She was furious not only for looking like an idiot at the SuperFresh but for wasting the time it took to do the damn shopping in the first place, and then knowing she'd have to turn around and do it all over again. She was sick of never knowing how much money was in their bank account, and she was fed up at his refusal to discuss finances with her.

"I'm sorry," he'd said, but he seemed more annoyed than sorry. "I'll transfer money into the household account now, and you can go back and get your groceries."

"My groceries? Oh, hell no. You go. I already wasted two hours. I have to figure out something to feed Devin for dinner now and get him to basketball practice by six thirty."

He gave her a look. "I'm not going to the store." He acted as if she'd not only asked him to do the grocery shopping but to do it wearing a sundress with a flower in his hair.

"Well, one of us has to go, and it isn't going to be me."

He slammed his fist onto the counter. "Jesus, Kate. You know I'm under a lot of stress right now."

"And I'm not? I just waited in a long line with people I've known most of my life, only to be told my card was rejected. I could hear the whispers starting behind me before I even knew what was happening. Do you know what people must think?"

"I don't give a fuck what they think."

"Well, I do. I'm the one who sees these people every day. I'm the one who lives here."

He glared down at her. "I don't live here?"

She snorted. "Hardly. And now you're trying to go back on the road, which means you'll be around even less." She threw her purse on the dining room table so hard it slid off the other side, dumping its contents all over the floor.

"I'm so tired of this." Now that the horse was out of the barn, she couldn't stop it from running away with her. "I'm tired of always being alone. I'm tired of being a single parent. I'm tired of never having any fucking money. For someone who's supposed to be a goddamn rock star, we never have any fucking money, and I'm sick of it. The house is falling down around our ears, and you just sit there and play your guitar like you're fucking Nero."

The ice in his blue-gray eyes matched the tone of his voice. "The house was falling down before we moved in. If you'll remember correctly, I didn't even want to move into this fucking house. I bought it for you. I hate this fucking place."

She wheeled around, ready to strike. "Nice. Maybe you wouldn't hate it so much if you'd get a regular job so we can fix it, and then maybe we might even be able to do something like go on a damn vacation once in a while."

"I do have a job, Kate." His voice was dripping with venom. "I'm a musician. I was a musician when you married me."

"I mean a real job." She was on dangerous ground but kept inching out farther. "Why can't you teach or something?"

"Because even if I wanted to do that, which I don't, I didn't finish college, and since so many years have passed, I'd have to start all over again. Doesn't seem very feasible to me, unless you plan to support us in the meantime. Why don't you get a job? Then you can't bitch at me because you don't have any money. Or maybe you'd rather I became a plumber or a mechanic."

His chest was heaving. She knew he was trying to control his temper, but she was out of control now too.

His words were measured. "I'm going through a rough patch right now. You know, this whole deal is for better or for worse."

"Yeah, well, I'm sick of always having the worse." As soon as the words left her mouth, she was sorry.

The muscle along his jaw twitched like mad. If she had been a man, he might have knocked her off her feet. She had gone too far.

"Really? Well, fuck you!"

He pushed past her, yanked open the closet, and snatched his jacket, sending the hanger clattering to the floor.

She grabbed his arm as he headed for the back door, but he pulled away.

"Back off, Kate," he said through clenched teeth, his voice low and threatening. "I'm warning you. Step back."

"Billy." She hadn't meant half of what she'd said. She was tired and stressed, and just as he'd been doing with her, she was taking it out on him. "Please."

She reached for him again.

"Back off. I mean it. Get the fuck away from me."

She'd never seen him so angry—not with her, anyway. He snatched the keys to his truck from the hook by the door and left.

Three days passed without even a phone call. He'd stormed off in the middle of a fight before, but this was the longest he'd ever been gone. She went from feeling guilty to being worried and through various degrees of anger. She could have called his cell phone, but she wasn't the one who'd left.

By the third evening, she began to wonder if she should report him missing. If he did return, after what he was putting her through, she was afraid she might strangle him.

She was too embarrassed to go back to the grocery store, so she went to the bank with the intention of taking cash from her household account and driving to the next town to do her shopping. But Billy had never transferred the money, leaving her with $18.57 to buy milk, food, and gas for her car, which was on empty. Grumbling the entire way, she walked to the small corner market in town to get milk and paid three times as much for a dozen eggs, a package of hot dogs, and a bag of rolls. If he didn't come home soon, they'd starve.

By the time she returned home, it had begun to snow. Flakes came down fat and fast. In no time, the ground was covered. Her anger grew with each passing hour. Rhiannon and Devin were fighting. All she wanted was to make dinner and go to bed. Not that she would sleep, between worry and anger and of course the unasked question: if he wasn't sleeping at home, where the hell was he sleeping?

She dumped a can of pork and beans into a small saucepan and turned the stove on to boil a pot of water for the hot dogs. There was a loud pop, and smoke began pouring from the front burner of the ancient range. The lights in the kitchen and dining room flickered and went out.

"What next?" she yelled.

The light outdoors was fading quickly, especially with the snowfall. She could barely see to yank the stove away from the wall to reach the plug.

She trudged through the dark stone basement, guided by a flashlight, and flipped the breaker for the two darkened rooms upstairs. With the stove now toast, she pulled on Billy's tall rubber boots near the back door and her mittens and went outside to start the grill.

It wouldn't start. After kicking the damn thing and nearly breaking a toe, she limped back inside to find matches. She wasn't anxious to light it manually, although the prospect of blowing herself up, along with the house, had its pluses and minuses.

She rolled a bit of newspaper into a long tube like she'd seen Billy do, lit the end, and turned on the gas. She reached around underneath with the lit paper. The flames swallowed the length of the newspaper, and she wondered why she hadn't used a tapered candle. It still didn't light. She pushed the last of the burning newspaper closer to the opening. The grill belched with a loud whoosh and a blast of flames that licked her face and melted her mascara, and she tumbled backward into the snow.

"Goddamn sonofabitch, sick and tired of this shit," she grumbled, angrily brushing off the snow. She threw all eight hotdogs onto the grill, determined she wouldn't be turning it on again anytime soon.

She was wondering how much she could get pawning a Fender Telecaster when she heard Billy's pickup in the driveway.

The truck door slammed. She refused to acknowledge him and kept staring at the grill, even when she sensed him standing behind her. She stabbed at the hot dogs—the cheap kind, because she couldn't afford the all-beef kind—and rolled them over so they could finish cooking before she froze to death. She gave the pot of beans a stir, although they didn't seem to be cooking at all.

"What are you doing?" he asked quietly behind her.

"What does it look like?" She sounded just as nasty, if not nastier, than before he left.

"It looks like you're having a cookout in the middle of February."

"Well, then, that's what I'm doing."

She jabbed at another hot dog but missed. It rolled off the grill and into the snow at her feet. She scooped it up with mittened fingers and threw it back on the grill.

"Jeez," he muttered.

She glared up at him.

"Why are you cooking outside?"

"Because the stove just blew up."

His head snapped up to the kitchen window, as if checking to see if it was on fire. "What happened?"

"I don't know. Do I look like an electrician?" *Keep it up, Kate, and he'll get right back in that truck, and it will be three weeks before you see him again.*

"Let me do this," he said gently. "Go inside."

"I'm fine. I don't need your help." She grabbed for the pot and bumped it, spilling half the beans into the workings of the grill and the rest onto the ground and her boots.

She started to cry.

"Okay," he said. "Give me that." He wrested the fork from her fingers. Then he turned off the grill, piled the hot dogs onto the plate, and balanced it on top of the empty pot. He opened the backdoor and held it, waiting for her to enter.

"Daddy's home!" Rhiannon cried from the kitchen.

Thunderous footsteps were heard on the stairs.

"Hey, Dad," shouted Devin. "Hot dogs!"

He grabbed a roll.

Rhiannon wrinkled her nose. "I hate hot dogs. Besides, I already ate."

Kate was too aggravated to argue.

"Then you can sit here while the rest of us eat," Billy said.

"Why? I have homework."

"Your homework can wait until after dinner. Sit down. I haven't seen you for a few days."

"That's not my fault." Rhiannon glared at her mother, indicating she knew exactly whose fault it was.

Kate wasn't in the mood for a go-round with either of them. She pulled off the boots and hung her wet coat on the rack by the back door.

"Where were you?" Devin asked, already reaching for another hot dog.

"I had business in the city."

Kate coughed, and Rhiannon muttered something under her breath.

"You have something to say, young lady?" Billy asked.

Her head shot up, surprised, but she gave him a smile that matched his own.

"No, Daddy. I'm just glad you're home."

"I thought so."

Kate spread some homemade relish on her hot dog and took a bite. She chewed and chewed, but the thing didn't want to go down.

"Your homework finished?" Billy asked Devin.

"Yep, did it as soon as I got home." He gave his sister a smug look. She made a face and rolled her eyes.

"Good. Then you can go grocery shopping with me after dinner."

"Grocery shopping?" Devin asked, his mouth hanging open. "Why do I have to go?"

"Someone needs to show me where the store is." He smiled at Kate, who was too surprised to respond.

"But that's Mom's job," Devin continued.

Rhiannon snorted softly.

"You can do the dishes," Billy told her.

"What? That's Mom's job," she cried, truly indignant.

Devin smirked into his plate.

"Speaking of jobs," Rhiannon said, "did Mom tell you she got a job?"

Kate shot her daughter a warning glance, but it was too late.

"What?" Billy looked from Rhiannon to Kate.

"Yeah," Devin chimed in. "Mom's going to be a reporter."

"Not a reporter, jerkface. She's going to be a typist." Rhiannon was eager to correct her brother.

Billy's smile faded. "You got a job?"

She fidgeted in her seat, wistful for the days before her children could speak.

"I did," she said, her voice low. She cleared her throat and stuck out her chin. "For the Belleville News and print shop."

"You're going to be a reporter?" He seemed more than a little surprised.

"I'm just going to work the counter at the print shop a few days a week for Mr. Holmes. Do some proofreading and typing for the paper, like birth announcements and weddings, stuff like that."

He pushed his plate with the half-eaten hot dog away. "You don't need a job. You can call him tomorrow and tell him never mind."

"But I do," she insisted. "Besides, I want this job."

He seemed about to argue but let it go. "We'll talk later." He turned to his son. "You ready there, buddy?"

Devin nodded, his cheeks puffed out with a fourth hot dog.

Rhiannon started clearing the table, while Devin went to fetch his boots and jacket. Kate stood and began gathering the rest of the plates.

Billy came up behind her and put his hand on her arm. "Let her do it. You look tired."

He looked tired too, but she wasn't about to exonerate him. Not yet, anyway.

He drew a finger along the side of her face. "I'm sorry." His voice was so low she could barely hear him.

She owed him an apology too and would have given it—three days earlier, before he'd walked out on her. Now, she wasn't in the mood to apologize.

He didn't seem to expect one, though. He kissed the top of her head and slipped into his jacket. "Let's go!" he called to Devin before telling Rhiannon to make her mother a cup of tea.

"What am I, the goddamn maid now?" Rhiannon said.

He rounded on her. "What did you say?"

"Nothing," she muttered, running hot water into the sink. "When are we going to get a dishwasher?"

"Keep it up," he warned, "and I'll tell you where I just found one."

Kate hid a smile at the long, low sigh from her daughter.

After a hot bath, Kate climbed into bed. She was reading when she heard the truck pull into the driveway. The deep bass of male voices could be heard coming from the kitchen below her as they put the groceries away.

The light was out, but she was still awake when Billy came to bed. He undressed quietly and climbed in beside her. She welcomed the familiar creak of the bedsprings and shift of weight beside her in spite of her residual anger. She had settled in far over on her side with barely an inch to spare, her back to him.

He was still for a while, then moved closer. "Katie."

He lay his hand atop the blanket covering her. She didn't move. He slid his hand underneath and touched the bare skin of her arm.

"Babe. You awake?"

She didn't answer, so he moved his hand up and down her arm, gently.

"Katie." His face, clean-shaven just days ago, bristled with whiskers against her ear. "I need you."

She let out a small sigh of exasperation.

He ran his hand over the curve of her waist and down her hip until he reached the hem of her nightgown. He slipped his hand beneath it. He traced his fingers over her back in small circles, just the way she liked. When she didn't respond, he moved his hand across her belly, then up, cupping her breast.

"What are you doing?" she asked finally.

His lips trailed along the curve of her neck and stopped just below her ear, where he planted soft, gentle kisses. She cursed the goose bumps that popped up under his touch.

"I need you," he said. "Please don't shut me out."

She rolled toward him. "Are you serious? Shut you out? You walk out on me, leaving me with nothing but eighteen dollars in the bank, no food in the house, no gas in my car, and you don't even call to tell me where you are or if you're okay? And four days later, you just show up and go to the grocery store and now you're the big hero, and I'm supposed to lie here and spread my legs like I'm grateful?"

"Don't be crude."

His response took her by surprise.

"You know it's not like that," he said. "It's never like that."

He kept his hand on her waist and pulled her closer.

"I was too angry," he whispered. "It scares me when I get that angry. I had to go." His voice was so soft he could have been speaking words of love, not justifying his actions. "Please, Katie. I need you." He kissed her temple, his whiskers tickling her cheek as he moved closer to her lips. "I'm sorry. I was wrong. I shouldn't have left. I was just so mad. I thought I should go before I did something."

She pushed against his chest, but he held her tightly.

"Baby, please, I need you." He sighed against her throat.

She pushed again, but not as hard. It was clear, no matter her opinion on the matter, that he meant to have her. And he was impossible to resist.

Her anger and resolve melted under the heat of his touch. He was on top of her now, her nightgown scrunched up about her neck, kissing and touching her, wearing her down to the place they could always go no matter what, the place they could get lost in each other and damn the rest of the world.

He knew she'd give in, and she did. And all of the last few days were forgotten, at least until morning.

Kate woke to the smell of coffee. When the edge of the bed dipped, she opened her eyes slowly. Billy handed her a cup. Surprised, she blinked several times, looking between him and the cup, and then nearly spilled it when she saw what time it was.

"I already took them to school."

She pulled herself into a sitting position and narrowed her eyes.

"Grocery shopping, taking the kids to school, making me coffee—
are we trading places?" Her voice was raspy with sleep. "I told you,
it's just a part-time job."

"And I told you that you don't need to work."

She gave him a baleful look over the top of the cup.

"I'm sorry about the other day."

"So am I. I don't want you to be a plumber."

The edge of his mouth curled into the grin she loved so much. It
faded before he spoke again. "About a month ago, I got an offer from
Pandemonium to go on tour, but I turned it down. I was trying to
focus on my own music . . ."

"It'll happen. It will."

"I don't know." He shook his head and sighed. "Anyway, when I
left the other day, I drank too much, and when I'd sobered up, I went
into the city to see if I could hook up with their manager, see if
they're still interested."

She cringed. A tour meant he would be away for weeks at a time.

"They hired someone already, but I kind of wore him down,
and . . ."

She exhaled slowly. "When do you leave?"

"Tuesday."

"How long?"

"Three weeks in Canada."

Not too bad. She nodded.

"Then five weeks in Europe, a week in Russia, a week in Japan,
then back to the West Coast to start the US leg of the tour."

"What?" Several drops of coffee splashed onto the comforter.

He took the cup from her. "I gotta take it. It's a good opportunity
and good money."

"That's such a long time," she said, trying to tamp down her anger
and disappointment. Anger at herself for pushing him to this.

"The good news, however . . ."

She folded her arms crossly and frowned.

" . . .the good news is that I called a couple of contractors to come out today and give us some prices on the addition we've talked about. With this tour, we can afford it now. We'll add on to the kitchen, put a bathroom upstairs for the kids, and add a master bedroom with your own bathroom."

All very nice. But still.

"Would you skip the tour if I told you I don't mind one bathroom for four people?"

He tucked a strand of hair behind her ear. "No, and you'd be lying. Besides, I already signed the contract. I have to go."

"That's that, I guess." She started to get up.

"So now, you see, you don't have to go to work. There'll be plenty of money."

"You'll give me the checkbook?"

He looked for a second as if he might lose his temper again. He shook his head. "I told you I'll take care of that. I'll have money deposited into your account regularly. You won't have to worry."

"Fine. But just so you understand: I already accepted the job. I'm taking it."

Over the next eight years, Kate regretted taking that job many times over. But never did she regret it as much as she had over the past ten months.

CHAPTER TWENTY-THREE

Jessie Jones, 1955 Beechnut Street, Houston, Texas

Kate didn't need the paper anymore. She had long since committed the address to memory. It had become a talisman. It not only gave her courage, but it kept her blood simmering at a low boil, right where she wanted it.

The plane lurched as it touched down. Her stomach was in knots. She'd told no one what she was doing or where she was going, and she'd almost turned back several times during her drive to the jetport. She'd either lost her mind or found her strength. Either way, she'd come too far to turn back.

She collected her bag from the overhead compartment and headed for the exit.

"Welcome to Houston," chirped a stewardess with a painted-on smile. "Enjoy your stay."

"We'll see," Kate answered honestly.

Less than an hour later, she was sitting in a taxi in front of 1955 Beechnut Street, a tan stucco, three-story apartment unit in a working-class neighborhood.

"Promise you'll wait for me," she implored the driver for the third time. "I wrote down your name and license number." She tried to sound threatening or at least like she meant business.

He glanced at her in the rearview mirror, then swiveled until he was facing her. "I'm not going anywhere. But just so's you know, it's twenty-four dollars an hour for waiting."

"I won't be that long. If I am, call the police."

There was no way of knowing what she would find or the reception she would receive. She didn't even know if Janet, or Jessie, or whatever the hell she was calling herself, was home.

She took a deep breath but made no move for the door.

"Do you want me to open the door for you?" he asked.

She shook her head and put her hand on the door handle. The driver watched her in the rearview mirror.

"Here goes nothing."

The building had a single entrance with a glass vestibule. Inside the vestibule was a list of names and call buttons. She scanned the first line. Nothing. Near end of the second row, she saw it: JONES/DONALDSON, APT. 3G

She stepped back. Janet could be using either name, but seeing both names like that made her wonder if Billy's father also lived here. Why hadn't she thought of that? This was a bad idea. She should just leave now, head back to the airport.

She glanced at the cab parked on the street. The driver gave her a thumbs-up and flicked his hand, motioning her forward.

Now what? She could push the button to be let inside, but when Jones/Donaldson asked who she was, what would she say? *Hello, I'm your long-lost daughter-in-law here to give you hell.*

A teenaged boy sauntered into the vestibule on the way out of the building. Kate stood to the side, reading the list of names, and once he passed, she scooted in. He hadn't even noticed her, his head bobbing rhythmically to the music blasting through his earbuds.

An elevator was located directly in front of her; corridors extended to the right and left. The hallways were dark and smelled of mildew, cigarettes, and the unmistakable combination of body odor and urine. Trying to calm her jittery nerves, she pushed the button for the elevator and waited. It made no sound. After trying two more times, she walked toward the end of the hall until she came to a set of double doors that led to a staircase.

Outside, the air had been steamy. Inside, it was stifling. How could anyone over fifty climb up and down three flights of stairs in the southeastern Texas heat? Kate huffed her way upward, focusing on why she was here. She was frightened and nervous, but she was also angry as hell. And this time, she was going to do something about it.

The third floor didn't smell quite as bad as the lower level, although it was far from pleasant. Stained beige carpet contrasted with the apartment doors, which were painted a bright, beachy turquoise.

Kate stood outside 3G, drawing on her anger to strengthen her. Loud country music seeped through the door.

A tiny voice inside her spoke as she lifted her hand to knock: *It's not too late to turn and run.*

"Yes, it is," she answered. "It's twenty years too late."

She knocked. Nothing. After a minute, she knocked again, harder this time.

The music stopped. "Jesus Christ." She heard a woman's muffled voice. "Hold your horses."

Heels clacked angrily across a tile floor. The door flew open. "Yeah?"

Kate recognized her immediately. She had aged, of course, and she looked as though she lived hard, despite her obvious use of Botox and lip injections. Given her unnaturally large, high breasts for a woman her age, it wasn't difficult to figure out how she spent a good portion of the money her son was giving her.

The one time Kate had seen Janet Donaldson, the woman had been wearing sunglasses. It was her eyes she found most unsettling now, a soft blue-gray with flecks of gold—Billy's eyes. A cigarette dangled from her lips, and she tightened the belt on her hand-painted silk kimono. Her hair was still long and blond, and she was made up like a drag queen.

Kate tried to speak, but nothing came out. Instead, she coughed.

"Can I help you?" Janet looked about two seconds away from slamming the door in her face.

It was now or never.

"Sorry. I had something in my throat." She coughed again, although she didn't have to fake it. The cigarette smoke floated around her head, burning her throat and eyes. "Jessie Jones, right?"

"Who wants to know?" She took another drag, stuck out her bottom lip, and blew it straight up into the air over her head.

"And you're also Janet Donaldson?" She felt braver now, even prepared to stick her foot in the door if need be.

Janet narrowed her eyes, looking at Kate as if trying to place her, then bent down suddenly to grab a small black cat that was about to stroll out into the hallway.

"Whaddaya want? I ain't got all day," she snapped, straightening up.

"I won't keep you long, I promise." Kate forced herself to smile. "May I come in? I have a business proposition for you."

Janet eyed her narrowly, squinting from the smoke that appeared to be burning her eyes as well.

"May I?" she mimicked Kate in a high-pitched, nasally whine. She laughed at her little insult, then leaned against the door. "Business proposition, huh?"

"I promise I won't stay too long. In fact, I have a cab waiting. So the longer it takes, the more it's costing me."

Janet stood back, opening the door wider. "C'mon in, then. Far be it from me to cost you any money."

Kate snorted involuntarily. *Oh, honey, you've cost me plenty.* It was the reminder she needed. The rest of her nervousness evaporated.

"Do I know you from somewhere?" Janet asked as she entered the apartment. "I never forget a face, and yours is familiar." She snubbed out her cigarette. When Kate didn't answer, she shrugged. "So you got a cab waiting. What's up?"

Kate cleared her throat. "We've met, only you told me your name was Jane. My name is Kate. Kate Donaldson."

"No shit." Janet dropped the cat. It landed with a thud on four paws and took off running.

Janet stepped into the tiny kitchen and helped herself to a beer. She popped the lid and surveyed Kate as she took a sip. "I knew you looked familiar. You still married to my son?"

It was possible she knew they were separated and had talked to Billy, but Kate nodded anyway.

"So to what do I owe the pleasure?"

"I want you to stop blackmailing Billy."

She cackled. "Blackmailing? Is that what he calls it?" She lit another cigarette, and blew the smoke away from Kate but glared at her all the same. "I call it helping his mother out. He's worth millions. Throwing me a few bucks here and there isn't gonna kill him." She took a long drag. "You must be one greedy little bitch to begrudge me a couple bucks in my old age."

For a woman, she had one hell of a set of balls. "Greedy? Me?" Kate almost laughed. "No, Janet, I'm not the greedy one. And it also wasn't a couple of bucks here and there. We both know that."

"So whaddaya want? He send you all the way down here to tell me he's cutting me off? Is he afraid to come see me himself?"

"To be honest, I don't think he thinks about you much at all, and I don't blame him." She almost choked on her own words. Being cruel wasn't in her nature, and although this woman didn't deserve any better, Kate still found it hard to be nasty. "Billy doesn't know I found out about your little arrangement. I'm telling you myself, it's going to stop."

"Says who?" Janet asked, although she didn't seem as smug as she had been a few moments earlier.

"I say. You're going to call and tell him you don't want any more money."

"Ha!" she laughed. "And who's gonna make me? You?"

"No. You're going to do it on your own, and I'll tell you why." Kate opened her purse and removed a manila envelope.

"This is a cashier's check for five thousand dollars. It's yours if you call him right now and tell him you no longer want his money." She watched Janet's face. "Then apologize for taking it all these years." The last part was unrehearsed, but Billy deserved it.

"What?"

"You tell him you don't want the money, and you apologize."

The face she made was almost comical. Kate continued, undaunted. "You might not care what I have to say, but I'm going to say it anyway."

To her credit, Janet composed herself rather quickly. The look on her face told Kate she had no fucks to give.

"He isn't worth millions. Far from it. Life has always been a struggle for Billy since long before I knew him, which I'm sure you're well aware of, having played an important part in that. We carved out a little happiness for ourselves, and I've been blessed to have him in my life, but it was never easy. He's been fighting demons all his life, and it's time to put this one to rest. I understand he was paying to keep you away from our family. But the jig is up. You can do as I ask, and I'll give you the five thousand as a final payment, and we'll keep this between you and me. Or you can ignore me, and I take my five thousand home and tell him I know. Either way, it's over. And you and Billy's father will continue to stay away from all of us."

She held up the envelope. "What's it going to be? I have a cab waiting, remember?"

Janet snorted, dropped her cigarette into an ashtray, and went into the kitchen to retrieve her cell phone. She started to punch numbers into the phone, but Kate stopped her.

"No. I'll dial. I want to know you're calling the right number."

Janet glared and handed her the phone. Kate set the phone on speaker, then punched in the numbers. She assumed Billy wouldn't answer, and he didn't. It was hard enough hearing his recorded voice. To listen to him live would have been unbearable.

She nodded at Janet after the beep.

"Billy." Janet cleared her throat. "It's your mother. Don't send me any more money. I, um, I don't really need it and I, uh, wanted to say . . . thanks for helping me out."

Kate pictured Billy listening to the message and tried to imagine the relief he might feel.

"And Billy . . ."

She held her breath.

" . . . I'm sorry. You were a good boy. You deserved better. Take care of yourself."

Kate pressed her hand to her chest. She couldn't have scripted it better herself. For a second, she almost felt bad for treating Billy's mother so harshly. She was about to say so, but Janet cut her off.

"There." Janet snapped her phone shut. The flicker of compassion she'd exhibited two seconds earlier was gone, leaving her dry-eyed and bitter.

Kate was stunned. "You didn't mean any of that, did you?"

"You told me to apologize and I'd get the five grand. That's what I did. Where's my money?"

Maybe Billy had been right to do whatever he needed to keep his mother away from her and their children. "So we have a deal, then? You and his father leave him alone, right?"

"I'm a woman of my word. And as far as Bill goes, he died in prison twelve years ago." She shrugged. "He finally pissed off the wrong person."

Kate almost staggered under the weight of it all. Her old self wanted to express her sympathy, but the other self—the self who had spontaneously boarded a plane and flown halfway across the country on a whim—wanted to scratch the bitch's eyes out.

What she actually did was hand Janet the check. "Don't bother him again."

Janet's eyes grew watery. She blinked a few times. "I don't think you understand how hard it's been to keep a roof over my head. I don't suppose you care how I'll get by now without a little help."

She didn't know if Billy's mother could sing, but her acting skills needed work. She took in the small, shabby apartment. "I hate to say this, but I don't care how you're going to get by. I really, truly don't give a damn."

With that, she walked out of the apartment and down the hall. The door slammed behind her, echoing through the empty corridor. She jumped but kept walking down the steps and outside to where her cab waited.

She climbed into the cab and collapsed against the seat.

"Oh my god." She grinned at the driver in amazement. "That may have been the hardest thing I've ever done, but it feels so good." She held out her arms. "And look! My hands aren't even shaking."

"That's good, I guess. I hope you didn't go in there and kill somebody." He sounded as if he was only half joking.

She couldn't stop grinning. "No bodies, nope. But I may have finally put a ghost to rest."

CHAPTER TWENTY-FOUR

Liz was dumbstruck when Kate told her about the spur-of-the-moment trip.

"That's amazing!" Liz exclaimed. "Although personally, I don't know that I would've given her any more money. But still."

"I wanted her to apologize," Kate said. "I know it won't take away forty years of hurt, but it's something. A little salve on a very deep wound."

"Why was that so important to you?"

She struggled to find the right words. "Because he's been hurt so much. There's this deep, beautiful soul inside him, but on the outside, he's hard and angry. He's ready to strike out at anyone and anything before it can hurt him first. I think I might finally understand the drinking and the drugs. He was numbing himself, trying to get away from it. But every month, he had to sit down and write that check and be reminded that she was still hurting him. I couldn't bear thinking of him like that. I wanted to make it go away."

Liz laced her fingers together and hooked them over her crossed knees. "Do you still love him, Kate?"

Tears welled up in her eyes. "Of course I do. I always will.

Everyone should have that one great love, and he was mine. I can't imagine ever loving someone like that again. I wouldn't want to."

"Why?"

Kate plucked a tissue from a nearby box. "First of all, I don't think I'll ever not love him. And second, a love like that is so encompassing it leaves no room for anything else. If the person loves you back, great, but if they don't . . . It's too painful."

"I'd like to focus on that relationship as we move forward, as well as your relationship with your children. You need to find a way to interact with all of them that's healthy for you. I think the time you've given yourself to heal has been good. I wasn't sure about that at first, hiding from your problems, but it seems to have worked for you. But you can't fully heal if you don't face them. You can only go so far, and I think you're getting to that point."

Kate shifted against the cushions. Facing Billy's mother had been easier than facing her children would be. She nervously clutched the tissue. "I know. I need to figure out how to fix things with Devin and Rhiannon, but Billy?" She wrapped her arms around her middle. "That scares me."

"Do you think he would hurt you again? Physically?"

She shook her head adamantly. "Oh, no. Once he realized what he'd done—afterward, I mean—I'm sure it hurt him more than it did me. Maybe it still does. I think the fact that he did that to me, that he was capable of that kind of violence—even though I know it was the drugs—scared him. Although . . ."

She shuddered, remembering the night of Joey's funeral when Billy had essentially raped her. "It was terrifying and awful, but I don't believe he meant to do me harm." She glanced over at Liz. "I know it sounds like I'm making excuses for him."

"A bit. Why are you afraid of dealing with your relationship?"

For all the time she'd given herself to reflect, to grieve, to prepare, it was still difficult to put any of it into words. "I think that if I were to sit down with Billy face to face and tell him I'm ready to work on us . . . I think he'll tell me it's over. And while I know that here"—she pointed to her head—"I'm not sure I'm ready to accept it here." She pressed an open palm to her heart. "He hurt me physically and emotionally. He cheated. He lied. He shut me out. He's done things, I'm sure, I can't even imagine. Yet the eighteen-year-old me still loves him and isn't ready to let go, even though I know it's time."

She closed her eyes and pressed a finger under her nose. If she didn't take a moment, she would start crying. Again. And she was so damn sick of crying.

"It's as simple as that. I'm afraid if I see him, it will either be over once and for all or it won't, and things will go right back to the way they had been. I can't deal with either right now." She opened her eyes. "I'm just not ready."

"We'll get there," said Liz. "I have faith in you."

CHAPTER TWENTY-FIVE

It was hot and muggy, even with the breeze off the ocean. Kate spent most of the day standing in the pool up to her shoulders, her book propped open on the concrete surround. It was the only place she could find any relief. The house had no air conditioning. So far she hadn't needed it, but the temperature was threatening to hit one hundred. On days like this, she was almost glad she'd cut off all her hair.

Jeff was visiting, and Harold had invited her to join them for dinner on his dock, where he'd turned his little fishing shack into a tiny, self-contained, open-air apartment of sorts. There was a refrigerator and a microwave and even a futon for sleeping when the hot, humid air in the house was too much. There were picnic tables on the deck, giving it the appearance of an outdoor dockside restaurant.

"This corn is pretty good," Kate said, helping herself to a second ear, "but when Tommy comes this weekend, I'm going to ask him to bring some Jersey corn and tomatoes. Then you'll see what really good corn tastes like."

"Do they have lobsters in New Jersey?" Harold asked.

"Of course they do," Jeff answered.

"I'm not talking to you."

Kate made a face. She could see Harold's point coming from a mile away. "Yes, they have lobsters."

"Maine lobsters?"

"Yes."

He seemed satisfied that New Jersey imported its lobsters from Maine but Mainers had their own corn, or something to that effect. She just shook her head.

A motorcycle roared up Spurwink Road.

"That's Shane," she said, addressing Harold's scowl. "It's his father's. He's probably visiting his grandmother. He's working days during the summer, so he comes in the evening."

"Damn hippie," Harold muttered.

"He's a nice boy. He's been a lifesaver for me."

"I've met him," Jeff said. "He's a nice young man, Dad."

"Humph," was all Harold said.

She finished her corn and wiped her hands on a paper napkin. "I have some news."

Jeff set down his lobster cracker, while Harold tipped his head back to drain the liquid out of a large claw.

"I went to the Portland Resource Center the other day and filled out an application to volunteer. I got a call today. I'm going to work in the kitchen a couple of days a week."

Harold scowled. "Good timing. Go work in a hot kitchen as soon as the temperature hits a hundred."

"I think that's wonderful," Jeff said.

"You would." Harold grabbed another ear of corn. He reached for the butter, but Jeff snatched it away.

Harold glared at his son, then at Kate. "That's not the best neighborhood, you know. You think about that?"

"There's lots of parking nearby."

"Of course there is," he argued, "because no one can afford a car. They just steal from the fools who park there."

"Dad—"

"No." Harold slammed the corn onto his plate. "You really think she should go downtown where all those immigrants and refugees are? It's not safe."

Kate's chest tightened. Maybe it wasn't such a good idea.

"I'm sure it's fine, Dad." Jeff's voice carried a note of warning.

Harold shook his head. "The only way I'm going to allow you to go is if I drive you and pick you up. Case closed."

"What?" she gasped.

"Dad!" Jeff said, loudly. "You can't tell her what to do."

"I'll say," she said.

"Case. Closed!" Harold rose and scraped his lobster shells and corn cob into a small trash can. "When do you start, and what time do we have to be there?"

Kate's mouth opened and closed several times. She looked at Jeff for help, but he also seemed speechless.

"You look like you're trying to catch flies," Harold said. "I asked you a question."

She crossed her arms and glared at him. "I don't believe this."

"Believe it." He took a sip of his beer.

Kate took a healthy swig of her own.

The conversation evaporated, but tension remained high. The only one unfazed was Harold, who helped himself to a second lobster.

"Kate!" a voice called. Charlie bolted up the stairs.

"Damn it," she yelled after him.

"Is that Shane?" Jeff asked.

"I don't think so."

"Kate! Are you down at the dock?"

"Oh my god!" She scrambled up from the picnic table. "It's Tommy. I thought he wasn't coming until Saturday."

She cupped her hands and called.

"C'mon down." She waved excitedly when Tom appeared at the top of the steep stairway. "It's okay, isn't it?" asked Harold.

He pushed up from the table. "I'll throw another lobster in the pot."

Tom gingerly picked his way down to the dock. "Wow, those are some stairs."

She threw her arms around him and gave him a long squeeze, then stood back to look at him. "I thought you were coming Saturday."

"And miss your birthday?"

She rolled her eyes. "I'm ignoring that this year. Remember?" She kept her voice low, hoping neither Harold nor Jeff had heard him.

"When's your birthday?" Jeff asked.

"Friday," Harold answered from the window of the dockside kitchen. "Lobster?" he asked, looking at Tom.

"Well, I did stop at Burger King on the turnpike."

Harold made a grumbling sound, which meant Tom would be eating lobster shortly. Kate pulled a Shipyard ale from the cooler and handed it to him, then went into the little kitchen to melt more butter.

"You know, I'm perfectly capable of driving myself to the resource center tomorrow," she said, her voice low but firm. "This is a big step for me. I appreciate your concern, Harold, but this is certainly a decision I can make on my own."

"Not gonna happen. Do you think he wants one lobster or two?"

Kate dumped a stick of butter into a bowl and popped it into the microwave. She slammed the door shut, a lot harder than was necessary. "You're a piece of work, you know that?"

"I certainly do."

———

BOTH HAROLD and Tom drove Kate to the resource center Tuesday morning. She sat in the back seat muttering all the way to Portland.

"You know what they say about people who talk to themselves, don't you?" Harold asked after a while, watching her from the rearview mirror.

"That they have high-handed friends?"

Tom laughed but didn't turn around. When Harold pulled up in front of the building, he asked if she would like him to walk her inside. She flashed him a dirty look.

"I'll be back to pick you up around two," he said. "Have a nice da—"

She slammed the door and headed toward the entrance. They were still there when she reached the building, waiting for her to enter before pulling away. She walked back to the car.

"Thanks for the ride. Now do me another favor and look around. The neighborhood is not that bad, and there is plenty of parking right by the building. It's perfectly safe. I don't need an escort."

"We'll see," Harold said.

"Insufferable." She spun around and headed inside.

When Tom picked her up three hours later, her arms were sore from peeling and chopping vegetables and her legs hurt from standing for so long, but for the first time in a long while she felt she had accomplished something worthwhile.

"How was it?" he asked as she climbed into his Lexus.

"Exhausting but good." She settled into the comfy, air-conditioned seat. "I was nervous at first, but everyone is nice, and it's so busy the time flew by. The food is kind of blah, and they need lots of supplies, but it's food. Fills the gut, right?"

"I guess," he answered, heading toward the highway. "You hungry?"

"No, I had some leftover lentil soup. What I would like is a nap."

"Poolside nap? Sounds perfect. How about I take you to dinner tonight?"

She crinkled her face. "I'm so tired. How about we eat in? We can go to The Channel Grill tomorrow night. I'm sure that's what you had in mind."

"It is. I'll drop you off, then run to the grocery store. I'll cook tonight."

She leaned against the headrest and closed her eyes. "Sounds wonderful."

"Good. It'll give us a chance to talk."

She cracked an eye open.

"Tommy." Her voice carried a warning note.

"You know, not everything is about you, Miss Thang," he answered, doing his best Joey Buccacino impression.

She laughed in spite of the pang of sadness that followed. "I'm sorry. You're right."

They drove for a few minutes in comfortable silence.

"Oh, hey! We're all set for your birthday."

"What?" She jerked forward so quickly the seat belt locked against her chest. "I don't even want to acknowledge my birthday. You know how the last one went. I'm done with birthdays."

"Nope. Not going to let you wallow."

"I'm not wallowing. I'm being realistic."

He shook his head. "We'll have a nice dinner at Sur Le Mer. Harold and Jeff are joining us. Very low-key, but I think you need to celebrate the fact that you survived the worst year of your life and that it's over."

"I don't want to. We can have dinner at home. Please, no fuss. I feel guilty."

He stole a quick glance. "Why would you feel guilty?"

"Because even though I'm trying not to think about it, I can't help but wonder about my kids and, you know, what they're thinking. I can't bear the thought that they may spend the day thinking about me and what I might be doing. The thought of actually celebrating just doesn't sit well with me."

"We're not talking party hats and noisemakers, Kate. We're talking about a nice dinner with people who care about you and want to see you happy and moving forward. That's all. If it was any other day, you wouldn't have a problem with going out to dinner, would you?"

She answered reluctantly. "I guess not."

"That's all it is. Dinner with friends."

"I guess. Not that what I say matters anyway."

"True."

She chewed on her lip and thought about it. "So, Sur Le Mer. Is that the old converted ferry in South Portland?

"That's the one."

"I've wanted to go there. Can we get a seat outside on the deck?"

"If you'd like."

"Good." She settled back into her seat. "And Tommy? Anyone comes out with a cake or sings 'Happy Birthday,' I'm jumping overboard."

"Duly noted."

———

AFTER A DINNER of barbecued chicken and tomato salad, they sat at the outdoor table, watching the pink rays of the setting sun deepen into an indigo sky. A sliver of moon rose over Cousins Island. Kate poured another splash of white zinfandel in her glass and topped Tom's off as well.

"That was lovely," she said. "I feel positively spoiled."

"I'm glad."

She stretched her legs out onto the empty chair beside her.

"You look good, Kate. Healthy, peaceful. I guess coming up here was the right thing after all."

It was the right thing—for her. And while she had dealt with much of the guilt she'd carried since the shooting, there was new guilt to face: the guilt from hurting her family by walking out on them.

"Liz has helped me so much. I've faced so many battles, both old and new, these past few months. I've come a long way from the person I was last November."

A chipmunk raced along the edge of the pavers and darted under the rosa rugosa. She lifted her glass and gave it a swirl, the wine mimicking the colors of the diluted sunset.

"Mentally, I'm doing better, but my heart is still broken. I don't think Liz can fix that. The best I can hope for is to be strong enough to live with a broken heart. At least I know it won't kill me."

And it wouldn't. She couldn't fix or change anything that had happened, but she would survive it.

"You said you wanted to talk."

He held up his index finger, took a fortifying sip of his wine, and set down the glass. "Stephanie wants a divorce."

"What?" She jerked forward, scrapping her shin along the edge of the metal chair and nearly toppling her glass. "Why?"

"She found someone else."

"Oh, Tommy." She searched his face for a clue on how to respond. "I'm sorry?"

He laughed. "I'm not."

"What about Lian?"

"It's all good. Years too late, but good. We'll share custody. She's keeping the house, but I may be relocating. Which is where you come in."

"Are you moving up here?"

He shook his head. "This isn't home for me. It's a nice place to visit as long as you're here, but I was thinking of New York."

"What about your practice?"

"After Stephanie told me about Steven, I told her about Joey. She was shocked. I mean, she'd figured out I was gay, but she had no idea that I had met the love of my life. To her credit, she actually cried when she realized what I've been through this past year and how I've had to keep everything a secret."

He stared into his glass and twirled the stem between his fingers. "She also convinced me to tell my parents."

"And?"

"Let's just say they took it better than I expected. They're not about to make an announcement at the country club, but they said they'll learn to accept it. And no matter what, they love me."

His voice cracked. Kate understood how bittersweet this was for him—the pain of having been unable to do this while Joey was still alive, and the joy of finally being able to be who he was with the people who loved him most.

She wrapped her arms around his neck and held onto him until he pulled himself together.

They sat quietly, watching night claim the last of the day's light.

"Joey's business needs more than someone to make sure payroll is met," he said. "I'd like to do that. I know what that business meant to him, and I'm hoping you want to keep it going as well. It's your call, because once everything is settled and the will is probated, it's yours. Joey had some ideas how he wanted it run in the future. We can go over that when you're ready. If it's okay with you, I'd like to move into the loft for the time being and get a better handle on running it. I don't know if it's what I want to do forever, but for now, I'd like to do this."

Relief at Tom's offer to take over the business, even for just awhile, didn't come close to describing the sudden unspooling of the tension and guilt she'd carried around for months. The thought of managing Joey's business had nagged at her like a pebble in her shoe —one she couldn't figure out how to remove. It was as if with just a few words, he'd erased months of stress dedicated to her inaction on something too important to be ignored, but that she'd ignored nonetheless.

"Of course it's okay. I'm beyond relieved, actually. I don't have a clue how to run a business."

"Not right now, but you will. I won't do anything without checking with you. I'm just worried that with no one really on top of everything day to day, we would lose ground. Joey had good people in place. I'd like to keep it that way."

"Absolutely." She squeezed his hand. "Now this is something we can celebrate on Friday."

He looked hopeful. "Cake?"

"Don't push it."

CHAPTER TWENTY-SIX

Harold shook his head in disgust. "I can't believe we're sitting on a ship in the middle of the ocean, and you're eating a steak."

"We're not in the middle of the ocean," Kate pointed out. "We're anchored to the dock. Probably more than anchored, as I don't believe this thing has been out of its slip in thirty years."

"Still. Smell that sea air. You should be eating seafood."

"So you're saying unless I smell manure, I shouldn't eat beef."

Jeff erupted in laughter, nearly spitting out his seafood scampi.

"Funny," Harold said. He cracked open the body of his lobster and scraped out something green and disgusting. "You don't know what you're missing."

"I have to ask *you* a question," she persisted. "You catch your own lobster any time you want. Why are you eating it now, when you could've had anything else?"

"Because I like it."

She speared a piece of her rib eye on her fork and waved it at him. "And I like steak."

While Jeff turned his attention to Tom, Harold surreptitiously dipped a forkful of lobster meat into Jeff's dish of melted butter and popped it into his mouth. "Suit yourself," he conceded with a grin. "It's your birthday."

"Yes. It is."

"Speaking of which." Jeff dipped into his pocket. "We bought you a little present."

It was too much. She had wanted to let the day pass without any acknowledgment, let alone a celebration. Her eyes flickered from Harold to Jeff. "Just spending time with all of you is special enough. A present is too much."

Ignoring her, Jeff set a box on the table. Her mouth dropped.

"Are you kidding?" She stared at the familiar blue box. "Tiffany's?" She shook her head. "I can't."

Harold pushed the box closer. "You didn't even open it. How do you know it's from Tiffany's? Maybe we're just recycling the box. You're going to feel pretty damn foolish then, aren't you?"

She didn't know whether to be embarrassed or annoyed, but she didn't want to look ungrateful, so she picked up the box and gave the white satin ribbon a tug. Inside nestled a pair of sterling silver earrings shaped like starfish.

"They're beautiful, and I love them, but I can't accept. This is too generous."

His harshness gone, Harold wrapped a calloused hand around hers. "We want you to have them. You're a blessing in our lives, Kate, and we want you to know that."

She shook her head, unable to find her words.

"Kate's been a blessing to a lot of people for as long as I've known her," Tom added.

Her mouth twisted. She felt the familiar prickle behind her eyes.

"Tell her, Jeff." Harold's voice returned to its usual gruffness.

"The starfish is symbolic—that's why we chose it," Jeff said. "The starfish represents the Virgin Mother, who is said to 'lovingly create safe travel over troubled water.' She's also an emblem of salvation during trying times."

The prickle turned into a burn. Her smile felt wobbly. "I've certainly had my share of troubled water and trying times."

"There's also a legend that says starfish are the reflections of stars in the sky that inhabit the ocean floor," Harold said. "And it's the symbol of rebirth. Did you know a starfish can drop one of its arms to escape and trick a predator and then grow back the lost appendage? It's even possible for the discarded arm to grow into another starfish."

"You people are too smart for me." Maybe if she kept joking, she wouldn't start crying.

The card that went along with the gift featured a painting of the Portland Head Light at sunrise. Inside, Jeff had written "The Story of the Starfish—author unknown."

She read it aloud, trying hard to keep her voice from cracking. "Once upon a time, there was a wise man who used to go to the ocean to do his writing. He had a habit of walking on the beach before he began his work. One day, he was walking along the shore. As he looked down the beach, he saw a human figure moving like a dancer. He smiled to himself to think of someone who would dance to the day. So he began to walk faster to catch up.

"As he got closer, he saw that it was a young man. The young man wasn't dancing; instead, he was reaching down to the shore, picking up something and very gently throwing it into the ocean.

"As he got closer he called out, 'Good morning! What are you doing?' The young man paused, looked up, and replied, 'Throwing starfish back into the ocean.'

"'Why are you throwing starfish into the ocean?'

"'The sun is up, and the tide is going out. If I don't throw them in, they'll die.'

"'But young man, don't you realize that there are miles and miles of beach with starfish all along it. You can't possibly make a difference!'

"The young man listened politely. Then he bent down, picked up another starfish, and threw it into the sea past the breaking waves and said, 'It made a difference for that one.'

"Happy birthday to someone who would not only rescue a starfish but has been known to save a lobster as well. Love, Harold and Jeff."

Although she laughed at the last part, she was so touched by their love and kindness, she could no longer hold back the tears. Even Tom seemed about to get emotional. He started to speak, but his phone began to vibrate.

"Excuse me a second." Tom walked to the rail that overlooked the marina and the multimillion-dollar yachts docked alongside the floating restaurant. He fired off a text. He watched his phone, and after a moment, he shot off another. Then he tucked the phone back into his pocket as he returned to his seat.

"Everything okay?" she asked.

"Fine." He reached under the table to give her hand a squeeze.

The message had been from Billy; she knew it.

Tom smiled. "So, as I started to say—"

Two waiters appeared, carrying a monumental confection covered with toasted coconut.

She gaped. "I said no cake."

"It's dessert," Tom pointed out, "and no one is singing. But just in case, Harold, if she gets up and makes for the railing, grab her."

Tom gave her an odd look and mouthed "Sorry."

The cake was huge; much too big for just the four of them. She scooped a fingerful of icing and popped it into her mouth. She closed her eyes and savored the sweetness of the coconut as it dissolved on her tongue. What the hell? She pinched off another dab of icing. It had been more than a few years, but if she was right, this was the cake to end all cakes. She was practically giddy.

"Is this from The Peninsula Grill? How did you know? This is my favorite!" She threw her arms around Tom's neck. "I want to kill you and kiss you at the same time."

He didn't answer, just bobbed his head and handed her a knife.

She couldn't stop grinning. "Let's cut this sucker."

She pointed the knife in Harold's direction. "You think lobster is good? Wait until you get a taste of this."

KATE WENT to bed not long after they returned from the restaurant. It had been a good birthday, all things considered, but she was feeling emotional and wrung out. She was still awake an hour later, staring at the dark ceiling, Charlie curled at her feet.

She slipped out of bed and tiptoed across the hall. A sliver of light stretched under the door of the master bedroom. She tapped lightly.

"Come in."

Tom set down his book and adjusted his glasses. "I was expecting you."

She sat on the edge of the bed, tugged her oversized T-shirt down over her thighs and looked into his calm, honey-colored eyes. "The cake wasn't from you, was it?"

"No."

"So he knows where I am?"

He shook his head adamantly. "Billy paid for the cake, and I made the arrangements for it to be sent with the understanding that it was private information. I wouldn't do that to you."

"Was that him texting?"

"At dinner? Yes. Although I received several texts today."

Several. Rhiannon and Devin. Maybe her son-in-law, Doug. How could she not feel guilty?

"I'm surprised they don't all hate me."

"No one hates you."

She shrugged. Maybe. Maybe not.

"What did Billy say?"

"Do you want to see?"

"I don't know." The tempo of her heart quickened. She did. But she was also afraid it would open a door she might not be able to close.

"It's up to you. I can tell you, or you can see for yourself."

By cutting off all communication with her family, she had been able to focus solely on herself. It had been selfish, but she believed it was what she'd needed. Was she ready to let them in, even just a fraction of an inch?

Baby steps. She pressed her lips together and opened her hand.

Tom picked up the phone from the nightstand, scrolled through several messages, and handed it to her.

Billy Donaldson: Pls tell me she's not alone.

She's not.

Billy Donaldson: You with her?

Yes.

Billy Donaldson: Tell her happy birthday & I love her & miss her.

Kate read the exchange several times, and not just because the words had become blurry. She handed Tom his phone. "You didn't tell him that you would tell me."

"Because I didn't know if you would let me. I'm not going to lie to him, Kate."

She stood to leave. "Tell him that you told me."

He nodded. "Anything else?"

Tell him that I love him and miss him too, her heart whispered.

"No."

"Okay. Good night, Kate. Happy birthday."

She kissed Tom's cheek and crossed the hall back to her room. But there was no point trying to sleep with coconut-flavored memories tugging at the corners of her mind.

Quietly, she slipped down the hall and into the kitchen. She filled a mug with water, dropped in a bag of Sleepytime tea, and popped it into the microwave. She slid the cake box from the bottom shelf of the refrigerator and cut herself a narrow sliver. When her tea was ready, she curled up on the couch in the darkened living room.

She lifted a forkful of cake and set it on her tongue. Closing her eyes, she let the sweetness transport her to another time, another place.

———

"WHAT'RE YOU DOING?" Billy stood in the doorway, his voice thick and deep with sleep.

Kate looked up from the peach velvet sofa where she sat cross-legged, a takeout box in her lap. "Eating cake," she mumbled, her mouth full of the decadent coconut cake left over from dinner.

He stretched languorously and sat in the club chair across from her, still half asleep.

He had called the day before from the road. He had two days off here in Charleston between concerts, and he'd begged her to come. It had been nearly impossible to get away, but Eileen, her neighbor and the kids' surrogate grandma, agreed to babysit, armed with a list of baseball practices and dance classes. That left Kate free to fly to South Carolina for what was essentially a booty call. Billy had booked a suite at an inn in the historic district, and they'd gone to dinner at The Peninsula Grill, although she knew there was really only one thing he wanted to do.

"I rolled over and reached for you, but the bed was empty," he said, watching her through eyes that were only halfway open. "I had to remember where the hell I was. I thought I'd only dreamed you were here." He leaned forward and kissed her on the forehead. "I don't like waking up not knowing where you are."

"I wake up almost every morning not knowing where you are," she pointed out a little too tartly.

"I know." He put his feet on the eighteenth-century reproduction coffee table. "I love what I do, but I hate being away from you so much. And I hate sleeping alone."

It was on the tip of her tongue to say she hoped that he was sleeping alone, but she swallowed the words along with the cake. The thought of anything different could suck the air right out of a room, even though he'd given her no reason to worry.

Move on, Kate.

"How can you sit on that naked?" She wrinkled her nose. "Don't you wonder if someone else was sitting there naked before you?"

"For what I'm paying, they should clean the upholstery between guests."

She took another forkful of cake, lifted her eyes heavenward, and moaned.

Billy pointed to the bedroom. "You should be in there making that face over me. I fly you all the way down here, put you up in an exorbitantly expensive hotel suite because I missed you and I'm horny and lonely, and when I wake up and reach for you, you're in the living room eating cake."

With a devilish look, she speared another forkful. "Want some?"

"No. I want you." He trailed his hand up her bare thigh.

"That was obvious when you walked into the room a moment ago." She pointed her fork at him. "You could hang your guitar on that thing."

He grinned. "And it's been that way since you stepped off the plane this morning, so come back to bed and let me show you how happy I am that you're here."

She wiggled the cake-laden fork in front of him.

"Come on," she coaxed, her voice deep and husky. "You know you want it."

"You know what I want." He moved from the chair to the sofa beside her. She continued to hold the utensil aloft. He leaned closer and opened his mouth, his eyes fixed on her. She slid the fork into his mouth and waited until he swallowed.

"Hmm . . . that is good, but I know something that's much better."

He lifted the box from her lap and set it on the coffee table. Then he pried the fork out of her unwilling fingers and set it in the box. His mouth moved down her neck, planting tender kisses as he tugged open the belt of her silk robe. He pulled it down, and his tongue traced a path along the sweep of her shoulders. His hair tickled her breasts. His tongue flicked over her nipple.

She pulled him closer. Gently, he pushed her backward, hooking his hands behind her knees and moving her lower, his warm mouth still on her, his tongue still teasing.

"You think anyone's ever been naked on this couch before?" he whispered between kisses.

She giggled.

When his lips brushed against her thighs, she shivered. He trailed his tongue against the backs of her knees and down to her ankles. The sweetness of the cake faded into the sweetness of the moment.

Illuminated by the dim light coming from the street below, he worked his way up her body back to where he'd started. She reached around the back of his head and slipped her hands through his hair, lost in the warmth of him. It felt like forever since they had been together this way. He kissed her over and over, nipping her lower lip and sucking on it.

When she had all but melted into the soft velvet, he sprang up, leaving her stunned and breathless.

"On second thought, this is good cake." He grabbed the box and fork, then dropped into the chair.

She lay on the couch, her robe and her mouth hanging open.

He grinned with the final bite. Rolling his eyes upward, he emitted an ecstatic groan, his mouth still full. "You don't know what you're missing."

She bolted upright. "You finished my cake!"

"I did," he said, pulling her to her feet. "Now come back to bed and show me how much you love me."

The empty box taunted her. "But my cake . . ."

He cupped her face in his big, warm hands. "I'll buy you more cake. I'll buy you a hundred coconut cakes. But tonight and tomorrow, you're all mine."

A few days later, Kate was back home and Billy was back on the road. The FedEx truck had come crunching up the long, narrow driveway with a special package for her—a coconut cake from The Peninsula Grill. The note was in Billy's handwriting. He'd ordered the cake before he'd left Charleston.

"Eat your fill, babe, because when I get home, you're all mine. Love, B."

THE MEMORY WAS SO vivid it could have happened ten days ago, rather than ten years ago. Kate finished her cake. This time when she climbed back into bed, sleep came quickly. She dreamed of making love beneath a sky filled with glowing starfish and then falling asleep in Billy's arms.

CHAPTER TWENTY-SEVEN

K ate had been working at the resource center for a couple of weeks, and although she wasn't used to being on her feet for long periods and it was often sweltering in the center's kitchen, she really did love it. In addition to feeling useful, it gave her an excuse not to think about her life, which hovered anxiously in the background, nagging her to make decisions, no longer content to sit on a shelf and be ignored.

Since they only needed her four days a week, on her off days, she made simple quilts for the babies and young children who lived in the nearby homeless shelter.

"I don't think I've ever seen such a dedicated volunteer," Amy, the center's director, said when Kate handed her the latest quilt. This one was made from fabric remnants she'd picked up at a quilt shop near Freeport. "Where do you find the time?"

Kate fidgeted in the doorway. "I don't have a whole lot going on right now." It wouldn't sound very noble to admit her largesse was in part a diversionary tactic. Not that she was trying to sound noble. She could feel the telltale flush staining her cheeks.

"I didn't mean to pry." Amy brushed a hand over the soft pastel quilt and set it on her desk. "It's just that you've been dedicating so much time to us since you started. I hope we're not taking you away from your family."

No, I did that all by myself. Kate gave Amy a wobbly smile and hooked a thumb in the direction of the kitchen. "I better get going. They'll be wondering where I am." She ducked into the hall and made a beeline for the back of the building.

There was a large group to feed that day, and they finished serving much later than usual. Samatar, the Somali cook, and the rest of the paid staff trundled off to a meeting. The other volunteer, Dorothy, who had to be well into her sixties, looked so bedraggled from the heat that Kate offered to finish by herself.

It wasn't like she had anything better to do.

The boom box over the prep table was still pumping out Miriam Makeba, so despite the heat and her self-imposed ban on music, she found herself moving along to the iconic South African singer's beat while she scrubbed baked-on barbecue sauce from a large roasting pan.

An occasional breeze floated in from the propped back door. Steam rose from the sink as she held the pan under hot water. Sweat trickled down her back and into her eyes. She set the pan on the rack, brushed a strand of damp hair from her face, picked up the next pan, and began to scrub. Between the music cranking, the dishwasher grinding, and the drone of running water, she didn't hear the voices in the alley until a wild-eyed woman appeared in the doorway.

"Help me!" the stranger cried. A toddler was wailing in her arms. "It's my husband. Please, I need to hide."

The fear on their faces propelled Kate forward. She pointed toward the dining room. "That way. Go!"

The woman darted through the kitchen as Kate lunged for the door. A man's voice reached her just as she kicked the wooden wedge from the door and slammed it shut.

"Sonja! Don't you fucking run from me!"

She locked the metal door and dropped the heavy latch into place. Moments later, the pounding started.

"Sonja! Get the fuck out here!"

The door was solid. He couldn't get through this way, but it wouldn't take long for him to make his way to the front of the building, which was open. Kate raced into the dining room to find the young woman pacing, holding her child tightly in her arms. Her lower lip was split open, and a bruise was forming below her left eye. Blood trickled from her naked left earlobe. A large hoop earring dangled from her right ear.

"Come with me," Kate said, fighting waves of nausea and panic. She led the girl into the hall. "The ladies room is on the right. Lock the door and stay there. I'll come back when it's safe."

At the sound of the clicking lock, she raced up the hall and burst into Amy's office. Amy, Samatar, and several others Kate didn't know were gathered around the conference table.

"What's wrong?" Amy said.

"I've got a young woman and a child locked in the restroom and an angry husband pounding on the kitchen door. She's hurt. I don't know how badly, but he's probably—"

Through the office window, Kate could see a man storming toward the entrance.

She pointed. "That might be him."

He was in his mid-twenties, of medium height and build, and wore a camouflage T-shirt, cargo shorts, and sneakers. The look on his face was one of pure rage.

Samatar was the first out of Amy's office.

The man burst through the front door, stopped, and scanned the lobby.

"Can I help you?" Samatar was a large man, well over six feet tall and solidly built. Kate knew him as a sensitive, gentle soul who always wore a smile. This Samatar, however, was intimidating.

"I just want to collect my wife and kid, and I'll be on my way," the man snarled.

"I don't think so." Samatar moved toward him and called to a woman who had followed him out of Amy's office. "Diane, call the police. Let's see if they can get this settled."

Before Diane could reach for the phone, Amy stepped forward. "On their way."

Amy was tall and slim, and there was nothing fearful about her. Right now? She looked determined, fierce. Mama bear, Kate thought.

"Fuck that." The man pointed at Samatar. "You tell that bitch I don't give a shit what she does, but she better bring my kid back or she'll be sorry." He kicked over a play table, breaking the leg, then shoved open the front door just as a police cruiser pulled up outside.

While one of the officers detained him, Kate led the other officer down the hall. But when they got to the restroom, it was empty. The door from the kitchen to the alley was unlocked.

Kate's heart sank. Why the hell would she run off?

"She's gone," the officer told his partner when he returned to the lobby. Kate trailed behind him, trying to make sense of why the girl would have left when help was just steps away.

"Then you have to let me go," the husband said with a smirk.

"Not necessarily," said the first officer. "Do you want to press charges for the damage to your property?" He pointed at the broken play table.

"I would," Amy said, "but it hardly seems worth it."

The husband snorted rudely.

"I would, however, like a trespass warning issued."

The officer filled out his report, and escorted the husband out of the building with a warning not to return.

"I can't believe she disappeared like that," Kate said as the squad car pulled away. "Why would she do that?"

"Sadly, sometimes these women don't realize they have options," Amy said. "Battered partners often believe they deserve the treatment they get, or they just don't know there's a safe place for them to go."

From where she stood, Kate could still see Sonja's husband at the end of the block. His swagger made her want to vomit. "I feel like I failed her somehow, and I'm not even sure what happened."

Amy slipped an arm around her shoulders. "You didn't fail her. Maybe she'll come back. Maybe she has a place to go and just needed the diversion to get away." With a sad smile, she cocked her head. "You okay?"

Although Kate's heart hadn't returned to its normal rhythm yet, she was surprisingly okay. She nodded. "I've been through worse."

A flicker of concern crossed Amy's face, but she didn't pry. "Samatar? Could you walk Kate to her car? I think she's had enough for one day."

"That's okay," Kate said. "I still have a few pans—"

"Absolutely not. And another thing: take a break tomorrow. I don't want you getting burned out. It happens fast here. That's how we lose our volunteers. Go to the beach. Go shopping. Do something fun."

CHAPTER TWENTY-EIGHT

K ate's "something fun" turned out to be a trip to Ogunquit.

"Of course there are places for her to go," Jeff said, as they strolled through the little garden behind the rectory. "The problem is these women don't usually know about them. And even if they do, they're either afraid to try and get away or don't believe they deserve better."

"I can't believe someone would actually think it's okay to be hurt and beaten."

He gave her an odd look. "Think about it."

"What?"

"You didn't think you deserved better."

Her spine stiffened. She hadn't told Jeff what happened the night Billy raped her. He'd been drunk and strung out on crystal meth, and even though she might never forgive him, she refused to believe he'd meant to hurt her. "My husband never— It's not the same."

Jeff watched her carefully as if trying to decipher her thoughts. "I didn't mean your husband," he said softly. "I meant your parents."

"My parents never beat me."

"Emotional or mental abuse is abuse. It's just harder to see."

She plucked the head off a stem of dill, crushed it between her fingers, and inhaled, letting the familiar tang and the scent of freshly mown grass ease some of the tension that had settled between her shoulders.

"Maybe you're right. It just kills me to think of another child being hurt, mentally or physically." She thought of the little boy from yesterday but pictured Billy. The chicken salad sandwich Jeff had made for their lunch churned uncomfortably in her stomach. "How can a person make a conscious decision to hurt another? You understand human nature. Explain this to me, because I don't get it."

"I wish I could." He paused to pluck a few dead blooms off a rose bush. "Maybe if we understood why people do what they do, we could help them."

"Why help them? It's their victims who need the help." She was feeling most ungenerous.

"If we could help them stop, aren't we also helping the victims?"

"I guess. But I'm more concerned with the victims."

His smile spread, which was odd, given the subject matter.

"What?" she asked.

"You keep saying you don't know what you want to do with your life. I think you do. Or at least, I think you know where you should begin looking to find your bliss."

"Find my bliss? Among emotionally and physically battered women and children? What kind of psycho do you take me for?"

"One with a huge heart. You can be as sarcastic as you want, but I think you know exactly what I'm talking about."

MONDAY MORNING, Kate parked her Saab on the street in front of the resource center. She was reaching into the back seat to pull out the bag with the two quilts she had completed over the weekend when she heard someone calling to her.

"Hey! You!" The young woman, Sonja, waved, then darted across the street. She was wearing sunglasses, but the remnants of a dark purple bruise below her eye were still visible. A bandage clung to her earlobe.

"How are you? Is everything all right? Are you okay?"

"Yeah, I just wanna thank you. I'm sorry I run off like that. I was scared, ya know. My husband gets pretty wired sometimes, and he was havin' a bad day."

Lots of people have bad days, Kate wanted to say, but that didn't give them the right to use their partner as a punching bag. "Where's your little boy?"

"With his dad. I told him I had to go to the store. I been looking for you, but you ain't been around."

"I don't work every day, and I took a day off."

"Must be nice, a day off." She smiled, and Kate saw that she was missing her left upper bicuspid. Her husband must be right-handed. The thought nauseated her.

"So you went back to him?" It wasn't her place to ask, and she knew she sounded accusing, but that didn't stop her from asking.

The girl's smile fell. "Hey, look! I didn't come for no lecture. I just wanted to say thanks. That's all. Like I said, he was havin' a bad day."

She couldn't stop pushing. "Do you need help? There are places where you can get help."

"Jesus, what's your problem?"

"Nothing." That wasn't exactly true, but still. "We can help you."

The girl waved her hand dismissively, then took off across the street.

Kate had to wait for a car to pass but called after her. "You might not get away next time. And what about your little boy? Huh?"

As soon as she could cross, she did. She followed Sonja down an alley, her voice echoing between the two buildings. "My husband's father nearly beat him to death when he wasn't much older. He almost died, but he got away, and he grew up to be a very talented musician."

The girl reached the end of the alley and hesitated, staring back at Kate.

"He even won a Grammy." Kate stepped closer. "Don't you want your little boy to grow up to be something special? Don't you deserve better too?"

"You're a crazy bitch," Sonja shouted. She slipped behind a box truck. By the time Kate reached the truck, she caught a glimpse of her as she disappeared down another alley, her voice echoing in Kate's head: *You're a crazy bitch.*

"Yeah, well . . . Tell me something I don't know."

ON THURSDAY, Kate arrived at the center early, sunburned from a day of doing nothing but floating in the pool with a pitcher of margaritas nearby. She had gotten so drunk from the combination of alcohol and sun that she'd flipped off her raft at one point.

"Whew!" Samatar laughed when she walked into the kitchen. "Look at you. I should melt some butter, Ms. Lobster." His quick, rolling speech made his words hard to understand, but she got the gist of it.

"Funny." Her bra strap dug into her tender shoulder as she raised her arm to put her purse in the cabinet above the counter. She grimaced.

He shook his head. "You want good color, you should be born Somali. Not try to cook yourself!"

Even frowning hurt. She had covered her face with aloe last night and again this morning, all the while hearing Joey's voice lecturing her about wrinkles and UV rays.

"I fell asleep in the sun," she said, hoping to end the conversation. She didn't mention she had been drinking and floating in her in-ground pool at her oceanfront home.

He teased her a few more minutes before interrupting himself. "Almost forgot. Amy wants to see you."

She tossed her apron on the counter and headed to the office. She was about to knock when Amy noticed her at the open door.

"Ouch! What happened to you?"

"This is what I get for taking it easy. I won't do that again."

"Seriously!" Amy rifled through some papers on her desk. "Here we go. Have a seat."

Kate eased herself down, wincing from the shock of the cold plastic chair against the heat of her well-done legs.

"We had a visitor," Amy said. "Do you remember the young woman who was here last week with the little boy? The one who was hiding from her husband?"

"Of course."

"She showed up yesterday morning, looking for refuge. We got her squared away in protective housing through the Domestic Abuse Resource Centers. She and her little boy are safe, thanks to you."

Kate studied Amy's face, unbelieving. Safe? Because of her? "Really?"

"She said you talked her into coming back." Amy folded her hands in front of her. "When did you see her?"

"The other day. I was getting out of my car, and she came from across the street. Said she wanted to thank me." Since it wasn't possible for her face to grow any redder, she plowed on. "I feel bad, but I kind of yelled at her. I asked where her son was, and when she said he was with his dad, I told her she might not be so lucky next time. I don't remember everything I said, but she didn't seem too receptive."

"Well, something hit home," Amy countered. "In fact, she wrote this out for you before they left. I hope you don't mind. I told her your first name." She handed Kate an envelope.

Dear Kate,

Thank you for caring about me and Tomas. I thought about what you said.

My boy likes music too.
Sonja
P.S. I'm sorry I called you a crazy bitch.

KATE SWIPED at her eyes and laughed.

"Feels good, doesn't it?"

She grabbed a tissue from the box on Amy's desk, grimacing when she tried to blow her sunburned nose. "I'm glad she listened. Where is she?"

"I don't know. DARC has several private homes throughout southern Maine that are used as protective housing for abused women. They can live there for a while until they can get on their feet. They can go back to school or get some training so they can get a job. They have access to day care and counseling. It's a wonderful system. Unfortunately, there isn't always room. We were lucky to get them situated so quickly."

Kate pushed herself from the chair. "You made my day, maybe even my year."

"I'm glad. You better get back before Samatar gives me hell for keeping you too long. He's really come to depend on you."

Kate clamped down on her lip to try and keep from grinning like a fool. It was a good feeling.

"Oh, one more thing," Amy called after her. "Sonja said you told her your husband was a famous musician."

Nope, nope, nope. Damn it. "I'm sure I didn't say famous."

"She said he won a Grammy."

Kate backed out the door. "That was a long time ago." She pointed toward the kitchen. "I got to—you know."

The mention of Billy, even if not by name, brought with it a glut of emotion. And even though it was unnerving to have Amy sniffing at the fringes of her personal life, her fear of discovery was overshadowed by the knowledge that she might actually have made a real difference in the life of a mother and her little boy.

CHAPTER TWENTY-NINE

Fog swirled around the field. The boulders had disappeared, and
there was no place to hide. It didn't matter; she was tired of
hiding. The beast rumbled in the distance, and the ground vibrated.
Cold rain hit her bare shoulders and trickled over the same strapless
leather dress she had worn a year earlier on her birthday. On her feet
were black stiletto boots.

Horses whickered. Two riders approached the clearing and
dismounted. The first removed his helmet. A tangle of dark curls
spilled forth.

"Joey!" She ran to him, arms outstretched, but he waved her off.

"There's no time." He tugged off his armor and slipped the chain
mail over her head. It dropped heavy and cold against her shoulders,
and she staggered under its weight. He handed her the helmet as the
other rider moved closer. Eileen! Kate hadn't seen her friend since the
night she died in a barrage of Sedge Stevens's bullets.

Kate tried to hug her, but like Joey, Eileen hastened Kate to ready
herself. She slipped her own breastplate over Kate's chain mail and
secured it in place, then handed her a great longsword. Kate could
scarcely lift it, let alone swing it through the air.

"What are you doing?" She pulled away. "I can't do this."

Her panic began to subside when the third rider appeared from the mist.

"Look! He's here." She tried to hand the sword back to Eileen.

"You must," Joey said.

"It's time," Eileen added.

"No, see. He's coming." Kate pointed toward the rider, who remained near the edge of the forest.

The beast roared from beyond the clearing. It was just a matter of time before he entered the circle.

Kate shook her head. "I can't do this. Call him." She pointed to the horseman. "He can't just sit there. I need him."

The ground shook so violently she nearly lost her footing. Familiar laughter sent shivers down her spine. She looked fearfully to the far end of the field and saw the tall, thin shadow, the one she thought was her mother.

Eileen mounted her horse. Joey remained close, but the third rider watched from the distance.

A frightening realization unfurled within her. "You're dead. So is Eileen." She pointed at the rider. "Is he dead? Is that why he's here?"

Joey ignored her questions and handed her a dagger as long as her forearm. He fastened a sheath about her waist.

"Stop that." She spun away from him and called out to the phantom rider.

"Aren't you going to help me? I need you!"

"Stop it, Kate." Joey grabbed her by the shoulders and shook her. "He can't save you. You knew this going in. You have to save yourself."

She pushed back. "I don't know what you're talking about. I knew no such thing!"

The laughter from across the circle grew louder. Crows cawed from the trees, alive with leaves of black.

"It's a fine day for the crows," a booming male voice called from across the way.

Her blood ran cold.

"This is it, Kate," Joey said. "It's you or them."

He motioned with his head toward the other side of the circle. The monster was now visible, snarling and pacing, not far from its two followers.

"I c-can't." She was near collapse from terror. "I can hardly walk." She gestured at her ridiculous boots.

"Use your wits. I have faith in you. We all do."

Joey mounted his horse and rode to the edge of the circle. When he reached Eileen, they swung around to face her. The third rider hadn't moved.

The ground shook. The monster had two horrid heads, both of them angled at her. It smelled of burned flesh and decay. Grasping the sword with both hands, she raised it onto her shoulder and took a step. Her heels sank into the ground, and she struggled to walk.

The beast charged, and as it closed in, she swung. She missed it and nearly pitched herself over with the heft of her sword. The monster lunged again, and she swung, catching its arm. The vibration of the blow ran up the shaft and into her arm, nearly causing her to drop the sword. The creature screamed, but across the clearing, she heard laughter. The cry of the crows grew louder.

She sidestepped, trying to remember how the warrior had fought the creature. She mimicked his moves, circling the beast. When it sprang forward, she shifted to the side and swung with all her might. The sword hit bone, digging in, and was wrenched free of her grip. The beast pulled it off with a horrid scream and flung it out of her reach. Then it dropped its two heads and rushed her.

Kate pulled the dagger from the sheath as it neared and jabbed it into a meaty shoulder. As the monster fell, it swiped her, lifting her off her feet and throwing her onto her back, knocking the wind out of her. She struggled to breathe as the creature circled her. It was bleeding, but it barely slowed in its pursuit.

Gasping for air, she rolled to her side, pulling her leg up and shielding her face as the monster descended. Pain shot through her leg and into her hip as it toppled onto her. It felt as if her leg had snapped *from the weight of the beast, which was now crushing her into the rocky ground. Her knee was pressed against her shoulder, and the muscles in her thigh burned as if they'd been set on fire. Liquid, warm and sticky, seeped over her shoulder and down her arm. The stench was nauseating.*

She pushed with all her might, but the monster wouldn't budge. She shimmied to the side and pushed with her uninjured leg, managing to wiggle until she was almost free. She looked for help, but she was alone. The mist had lifted, and the rain had stopped. The sun shone down through the trees, once barren and bare but now in full leaf. She pulled and twisted her painful leg, gaining movement as her foot began to slip from the boot. She dragged herself along the ground, covered in blood and dirt. With no small effort, she pushed until finally her foot jerked free of the boot and the monster. She rested on her elbows, panting. She tugged off the other boot and stood.

Barefoot and bloodied, she staggered toward the longsword and picked it up. Then she hobbled back to the monster and poked it carefully, making certain it was dead.

She leaned closer. "I'll be damned."

Sticking out from the creature's chest just about where its heart would be was the sharp, stiletto heel of her boot. It had snapped off in the monster's chest, piercing its heart and killing it instantly.

Joey had said to use her wits, although it seemed more as if her instinct for survival had finally roared to life, or maybe just dumb luck. Regardless, the beast was dead. It hadn't slunk off the field to fight again.

It was over.

She was alone. Joey, Eileen, and the mysterious warrior had vanished. The specters that accompanied the monster were also gone. In their place stood two stone pillars.

Kate limped from the clearing and set out in the direction from which Joey and Eileen had come. She kept moving until she heard the sound of rushing water and followed it into the woods until she came upon a stream. First, she drank. Then she pulled off the armor and waded in, splashing and scrubbing until she had removed all of the monster's blood. When she finished, she fastened the dagger around her waist, lifted the great sword, and climbed the embankment. Her body ached and she still couldn't feel her leg, but she was no longer afraid.

She'd nearly reached the path when she heard the stomp and whicker of horses. Moving as fast as her numbed leg would allow, she emerged from the forest to find Billy standing beside two horses. He looked as young and beautiful as the first time she laid eyes on him.

"I knew it was you."

He held out the reins to the white horse. Unable to feel her leg to climb into the saddle, Billy lifted her easily and set her atop the horse.

"Why are you helping me now, but you wouldn't help me before?"

He climbed onto his own horse before answering. "I'll always be there if you want me, but only you can fight your demons. Otherwise, they'll just keep coming back."

He made a noise, and the horses began to move.

"Where are we going?"

"Home."

KATE WOKE WITH A START. Electric pins and needles shot through her right leg. She couldn't move, and for the briefest second, she couldn't remember where she was or if there might actually be a monster on top of her. She pulled herself up, and her arm sliced the dark until her fingers found the lamp.

The monster turned out to be Charlie. Snoring away, he lay draped over her leg, which had fallen asleep. She wrenched herself free and tried to stand to get her circulation moving again. Then she limped into the kitchen and poured herself a glass of water. She carried it out onto the deck and sat in the rocker.

A riot of stars pierced the moonless night sky. The ocean was black as well. High tide. She'd come to know its rhythm as well as she knew her own.

Home.

This was home. Yet there remained an ache inside her that no therapy or medication could mend. Knowing her family was well was no longer enough. But was she ready to face them?

"Jesus, Kate. You killed a goddamn monster. You should at least be able to figure out how to apologize to people who love you."

She ducked inside and picked up her cell phone: two forty-five a.m. Without giving herself time to rationalize or debate, she punched in the numbers.

It rang. Once. Twice. Three times. And when a sleepy male voice answered, it took every ounce of strength she had not to hang up.

CHAPTER THIRTY

It was already too late, but that didn't stop Kate from doubting if she was ready to tackle her past. At her next session, Liz insisted she was.

"I don't think you would have acted on that impulse if you weren't truly ready."

"Yeah, but what if I was just responding to the dream and thought I was strong enough?"

"A dream is just a little play your subconscious puts on in your head. It gives you the opportunity to role-play, if you will, and resolve issues in a way you can't always resolve when you're awake. From what you've told me about your son, he's supportive and sensible. Do you really think you have anything to fear seeing him face to face?"

"Fear? No. I'm just afraid he might try to convince me to go home. I'm not ready. I don't want to go back."

"Those are two different things," Liz said. "Not ready is one thing. Not wanting to is very different."

Was that it? She didn't want to go back? At this moment, no, she didn't. She wasn't the same person she was a year ago, not by a long shot, and she still had a lot of baggage to address.

"I'm not sure which," she said finally. "Maybe a little of both."

"You'll figure it out. I think you've exorcised most of your demons, don't you?"

"You may be right."

"How about we try to exorcise one more?" Without waiting for an answer, Liz moved another chair directly across from Kate and gave her an encouraging smile that didn't stop the prickly nerves creeping up Kate's spine.

Liz settled back into her own seat and pointed to the empty chair. "If your mother were sitting there right now, what would you say to her? Tell me what you see and what would you say."

Her mother had been gone for almost fifteen years now, and even theoretically, she wasn't sure she wanted to bring her back. But if it brought some closure and helped bring her closer to becoming whole, maybe it was worth a shot. Despite an uncomfortable tightness in her chest, she closed her eyes and tried to focus.

Her mother eventually swam into her consciousness, frowning and looking as if Kate had interrupted something important. And as ridiculous as it was, she immediately felt defensive. She inhaled deeply and tried to unclench her entire body.

"She's sitting with her legs crossed, and her hands are folded just so." Kate demonstrated, resting her right hand lightly on the left. "She's wearing a suit with my grandmother's brooch on the lapel. Her hair—" Her voice wavered. "It's still beautiful and thick, cut just below her jawline. It's a medium brown with highlights around her face. Never a gray hair." Kate caught herself smiling, and just as quickly, it faded. "She's watching me, smug-like. I can almost hear her. 'Go ahead, Kate, say what you want. No one will believe you anyway.'"

The disapproval felt so real she struggled to continue. It was as if she'd truly conjured her mother's presence. Part of her wanted to curl into a ball. But she didn't. She just squeezed the fabric of her sundress in her clenched fists.

"Is there anything you want to tell her?" Liz asked gently.

Eyes still closed, Kate nodded. She took in as much air as her lungs would hold and then exhaled slowly. She forced her hands open, smoothed them over her thighs, and ran them back and forth until she felt calmer.

When the words finally came, they fell from her lips, fast and furious. "I'm sorry your life didn't turn out the way you wanted, but it wasn't my fault. If it was anyone's fault, it was your own. I didn't ask to be born, but I'm glad I was, because even though my life didn't turn out the way I expected, I'm glad I'm here.

"You could've written your books if you'd wanted. There's always a way. You used me as an excuse because you were afraid to fail. Evelyn Daniels could not be a failure. It was much easier to blame me and Dad, wasn't it?

"I'm sorry you never wanted to be a mother—never really were a mother, either, other than the biology of it. Becoming a mother was the best thing I've ever done."

Her voice cracked, but she couldn't stop. "You missed out on so much. You chose to be unhappy. God gave you a beautiful life—a husband who adored you no matter how you treated him and an obedient, loving daughter who looked up to you. I tried so hard to be good, to be everything you expected, but I failed." She swallowed a sob. "Scratch that. I wasn't a failure. Only in your eyes. God only knows how, but I grew up to love and care about others. I've tried to be kind, to help people when I could and sometimes even when I couldn't. I was a good mother. Or at least I tried to be. I love my children, and I loved my husband."

She licked her lips, and it was only when she tasted the salt of her tears did she realize she'd been crying. "I feel sorry for you, Mom, but you lived your life the way you chose. It wasn't my fault. I never deserved the way you treated me. Never."

She dropped her face into her hands and sobbed. Liz let her be. When she was all cried out, and trusted herself to look up, the chair was empty.

"She's gone," she croaked out.

"How do you feel?"

Kate snatched a tissue from the ever-present box, and wiped her eyes and blew her nose. "Okay. Lighter." She pressed her hand against her chest. "Here. I feel lighter."

"Are you ready to see your son?"

"I am—or I will be by the time he gets here." She dabbed at her eyes and laughed. "I've got a lot of cooking to do. He's a big boy. I can't imagine he's gotten any smaller in the past year."

CHAPTER THIRTY-ONE

It was going to be a beautiful day. The cloudless sky was a brilliant shade of azure and the ocean reflected a deeper, darker blue. It was warm but not humid. The pool hedge was in full bloom, and the heady scent of beach roses reached all the way to the front door. Birds were singing, and the chipmunks and squirrels on the deck and around the pool skittered about as if they too were preparing for a special visitor. Even the resident eagle made an appearance at low tide, balancing on a large boulder, a general making a final inspection of the troops.

Kate had spent most of the past few days in the kitchen. She'd baked Devin's favorite chocolate chip cookies and made blueberry and peach pies. She'd made vegetable beef soup and chicken parmigiana and spent hours making cavatelli from scratch, hand-mixing the pasta and rolling the dough into tubes, cutting it into pieces, and fashioning each one into a shell with her thumb. And of course, there would be homemade marinara to serve over it.

Harold promised fresh lobster and clams whenever Devin wanted and anything else Kate needed. He seemed almost as excited as she was and had already cut her grass twice. She caught him sweeping her dock and using his Weedwacker around the boat house just to "neaten it up a bit."

When she wasn't cooking, she was cleaning. The guest room downstairs, which offered a view of the ocean, was ready. There were fresh sheets on the bed and a handmade quilt. She cut a bouquet of coneflowers, cosmos, and black-eyed Susans from the garden and set them in a vase on the chest in front of the window.

At a few minutes before three, she settled on the front steps and waited. Then she paced. When she caught a glimpse of Billy's black truck, she panicked. She wanted to run, but her feet seemed fixed to the brick walkway.

The truck neared, and she could see there was just one person in the cab. And instead of a blond ponytail, his hair was short and dark, just like hers.

———

DEVIN WAS ALMOST to the end of the dead-end street before he realized he'd been practically holding his breath for the last mile. He let it out with a whoosh when he saw his mother standing in the yard, holding Charlie on his leash. From what he could see, she looked good. Tom had said she was getting better, but it wasn't the same as seeing for himself.

He parked the truck beside the garage and climbed out, stretching his cramped legs. Before he could take two steps, Charlie practically tackled him. He leaned over to hug him and the dog responded by licking his face.

"Oh, yuck!" his mother scolded. "Let me get my kisses in first."

She stood before him, a shy smile on her face. "I think you've grown. I didn't think that was possible."

"I'm taller than Dad now. Six foot five."

"You're a whole foot taller than me," she said, laughing. He'd missed that sound.

"You look good, Mom. You've gained weight."

She jammed a finger into his ribs. "Devin Donaldson! You don't ever tell a woman she gained weight!"

"Sorry, but it looks good on you."

"Still." In truth, she looked pleased, but her expression faded as she lightly touched the side of the truck.

"Your father lent you his truck and you didn't have to tell him where you were going?"

He tugged his suitcase from the back seat. "It's mine. He gave it to me for graduation. He gave me other stuff too, but since he got a new pickup, he gave me this one."

Her head dropped, and in that moment it seemed she'd drawn into herself so tightly that she actually became smaller. "I'm sorry I missed it." She looked as if she were about to cry.

He was at a loss. Because she hadn't been there to watch him get his diploma, he had refused to participate in the ceremony. The only walk he'd done was down their long driveway to the mailbox. Although his father had tried to change his mind, Devin believed he'd secretly been relieved not to have to sit through the commencement exercises alone.

It would probably make her feel worse to know that he had missed his own graduation, so he made a split-second decision not to tell her. "It was no big deal, Mom. Just promise you'll come to the next one. I start my master's program at Rutgers next week."

She nodded and smiled. "Family tradition, huh?"

"That and it's a good program for school psychology."

"I'm proud of you, Devin, and I promise, nothing will keep me from the next one." She opened her arms. "Can I hug you?"

He wasn't a little kid anymore, but he felt like one. He was trying his damnedest not to cry, but when she wrapped her arms around him and squeezed, he couldn't hold back. Neither could she. They stayed that way for a good long while, her tears dampening his faded Shinedown T-shirt.

He pulled away first and scanned the yard, taking in the sloping lawn and the small grove of tall pine trees, the outbuildings, and the ocean view.

"This is where you live?"

She nodded, dabbing her index fingers under her eyes. "Yep. This is home—for now."

"Is it Mr. Reilly's house?"

"Something like that."

"THIS PLACE ROCKS," Devin called over his shoulder from the upstairs deck. Kate had given him a quick tour and they'd walked down to the dock before she'd set about making his favorite dinner. "No wonder you don't want to come home."

She cringed. The remark stung, but she understood.

"I didn't mean that the way it sounded," he said contritely, stepping inside. "Where do you want me to sit?"

She pointed to the head of the table. "You can sit there."

Devin hesitated before pulling out the chair. The head of the table had always been Billy's place, even when he wasn't home. She didn't want to think about it or know what her son might be thinking. She poured herself a glass of wine.

"Wine, beer, or iced tea?"

"Beer's fine."

She pulled out a bottle of Shipyard. "Glass or bottle?"

"Bottle." He helped himself to the salad. "I can't believe you made cavatelli. I haven't had this since—" Brushing off his embarrassment, he dove into his salad. "Man, this is good."

"It's salad, Devin," she said as she piled the dressed greens onto her own plate. "Not that difficult."

"I know, but no one does the oil and vinegar like you. I mean, Dad's getting better, but he can't cook like you."

She rose so quickly, afraid he might continue talking about his father, that she almost knocked over her wine glass. "More bread?"

He shook his head, mouth full, and held up the nearly full basket.

"More butter, then." She darted into the kitchen and returned with a second full stick of butter. "How was Colorado?"

"I didn't go this year. Didn't Tom tell you? I thought it best I stay home with . . . you know."

"Oh. I'm sorry." There was so much to apologize for that she might be saying those two words every day for the rest of her life.

"It's okay. I got a job as assistant manager at the town pool. I set up programs for the kids, swimming lessons, stuff like that. It was good. I like working with kids, and to be honest, there was a lot less stress this year than dealing with kids with behavior problems or addictions."

"I can imagine," she said softly.

"Danielle stayed local this summer too, so that was good."

"You're still together? That's wonderful. She seemed very nice."

He nodded. "I'm pretty sure she's the one."

All kinds of thoughts and emotions rushed over her, and she pressed her napkin to her mouth. Of course he was too young, but that wasn't the worst of it. The worst of it was that he had met and fallen in love with a girl, and she had missed almost all of it. She had no right to lecture him or warn him that he was too young, that he needed to do more before he settled down. She'd given up that right when she walked away from him and Rhiannon and their father. It wouldn't be fair to try and snatch it back.

"What have you been doing?" he asked after dinner as he helped clear the table.

"Hmm. I do some volunteer work, which I enjoy, and I see a psychiatrist of course. She's great. I didn't realize how many things I needed to confront—not just what happened to Uncle Joey and Eileen, and you know, abandoning my family." She covered the rest of the pasta with plastic wrap and set it in the refrigerator. "My problems go back to when I was a little girl."

"Yeah, I know. Dad said your mother was a witch."

The remark was unexpected, and her face must have said so.

"Sorry." He looked embarrassed.

"No. She was a witch, among other things. Your dad had it a lot worse, though."

"Honestly, I don't ever remember Dad saying anything about his parents, just his grandparents now and then. I mean, really, he's my father, but I don't know him very well. I mean, I know him." He raised the beer bottle to his lips. "But still."

Kate motioned him out to the deck and handed him a can of bug spray.

"Use it, or you'll be sorry."

"Mosquitoes?"

"Who knows? They call them no-see-ums up here, and that's the truth. You don't see them, but by tomorrow afternoon, you'll know they were here." As proof, she displayed one of her ankles. No raw spots or scabs were visible, but lots of dark pink spots remained from earlier attacks.

Outside on the deck, they rocked in silence. She knew the question was coming, but despite almost three glasses of wine, she still wasn't prepared when he brought it up.

"So speaking of Dad . . ."

"Were we?" she said with a sigh.

"What about you and Dad?"

"Right for the heart, huh?"

"I'm not a little kid, Mom. It's a fair question."

"It might be a fair question, but I don't think I can give you an answer. At least not the one you're looking for."

He set the beer bottle down so heavily it rattled the slate-topped table. "So you just stopped loving him?"

"My god, Devin!" She stopped rocking. "Of course not. I've loved him almost from the moment we met. We just aren't good for each other."

"He still loves you."

She laughed softly. "How would you know that? Did he say that?"

"All the time."

Her insides twisted into a tight coil. "And what would you expect him to say? That he doesn't love me anymore and that he's found someone else? He's not going to tell his children that, sweetheart."

"I don't think he would lie."

The moon cast a path along the water. Kate followed the flight of a bat as it swooped across the moonbeams and down to the dock, seeking its fill of the nighttime smorgasbord.

How could she talk with Devin about his father? But he was right; he did deserve some answers.

"I honestly don't know how your father feels about me. Does he still love me? I don't think so. Maybe not for a long time. I think what he felt may have been pity. Or guilt. I really don't know."

"I know. I know he loves you."

She nodded. "I know you want to believe that. And I know he did. Once. He loved me as much as it was possible for him to love anyone. I just think he loved himself more."

They sat quietly, each lost in their own thoughts, until Devin interrupted the silence.

"Is there someone else?"

She laughed softly. "Me? No. Once was enough. Falling in love with your father was the best thing that ever happened to me, other than you and your sister." She squeezed his arm. "I knew from the beginning he was it for me. I think I can be content again, tolerate my life, maybe even find some joy. But fall in love again? No, that I can't do. I gave my heart away twenty-five years ago. He never gave it back."

"Do you want it back?"

She drew her knees up under her chin and stared out over the cove. "No. It's his. I could never love that way again. It's too powerful. I think we're built for one great love in our lives. Your father was mine."

Even in the dark, she saw the sadness in his eyes. She ran her thumb over his cheek. He looked so much like Billy it nearly broke her heart.

"But I'm okay with that," she said, unsure who she was trying to convince, herself or Devin. "How many people go through life and never have anything close to what we had? My life didn't turn out like I expected, and there are things I would change, obviously. But falling in love with Billy McDonald? I wouldn't change that for anything."

THE REST of Devin's visit went quickly. By the time Friday morning rolled around, she was sad to see him leave. They had crammed a month's worth of sightseeing into five days. They'd visited six lighthouses, gone shopping in the Old Port, picnicked at Popham Beach, and hunted for sea glass at Spring Point. She'd kept him so busy, she hoped he didn't mind that she had no cable or internet for watching the Phillies or checking email.

He was loading a cooler packed with lobsters from Harold and ready for the seven-hour ride when she told him he couldn't bring them home.

"Don't worry," he said, sighing. "I'm going straight to Danielle's place in the Poconos. We'll eat them tonight. No one will be the wiser."

"I'm sorry."

"I get it. But you know, you'll have to deal with Dad and Rhiannon sooner or later—and it's already later."

"I will, I promise. Just seeing you was a big step for me."

"I think it went well." He flashed her a sly smile.

"It did, and I promise, I'll keep working on it."

She stood at the end of the driveway, watching long after the black truck was out of sight.

"Fair winds and following seas, my boy," she whispered. If it was possible, she felt even lonelier than when she'd first arrived.

CHAPTER THIRTY-TWO

S ummer faded into fall. Harold would be leaving for Boston
soon.

"For now," Kate said when he asked if she was going to stay. "I'm
good at avoiding things."

"I see that. Although for the life of me, I don't know what you're
hiding from anymore. You take care of yourself well. Sure as hell
don't hesitate to give me a hard time."

"Give you a hard time? That's your specialty, old man."

He snorted, and she knew enough not to argue with him or she'd
be late for work. There was no winning an argument with Harold.
Better to move on to a more difficult topic, for her at least.

She swallowed back the lump forming in her throat, and asked
when he would be leaving.

"The sixth. Jeff has a wedding at Sacred Heart the fifth, so he's
coming up Friday. We'll head back to Ogunquit on Sunday. I'll leave
from there for Boston."

"It'll be too quiet without you."

"You still got that goddamn hippie racing up and down the street
on that crotch rocket," he snarled.

"That's not the same, and you know it."

"Yeah, well." He shuffled his feet uncomfortably. "You better get going, or there won't be anybody to feed those tired, poor huddled masses of freeloaders."

She climbed into her car. "I know you don't mean that."

"From your lips to God's ears," he called over his shoulder.

There were more than the usual amount of huddled masses at the shelter that afternoon, and by the time Kate had finished up in the kitchen, her feet were killing her. A new nail salon had opened in Falmouth and thoughts of soaking her feet in a warm, jetted spa and then a foot rub was all she could think about. It had been ages since she'd treated herself to a pedicure; she was due.

"Did you pick a polish?" the nail tech asked.

"Crap." Her tired feet were already ankle deep in heaven. No way was she getting up now. "I'm sorry. What's popular now?"

"Chocolates, purples, all kinds of grays, emerald, navy."

Kate lifted her tanned feet from the bubbly water and wiggled her toes. None of those colors sounded appealing. "How about a strawberry pink?"

The girl shrugged and went in search of an old standby color while Kate rested her eyes.

As the nail tech began to remove the old polish, someone climbed into the chair across from her. Kate opened her eyes and smiled. She was adjusting the massage option on her chair when the woman spoke.

"Have you been here before?"

Kate shook her head.

"Me neither. Just thought I'd check it out. I usually go to a place in Portland, but I had a coupon."

Kate tried a different speed on the chair, but when it felt as though it would hurl her right onto the floor, she gave up. As long as her feet were happy, that's all that mattered.

"Do you have a coupon?"

"Me?" Kate asked. "No."

"I might have another. I got mine out of the paper the other day. I have this one, though." She pulled Sunday's *Boston Tribune* from her purse and began paging through it.

"That's okay."

"Are you sure? I don't mind looking."

"Really, I'm good. But thanks."

"Okay, but if I find it . . ."

The woman mumbled softly as she flipped through her newspaper, rattling the pages. Kate thumbed through a magazine, finding it difficult to concentrate. When the woman had finally settled in and the only sound was the tinkle of some new-agey music and the hum of the pedicure spas, Kate risked a glance. A familiar pair of blue-gray eyes stared back at her.

"Oh my god." She craned her neck and leaned forward, nearly dropping her magazine into the water.

The woman lowered the paper. "Are you all right?"

Kate waved off the nail tech and pulled her feet from the soapy water.

"Your newspaper," she said, her voice barely audible. "I need to see your newspaper."

The woman clutched it to her chest. "There's not another coupon. I looked."

"It's not that. Please? I'll pay you. I need your newspaper."

The woman looked at Kate as if she'd gone mad. She glanced around for reinforcements and, finding none, handed Kate the paper, reminding her that she hadn't finished it, against the increasingly likely event that Kate might make a mad dash for the door, leaving her shoes and purse behind but stealing the woman's days-old newspaper.

Kate stared at photo, unable to move.

The woman leaned over to see what had caught her attention and sighed. "I'm not into that loud, grungy music, but I have to admit, he's gorgeous. My daughter just loves him."

Kate's hands began to shake.

"So does mine," she whispered.

There he was on the front of the entertainment section of *The Boston Tribune*, above the fold, five columns wide in full color. He looked good. A little tired, maybe. His forehead was lined, and some well-trimmed scruff ran along his jaw. An early beard, perhaps. His hair, still long and multiple shades of gold and light brown, hung past his shoulders. Dressed in black, he leaned back into an ornate velvet armchair, his hands folded in his lap, looking up at the photographer. He wasn't smiling. He looked pensive, perhaps even sad— much too serious for someone finally on the cusp of his dream come true.

'WITHOUT YOU' PROPELS ROCK VETERAN INTO TOP SPOT ON POP CHARTS

By Gillian Wood

One of the biggest new stars on the pop horizon is no newcomer. He's a grandfather with more than 25 years under his low-slung leather belt, and he's played with some of the biggest names to ever strap on a Fender.

With a hit single that debuted last week at number one on the charts, Billy McDonald is finally getting his due. His new album, "Wasted Time," comes out next week. A U.S. tour that starts in late October is already selling out concert venues across the country.

"Wasted Time" is a complete reversal for McDonald, whose blistering lead work can be found on numerous albums, from hard rock to big city blues. McDonald was front man for Pernicious Anemia for several years before trying unsuccessfully to break out on his own again in 2005.

"Without You," the first hit off the new CD, is a heart-wrenching piano ballad penned by McDonald, a classically trained pianist as well as a dynamic guitar player. The rest of the album is a mix of love letters with a rock 'n' roll flavor as well as the type of searing, angry

rhythms that kept McDonald number one on every record producer's list as one of the top studio musicians for the past 20-some years.

In 1991, McDonald won a Grammy for his recording of rock-a-bye lullabies titled "Rockin' My Baby," but his solo career never took off.

Word is that "Wasted Time" is dedicated to Kate Donaldson, McDonald's wife of 24 years. Ever mindful of his privacy, he refused to talk about that or anything about his personal life during our discussion. In fact, before he consented to the interview, we were warned that all questions were to remain focused on the music and McDonald's career and that no personal questions would be entertained. True enough, when a question was deemed too personal, his manager threatened to pull the plug.

We caught up with McDonald in New York City. In spite of the sweltering temperatures of the Big Apple, he seemed unfazed in black, his shoulder-length blond mane loose and sporting a few days' scruff. McDonald remains, after all these years, one of the best-looking enigmas in rock.

BT: "Wasted Time" is a real departure for you, compared to the heavy metal and grunge rock you've dedicated yourself to over the years. Why the change?

BM: This past year has been a difficult one for me personally, and I found myself reevaluating what I was doing with my life. Music is and always will be what I do, but I needed to be able to express myself on my own terms. I think I've done that.

BT: Is that where the title song comes from? Have you been wasting your time?

BM: Yes and no. I don't believe that any experience is wasted. Everything life throws your way can be a valuable opportunity to learn, grow, and change if you must. I realized it was time for some changes. Were there things I should have done differently? Absolutely, but I learned from them all.

BT: I understand the album is dedicated to your wife, Katie. At least half of the songs on "Wasted Time" are heartbreak or love songs. Is there a message in there somewhere?

BM: I won't discuss my wife. However, the songs are real to me, regardless of what messages someone may or may not see in them or choose to read into them.

BT: Your "Wasted Time" tour starts in October. You've been touring throughout your entire career, but this will be the first major tour featuring all your own music. Would you say this is the best thing that's ever happened to you?

BM: No, I've experienced much better things in my life. I just didn't always realize it at the time.

McDonald wouldn't elaborate, and with that cryptic statement, the interview was over.

The 48-year-old rocker has remained a mystery throughout much of his career. His family has rarely been in the public eye, although his wife did make headlines last year when she was the target of a madman's bullets. Eight people died at a New Jersey municipal meeting she was covering as a reporter for a northern New Jersey newspaper, although she remained physically unscathed. Donaldson has not been seen publicly since the incident, and several sources close to the McDonald camp confirm that the couple separated late last year.

Another industry insider has said that McDonald's career suffered at his own hands, given that he is difficult to work with and has a violent temper as well as a problem with drugs and alcohol. Public records show that McDonald was arrested last year for aggravated assault and served 90 days in county jail earlier this year after pleading guilty in a plea agreement in county court in Andrewsville, N.J. Part of that time was split between jail and rehab.

Regardless of his past, McDonald appears to be on top of his game with this latest effort. If he continues to produce work of this caliber, this is likely just the beginning—again.

IT WAS like reading about someone she used to know. He had gone to jail and rehab, written at least a dozen songs, recorded an album, and scheduled an upcoming tour—all since she'd been gone. He'd achieved all he'd ever wanted now that she was out of the picture.

No wonder he dedicated the album to her. He should have called it "Good Riddance."

She shoved her feet back into the bubbling water. It was time she faced facts. Billy was moving on with his life.

It was time for her to do the same.

CHAPTER THIRTY-THREE

The sky was clear and cloudless as the first stains of pink unspooled across Broad Cove. The early October air was still. The night birds were long gone and the chickadees, grosbeaks, and nuthatches not yet awake. Now and then a truck or car from the main road interrupted the silence, but overall, the peace and solitude of the morning was almost spiritual.

Days like these held such promise.

From her chair on the upper deck, Kate surveyed the remnants of the garden in the dawning light. Most of the flowers were past their prime, but a few roses remained, stubbornly unaware their time had come. The stands of rosa rugosas lining the fence were dotted with bright red rose hips. A handful of deep-pink blooms clung to the branches. Should she cut herself a final bouquet? Better to let them linger. The weather would turn soon. Might as well enjoy that last bit of color as long as she could.

Today promised to be glorious. The temperature was expected to rise into the eighties. There was a slight chance of rain later, but for now, it was perfect. With the early sun already warming her bare legs, Kate sipped her coffee and watched the seagulls dive over the mud flat ahead of the rising tide.

She was on her second cup of coffee when she heard Harold's ride-on lawnmower start up. As the whir of the engine drew closer, she rose from the rocker, rubbing at the slat marks on the backs of her thighs, and dashed to the bedroom for her robe. It wouldn't be long before he was yelling to her from outside the kitchen window. The clock on her nightstand said it wasn't much past eight. Good thing she was an early riser.

"Up for a boat ride this afternoon?" Harold asked after she opened the front door. "Taking it out of the water tomorrow. This is the last day for a ride."

"You don't have to ask me twice." It was a day made for being on the water.

He tapped his forehead in a salute. "We'll meet you at your dock about eleven thirty. We have to be back by four." With a nod, he was off, but not before making a few neat passes up and down the side yard.

She took a quick shower and dried her hair. It reached just below her jaw now, and she wore it in a bob with bangs. She drew on a little eyeliner and a touch of mascara and slipped into a pair of capris and a long-sleeved T-shirt. After she was dressed, she made a quick trip to Hannaford's for some fried chicken, potato salad, and a bottle of wine. If Harold and Jeff were kind enough to include her in one last ride, the least she could do was feed them.

When she returned, she packed the food and wine into a small cooler with a few bottles of water and two wine glasses. Jeff didn't drink when they were boating, but Harold was never one to turn down a nice chardonnay. She tossed a heavy sweater into her tote along with a can of bug repellent.

After locking up the house, she hoisted the canvas bag over her shoulder, grabbed the cooler, and picked her way down the steep path to her dock. Charlie raced up and down, trying to hurry her along.

Most of the leaves retained their summer green, but several trees were burnished with autumn reds and golds. In spite of fall's less-than-full onslaught, a lack of rain had caused some of the trees to go straight from green to brown, their leaves already littering the path. Vines sporting berries of red or yellow wrapped around the trunks between splashes of purple from wild asters.

She reached her dock just as Jeff was firing up the motor on Harold's Bayliner. Tomorrow it would be taken out of the water and stored alongside his house. The canoes, kayaks, and Zodiac had already been put away until spring. Jeff navigated away from his father's dock and steered toward Kate.

Even more excited at the prospect of a ride than she, Charlie raced up and down the dock, barking.

"Calm down, you nut ball!" He obediently sat beside her, but seconds later, his tail was wagging furiously again and his body along with it. Before she could stop him, he dove into the water. She yelled, but it was pointless. He paddled around happily and swam out to meet the boat. As Jeff pulled up, Charlie climbed ashore, raced up the dock, and bounded into the boat. For an encore, he shook himself happily, spraying seawater over the three of them.

Kate grabbed his collar and yanked him down beside her.

"Always happy to see someone excited to sail," Harold said, excusing the dog's poor behavior.

Kate swiped her arm over her face. "I'm sorry. We haven't even made it out of the cove, and we're all wet. Charlie, sit." She pointed to a spot in the middle of the boat, and the wet dog obligingly sat, blinking back at her innocently.

She grabbed a cushion and took a seat in the bow. Harold sat across from her, and Jeff moved back to man the wheel.

"What have you got there?" Harold eyed the cooler curiously.

"Fried chicken, potato salad, some fruit, some wine for me and you, and for Jeff, water."

"Fried chicken, you say?"

"In case we want to stop for a little picnic."

Harold winked as he pulled the wine glasses from her bag, then reached into the cooler and poured the wine. He tossed a bottle of water over his shoulder. Jeff caught it one-handed.

"Can't wait until noon, Dad?"

"It's noon somewhere, right Kate?"

The afternoon passed quickly. They ate their picnic on a small island, and while Harold stretched out for a siesta, Kate and Jeff walked along the beach. Charlie raced ahead, chasing seagulls and diving into the water after whatever caught his eye.

"Have you really thought this through?" Jeff asked when she told him she was thinking about filing for divorce. "How would you feel if the shoe were on the other foot? If he did that without talking to you first?"

"Furious—but that would be different."

"How so?"

"Because he didn't go through what I did, not to mention I never cheated on him."

"Didn't he kind of go through what you did?"

"How could he 'kind of' go through it? That doesn't even make sense."

"I don't know. You said he was by your side when your friend died. He slipped into an active crime scene after the shooting, searching for you, terrified that you might have been shot or killed. Do you think that had an effect on him?"

Warming up either from the walk or the scrutiny, she pushed her sleeves up her arms. "Since when do priests play devil's advocate?"

"Who better?" he asked with a wry, crooked smile.

She picked up a deep-pink speckled rock, examined it, and slipped it into her pocket. "I think it's ridiculous the way you men stick together even when you don't know each other."

"I'm just saying, don't file for a divorce before you talk to him. What's the rush? You've waited this long. Why now?"

"Because it's time. Actually, it's past time. I know we Catholics aren't supposed to believe in divorce. Are you trying to talk me out of it because that's what you're supposed to say?"

The look he gave her was pure disappointment. "I think you know me better than that. Do you really think I'd advise you to stay in a bad situation because the rules tell me to?"

She shrugged. "So you've never advised someone to stay in a failed marriage because it's a sin to get a divorce?"

"No, I can honestly say I haven't. But I have advised people to try every means of fixing their relationships first, especially when they haven't even talked things over."

"Here I am thinking I've finally come to some kind of decision, and you're telling me to think some more. Tom says the same thing. Even Liz wants me to map out my reasons for and against it."

She picked up a piece of driftwood and threw it. Charlie immediately bounded after it and brought it back. She threw it again, letting some of her frustration sail along with it.

"Maybe you're right. I guess it's not fair to just send him divorce papers. Although in the long run, that's the easiest way to do it."

"Since when was it okay to do things the easy way?"

"What I mean is, I'm afraid to be around him. I'm afraid if he doesn't want a divorce, he'll talk me into coming back, even if it's not what I want."

"Do really think he can make you do something you don't want to do?"

"Yeah. Maybe. Probably." She shrugged. "I don't know."

"Well, that was the most convincing thing I've ever heard."

She rolled her eyes.

They had walked the circumference of the island, and as they approached the boat from the other side, they saw Harold heading in the opposite direction. Jeff called to him several times before he heard.

Harold jogged toward them, waving his arms. "If we don't get moving, we're not going to get back to the dock before low tide."

The front of the Bayliner was sitting on the muddy shoreline.

Jeff checked his watch. "Oh, crap."

He grabbed the cooler and darted into the water while Kate gathered the rest of her things. Harold climbed in and Jeff lifted Charlie, who wiggled to get free, and set him into the boat with Harold.

"You're going to have to help me push the boat into deeper water," Jeff told Kate. "I don't want Dad to have to climb in."

"I'm fine," Harold barked, throwing a leg over the side. "Stop treating me like an invalid."

Kate shook a threatening finger. "Don't do it, old man. I'm already soaked up to my knees. You just hold onto that damn dog." Charlie looked ready to bolt.

By the time they got the boat out far enough for Jeff to start the engine, she was soaked up to her thighs. Harold handed her a blanket from under the seat to wrap around her legs.

"It's going to get chilly as soon as we get moving," he said. "We're going to have to fly."

They made it to Harold's dock with nothing but chicken bones, an empty wine bottle, and a few inches of water remaining with the tide. The three of them had to drag the boat in the rest of the way. Harold headed for the house to heed a call of nature, and Charlie bounded after him, as excited to be on dry land as he had been to set sail.

"I'll be sad to see the boats out of the water," Kate said, standing on the dock, hosing the muck from her bare feet. "And I'm going to miss you and your father. It's going to be awfully quiet around here."

"You're really going to stay?"

"I think so," she said with a shrug that was more casual than what she was truly feeling. "My life is here now."

Jeff rested a hand on her shoulder. The look he gave her was sad, but sincere. "Not really, Kate. Not yet, anyway."

She turned off the water and tightened the spigot with a small grunt. "Maybe not, but it feels like home. I think this is where I belong."

"That may be, but you have a lot of unfinished business."

Thinking about the mess with Billy made the heaviness of Harold's imminent departure feel that much worse. She slipped her canvas bag over her shoulder, while Jeff lifted the cooler.

"You're not going to have any answers until you face him," he said as they made their way up the steep steps from the dock.

"I know. Maybe I'll call Devin, see if I can find out what to expect if I do go back."

She stopped talking as she made her way up the last section of steps, huffing and puffing. "Jeez, these are a killer. I don't know how your father does this every day."

"He's a tough old bird."

"Speak of the devil."

"What took you so long?" Harold strolled toward them, carrying two empty wine bottles. Charlie trotted happily alongside him.

"If you finished off two bottles of wine, we took a lot longer than I realized," Jeff said with a shake of his head.

"I like a little wine with dinner," Harold answered. "Kate, honey, can you put these in with your returns? I missed these when I went to the redemption center."

"Absolutely." She tucked the two bottles under her arm along with the empty one she was already carrying. "What time are you leaving Sunday?"

"Early," Jeff said. "I have to be in Ogunquit for eight-o'clock Mass. I was thinking of leaving tomorrow after the wedding, but they want me to come to the reception and say the blessing. We'll just leave in the morning."

A motorcycle roared past the house, prompting Harold to turn and shake his fist. "Damn hoodlum."

Jeff rolled his eyes. "Just because he rides a motorcycle doesn't make him a hoodlum."

"No? What does it make him?"

"Ecological? Adventurous?"

"Pah!" Harold waved him off.

Kate debated giving Harold a hug, which would either annoy or embarrass him, but in the end, she couldn't help herself. She chased after him as he made his way toward the house.

"Harold!" She threw her free arm around his neck. "In case I don't see you, thank you for everything." Her voice broke. "Thank you both. I don't know where I'd be without you."

Harold's face softened, and his arms looped around her. "You have my number, and remember, you promised to come to Boston and visit. No excuses." He followed up with a quick pat on her back and let go. "You better go after that crazy dog of yours." He pulled a handkerchief from his pocket and rubbed it under his nose and across his eyes. "Damn allergies."

Unable to speak, Kate nodded. She felt some allergies coming on as well.

Relishing the cool grass beneath her bare feet, Kate walked beside Jeff, while Charlie galloped on ahead of them. It was nearly four thirty, and the temperature had dropped since morning. The sun, partly obscured by gathering rain clouds, had dipped behind the tall pines.

Charlie disappeared behind the trees, barking over the idling of Shane's motorcycle. She'd call him, but why bother? He'd only ignore her. If she was going to live here permanently, she would have to start tying Charlie up when he was outside or put in an electric fence, since Harold wouldn't be around to shoo him back home when he went wandering.

"Damn dog. He must be in Rhonda's yard. Probably won't let the poor kid get off his bike."

After the engine cut off, Jeff gave a loud whistle. Charlie bounded around the copse of pines that separated the two properties.

"Come here, you knucklehead!" she yelled. He ran past her, drew up behind them, and galloped back toward the house at full speed.

Jeff laughed. "I bet he's good company."

"When I'm not chasing him all over the neighborhood."

Charlie disappeared, and the barking started again.

"I'm coming. Don't rush me!" She was still laughing at her maniac of a dog as they cleared the trees.

The biker standing in her driveway was a good half-foot taller than Shane and was dressed in black from his helmet to his boots. Lost, most likely. But then he turned toward her and removed his helmet.

A shaft of lowering sunlight pierced the pines like a spotlight, illuminating the place where he stood and reflecting the mass of blond waves that tumbled gently over his shoulders.

This time, she knew she wasn't dreaming.

CHAPTER THIRTY-FOUR

When he woke that morning, Billy had no idea that by late afternoon, he would find his wife—not only find her, but find her with another man. His heart was about to punch its way through his chest. He looped his thumbs into the front pockets of his jeans, spread his fingers across the tops of his thighs, and concentrated on keeping them there. It took everything in his power to stay under control, but he'd worked too hard and waited too long to lose it now.

His eyes drank her in. His beautiful Katie! She was still thin, but she'd regained some of the weight she'd lost. Her cheeks were fuller, and the sharp angles of her shoulders and hips had been replaced with the soft, gentle curves he remembered. Her hair was shorter than he'd ever seen, but it in no way diminished her beauty.

The real difference, however, was that she had been laughing. A sound he hadn't heard since before he'd gone out on tour with Stonestreet almost a year and a half ago. It was good to see her looking almost like herself, but it fucking killed him to see her that way with someone else.

Recognition swept across her face, and she resembled a deer in the headlights. Maybe this wasn't a good idea. Maybe he should have told Devin to let her know he was coming. She moved closer, and he saw she was carrying empty wine bottles and glasses. Bile rose in his throat. Had he interrupted something?

Charlie darted toward him, raced to Kate, then back again, barking wildly.

Billy stood on the brick-paved walkway, grateful to be wearing shades. Not for the sun, but to hide any emotion he couldn't control. She was also wearing sunglasses. He wouldn't know what she was thinking either, although the way she chewed on her lip gave him a clue. It also made him weak in the knees.

She was barefoot. Her cropped slacks were damp above her knees. Grass clippings clung to her feet and ankles.

When she spoke, her voice was soft and low, pouring over him like warm honey. "Hello, Billy."

He swallowed. "Katie."

Charlie had no trouble showing his emotions. He barked and jumped and wove in and out around their legs.

"Charlie!" the three of them yelled at the same time.

He glared at Kate's friend. With a whimper, Charlie plopped onto the grass and rested his head on his front paws, looking expectantly from Kate to Billy.

Kate's dark glasses made it difficult to tell if she was looking at him. He didn't want to take his eyes off her lest she disappear, but her friend forced him by setting down the cooler and extending his hand.

"I'm Jeff." The bastard was smiling.

Jeff was shorter than Billy by several inches, and had close-cropped, sand-colored hair. He was dressed neatly, right down to an Izod polo shirt tucked into a pair of khaki shorts and a thin, woven belt that might actually have had lobsters on it. A yellow sweater was tied around his shoulders.

Who the fuck wore a yellow sweater? Or fucking lobsters, for that matter? A stockbroker, maybe. Or an accountant. Billy's already low spirits plummeted. The kind of guy Kate should have been with all along, that's who. Not some alcoholic musician with a bad attitude and a hot temper.

In spite of his preference for punching the guy in his crooked nose, Billy shook his hand. "Nice to meet you."

"I'm sorry." Kate looked nervous, as if she'd expected him to deck the guy. "Jeff, you've heard me speak of Billy. My husband."

Billy tried to read her but couldn't.

"Jeff's my neighbor's son and a good friend."

No one moved. Billy stared at Kate. She stared at her feet. And her friend stared at him.

After an uncomfortable few seconds, Jeff cleared his throat. "I should be going. I have that rehearsal tonight. Kate? You good here?"

"She's fine." Billy couldn't stop himself, nor could he hide the irritation in his voice. He only slightly regretted it when Kate's head jerked up.

She smiled sweetly and nodded. "Please thank your dad again." She reached up to kiss Jeff's cheek, and Billy's fingers curled into fists.

Rehearsal? So he was a musician. Billy assessed him again. Probably played with some orchestra.

"It was nice meeting you." Walking backward, Jeff gave a little wave before turning and sprinting across the lawn with Charlie in close pursuit.

Billy whistled. The dog stopped in his tracks and trotted back to Billy, looking up at Kate as if she were encroaching on their territory.

"Someone's got to teach me how to do that," she mumbled.

The last of the sunlight had vanished. Kate stood close enough to touch, but neither of them moved. Finally, Billy slipped off his sunglasses, folded them, and tucked them into the neck of his T-shirt. With both hands, he removed Kate's, folded them, and dropped them into her canvas bag.

He looked for a spark and found himself tumbling into eyes the color of a stormy sea, and then he smiled.

"Hello, Katie. I've missed you."

KATE'S HEART ricocheted against her ribs. When Billy removed her glasses, it was all she could do to stay on her feet. He didn't touch her, but she felt warmth radiating off his hands and onto her cheeks. She inhaled sharply.

"Are you okay?"

She nodded. Damn, he looked good. The lines on his face were deeper and there were a few silver hairs in his unshaven scruff, but his eyes were clear. Eyes she still saw each night when she closed her own. A thousand thoughts and memories raced through her mind, but not a single word sprang to her lips.

"I'm sorry to surprise you," he said. "I should've asked Devin to let you know I was on my way, but I was afraid you'd tell him to stop me."

Is that what she would have done? Probably. What she needed to do now was to get a grip.

"Nice bike." She tried to keep the snark from her voice. She hated motorcycles, and he knew it. "Yours?"

"It is." At least he had the decency to look sheepish, even if she had no right to an opinion.

"You have a license?"

"Of course."

He hadn't had one for the past couple of years, so why would she assume differently? She pressed the bottles closer to her chest. "Where are you staying?"

Billy's face clouded. "I don't know. I didn't think that far ahead." He dragged a hand through his hair. "When I found out where you were, I grabbed the keys and jumped on my bike. I would've been here sooner, but I hit rain in Massachusetts and ended up parked under an overpass for a while."

Her mouth fell open. Still not getting a grip. "You just found out? Today?"

He glanced at his watch. "About seven hours ago."

It would have taken him at least six, six and a half hours to get there with no traffic.

"Who told you? Devin?"

Billy nodded, but lowered his eyes. "Has he known all along?"

"No. Just a few weeks. No one knew except Tom."

"Yeah, and the bastard wasn't talking."

"He was doing what I asked."

Billy nodded.

A mosquito landed on her hand, and she shooed it away.

"Do you want to come inside?" She was afraid of what might happen if they were alone together, but she wasn't in the mood to be eaten alive. "Or you can hold these and let me spray myself."

"Inside. If that's okay."

As she fumbled through her canvas bag for the house keys, the empty bottles slipped from her arm and shattered on the brick sidewalk.

"Oh crap!"

Shards of broken glass glittered around her feet.

"Don't move," he ordered. "Just hand me the keys."

Before she could protest, he scooped her up and carried her up the steps. Holding her, he squatted low enough to slide the key in the lock.

"You could put me down now," she said nervously. "The glass is down there, not up here."

Ignoring her, he proceeded into the house and set her down on the floor in the foyer. "If you get me a broom, I'll clean that up for you."

She fetched the broom and dustpan, and while Billy swept up the broken glass, she stood in the kitchen, gripping the edge of the granite countertop like a lifeline. The pounding of her heart filled her ears, nearly drowning the rhythmic swish of the broom outside. She felt dizzy and for a moment, she thought she might faint. An electric current had shot through her when Billy picked her up. It was so strong he had to have felt it himself.

But what if he hadn't? She was doomed, that's what.

BILLY WAS careful to get every last bit of the glass. Kate often went barefoot, and he didn't want her or Charlie to step on a piece he might have missed. He was guiding the last shard into the dustpan when someone called his name.

Kate's friend darted across the lawn like a preppie mobster in a black suit with a black shirt. He held out a key. "My dad forgot to give this to Kate. So she could look after the house. You know, if she's still here."

What Billy wanted to do was tell Jeff that she wouldn't be able to do that since she'd be back in Jersey. With him. But he didn't; he just pocketed the key.

"So what do you play?" Billy asked, leaning on the broom.

"Play?"

"Yeah. What instrument do you play?"

Jeff rubbed a hand across the back of his neck. "I studied piano as a kid, but I'd hardly call that playing." He laughed. "In fact, I'm certain my piano teacher would definitely not call what I did playing."

"You said you had a rehearsal."

"Oh. Sorry. Wedding rehearsal." He held up a white clerical collar; something that Billy had failed to notice. "I'm a priest."

A priest? Relief filtered through his veins and he had an overwhelming desire to laugh. Fortunately, he was able to control himself. "Ah. Well, you have fun!"

He was more than certain he'd already cleaned up every last sliver of glass before, but kept sweeping until he could control the grin covering his face.

Was this actually happening?

Less than eight hours ago, he'd been sitting at the kitchen counter with his head in his hands.

"What's wrong?" Devin had asked.

Billy had wiped his damp cheeks and shook his head. "Nothing."

"Is it Mom?"

"No. Sorry." He forced a smile. "Actually, it's good news."

Devin looked skeptical.

"Really."

"Okay." Devin poured himself a cup of coffee.

Billy pushed off the stool and pulled a carton of eggs from the refrigerator. "How about scrambled eggs and toast?"

"You don't have to make my breakfast. I'm not a little kid."

"I don't mind." He cracked a few eggs into a bowl as Devin settled onto a stool. Billy could feel his son's eyes on him as he beat the eggs into a froth.

"Well?"

The frustration he'd been feeling that morning had taken over his arm, and at the rate he was beating the eggs, Devin might end up with a soufflé for breakfast.

"I just got a call from my producer. The single's gone platinum. They're expanding the tour."

"That's great. I'm confused, though."

His mouth quivered as he poured the foamy mixture into a hot pan. "It's all I ever wanted. But without your mother, it doesn't seem important anymore. I've been hoping she'd hear the song on the radio and call or text me. Anything." He shook his head and shrugged. "Well, at least you and I are cool now. I know I can't go back and fix all those times I fucked up when you were a kid, but you know, I like where we're at now."

Devin set his cup down. "I'm proud of you, Dad. You weren't always the best, but you sure as hell weren't the worst."

"A lot of good that does me. What's that saying, too late smart? Whatever I am, I'm too late."

"Maybe not."

"It's almost a year, and we've heard nothing from her. At least Tom says she's okay. I would've lost my mind by now if I didn't know anything. Some days I'm so fucking pissed that she left, but most of the time, I miss her so much I don't care. I just want her back."

Devin plucked a piece of toast from the toaster and slathered it with butter. "When does the tour start?"

"Not till the end of the month. I have to be in Portland by the twenty-fourth."

"Oregon?"

"Maine. I've got two dates there, then Boston, New York, a few gigs in Pennsylvania, then Baltimore. I'll be home for Thanksgiving. I guess we'll go to Rhiannon's, and then I head out again the following Tuesday."

"Rhiannon's, huh? I'm not eating tofurkey."

"At least we'll be together." He poured himself a second cup of coffee.

Devin took a bite of his toast, then cleared his throat. "Look, you're going to be pissed, but I'm going to tell you anyway."

"I get that you want to spend Thanksgiving with Danielle—"

"It's not that. It's Mom."

The hand carrying his cup paused halfway to his mouth. "What about her?"

"I know where she is."

It was possible his heart might have stopped. "What?"

Devin pushed the plate of eggs away and glanced nervously at him from across the counter.

"I know where she is."

"I *heard* that. Where?"

"She's in Maine."

"How do you know?"

"I saw her back in August."

He slammed the cup down so hard coffee sloshed out, burning his hand and splashing onto the counter.

"You've known where she is and you didn't say anything?" His voice was getting louder. "Does Rhiannon know?"

Devin shook his head. "No. Just me. Mom still doesn't think she's ready to deal with everything, and I promised not to say anything."

"You mean me. She isn't ready to deal with me." He wanted to throw the mug across the room. "You need to tell me where she is."

"I will," Devin said, pulling out his wallet. He removed a slip of paper and handed it to him. The few words were jumping around, but Billy zeroed in on the most important one. "Cumberland? How far?"

"Just outside of Portland. About six, seven hours."

He shoved the paper into his pocket and felt for his keys and his wallet. He stormed down the stairs and grabbed his helmet and jacket from the shelf near the back door.

Devin followed. "What're you doing? You're going now?"

Billy kicked the screen door open. "What the fuck do you think?"

He pounded down the walkway, Devin and the world around him a blur. There was one thing in his mind and one thing only.

Katie.

Half an hour later, he was soaring up Route 80 when he veered the Harley onto the shoulder and into the grass so hard he nearly upset the bike. His heart was racing. He was having trouble breathing. He yanked off his helmet and tossed it onto the grass. Leaning forward, he took in huge gulps of air.

He couldn't believe it; he was having a fucking panic attack.

If he could slow his breathing, maybe his heart would follow. He walked toward a cluster of trees, ignoring the roar of the highway. When he'd calmed himself enough to speak without panting, he pulled out his cell phone.

Devin answered after four rings. "Yeah?"

"I'm sorry."

Nothing. *Shit.*

"I shouldn't have lost it like that. You did the right thing. You were protecting your mother. I'm proud of you. She raised you to be a good man."

A few seconds of silence. "Thanks."

"We were making progress. I hope I didn't blow it."

"I understand."

Billy chuckled halfheartedly. "Do you? 'Cause I sure as hell don't."

"I get it, Dad. You're worried."

"I'm trying to do better. I am."

"That's the only reason I told you. If I hadn't believed you were trying so hard and if I hadn't seen for myself that she's doing better, I never would've told you."

"Is she . . ." He tried to speak around the rock lodged in his throat. "Is she really doing better?"

"Yeah. She is."

"Good." A tear rolled down his cheek. "I guess I'll see for myself soon enough."

"Dad?"

"Yeah?"

"Hurt her again, and you and I are done. You understand?"

A sob escaped when he opened his mouth. "Understood."

He tucked his cell phone into his pocket and dropped to the grass. He pressed his palms against his eyes to stop the tears, but it was no use.

The hurt and fear of the past ten months rushed him all at once. When he reached his destination, it might mean the end of months of living on edge and a chance to rebuild their marriage—or it might mean the end, once and for all. Either way, he had to be ready. Yet here he was, less than thirty minutes down the road, and he was already having a meltdown.

He wiped his face with the hem of his shirt and climbed back on the bike. He slipped on his helmet, adjusted the mirrors, and roared off toward the unknown.

CHAPTER THIRTY-FIVE

"It's going to rain." Kate stood in the doorway leading into the house from the garage and watched Billy empty the contents of the dustpan into the garbage. "Do you want to bring your bike in?"

"If you don't mind."

"Of course not. Are you hungry?"

He ran a hand over his stomach, and she followed it with her eyes, her face growing warm at the memory of her own hand touching the skin beneath his T-shirt.

"Kind of. I haven't eaten since this morning, but I don't want you to go to any trouble."

"It's no trouble. Let me see what I can whip up."

She was poking around in the refrigerator when he came inside.

"I'm trying to see how creative I can be. I don't get much comp—" She averted her gaze, but not before she'd caught the look of hurt in his eyes. "Not that you're company. It's just . . ." *Shut up, Kate. Just shut your mouth.* She tried to smile but wasn't quite sure she'd pulled it off.

"Anything is good. Toast, crackers. Just something to put in my stomach."

"I can do better than toast."

He sauntered into the dining room, stood in front of the patio door, and whistled softly. "This is amazing. What a view."

For some reason, it made her happy that he liked it, which surprised her. She stopped rummaging long enough to follow his gaze.

"It is, isn't it? You should see the sunrise. It comes up right over those trees. It's beautiful."

"May I?" Her legs felt rubbery when he smiled. "May I see the sunrise?"

She ducked her head back into the refrigerator and made a big show of pulling out a container of organic greens and a cucumber.

That answered the question of where he was staying.

"I guess," she said, focusing on the salad ingredients and not the achingly beautiful man standing in her kitchen, "if you can get up early enough."

Billy opened the slider and stepped out onto the deck. It was still clear enough to see the yard below, the garden, and the drop-off to the cove.

"Where's the water?" he asked when she stepped out beside him.

"It's low tide. By the time you get up, the tide will have come in, gone out, and come in again. It's comforting. No matter what else happens, the tide comes in and goes out, and no matter how barren and muddy it looks, in just a little while, it will be beautiful again."

"It's beautiful now."

He wasn't looking at the view.

"Wait, you'll see," she answered, as if he were.

Billy scanned the rocking chairs on the deck, the colorful mums in the large containers, and the pool below. "A built-in pool?"

"Comes with the house. C'mon, I'll give you a quick tour."

She showed him the living room and took him downstairs and through the family room. They were headed outside when her cell phone began to ring.

"I'll be right back." She darted for the stairs. "I have a feeling this is someone I'll want to speak with."

"Go ahead. I'll just poke around."

She reached the phone just as it stopped ringing. Devin. Just as she suspected. She dialed his number.

"Hi, Mom!" He sounded forcibly chipper.

She dropped onto the edge of her bed. "Start explaining."

"I guess he made it."

"Why is your father here?"

"Look, Mom, I'm sorry I— You know what? I take that back. I'm not sorry."

Trapped. And unprepared. She couldn't deal with Billy yet and he knew it. "You promised."

"And I meant it, but things have changed. We've changed."

"I'm not ready—"

"Yes, you are," he insisted. "And he's ready. This can't go on forever. You need to sit down and talk. You two aren't the only ones in limbo here. Do you have any idea what it's been like watching him the last ten months? At least he hasn't been sitting around feeling sorry for himself—"

"Oh, I'm sure of that," she answered snidely.

"Stop it, Mom. You wouldn't let me say anything when I came to visit, but you need to listen now. He's changed."

She sighed. "You know what they say about leopards."

"Bullshit! I'm not talking about leopards. I'm talking about my father. I'm talking about a man who's done all the hard work this past year. He almost died when you tossed him out last summer. He OD'd on heroin. If I hadn't found him when I did . . . Let's just say we wouldn't be having this conversation. Given the shape you were in back then, I probably wouldn't have a father or a mother. Which is why we never told you."

Jesus! Heroin? The room had begun to spin, her life somehow whirling past her along with it. Had she been that clueless? She groped for a pillow and crushed it in her arms, holding on for dear life.

"All he wanted was you. He kept asking for you, but I refused to let anyone call you. I'd had it with him by then. After you left, he was lost. We all were. He went straight into rehab, and then he made a deal with the DA and served his time. He's been clean and sober since. He even goes to AA every day. I'm proud of him, Mom."

"I didn't know—"

"Of course you didn't. And it's okay, because you had to do what you had to do. I'm proud of you too, but it's time you started facing reality. You have a family, and every one of us loves you, and we want you back. Even if you don't want to be married anymore. That's your business. I think Dad is finally at a point he can deal with that now without falling apart. If I didn't believe that, I'd have never told him where you were."

She gripped the pillow tightly. Maybe Devin was right. It was time to make a decision. She owed it to Billy, and she owed it to her children.

Most importantly, she owed it to herself.

"Are you okay?"

She cleared her throat. "I will be."

"Do you know what you're going to do?"

"No. But I'll listen, and I'll talk. That's all I can promise."

"That's all I ask."

She sat in the dark after hanging up, trying to gather her thoughts. Could Billy have changed that much? She had. Anything was possible.

There was a soft tap on the door. "Katie?" Billy pushed it open. "Everything okay?"

She released the pillow and set the phone on her nightstand. "I was talking with a very tall stool pigeon."

"Did you tell him I made it?"

"Yeah. I told him several other things too."

He chuckled. "I can imagine."

"He told me a few things as well."

"I'm not surprised."

Billy stepped into the room and held up a plastic grocery sack. When its contents moved, she frowned.

"What's in the bag?"

"Some old guy came to the door and said to give these to you. He said you'd know what to do with them."

She peeked into the bag and rolled her eyes. "Harold."

He opened the bag wider. "Which one is Harold?"

She laughed, and some of the tension slipped away. "No. Harold is my neighbor. Jeff's father."

"I introduced myself, but he said he already knew who I was. Then he shoved the bag in my hand." He cocked an eyebrow. "He also said to tell you not to set them free."

She laughed again and began moving toward the kitchen again. "Long story."

"Doesn't he know you don't eat lobster?"

"Yes, but he knows you love them."

"Wow. That was nice."

"He can be a bit abrasive, but he's been good to me. I'll miss him."

"I think he called me a damn hippie."

"That's Harold."

Billy set the bag of lobsters on the kitchen counter. "Do you mind if I get out of these clothes?"

Was he kidding? "Um . . ."

"I'm still wet from getting caught in the rain, and I think I'm chafing." He squirmed to prove how uncomfortable he was.

She felt her skin heat. "Oh. Sure. Why don't you grab a hot shower? You can use my bathroom, and I'll dry your clothes in the meantime."

While he was in the shower, she pulled out a pair of cargo shorts Devin had forgotten. She also had one of Billy's old shirts. She left them on the bed in the guest room.

She was waiting for the water to boil when he walked in wearing nothing but a white towel around his waist.

She gasped. "You startled me."

"Sorry."

Averting her eyes to look at anything but his toned and inked chest, she returned her attention to the lobsters crawling over each other in the kitchen sink. "I put some clothes for you on the bed in the guest room."

"Whose clothes?" His voice turned tight.

"Devin left a pair of shorts, and I had an old shirt of yours. No underwear, unless you want to squeeze into a pair of mine." She expected a remark about getting into her pants, but he didn't bite.

"That's okay. I'll go commando."

"We can run to the mall after we eat, but we're going to be pushing it."

He shook his head. "I'm fine. I'd rather spend the time with you. I didn't drive all the way up here to go shopping."

"Okay." Two syllables. Even to her own ears, they seemed to be saying much more.

"I just wish I'd thought far enough ahead to grab a toothbrush."

"That I can help you with." She put a lid on the pot to help the water boil faster and led him to the guest room. "There are the clothes. I think there are extra toothbrushes in the drawer in the bathroom."

He made a face.

"Not used ones," she added.

She flipped on the light in the small bathroom and rooted through the drawers until she found a handful of wrapped toothbrushes. "Here you go." She held them up as she stepped into the bedroom. "You even have a choice of col—Billy!"

His back to her, he had dropped the towel and was slipping into the shorts. He zipped them up and turned around.

"Sorry." The shorts hung low on his waist, exposing the head of the serpent inked on the sharp V below his waist and threatening to expose even more. Not that she hadn't just gotten a bird's-eye view of his ass.

He pulled on the shirt and sniffed the sleeve. "Do you still sleep in my shirts?"

It was embarrassing, but she felt compelled to answer honestly. "Sometimes. I only have the one. It stopped smelling like you a long time ago, but I still wear it."

"It smells like you now." Even in the dim light, she could see the flash of his smile. "Sweet and orangey."

Warmth crept up her neck and into her cheeks. Her goddamn husband of twenty-four years was making her blush. Unbelievable.

"That water should be boiling by now," she said, making a hasty exit.

He followed her into the kitchen and slipped an oven mitt on one hand. "I'll do this." The corner of his mouth quirked up into a smile as he lifted the lid of the pot. "You've had enough drama for one day, and I'm too hungry to have to chase my dinner."

She waved an index finger at him. "Just stick them in head first."

He lifted a particularly feisty crustacean out of the bag. "Do they really scream?"

"I have no idea, but I don't want to find out."

———

EVERY TIME KATE LOOKED AWAY, Billy stole another glance. Twelve hours ago, he hadn't known where she was. Now he was in Maine in a house on the ocean, and they were eating dinner. Together.

There was something different about her. Not just her hair, and she was still as beautiful as ever. She was different in other ways. Despite her initial distress at seeing him—and he didn't blame her—he sensed an underlying confidence. It was a good thing, but it scared him. Could she have changed enough to realize life was easier without him or that she no longer loved him?

The succulent mouthful of lobster he'd just swallowed went down like a piece of shell.

"Went down the wrong way," he sputtered. He picked up his glass and drained it.

She looked concerned until she he'd convinced her that he wasn't about to choke to death.

"Do you want more water?"

"Yes, please." He handed her his glass and gulped down half of it as soon as she set the refilled glass before him.

"Are you always this thirsty?"

He picked up the lobster cracker and went to work on the second claw. "Probably from being on the bike all day."

"Riding a motorcycle makes you thirsty?"

"I guess," he stammered. "I've only had it a little while. I never took such a long trip with it."

She eyed him warily. "You may want to get that checked when you get home."

Home—his home, not hers. His heart took a nose dive. "I will."

They chewed in silence, Billy still stealing glances and Kate pushing pieces of cucumber and lettuce around her plate. The silence grew uncomfortable.

"I don't ever remember lobster tasting this good," he said, wiping melted butter from his hands.

She looked almost relieved he had spoken.

"Devin said the same thing." She pointed to the cove with the tip of her fork. "The fact that earlier today it was still swimming in the back yard helps. Plus you said you hadn't eaten since this morning. An old shoe drenched in butter would probably taste good about now."

He popped a piece of the tender white meat into his mouth. "Doubt it. You sure you don't want to try?"

"Positive." She drained her wine glass, picked up the bottle, and poured more. "Are you sure I can't get you something else? I have seltzer or I can make some iced tea . . ."

"No, thanks."

"Coffee? More water?"

"I'm fine, Katie, really. I don't need a thing."

That was a lie. He needed her. The look he tried to convey said as much.

In the soft light, it seemed she was blushing, but it could have been from spending the day on a boat. When she took a large mouthful of wine, he was convinced it was the former.

"Well, I could go for some coffee." She jumped up. "Coffee? All I have is decaf."

"If you're making it, I'll have some."

As she reached for his plate, he curled his hand around her wrist. "Are you okay? I didn't mean to freak you out. But you were here, and I had to see you."

She stared down at his hand. "I'm okay." She nodded a little too enthusiastically. "I am."

As soon as he let go, she darted into the kitchen. She reminded him of a hummingbird.

"Would you like me to set a fire?" He brought the remaining dishes in behind her and set them next to the sink.

She began rinsing them and loading them into the dishwasher. "Sure. That would be nice."

When the coffee finished brewing, she joined him in the living room. She handed him a large mug and curled up on the other sofa, about as far away from him as she could get.

"It's unusually warm for this time of year," she said. "Here, I mean. In Maine. Although I guess it's warm back in New Jersey too."

"Pretty much."

"I guess the weather isn't all that different here unless you go farther north or inland. You go inland, it gets pretty cold."

They hadn't seen or spoken to each other in over ten months, but if she wanted to talk about the weather, then they would talk about the weather.

"I noticed most of the trees are still green," he said, giving her what she wanted. "The leaves are already turning back home. I thought New England was all about the amazing foliage."

"It's been a strange year," she said, quickly adding, "weather-wise."

"It certainly has." His response had nothing to do with the weather.

When she caught him looking at her, she averted her gaze to the fire.

"You look good, Katie."

She shifted uncomfortably. "Thank you. So do you."

"Thank you." The conversation was so strained it was painful yet funny at the same time. Either that or his nerves were getting the best of him.

"How are you? Really?" he asked.

"I'm okay. Better." She sipped her coffee. She didn't speak again at first, so he thought she was done, but then she surprised him. "It's been like peeling an onion. I had to go all the way back to the beginning to get to the heart of it all. The cracks in my foundation were so deep, it took a while to get there, but I did it."

"Back to our beginning?"

"Way before that, actually. Back to when I was a very sad, very lonely little girl. I never realized how much I'd buried."

"I'm sorry." A lump formed in his throat. "You didn't deserve it."

The fire turned her hair a reddish brown and cast shimmering golden light across her face. She looked like a goddess. "You're right." Her voice was soft, but confident. "I didn't deserve any of it."

He set the mug on the coffee table and leaned forward. "Look, babe . . ." He tried to swallow the endearment.

Before he could continue, Kate cut him off. "Not tonight. We'll talk tomorrow. Let's just be here for now."

"Okay." He dropped back against the cushions. "Tomorrow, then."

CHAPTER THIRTY-SIX

The house was silent except for the tick of the grandfather clock in the dining room, which, Billy noticed, chimed randomly. At least it was random according to his watch. His body cried out from exhaustion. The muscles in his legs and thighs vibrated and his back was stiff and sore, yet his brain was in overdrive, playing every possible scenario on rewind. Sleep seemed unlikely, especially with Kate less than twenty feet away. So close, yet still so far.

He picked up the clock on the bedside table and was shocked to see it was after six, until he noticed the second hand wasn't moving. He felt his way to the bathroom, flicked on the light, and squinted at himself in the mirror. He ran his fingers through his hair. It was time for a trim. And he'd have to pick up a razor tomorrow, and some underwear at the very least.

Of course, that would depend on how their talk went. Kate might send him home. He'd seen a small crack in her resolve, and although she'd been shocked, she wasn't angry. At least he had that going for him.

He turned off the light and climbed back into bed. It was comfortable enough, but his mind wouldn't simmer down. He rolled over, punched the pillow, scrunched it up under his neck, and lay back down. When that didn't help, he threw off the covers. There was a bit of a chill in the house, so he pulled on the shorts and his old shirt and headed for the kitchen.

Illuminated only by the dimmed sconce lights and the blue flame flickering under the tea kettle, he rummaged through the cabinets until he found a box of Sleepytime. He found a mug, dropped in a tea bag, and leaned against the kitchen sink, staring at his reflection in the wall of glass while he waited for the water to boil.

"Can't sleep?"

He jumped. "Jeez. You scared the shit out of me."

"Sorry." Kate gave him a sleepy smile. She was wearing a white robe covered with tiny pink flowers and ruffles around the neck. He'd never seen it before, and it was a painful reminder that she had a different life now, one without him. A hank of hair stood up at the back of her head. He crossed his arms and tucked his hands against his ribs to keep from reaching out to smooth it.

"Can't you sleep?" he asked.

"Not really." She pulled a chair from the dining room table, then sat with her knees tucked under her chin.

He pulled down another cup and dropped in a tea bag. He poured the boiling water into both mugs and added a dollop of honey to Kate's. The grandfather clock in the dining room proclaimed it was almost four as he carried the cups to the table.

She blew on her tea and took a cautious sip. The silence between them was filled by a loud chorus of wind chimes outside the window. When he looked up, she was watching him over the rim of her cup.

"Why didn't you come for me?" she asked quietly.

She couldn't be serious. Hadn't she insisted none of them come looking for her? How could she even ask him that?

"I didn't know where you were. Not till today. I left the minute I found out, honest."

"No, when I was in the hospital—in the psych ward. Why didn't you come? You didn't even call."

His mouth dropped open. "I didn't know until after you'd already disappeared."

She rolled her eyes and looked away.

He was trying not to lose his shit, but it was difficult. "I mean it. No one told me."

"Billy," she said, her voice measured, "other than the past ten months, when did you ever go more than a few days without speaking to me? You mean to tell me you didn't talk to me for what, a week, and you didn't think something was wrong?"

"Of course I thought something was wrong! I called you every day. Several times a day, in fact." He tried to snuff out the fire that had ignited inside him as he struggled to recall what had happened. "Rhiannon told me you were angry that we'd made you see a psychiatrist. She said you were punishing me."

"Does that sound like something I would do?"

He reached for her hand, but she snatched it away.

"No," he answered, surprised at how calm he sounded. "It doesn't. However, you must admit, your behavior hadn't been exactly normal. It bugged the shit out of me, but she swore you were okay. Why would I think she was lying?"

She gave him a baleful stare.

"You're right," he said. "I'm sure she lied plenty over the years. She went too far this time, though. She was texting me from your phone, posing as you and telling me you were fine but you didn't want to talk to me."

Kate's jaw pretty much unhinged. "What?"

"Yeah." He was still furious with Rhiannon, and he had to focus on finding his center before he was able to speak again. "Katie, believe me. If I'd known what had happened and where you were, they couldn't have kept me away. I would have flown home in a heartbeat, and I would have torn that hospital apart brick by brick to get to you."

She chewed on her lower lip. Was any of this getting through?

"I mean it. If I'd known what you had done and that you needed me, I would've been there. I didn't realize how bad . . ." He remembered Rhiannon's hysterical description of how she had found her mother, trying to justify what she had done and not done in keeping it from him.

He reached for Kate's hand again. This time, she didn't pull away.

"Listen to me." He leveled his gaze with hers. "First of all, I never should've left. I was wrong, and for that, I'll never forgive myself. But beyond that, you needed to be in that hospital. I would've been wrong to take you out, no matter how much you hated it. And as much as it would've killed me to see you there, the alternative would have been worse."

He couldn't say the words out loud. He'd barely been able to think them, knowing she had wanted to die.

Her eyes remained locked with his. Then she blinked and looked away. When she looked at him again, she wore the ghost of a smile.

"Good answer."

They finished their tea in silence. He picked up both cups and set them in the sink just as the clock chimed. It was 4:18.

He snorted. "That is definitely your kind of clock."

"'A watch is always too fast or too slow. I cannot be dictated to by a watch.' Jane Austen wrote that in *Mansfield Park*. Suits me, doesn't it?"

"It certainly does."

"There must be something in my genetic makeup that opposes time. I can't seem to function within its boundaries."

She flipped off the light, and they headed toward the bedrooms. Billy stopped at the door to the guest room.

"Well, good night again," he said.

She made no move to continue to her room, and it was all he could do to keep from reaching for her. He buried his hands in his pockets. For a moment, she looked as if she would say or do something, and he waited, hoping she would take the first step.

She just smiled and nodded. "Night."

He leaned against the doorjamb, watching as she continued down the hall. Before she stepped into her room, she glanced over her shoulder.

"Just want to make sure you get home safely."

She laughed, and he relished the sound.

She gave an awkward little wave. "Good night, Billy." She was still smiling when the door closed.

"Good night, Katie."

CHAPTER THIRTY-SEVEN

K ate slapped at the button on her alarm clock. She'd barely had three hours of sleep. The last thing she felt like doing was waking up. She rolled over and closed her eyes until reality poked a finger at her muddied brain via the aroma of freshly brewed coffee wafting through her open bedroom door.

Her head snapped up. Charlie, who always slept at the foot of her bed, was gone.

She flipped onto her back and tried to sort through the past twenty-four hours, but before she could give it much thought, she remembered why she'd set the alarm in the first place.

"Shit." She threw off the covers and groped for her robe.

She was supposed to cover for one of the volunteers who had a wedding upstate. She grabbed her things and ducked into the shower. When she was done, she drew on a quick sweep of eyeliner and a light brush of mascara. She found a pot of lip gloss in one of the drawers in the vanity and dotted some of that on as well, all the while trying to convince herself she wasn't doing it for anyone but herself.

Although she looked somewhat brighter, she frowned at her reflection. "You're not fooling anyone, missy."

She wiped off the lip gloss.

The door to the guest room was open and she was surprised to see that the bed had been made. A half a pot of coffee awaited her in the kitchen. She gave it a sniff. Still fresh. She poured some into a travel mug.

It was going to be another gorgeous day. The tide was coming in, and the sunlight sparkled on the gentle ripples. She grabbed her purse, keys, and coffee and stepped outside.

Charlie lay stretched out in the sun. Not far from him was Billy, wearing nothing but the baggy cargo shorts, his hair pulled into a man bun as he worked through a series of movements using a long orange stick. She squinted. Was that her broom handle? His muscles rippled as he moved, and the pants, at least a size too big, threatened to slip over his hips. She was having a hard time remembering there was someplace she had to be.

When he swung around and saw her, he smiled but continued whatever he was doing through a few more movements. Then he bowed toward the water.

"You look nice," he said, glistening and just a bit out of breath as she approached.

"So do you." She immediately wanted to bite off her tongue. She anchored her eyes on his face, refusing to allow them to drift over his bare chest, which was definitely boasting some new ink.

"Heading out?"

She nodded and took a sip of her coffee, praying for a modicum of composure. "I don't usually work Saturdays, but I agreed to fill in for someone. I should be back by two."

"It's okay. Charlie and I are getting reacquainted." He hooked a thumb at the beast snoring in the sunshine. "Maybe we'll take a walk, go check out that back yard."

When he smiled, her blood grew dangerously warmer.

"I can see if they can find someone else," she offered, immediately wanting to kick herself.

He shook his head. "I'm fine."

"Do you need anything while I'm out?"

"Nah, I'm good. Do you mind if I get on your computer? I'm having trouble connecting to Wi-Fi on my cell."

"Sorry. No computer. No internet. No cable."

"Seriously? It's like living in the Stone Age."

"Kind of. Harold should be home most of the day. He could probably let you use his computer."

"Sounds good." Billy glanced up at the house and then out at the ocean. "So, what exactly do you do?"

"Do?"

The corner of his mouth pulled up, and she felt her knees wobble a little. "Yeah. Do. Whatever it is, it must pay pretty well."

"Oh." She followed his gaze around her yard. "It's kind of a long story. We can talk later."

"Hope it's nothing illegal."

She laughed nervously. "Yeah, I'm hooking on the side."

He didn't seem to find that funny at all.

"I'm kidding. My new best friend is a priest. Think about it."

As she turned to leave, Billy caught her arm. He leaned forward and brushed his lips across her forehead. Her eyes closed and breathed deep, the salty ocean air combining with the scent of sweat and pine from the nearby trees. Her heart galloping, she gave him a dismissive nod.

"I'll see you later," she said, nearly tripping over her own feet. "Make yourself at home."

SNOOPING PROBABLY DIDN'T QUALIFY as making oneself at home, but Billy knew so little about what Kate had been doing since she left, familiarizing himself with her surroundings might give him an idea.

He poured another cup of coffee, then headed downstairs. After poking around in the rooms off the main living area, he decided to check out the rest of the yard. Barefoot, he picked his way down a steep trail that followed the path of a creek that ran into the cove. Rounding the embankment, he came to a small boathouse and beyond that, a dock.

Charlie, who had meandered down alongside him, suddenly shot down the ramp and across the dock and dove into the water like Michael Phelps.

"Charlie! Damn it! Get up here." The dog paddled around the dock, swam past him, then back out again. He whistled. Charlie lifted his head, but he seemed more intent on a quick swim. Billy wasn't about to go in after him, but he was ready to strangle him. He whistled again, but Charlie kept swimming in circles until he caught sight of the neighbor and made a beeline straight for him. He climbed up the bank and then trotted out onto his dock, shaking off the water.

Goddamn it. Billy could see no way to get over there without getting in the water.

While he was still trying to determine how cold the water was and if he could wade over to the next dock, Harold climbed into a motorboat and started it up. Charlie hopped in beside him.

"How about a ride?" Harold called. "I have to take the boat up to the town landing so we can take her out of the water. Give you a little look-see of the cove, if you'd like."

"Sure, why not?"

The old man pulled alongside the dock and took out his cell phone. "I can call Kate, let her know."

"That's okay." Billy stepped down into the boat. "She had to work. She won't be back until this afternoon."

"Pah!" The old man seemed disgusted, but he didn't give Billy a chance to ask why. He opened up the throttle and they picked up speed, causing Billy to lurch backward. He sat quickly before he found himself in the water, and to make sure there weren't any more unscheduled swims, he grabbed hold of Charlie's collar and held on tight.

The ride was short, so he didn't see much, but what he did see was impressive. Grand waterfront homes surrounded with mature trees and evergreens sat poised near the waterfront, so unlike the Jersey shore with its miles of built-up properties and amusement piers.

As they neared a small marina and boat launch, Harold cut the engine. They bobbed gently, the water's lapping against the boat and the occasional cry of a seagull the only sounds.

"What're you doing here?" Harold asked.

"What?"

"Why are you here? Kate's been here for nearly a year. You just decided to show up now?"

Who the fuck did this guy think he was? "I don't think that's any of your business," Billy answered.

Jeff was waving from the shore, but Harold ignored him. A motor roared to life along the shoreline. Harold pulled out a penknife, opened it, and started cleaning his nails.

Oh, for fuck's sake. "Are we seriously going to just sit here?" This crazy old bird might be Kate's friend, but that didn't keep Billy from wanting to pop the motherfucker.

"Dad!" Jeff yelled.

The bastard didn't move. He just glared.

"I don't know what all went on between the two of you, but I know whatever it was, hurt her badly. And maybe you don't think it's any of my business, but I'm making it my business. Kate's become like a daughter to me. So if you're just here to stir up trouble, I suggest you head on home and leave her be."

Despite being at least twenty years older, and at least six inches shorter, the old man looked ready to go a few rounds and then some. Unbelievable!

"Jesus Christ! Katie's my wife, and I love her. I'm not here to hurt her."

Harold folded the knife and slipped it into his pocket. "You better not. I'm warning you."

"Dad!" Jeff cupped his hands and yelled louder. "Bring her in! Now! Whatever you're doing, knock it off!"

Billy eyed the old man. "You can either take this tub in, or I'll swim in."

"No need." Harold reached for the ignition. "Just so's were clear."

"We're clear."

CHAPTER THIRTY-EIGHT

Billy didn't let go of Charlie's collar until they were in the fenced-in area by the pool.

"That's the last time I take you anywhere near that water without a leash!" The dog dropped down in a sunny spot, rested his head on his front paws, and blinked. A canine version of an apology.

"Nice try."

Leaving Charlie by the pool to dry off, Billy went inside to change. Then he pulled out his phone and called the AA hotline. There was a meeting starting in Portland in forty-five minutes.

New meetings could be uncomfortable. He never knew if anyone would recognize him, and it had gotten harder with the recent spate of publicity. He didn't care who knew he went to AA. He wasn't ashamed, but he didn't want word getting out that he was in Maine. A few heads turned to stare and he heard some whispering, but he chalked it up to being the new guy. He introduced himself as Bill and declined to speak. At this point, just going to meetings and remembering why was enough for him.

On the way back, he stopped at a Wal-Mart and picked up a pair of jeans, a couple of T-shirts, some briefs, shampoo, and a razor.

When he passed a Harley dealer, he stopped and bought another helmet on the off chance he could talk Kate into getting on the bike. Helmets weren't required in Maine, but he knew she would never go without one and would freak out if he did. At least he hoped she still cared enough to freak out.

Back at the house, he tossed his bags on the bed in the guest room. Although Kate had said she wouldn't be back until after two, the door to her room was open. Thinking she might be resting, he peeked inside to find Charlie stretched across the bed.

"You're living the life of Reilly, aren't you?" The dog gave him a lazy blink, yawned, then drifted back to sleep. "I hope you're only this mellow because I'm here. Otherwise, you're useless as a watchdog."

It felt strangely odd and uncomfortable to be in Kate's room, but not enough to stop him from taking a look around. The bed was unmade. A patchwork quilt trailed from the end onto the floor, and several pillows were bunched at the top. He raised one of her pillows to his face. Clementines. He closed his eyes and pressed it to his cheek. On her nightstand was a stack of books and next to it, a small ceramic dish held a bar of soap. He held the soap to his nose. Lemongrass. His scent. Kate might not be sure what she wanted, but he'd like to think he was still in the running.

He chased Charlie off the bed and closed the door behind him. There was another door at the end of the hall. A closet, maybe, or another bedroom.

When he pushed the door open, it was like walking into another dimension. Most of the house looked like a Pottery Barn catalog, with comfortable, oversized furniture and neutral backgrounds. There were books everywhere, knickknacks, art pieces, collections of shells, and glass. It looked loved and lived in.

But this room? It could have been plucked right out of a Manhattan high-rise. It was sterile and minimalistic, and other than the photos on the wall, it was devoid of any warmth or personality.

Heavy curtains covered the windows, making it dark, despite the bright, sunny afternoon.

Billy switched on the lamp and took a closer look at an artfully arranged grouping of photographs of the male body. It was an evocative collection that could have come from some Soho gallery. And while he was sure he'd never seen them before, there was something strangely familiar. He scanned the room for clues, but when he came up empty, he stared at the photos again.

"Whose fucking house is this?"

THE LUNCH CROWD WAS LIGHT, so Kate finished earlier than expected. Good thing, because all she could think about was Billy. On her way home, she stopped at the Maine Mall, where she darted into Macy's and picked up some jeans, sweaters, a dress shirt and a pair of slacks for Billy, as well as socks and underwear.

She expected to hear sounds of life as she came in through the garage and was disappointed when she didn't. She was used to the quiet, but with Billy there, she had hoped—

Actually, she had no idea what she was hoping.

The click of Charlie's nails on the wooden floor was the only sound to greet her as she piled the bags on the dining room table.

"Hey, buddy." She scratched behind his ear. "Where's Daddy?"

Charlie yawned and plopped down at her feet.

There was no sign of Billy by the pool, and he wasn't in the family room. The door to the guest room was partway open. Judging by the even hum of his breathing, he was asleep.

She leaned against the doorjamb. His back was to her and he was shirtless, and she assumed, naked beneath the sheet. His hair was loose and spilled over the pillow. She watched his shoulder rise and fall.

You can either stand here like a creeper, get undressed, climb in beside him, and have wild make-up sex, or you can go climb into your own bed alone and figure out what the hell it is you really want and whether you will ever forgive him.

If she had offered the different parts of her body a vote and the majority ruled, she would have been on him in a flash. But she didn't. She climbed into her own bed in her boring bra and panties, wondering why she hadn't invested in something fancier at the mall, just in case. Victoria's Secret was right next to Macy's, after all.

"Knock it off, Kate," she muttered under her breath, her body still at war with her brain.

She set the alarm for five and pulled the covers over her head. When it went off a little while later, she reached over, hit it, and rolled onto her side to find Billy standing in the doorway, watching her.

How come it wasn't creepy when he did it?

"Morning, sunshine." He was wearing jeans and a New England Patriots T-shirt, and judging from the aroma, the mug in his hand held fresh coffee. "You could've napped with me, you know. That is, unless you still snore."

"I don't snore."

"Coffee?"

"Yes, please."

He pushed off the door and headed for the kitchen. She slipped out of bed, grabbed her robe, and followed him into the kitchen.

"You went shopping?" He gestured at the bags on the dining room table.

"I guess you did, too." She took the mug of coffee from him. "And don't let your son see that." She pointed to his T-shirt.

"I'm trying to immerse myself in the culture and act like a native."

"Then you better work on that Midwestern accent."

He grinned. "Okay, Jersey Girl."

"Yeah, right," she said as she dumped the contents of the bags onto the table. "I got you a few things: jeans, socks, sweaters. Just some stuff."

He palmed his forehead. "I forgot socks."

"I see you didn't forget a razor." He still had the goatee, but the rest of the scruff was gone.

"I know you're not a fan."

"You didn't have to do that for me." Color rose in her cheeks as she recalled the feeling of stubble on her face and neck, not to mention other places. Not daring to look at him, she grabbed the last bag. "I also got you a pair of dress slacks and a button-down. I thought we'd go out for dinner. You can wear jeans if you want, but it's a nice place."

"Whatever you suggest."

"Look over this stuff first. Anything you don't want, I can take back."

Billy picked up one of the sweaters. "It's 80 degrees outside."

Why had she bought sweaters? "I, um, didn't know how long you were staying. In case it gets cold. I can take them back. No biggie."

He shook his head. "They're great. Thank you."

He pulled out a pair of jeans and a black button-down shirt and tugged off his T-shirt. She'd seen his new tattoo earlier but hadn't wanted to stare. Now, just a foot away, she could see it was her name embedded in a Celtic symbol, surrounded with words she didn't understand: "Katie. Bidh gaol agam ort fad mo bheatha, thusa's gun duine eile."

"What is that?" She pointed.

His eyes followed her finger, although he had to know what she was asking about. This time, she thought he might be the one to blush.

"It's a Celtic heart knot. And that's Scots Gaelic." His grandparents had been Scottish. His father's side was more of a mix, predominantly Scottish and Norwegian.

"What's it say?"

His eyes met hers. "Katie. I will love you my whole life, you and no other."

She pressed her lips together until she could speak without her voice betraying her. "When did you get it?"

"In the spring after I got out of jail. I haven't changed my mind, you know."

She wanted to ask how someone who felt that way could have found himself with another woman, but she bit her tongue.

Her eyes fell on the words inked along his rib cage proclaiming that he would always want her, always love her. Then there was her name tattooed around the ring finger on his left hand, and their wedding date and part of his vows to her across the thumb and wrist of his right hand.

Had he really needed so many reminders of how he was supposed to feel about the woman he'd married?

"I'm going to iron your shirt. If you want to call and make reservations, the number is on the refrigerator—The Channel Grill."

The ironing board was in the little room at the end of the hall she used as an overflow closet. Not that she had that many clothes, but it was a good place to keep an iron and her sewing machine. She had just finished pressing the shirt when Billy appeared in the doorway.

He was holding up a slip of paper. "Where did you get this?"

She couldn't read it from where she stood, but she didn't need to. She recognized the stained piece of paper that had been hanging on her refrigerator for the past few months.

Oh, shit.

"Where did you get this?" he asked again, his voice sharper.

"You don't have any right to be upset with me over that."

"I'm not upset with you, but I might kill her."

She unplugged the iron, took his hand, and led him into her room. She sat on the edge of the bed and pulled him down beside her.

"Let me explain."

He looked as if he was going to be sick.

"Last year, right after Thanksgiving, I was looking for some Christmas stuff up in the attic, and I found the box of canceled checks that were all made out to Jessie Jones."

Billy didn't look as if he was breathing.

"The way my mind was working back then, I thought the worst. I thought that you had another child somewhere, or a girlfriend you were supporting."

"Jesus, Katie."

She pressed her fingers to his lips while she tried to think how to proceed. She could tell him those checks had been what pushed her over the edge, what made her finally act on her suicidal thoughts, but it would only hurt him. And what good would that do?

The moment she took her fingers away, he spoke. "Why didn't you just ask me?"

She raised her eyebrows. "Why didn't you just tell me?"

His hand curled into a fist and he pressed it hard against his thigh.

"I couldn't stop thinking about it, so not long after I got here, I asked Tom to find out who Jessie Jones was. He hired a private investigator who discovered she was your mother. I didn't even know she was still alive, let alone had a stage name."

"Yeah, her 'stage name,'" he said with a guffaw. "What a load of crap."

"Perhaps. It didn't take very long for the detective to find out that she was . . . that she had threatened—"

"She was blackmailing me. I was paying her to stay away from our family and, more importantly, not to ever let my father know where we were."

She nodded. "I know. Tom gave me the name and address, and I tried several times to write to her, to tell her I knew and to ask her to leave you alone."

"Ha! Like she would've listened to you."

"Maybe, maybe not. But I just couldn't say what I had to in a letter. I couldn't express my anger the way I needed to and make her listen."

He rubbed his hand hard across his face.

"So, anyway—"

"There's more?"

"Like I said, I was too upset to express that in a letter. So I went to see her."

"Jesus, Katie." His fingers tightened around hers. "When?"

"In June. It was crazy and impulsive, and I probably shouldn't have gone, but on the other hand, it felt so good to be able to grab something by the short hairs and deal with it. I wanted her to stop hurting you."

He pressed her hand to his lips, then folded it in his much larger one. "How did you know she'd follow through?"

"Because I made her call you while I was there." She paused for a moment. "I don't really even want to tell you this part, but if we're going to be honest with each other, I kind of bribed her."

A pained expression crossed his face. "At least you were speaking her language."

"I guess. I gave her two options. I told her she could call and tell you to stop sending her money, or I would tell you I knew. Either way, it was over. But if she called, she had to apologize, and for that, I would give her money."

"And she wanted the money?"

She nodded.

"How much?"

She felt uncomfortable. "Too much. But I did it for you. It was important to me that she apologize. Everything else she said of her own volition."

"Do you think I believed her?"

"Probably not."

"Not for one second. I've been waiting for the other shoe to drop, although for the life of me, I couldn't figure out what it could be."

"Well, it's over. She won't bother you anymore." She traced a finger over the tattoo on his wrist. "There's something else she told me."

"I can only imagine."

"She said your father died about twelve years ago. I'm sorry."

He laughed. It was a hard, angry sound. "I'm not sure if I should believe that either. How?"

"All she said was that it happened in prison. I got the impression it may have been from a fight."

"Live by the sword, die by the sword," he mumbled, following up with a weak smile. "So are you going to tell me how much you gave her?"

"It was worth every penny," she said defensively.

"That much?"

She winced.

"Maybe I don't want to know," he said.

"That's probably for the best."

He kissed her on the forehead. "Thank you."

"For what?"

"For dealing with my mother. I'm sorry you had to do it, and I'm sorry I didn't tell you."

She nodded. "Me too."

CHAPTER THIRTY-NINE

Billy scanned the menu, and since Kate already knew what she would order, it gave her a better chance to get a good look at him. His hair was a little shorter than the last time she'd seen him, but still long, thick and blond. His goatee was a little grayer. And his body, a little bigger, beefier. Whatever weight he'd gained must have been all muscle.

"So what's good here?" Billy asked, flipping his menu over to read the other side.

"If you want seafood, Tom says the mussels are good, and the lobster bisque. Although according to Harold, I make a damn good lobster bisque."

"I'm not surprised. You're a great cook, although you never made fish or seafood."

She shrugged. "He kept bringing me lobsters. Then he started bringing recipes to go with them. I made soup, and I'd freeze some and give him the rest—that is, until I went over there one day and found him having an apparent heart attack."

Billy lowered his menu. "Seriously?"

"Turns out he has pancreatitis and isn't supposed to be eating all that rich food. Scared the daylights out of me. But on the plus side, it got me to step out of my comfort zone, which had shrunk to about a two-foot perimeter around me."

She was about to tell him about going to Portland and finding the resource center when a young woman approached.

"Excuse me, I'm sorry to bother you, but would you mind terribly?" she said nervously to Billy. "My boyfriend's a huge fan, and he'll just die when he finds out you were here." She glanced at Kate, then swiveled back to Billy. "We just love the new CD."

She pushed a cocktail napkin toward him.

"I'm sorry," he said. "I don't have a pen."

"I do." Kate pulled a pen from her purse.

"Are you Katie?" the woman asked, but before Kate could answer, she continued. "You must be thrilled."

After the woman returned to her seat, Billy encouraged Kate to continue, but before she had the chance, the waiter appeared. He read through the list of specials and took their drink orders. Billy ordered a club soda. Kate hesitated and then ordered the same.

"You didn't have to do that," he said after the waiter walked away.

"I don't mind. It's not like I need it." She grimaced. "Sorry. That didn't come out right."

"It's fine. I know what you meant."

"I'm sorry to bother you." Another woman was standing next to their table. Kate guessed this one was in her mid- to late thirties. "Are you Billy McDonald?"

He shot Kate an apologetic look, then nodded.

The woman twisted back to her companions at a nearby table and squealed "I told you!" She was practically purring as she handed Billy a pen and a piece of paper. "Would you mind?"

After he signed his name, she pulled out her cell phone and asked if she could take a selfie with him. By the time she returned to her table, the hum of conversation in the restaurant had become more of a loud buzz.

"I'm sorry," he said. "Do you want to go somewhere else?"

Kate shook her head. "It's a little annoying, but you deserve it. I am a little worried, though. I don't want Rhiannon finding out where I am by reading it on Just Jared or TMZ."

Billy tossed his napkin on the table. "Just a sec."

He approached the woman who'd asked for the selfie, spoke to her for a few moments, then pulled out his iPhone and keyed in something she was telling him.

"What was that about?" Kate asked when he'd returned to their table.

"I asked her not to share that photo on social media for the next few weeks, and if she agrees, I'll have concert tickets waiting for her and her friends at will call."

Kate sighed with relief. "Thank you."

When the waiter returned with their drinks, Billy ordered a charcuterie board as an appetizer, since he still hadn't had a chance to study the menu.

"Congratulations on the new album," Kate said when they were alone again. "It's been a long time coming, and you deserve this. You've worked really hard."

"I've played pretty hard too. And there were other things working against me." His jaw tightened, but when he looked up, he smiled. "Maybe I needed to do a bit of growing up as well."

"I'm proud of you. I don't know if I still have the right to say that, but it's how I feel."

He reached across the table and squeezed her hand. "Thank you. That means a lot to me."

"Excuse me, Mr. McDonald?" A polished young man stood beside their table. He had a hint of a French-Canadian accent. "My name is André Cloutier. I'm the manager here at The Channel Grill. I wish to apologize for all of the interruptions. If you would like, we can move you to another table where you might not be so visible."

Billy deferred to Kate.

"I think at this point, it wouldn't really make a difference," she said.

"If you're sure," he said. "I'm okay with just getting dinner to go."

"Please, Mr. McDonald, we would love for you to stay. We will do our best to see that you enjoy your dinner without any further distractions."

"That would be nice," Billy said. "Thank you."

"Thank you, sir. Again, my name is André, and if there is anything I can do to enhance your dining experience, please let me know."

"Wow." Kate stifled a laugh after André backed away from their table. "I thought he was going to bow."

Billy dipped his head. "Now that would've been embarrassing."

"I guess you better get used to all this attention."

"I'm not going to let it go to my head yet."

"Yet? So you will eventually?"

He grinned, and her spine tingled. "Maybe."

The waiter brought the charcuterie board and took their order. Next they were interrupted by the sommelier with a bottle of white wine, compliments of Mr. Cloutier. Kate was going to refuse it, but Billy insisted.

"None for me," he instructed the waiter who followed close behind with two wine glasses. "But the lady will have some."

He was being too considerate at his own cost. When they were alone again, Kate insisted she didn't want to drink in front of him.

"Katie, please. I can handle it. I've been sober for ten months. It's not easy, but I'm okay. And sitting across from you makes it all worthwhile."

There was a sad sort of desperation in his eyes that somehow made it easier to reach for the wine. She was no clearer on what she wanted for their marriage than she had been a day, a week, or even a year ago.

The Sancerre was crisp and delicious, and in a very short time, or maybe because she was drinking too fast, she felt less jittery. By the time they left the restaurant, her nervousness had disappeared along with most of the bottle.

When the valet brought the car around, Billy took the keys and held the passenger side door open for her. "I'll drive."

"You don't know where we're going."

"I found you, didn't I?"

BILLY GOT Kate settled into the passenger seat, then climbed in behind the wheel and slipped the key into the ignition. She gave him a loopy smile that he felt down to his toes.

"It's beautiful tonight. Put the top down."

When he pointed out it might be a little too chilly, she told him to "blast the heat."

He recognized his way back to the house, but as they neared the turn toward Cousins Island, Kate directed him to take it.

"You sure?"

"This is the scenic route," she insisted.

They drove for a while before they came to the end of the road, looking out toward the ocean. Billy parked and cut the engine. The night smelled of wood smoke, ocean air, and the sweetness of oranges. Lights glowed on the distant horizon, and the stars overhead twinkled like diamonds on a field of black velvet.

Kate's sigh wrapped around him like a warm honey. She tilted her face up at the sky. "Isn't it beaut—"

He leaned across the console and kissed her. He'd taken her by surprise, but she didn't stop him. Her lips were warm and tasted of wine. When she didn't push him away, he kissed her again. His hand snaked up her arm and along her neck. Cradling her head, he pulled her closer, careful of the gearshift between them.

When she ran her fingers along the side of his face, he thought he might cry. Her hand dropped to his chest and gripped his shirt. Then gently, she pushed him away. He tried to see her eyes, but it was too dark. All he could hear was the gentle lapping of water against the shore and the sound of Kate's breathing.

"Take me home." Her voice was low and thick. "Please."

His heart sank. His fingers thrummed nervously on the steering wheel as he navigated back to the highway. Less than ten minutes later, he was nosing her Saab into the garage.

They sat in the car as the garage door closed behind them.

"I'm sorry," he said, wanting to remind her that she'd kissed him back. But he didn't, he just savored the taste of wine on his tongue, not because it was wine but because it was Kate. Just as the tang of salty air was now Kate, along with the familiar scent of oranges.

He got out of the car, opened her door, and helped her to her feet. Her eyes were pink and glassy.

Charlie was waiting in the laundry room. Kate gave him a quick scratch, then staggered slightly and braced herself against the wall before heading for her room.

Jesus, all he'd done was kiss her, and he needed more. Just seeing her was enough to send him over the edge. He knew he shouldn't overwhelm her, but that was exactly what he'd done. He needed to rein himself in. If he pushed her too hard, it could all blow up in his face, and then what?

He led the dog through the garage, warned him not to run off again, and opened the door to let him out. Charlie nosed around the pines, then trotted over to the tall maple near the edge of the yard. He barked at something in the hedges, then moved on to mark several trees and nearby shrubs. When Billy felt he had pulled himself together enough to go back inside, he gave a sharp whistle. Charlie came charging back.

"Good boy," he said, hoping there were treats somewhere to reward Charlie for listening. There was nothing in the kitchen, so he searched the pantry, where he found not only a large glass canister with dog treats but Kate's stash of alcohol.

"Fuck." He said it so softly he wasn't certain if he'd actually spoken it aloud. In addition to a variety of liqueurs, there were bottles of Tanqueray, Ketel One, and a very pricey, unopened bourbon. Kate didn't drink gin or bourbon. Was this stuff that had been left in the house before she moved in, or had she been entertaining someone else?

The last thought made him want to grab one of the bottles—it didn't matter which. Instead, he reached for the canister of dog treats and gave Charlie two, then set the jar on the kitchen counter so he wouldn't have to go back in the pantry. He refilled the dog's water dish, then took a peek down the hall.

Kate's door was closed.

"Damn it," he said aloud, his fist curling, wanting to hit something. He tried to focus on a calming image. The technique, learned while in rehab, had been a godsend in helping him manage his triggers.

Although the night was dark, he stepped out onto the deck and tried to envision the water in the cove. It was a new image, but it worked as well as the others he had at his disposal.

All was not lost. It couldn't be.

But just to be safe, he took out his cell phone and dialed his sponsor.

FIFTEEN MINUTES of talking with Reese saw him through his temptation, and the urge had passed. His fear of blowing it with Kate, however, had not. Guessing that sleep would evade him again, especially after the afternoon nap, he put the kettle on and took down two cups. He'd make one for Kate. He would knock on her door, and if she didn't want it, she didn't have to drink it.

He was so lost in thought he didn't realize she had come into the kitchen until he felt her standing behind him. She had changed into a simple cotton nightgown. Her eye makeup was smudged, and she was clearly more than a little drunk.

"Do you want some tea?"

She stared at the cups on the counter. Then she lifted her hands to his neck. She pressed her body against his and pulled his lips toward hers. He obeyed, stunned when her small tongue darted inside his mouth. He pulled her closer and wrapped her in his arms, ignoring the angry whistle of the kettle behind him.

He was nearly out of breath when he finally forced himself to pull away. Her fingers curled around his belt and tugged clumsily at the buckle.

"Katie." Soon there would be no turning back. "Stop. Stop." He reached for her hand. "Listen to me."

Her eyes were narrow with the effects of too much alcohol and too little self-control.

"Babe, you've had a lot to drink. I don't want you to do something you're not sure you want." Certain parts of him screamed silent obscenities. "I don't want you to be sorry later."

Her nerves must have been on overdrive as well. She pulled her hands away and slid them under his shirt against his skin.

He grabbed her wrists.

"Katie, stop. I love you more than anything in this world, and I'd give anything to have you right now, but I can't do this unless I know it's for real. That it's forever." He pulled back. "If you can look at me right now and tell me for certain that you still want to be my wife and that you forgive me and will come home, then I'll carry you into that bedroom right now and no one will see us for weeks. But if you can't, if you still don't know what you want and you're not ready to commit to me—to us—one hundred percent, then I can't do this. I won't."

She gaped as if he had lost his mind. "Are you really turning me down?"

"I don't know." He exhaled slowly. "Do you love me?"

"Of course I love you, you jackass," she spat. "It's never been about whether or not I love you."

"Do you still want to be my wife?"

She blinked up at him, her eyes going from hard and angry to wet. Her shoulders drooped.

"I don't know," she said, her voice rising. "God, Billy! I'm still so hurt over some of the things you've done. All I know is that right now, I want you. Doesn't that mean something?"

"It means a lot." He brushed the hair out of her eyes and ran his thumb along her cheek. "It's more than I deserve, but it's not enough. I know I've hurt you. I live with that every single day. But I've been hurt too. Losing you was the worst thing I've ever been through. I can't have you back just to lose you again. I won't survive it a second time, Katie. I'm not that strong."

She put her hands on either side of his face. "Kiss me good night."

He leaned down, slipped his arms around her waist, and touched his lips to hers. As he did, she slipped her hand between his legs and cupped him gently. He should've stopped her, but he didn't. He moaned against her mouth, ready to deepen the kiss, when she stepped back. Wearing a smug look, she pulled the nightgown over her head and dropped it on the kitchen floor.

"There. That's what you're missing." Then she half flounced, half listed out of the room.

"I know what I'm missing," he called after her, his jeans uncomfortably tight. "Trust me."

"Ha!" she called from somewhere down the hall.

Her bedroom door slammed with a bang loud enough to shake the pictures on the walls.

The kettle was still screaming, and the tea bags mocked him from the bottom of the empty cups. If he had any hope of getting to sleep, he needed more than a hot cup of tea. What he needed was a very cold shower.

CHAPTER FORTY

K ate pried one eye open and immediately shut it, trying to will
away the sharp, stabbing pain in her temples. She grabbed the
extra pillow beside her and sandwiched her aching head between the
two, as if cushioning it would provide a shred of relief. She wanted—
no, she needed—to go back to sleep. Unfortunately, a little pea-sized
nugget of regret had woken as well.

What the hell had come over her last night? Bad enough she'd
practically thrown herself at Billy, but then the bastard had turned
her away. Not once throughout their entire marriage had he ever
rejected her.

She slipped further under the covers, determined to stay there
forever. Her bladder had something else in mind. She eased herself
up and shimmied to the edge of the bed. When the room stopped
spinning, she staggered to the bathroom.

"What the hell?" she muttered, catching a glimpse of herself in
the mirror. Mascara trailed beneath her bloodshot eyes, and her hair
practically stood straight up in the back. She scrubbed her face,
mumbling and grousing under her breath. "Jesus, Billy. You're here
two days and I'm already talking to myself and getting drunk."

You're going to blame him for this? How is your drinking too much his fault? How is his rejecting you, when you won't let him know how you feel, his fault?

She glared at her reflection. "Oh, shut up."

She squirted some drops into her red, swollen eyes and, after another mini-war with herself, swiped on a little mascara and eyeliner.

Old habits died hard.

She frowned at her reflection. She might not look like herself, but she looked better than she had a few minutes ago.

She pulled on a pair of jeans and a sweatshirt and headed for the kitchen in search of aspirin and caffeine. The door to the guest room was open and again, the bed was made. She could count on one hand the number of times Billy had made the bed in the past, and both times had entailed her giving birth.

The kitchen was empty, but a note taped to the coffeemaker instructed her to "press the button." Her largest mug sat nearby along with a spoon, a glass of orange juice, and, thankfully, a bottle of aspirin. As the rich, dark liquid filled the carafe, she inhaled deeply, trying to jump-start her caffeine fix. She tapped out three aspirin, tossed them back, and drained the glass of orange juice.

From where she stood, she could see Billy outside moving through a series of martial arts forms again with her broom handle. Charlie, who had mellowed considerably since Billy's arrival, napped under a maple in the corner of the yard.

Kate filled her mug to the brim, slipped on a pair of her darkest sunglasses, and stepped outside. She wasn't any closer to knowing what to do about Billy than she'd been the day before. And watching him shirtless, with his muscles rippling and glistening, wasn't help-ing. The only thing she knew for sure was that spending the day alone in the house with him was likely to result in a repeat of last night's behavior. She should've just stayed in bed.

Yeah, right.

For months, she'd pushed almost all thoughts of sex from her mind, and other than her dreams, she'd been successful. Now with Billy here, looking and smelling so good, she couldn't stop thinking about it. She was forty-three! It shouldn't even be about the sex anymore. Right?

Ha!

What she needed was an appointment with Liz. She'd left her a message on her way to Portland Saturday, but hadn't heard back. Kate knew she needed to talk to Billy, but was she ready? She wanted to know about Christa, yet she didn't. Having Liz as a buffer or a mediator, or whatever, might make it easier, if that were even possible.

All this thinking was making her head hurt.

She called softly for Charlie. He lifted his head, but other than wagging his tail once or twice, he remained where he was, close to his master. Traitor.

Billy continued his workout, moving fluidly through pose after pose. He had always been long and lean, and until the last year they'd been together, he had been in great shape. But in that final year, much of it spent on the road, he'd grown thin. Through the benefit of time and distance she accepted that he was an alcoholic and if not a full-blown drug addict, he'd been dangerously close. But the man she watched barefoot in the damp grass moved like a trained athlete. This was not the man she'd left ten months ago, not physically, at least. This Billy was strong and healthy. He said he had been trying, and on the outside, he looked to be succeeding.

When he finished the last series of movements, he bowed deeply, then picked up a towel he'd left lying in the grass. He mopped his face and chest, picked up her broom handle, and whistled for Charlie, who came bounding after him.

"Morning," he said, a sly smile on his face. "How are we feeling?"

The sun had moved toward the center of the sky. Kate shielded her eyes. The glare was painful despite the dark glasses.

"I don't know how *we're* feeling, but *I* feel like shit."

"Did you take some aspirin?" He gripped the towel draped

around his neck, causing the veins to stand out along his forearms. Between that and his muscled chest and abdomen, she was almost a goner. Good thing she was nearly incapacitated. "I did. It didn't help."

"How about some breakfast?"

She stood and brushed off the back of her jeans. "Sure. What would you like?"

He dipped his head and laughed. "I meant, what would you like me to make you?"

"Seriously?"

"Yeah. What do you want? Eggs, pancakes, French toast, oatmeal?"

"Oatmeal?" He had to be kidding.

"It's good for you, you know."

"I do know. I always told you that, but you hate it."

"So do you."

"True." If he was offering to cook, she was taking him up on it. "Out of respect for my hangover, how about some scrambled eggs? The protein might help."

He took her empty mug.

"Scrambled eggs it is. Let me grab a quick shower, and then I'll make us some breakfast. I'll be right back."

He returned a minute later with a large glass of ice water. "Drink this. It'll help your hangover."

She squinted up at him. Even with the dark glasses, it still felt as if the sun might cause her head to explode. "Coffee."

"You're dehydrated. Drink a few glasses of water. It'll help, trust me."

Too queasy to argue, she took a sip of the water. By the time she finished, Billy was done with his shower.

"Feeling any better?" He had changed into a pair of jeans and a black T-shirt. His hair was wet, and he smelled of lemongrass. He must have taken one of the bars from the dish in the hall bath.

She held her thumb and forefinger about an inch apart.

"Good. Go sit, and I'll make you some eggs and toast."

He took the glass, filled it again, and handed it to her.

"Coffee."

"Water. If you can get another one in after this, you'll feel much better. I promise."

What did he think she was, a camel? She sat at the dining room table, grumbling and sipping her water. She was still wearing her sunglasses—not that she needed them in the house, but it kept her from having to make eye contact—and watched as he busied himself in the kitchen. When the toast popped, he spread it with a little honey, plated it with her eggs, and set it in front of her. Then he poured her more coffee. He returned a second later with a bowl of oatmeal with a dollop of honey in the center.

"Who are you?" she asked as he took a big gulp of orange juice.

"I'm still me." The grin made her insides turn to goo. "Only new and improved."

She almost had to sit on her hands to keep from reaching out to touch the dimple on his cheek.

"Up before noon, making breakfast, eating healthy, exercising. Not to mention, turning down a sure thing." She tried to keep the edge from her voice but failed.

"I told you, I've changed. I don't ever want to look at you again as a sure thing. When you come to me—" He dropped his gaze. "*If you come to me, it has to be for the right reasons.*"

He touched a finger to her wrist and drew it back and forth. "We need to talk, Katie, and try to figure out where we are and where we're going. I know what I want. I need to know what you want."

It would be so easy to give in right then, but what if she could never truly forgive him? What kind of marriage was that? But at that moment, if her head hadn't been threatening to roll off onto the floor and her stomach hadn't been lurching as if she were out on a storm-tossed sea, she'd still have tried to drag him off to bed. Hell, she'd do it right on the dining room table.

His thumb massaged a small circle on her forearm. "What are you thinking?"

A slow burn crept up her neck. "Umm . . ." She pushed her eggs around her plate, then scooped some onto her fork and shoveled them into her mouth.

"These are good," she mumbled, her mouth full. "Thank you."

Clearly disappointed with her response, he went back to his oatmeal.

Not knowing what to say, she suggested an outing. What she really wanted, other than throw-me-down-tear-off-my-clothes-and-ravage-me sex, was to go back to bed and bury her head under her pillow for a multitude of reasons, not the least of which was getting her hormones under control.

"How about we play tourist this afternoon?" She wasn't good at hiding her emotions, and Billy knew that.

He gave her a tight smile. "You up for that?"

Definitely not. "Sure."

He lifted a spoonful of oatmeal to his mouth. "Sounds great."

CHAPTER FORTY-ONE

Kate was feeling much better after breakfast and four glasses of water, and she was eager to push aside anything of consequence in order to show Billy some of the places she loved. And her adopted state was in full cooperation, serving up warm sunshine, azure skies, and ocean views that went on for miles. The two picturesque lighthouses made their last stop just perfect. Or as perfect as it could be for someone trying to avoid a difficult conversation.

"Wow," Billy said as they stepped onto the small, crescent-shaped beach near Two Lights.

"Just wait. C'mon."

He reached out to hand her the keys, but she shook her head.

"Keep them," she said. "If you don't mind, you can drive."

He had tried to convince her to ride the Harley—he'd even bought an extra helmet for her—but she'd refused. Instead, she had handed him the keys to the Saab and asked him to drive.

Her reflection looked back at her from his mirrored aviator sunglasses. What did he see when he looked at her? She was used to the shorter hair; he'd barely had a day, yet he seemed to have taken it in stride. Rhiannon must have told him how she'd looked when she'd found her. He was probably glad she wasn't still practically bald.

She crammed her hands into the pockets of her jacket, and Billy did the same as they walked side by side up the short ridge. They continued past The Lobster Shack and out onto the rocky coastline. The open ocean stretched out before them.

"Let's walk out on the ledge." She pointed to a narrow finger of metamorphic rock.

Billy followed as she navigated along a path lined with stunted clusters of beach roses groaning under the weight of fat, red rosehips. Random deep-pink blossoms greeted them, vestiges of the unusually mild autumn. At the end of the path, she waited as Billy picked his way among the jagged rocks. The sun glinted off the strands of hair that had blown loose from his ponytail.

"So now you're a mountain goat?" he asked when he caught up with her.

"Joey and I used to climb up here and out to the edge of the point." She touched his arm and pointed to the small expanse of sand and rock below them. "The beach down there, that's where we would search for sea glass. It's best when the tide's out. We found tons of stuff—shells, driftwood, I even started hauling broken lobster buoys off the beach, but they never made it home with us. My mother would toss them before we left, and we wouldn't find out until we were back in Belleville. That's why I started stashing my sea glass in my suitcase. I amassed quite a collection over the years."

She swallowed the twinge of sadness that settled over her whenever she thought of Joey and focused on a sailboat cutting around the point and heading for Casco Bay. Billy didn't speak. He just stood beside her, staring out to sea.

"You hungry? Thirsty?" he asked after several minutes. "You should probably drink more water."

"Maybe thirsty. If you get something, I'll just share. If that's okay."

He purchased a bottle of water and followed her out to the carved ledge.

She wandered to a large, flat rock and sat. "Isn't it beautiful?"

The sky was a deep, clear blue, unmarred save for a few wispy mares' tails.

Billy stretched out on a rock beside her and leaned back. Neither of them spoke. She couldn't help stealing furtive glances at him. She wanted to touch him, to trace the black swirl of the tribal tattoo on his forearm, to feel the silky softness of his hair on her fingers, but she didn't dare.

"I still can't believe you're here," she said when she could trust herself to speak.

It was impossible to see past his sunglasses to tell what was in his eyes. He lifted her hand and folded it in his. Seconds earlier, she'd ached to touch him, but her heart and brain were still at odds, and until she came to terms with one or the other, holding hands was off limits. She wriggled free and began chattering about the geologic history of the rocks they were sitting on. Then she told him that Joan Crawford or Bette Davis, she couldn't remember which, had once lived in the house where the second of two lighthouses had been, and did he know one of their husbands, Joan or Bette, she still couldn't remember which, had sat on the board of Pepsi? Or maybe it was Coca-Cola.

Her heart thumped wildly with the nearness of him. It was as if she were eighteen again, only this time, she had seen the future. If she'd known then what she knew now, would she have walked back to her dorm through the snowstorm the morning after they'd met, or would she have fallen just as deeply in love?

The answer was immediate. She would have chosen love. It was a no-brainer. Too bad knowing that still didn't help her figure out what she was doing now.

A light breeze blew off the water, but the air was warm. Billy took off his jacket, balled it up, and lay back, using it as a pillow. He pushed his glasses up over his head and closed his eyes. Despite years of drug and alcohol abuse, he was still incredibly handsome: strong, chiseled jaw, straight nose, full lips. To this day, she couldn't think of anyone who came close to Billy in looks, other than Devin, of course. Although Devin had her dark hair, he was as heartbreakingly hand-some as his father. And while Billy had certainly broken her heart and most certainly scores of others, her son would never knowingly hurt anyone.

She missed her children and grandchildren. Their absence had begun to weigh heavily now that Billy's arrival had stripped away her ability to ignore her past life.

She exhaled loudly, trying to lift some of the weight centered on her chest.

Billy squinted up at her. "You okay?"

"Yeah. I was just thinking."

"Here." He stretched his arm out, offering it up as a cushion for her head. "Lie back. The sun feels good."

"Um, I like watching the waves." It was tempting to lie beside him, to tuck her body against his. This was proving far too difficult.

He folded his hands across his stomach and closed his eyes.

She continued to study his face. "Billy?"

"Hmmm?" He didn't open his eyes this time.

"Was it bad? Jail, I mean. Was it hard?"

He let go a low chuckle. "You mean like hard time? Chain gang stuff?"

She poked him in the ribs. "No. Was it hard going to jail? You've been arrested before, but you never had to stay more than a few hours."

Squinting against the bright sunshine, he lifted up to his elbows. "Was it hard? Yeah. It was also humiliating, but it was a lot easier than being home without you."

He sat up, gently lifted her glasses from her face, and cupped his hand to her cheek so she couldn't turn away.

"It was easier to be locked up, knowing I wouldn't be able to see you anyway, than it was to be home every day in a house that echoed so loudly with your absence it was almost unbearable. I flew home as soon as Rhiannon called and told me you were gone. After I'd gone to see Tom and he wouldn't tell me where you were, I had Doug find me a rehab facility. They couldn't take me for a few days. If C.J., hadn't been so cool about it—if my own damn manager hadn't come to stay with me until then—who knows what I might've done? I thought I was going to lose my mind."

She chewed hard on the pad of her thumb, uncomfortable with the guilt of causing him so much pain. "I should've been there for you."

He smiled, but it was a sad smile. He tucked a strand of hair behind her ear. "Why? Would you have baked me a cake with a file in it?"

A fat tear slipped down her cheek. He caught it on the edge of his thumb and brushed it away. "No, babe. I was in desperate need of a wake-up call, and I finally got one. I needed to go to jail and to rehab. I needed to fix myself so that I could finally be worthy of you."

He gently guided her so that she faced him straight on and took both of her hands in his. "When I look into your eyes and see myself reflected there, I want to be the man you fell in love with. The man you need me to be. The man you deserve."

Every word pierced her heart like arrows, as if he were trying to reinsert himself there. What he didn't understand was that he already lived there. He would always live there, whether she wanted him there or not.

"The past year and a half has been the worst time of my life," she said. "But I've dealt with almost all of it: Joey's death, Eileen's death, the shooting, this fucked-up world we live in. I've even come to grips with my shitty childhood. I've processed it all—except you." A painful little cry slipped past her lips. "I don't know how to process you or what you've done. I don't know if I can."

"I don't want to be dealt with or processed, Katie." Agitation fueled his voice. "I want to be forgiven, and I want you to love me again."

She shook her head. "It's never been about love, Billy, I told you that. In spite of everything, I've never stopped loving you. I just don't know if I can forgive you. Or trust you."

"If you love me, don't you owe me a chance?"

"Owe you? Didn't you owe me something? Didn't you owe me your honesty and fidelity?"

"I did. I still do. I can't change what happened. It was one time, and in the scheme of things, it was almost insignificant, but—"

"No, Billy. It was never insignificant."

"You know what I mean. No one died."

"Maybe something died."

He touched his forehead to hers. "Can we try to fix this, Katie? Please?"

Her heart hurt. She wanted to fix what they'd had. She just wasn't sure it was possible. "I don't know."

When she tried to pull away, he let her. She drew her knees up and clasped her arms around them, curling in on herself. The waves crashed against the rocks below, and for a while, that and the cry of sea gulls hovering nearby were all she heard.

"I hope this doesn't come out wrong, but please just listen," Billy said. He straightened his legs out before him. "Over the past year, I've learned a lot about myself. I overdosed on heroin. I went to jail. And I hurt and lost the person I love most in the world. I've come face to face with my demons, but I confronted them and I won. I am a better person. I've been to rehab, and I go to AA. I've been sober for ten months. I'm working on being a real father. I've made my peace with everyone, Katie, everyone except you. Not a night goes by that I don't look out at the sky, knowing the same stars are shining down on you wherever you are, and ask your forgiveness."

The needy part of her wanted nothing more than to tell him all was forgiven. The other part, the newer, stronger part, wouldn't let her.

"The thing is," he continued, "after going through all of that, the therapy and learning to control my temper and my weaknesses, I've forgiven myself. Holding on to all that guilt did nothing but destroy me, and in turn, I destroyed everyone around me—especially you. Guilt serves no purpose. I'm still sorry for what I did, and I'll always be sorry for hurting you, but I had to forgive myself or I could never move forward. This past year has shown me that I'm not the horrible sonofabitch I thought I was. I also learned . . ." He swallowed and stared into her eyes. "I learned I can live without you. I'll survive, and obviously you will too. And that's a good thing. I don't want to live the rest of my life without you, but if that's what you want, I'll respect that. If you want a divorce, Katie, I won't fight you."

His words stung as if he'd slapped her. She'd told Jeff just the other day she was considering a divorce, but to hear Billy say it shook her to her very core.

A seagull swooped down and landed in front of her, looking as if it too was waiting for an answer. She shouldn't be shocked; she'd even believed when she'd left in December that he had wanted out of their marriage. But that's not what he was saying. The opposite was true. He just said he didn't want to live without her, only that he could if he had to. Which left her in almost exactly the same place she'd been for months. What did she want?

She brushed a finger over a patch of yellow lichen clinging to the rock on which they sat. Lichens, she'd read, were one of the toughest organisms on Earth. That's what she needed, to toughen up. Her heart was leaning toward reconciliation, maybe even more than she was willing to admit, but what if she were wrong? How could she be sure she could trust him again? She didn't even trust herself to make a decision.

"Would you do something for me?" she asked, her throat dry and her voice raspy.

"If I can."

"Will you go to the psychiatrist with me?"

He lowered his head until his eyes were level with hers. "Yes. Absolutely."

CHAPTER FORTY-TWO

Other than a brief rain shower the night he'd arrived, the weather had been postcard-perfect. But this morning, the sky was dark and leaden. The wind whipped leaves from the trees and angry whitecaps turned the placid cove outside the window into a boiling cauldron.

A sign of things to come? God, he hoped not.

Billy sat across from Kate in the doctor's office and pressed his elbows into the tops of his thighs. This had been Katie's idea, but picking at scabs, even with the help of a professional, was going to be difficult for both of them.

"Are you willing to answer any questions Kate may have, Billy?" the doctor asked. "No matter how painful it is for you or how painful you think it might be for her?"

He tried to gauge what Kate might be thinking, but she was no longer an open book—not to him, anyway. The last thing he wanted was to hurt her any more than she'd already been hurt. But if this was a way for them to heal, he'd do whatever he could.

The only thing he had refused to do was make love to her. Jesus, that had been hard. He burned at the sight of her. To be so close, to graze her arm, to catch a whiff of her hair had been torture. But to give in now would put them both on dangerous ground, maybe even set them up for failure. They could fall back into old, unhealthy habits. They couldn't go backward if they were to survive. It wasn't possible.

"Yeah." He nodded, looking at Kate. "If it'll help. I just don't want to make it worse."

Kate winced.

"That's a possibility," the doctor explained. "However, there's also a good chance that what Kate's imagined is worse than the reality."

He hadn't thought of that. What had happened with Christa was wrong, definitely, and no excuse from him could change what he'd done. But it had meant nothing to him. It had been a stupid, drunken mistake, and he'd never even come close to repeating it, with Christa or anyone else. Since Kate had never permitted him to explain, maybe she really thought there had been some ongoing relationship. He was both nauseated and hopeful.

He brushed a hand across his face, the smooth skin beneath his palm still unexpected. He'd shaved that morning, even his goatee was gone. Kate had always preferred him clean shaven. The act was small, desperate. *Look at me, babe. I shaved. Just for you. Will you forgive me now?*

Yeah. He was that pathetic.

Dr. Crane—Liz, she had said to call her—settled into a comfortable-looking wing chair. Kate sat on the far end of a leather sofa close to a window that offered a view of the sheltered cove. Billy faced the both of them, forming a lopsided triangle.

"Go ahead," Liz urged Kate. "You can handle this."

Kate's eyes darted between him and Liz. She gnawed on her lower lip and picked at an invisible spot on her jeans.

"How many?" she asked, her voice so low he wasn't sure he heard, let alone understood.

"I'm sorry, babe. What?"

His easy use of a pet name seemed to cause her some distress. She stared up at the ceiling and repeated her question, louder this time. "How. Many?"

Two seconds into this, and he was already at a loss. He looked to the doctor for guidance. "I don't understand."

Then it hit him. Was she fucking kidding?

"Wait? How many women? Is that it? How many women have I been with since we met?"

The idea that not only was this a question she needed to ask but the most important one of all proved that she expected the worst.

"One. And before you ask, once."

The eyes that pinned him to his chair were cold, hard emeralds.

"I mean it!" His voice was loud and shaky. "Once. It was just Chr —" He didn't want to say her name. He didn't want to breathe life into her or bring her anywhere near either of them. "You know who. And it was the one time."

"Let's not assume Kate does or doesn't know something," Liz said. "This way, it's all out in the open. I think that's what she wants."

"Thank you," Kate mumbled.

He huffed loudly. "Fine. Christa Dunphy, and it was one time. If that."

The silence filling the room was uncomfortable.

"One time." Kate glared at him. "You want me to believe in twenty-some years, you only cheated on me one time?"

He stared right back. "Why? How many times have you cheated on me in twenty-some years?"

She reared back. "Never!"

"Am I supposed to believe that?"

Her mouth dropped open, and her gaze flicked from him to Liz and back.

"Yes, once." He lowered his voice. "And I believe you. Why can't you believe me?"

"Okay," she said, humoring him. "It was just once. Why? Why that one time? What did I do to make you go running to her?"

It was the same question he'd asked himself a thousand times. "It wasn't like that. You didn't do anything. You're not to blame at all."

She turned away, but not before he saw a tear run down her cheek.

He threw his hands up. "I can't hurt her like this. I don't see the point."

"Kate, do you want to continue?" Liz asked.

A few quiet seconds ticked by. Kate cleared her throat. "I know this is hard for you too, Billy, but I can't see past this right now. This . . . this boulder is standing between us, and there's no hope of moving forward together unless we move it out of the way, and even then . . ."

Billy twisted the rubber band around his wrist and tugged. He needed to find his center, needed something to focus on; he was unraveling fast. He kept twisting until he'd practically cut off his circulation, then he eased off slowly.

"What do you want to hear?" he asked quietly. "You know who. What else? You tell me what you want to know, and I'll tell you, if you really believe this will help us."

He searched her eyes to gauge if what she was asking was what she really wanted. He wished he could still see through to her soul, but that door was slammed shut and locked tight. It was a cruel reminder of the damage she had suffered.

"All of it." Kate lifted her chin. "All of it, until I tell you to stop."

He could be stubborn too. "Okay, but when I'm done, you need to listen to what I have to say about it."

She seemed about to argue, but Liz cut her off. "Can you agree with that, Kate?"

"I don't know that making excuses for your behavior is going to help what we're—"

"I never said anything about making excuses. That's not what I mean. I just want to try to explain some things. I mean, if we're putting it all out on the table."

She mulled over his request and shrugged. "Go ahead."

"It was the night of the Grammys, the night Devin was born."

Her painful whimper was like a knife in his chest, and the look on her face broke his heart. He glanced at Liz, and she nodded for him to continue. He did without looking at Kate. He couldn't.

"You'd been complaining all week that you didn't want to go. You thought you looked fat, said I should be embarrassed to be seen with you." He looked at the doctor. "It wasn't true. She was as beautiful as ever. She had this dress that matched her eyes. Jade green velvet."

He rubbed his thumb over the ridges of his black titanium wedding band.

"Anyway, Devin was a big baby, and she was carrying him much bigger and lower than she did Rhiannon, but she wasn't fat." He could see her as clearly as if it were yesterday. "She looked ripe like an apricot, and she was just as beautiful as the day we met. She still is."

Kate seemed to have zoned out. It was hard to tell if she was even listening.

"So that morning, she starts making excuses about not going—"

Her head jerked up. "I was in labor."

What the hell? He glared right back at her. "And you know I didn't know. You said you had a headache. Then you said you thought you were going to throw up. It all sounded like excuses. Why didn't you just tell me you thought you were in labor? Why weren't you honest with me?"

She slammed the pillow she'd been holding against the back of the couch and leaned forward. "Two reasons. First, I thought you wouldn't go if I said there was a chance I was in labor, and I'd feel guilty that I caused you to miss the most important night of your life. And second . . ." Her voice dropped. "Because I was afraid you might go even if I was in labor. I didn't want to be hurt if you didn't choose me."

Twenty years later, and the words still stung.

He licked his lips. "You're right about one thing. I wouldn't have gone. But I would've never made you feel guilty for missing that and being there for the birth of my son. And it was never the most important night of my life. Not without you there."

The corners of her mouth drooped along with her shoulders. The room grew silent.

"Go on," Liz said.

"I thought she was looking for an excuse not to go. Then she tells me Joey was coming over to hang out with her. To my overly inflated ego, it seemed like she'd rather spend the evening with him than go with me. So yeah, I had my nose out of joint. I'm not proud of it, but I was feeling sorry for myself."

"So you slept with another woman to make up for it?" Kate's face may have been unreadable, but the anguish in her voice was clear.

He shook his head. "That's not what happened."

"So now you're saying you never slept with her?"

"I never said I *slept* with her." He chose his words carefully. "I never *slept* with her. Actually, I didn't do anything." His voice was barely a whisper. "But I didn't stop her, either."

It took about two seconds for Kate to figure out what he was implying. The look on her face was one of pure disappointment. "I think you need to back up, unless you expect me to believe she went down on you in the middle of Radio City Music Hall."

She spoke with such malice that it was his turn to wince. He steadied himself and addressed his comments to Liz, which somehow made what he was about to say slightly easier.

"Christa found out from Joey that Katie wasn't going, so she offered to sit with me so it wouldn't look like I was alone. I was okay with that because I didn't want to be alone. Christa said Joey had told her Kate didn't want to go to the ceremony, and he was just going to hang out with her instead. I realize now she was probably yanking my chain, but at the time, it sounded plausible. The more I thought about Kate's excuses, the angrier I got." He shrugged. "I know that was stupid, even if she just didn't want to go, but I wasn't thinking. Or I was only thinking about myself, which I was always good at."

"Address your comments to Kate, Billy," Liz said with a gentle gesture toward the couch. "You're telling her what happened. I'm just an objective listener."

He glanced at Kate. Legs crossed, her arms folded tightly, she stared at the toe of her sneaker. She wasn't saying much, but her body language was speaking volumes.

"When I won and they called my name, my first thought was how sorry I was that you weren't with me. You were the only person I wanted to share that with, and you weren't there. And then I really screwed up. I hadn't written anything down because I didn't expect to win, and when I got up there, I was just winging it. I'm looking out at just about every music legend I've ever worshiped, all staring back at me, and I couldn't even remember my own fucking name, let alone anyone else's. I remembered to thank Joey. I mean, the whole album was his idea. And then I was just stumbling over my words, and I saw Christa, and I thanked her." He glanced at Liz. "Christa was my agent at the time."

Kate was fully watching him now.

"And I forgot you. I still don't know how I could've done that. You're always right here." He pressed his fist to the spot over his heart. "I realized it as soon as I stepped away from the mic, but when I turned to go back, it was too late. I couldn't believe I'd been that stupid. I tried to call you as soon as I could, although honestly, I was afraid because I figured you'd be hurt. And I didn't blame you. Anyway, there were pictures and interviews. I didn't finish backstage for about a half an hour. I went to the phones and tried to call, but the line was busy. The only person you ever talked to that late was Joey, and he was with you." He tugged his hand through his hair. "So I assumed you were mad and had taken the phone off the hook."

Her hand had started doing that nervous thing again, rubbing up and down her thigh. "Does that sound like something I'd do?"

He shook his head. "No. That's what makes it worse. You might have been hurt, and rightfully so, but I know you wouldn't have done that. I wasn't thinking."

He glanced over at Liz. "Turns out she never saw it, anyway."

"I saw it," Kate said, her voice dull.

"Joey said you didn't. He said the doctors and nurses were in the room and everything was going downhill—"

"I didn't see it that night, but my mother did." She arched an eyebrow. "She found someone who had recorded it and had a copy made and sent it to me. She didn't want me to miss your big night."

It just got worse and worse. "You never told me."

"Why? I assumed you already felt bad." She pushed herself from the sofa and moved over to the window.

Fair enough. It would be a lot easier talking to her back, anyway.

"Well, I thought you were mad at me. Using that as a lame excuse, and combined with still being bent out of shape that you hadn't come with me, I went to a party with Christa at some record exec's place. I was going to have one drink and then go home, but as I've proven too many times over the years, I don't know when to stop. I was drinking, and there was a lot of coke and all kinds of shit, I can't remember what else, but I was wasted. And then . . . it just . . ." He didn't want to continue. "It happened. Okay?"

He threw his hands up in the air as if that would put an end to the conversation and glared at Liz as if he could transfer ownership of this nightmare to her. She was irrationally calm, as far as he was concerned.

And then she motioned for him to continue.

"It's just going to make things worse," he said frantically.

"It might," she said. "But whatever you have to say, Kate can handle it."

Kate hadn't moved from the window. Her body was so stiff that he couldn't tell if she was breathing.

He kept his voice low, as if that might make it easier. "Christa had been coming on to me all night. Actually, for years. It started soon as I met her, but nothing ever happened. Not even close."

"She's a beautiful, sexy woman," Kate said to the window. "She still is."

"She's a slut and a bitch." He was practically snarling.

Liz looked surprised. "You still see her?"

"Not if I can help it." He gripped the arms of the chair. "She was at Joey's funeral. She was one of his clients."

"You were talking with her." Kate spun around. "I saw you. You two looked pretty cozy."

He shook his head. "She was trying to start something, and I put her in her place. So she had to throw her digs in about my failed career, which she's played a big part in over the years."

"I think we're getting a little off topic," Liz interrupted. "Kate, do you want him to continue?"

The look Kate gave him should have dropped the temperature at least twenty degrees. "I want to know what happened the night our son was born."

He tugged at the cuffs of his sweater. His throat was dry, and he needed a drink. A real drink. "Like I said, Christa had been hanging all over me. She took me around, introduced me to all the big brass. Big names. People I'd heard of but never thought I'd meet. I'd gone from feeling sorry for myself to this amazing moment when I won and then right back to feeling alone again. But she just swept in and took over. She kept pushing the drinks, and I was getting pretty fucked up."

Parts of that night were still hazy. He groped through the memories for Katie's sake. Although at this point, things were unraveling fast and she was drifting farther away, not getting closer.

"It was crowded and noisy, and I was wasted. We were in some back room doing coke. I don't think I even realized we were alone. It's all pretty hazy. I was drunk and dusted, and I didn't know shit."

Kate was facing the window again, but by the way she hugged herself around the middle, he knew she was listening.

"We did a few more lines, and I guess I was—"

"Did you kiss her?" She hadn't turned; she just kept staring out the window.

He wanted to vomit. "I don't know. Maybe. I doubt it. But if you want me to be honest, Katie, I can't swear to that."

Her shoulders slumped, and his did as well.

He waited. Another nod from Liz.

"She found something that didn't require any participation on my part, and that's what happened. I didn't touch her."

The clock on the mantel ticked for close to a minute before Kate spoke again. Her words sliced through him. "Did you come?"

The blood in his veins turned to sludge; his outer extremities tingled like they'd fallen asleep. How the hell was this fucking conversation going to fix anything?

"Katie—"

She whirled around. "Did you come, Billy?" She took a step toward him, her hands balled into fists and her voice rising. "A simple yes or no. Did you come in that whore's mouth?"

His heart lurched so hard it felt as if it had somehow stumbled. Why didn't Liz stop her? Couldn't she see this wasn't helping? How could he answer that question? He was a guy, for fuck's sake. His dick had a mind of its own.

"Katie, please—"

"God, Billy! I want to punch you. I want to hit you so hard!"

He bolted from his chair. "Go ahead. Hit me. If that'll make you feel better, I want you to hit me." He wanted her to beat the shit out of him if it would make her feel better.

"Whoa, whoa, whoa!" Liz jumped to her feet. *Now she steps in.* "Nobody is hitting anybody."

"It's okay." His eyes remained locked on Kate's. "If you wanna hit me, Katie, go ahead. I deserve it."

"Kate." Liz carried a warning note in her voice.

Kate spun back toward the window.

Liz aimed a finger at his chair, so he sat. Helpless and nauseated, he stared at Kate's back, wanting to go to her but afraid she would push him away for good.

The clock continued to tick.

"Kate," Liz said finally, "do you want to continue?"

She didn't answer right away, and when she did, she sounded broken. "I guess. That's what we're here for, right?"

Liz nodded at Billy. "Go on."

"There's not much more to tell. I pulled myself together, and I got the hell out of there. I walked for a long time, sick to my stomach, and not just from the alcohol. I was ashamed and disgusted, I threw up in the street. I hated myself." His throat was as dry and sore as if he'd been swallowing daggers. "When my head was a little clearer, I called for my ride, and then I came home, wondering how I would ever face you, only to find out that while I was out fucking around, you'd not only given birth to our son, you'd almost died."

It was as if someone had thrown a switch. The torrent of tears he'd been holding back for far too long burst forth. He couldn't stop them; he wasn't even sure he wanted to stop them.

Liz handed him a box of tissues, but Kate didn't move. He could see she was watching him in the reflection in the glass, as grief-stricken as he was.

No one spoke for a long time.

"Is that why you bought the house?" she asked.

He nodded. "Pretty much. I'd been thinking about it, even though I thought it wouldn't be good for you to live so close to your parents. But after what I'd done, I figured I owed you."

He blew his nose and grabbed another tissue. "As for Christa, I fired her the next day. She kept calling me, and when I didn't respond, she sent a message through Denny that I had better meet with her or else. So I did." He balled up the tissues and tossed them onto the table. "She offered me my choice of two recording contracts, each one worth more than anything I've seen since. The deal was that she'd remain my agent, and I'd be at her beck and call until she grew tired of me. If I turned her down, she threatened to go to you."

Kate shifted away from the window enough to meet his gaze. "I guess we know which option you took, since she never came to me."

His anger at Christa was as strong as if it had been yesterday, and he had to restrain himself to keep from driving his fist into the coffee table. "That's not what happened. I went to see Joey."

"Joey?" Her head shot up. "Why Joey?"

"Because I needed his help. I told him everything, and then I begged him to get Christa to stay away from you."

She snorted. "Joey would've never gone along with that."

"He did. It took some convincing, but he did. He did because he loved you, Katie, and he didn't want to see you hurt any more than I did. I told him I didn't care what Christa did to me or my career, but he had to convince her to stay away from you. And he did. He may have hated my guts, but he did it for you. Christa promised to make sure my career stayed as dead-end as I was, and to her credit, she's done exactly that."

Kate turned, and he could see that her face was pale and strained. "How? What has she done?"

"No one in any of the big New York or LA firms will represent me, even the ones who've courted me. Whenever I get close to a contract, Christa gets wind of it, and they pull out. Sometimes her name comes up. Others don't say anything, but I already know. Same thing with some of the gigs I audition for. If she hears I'm up for a job, she steps in and makes sure it doesn't happen. I know it's her because she calls me, and since I don't take her calls, she leaves messages asking how it went."

"So all these years, she's made it her business to sabotage you?" Kate asked angrily. "Why would she even do that? She got what she wanted."

"No, she didn't. She wanted me. She never had me. She had five minutes alone with a shadow of me. When I cut off communication with her, she decided to get even. The afternoon of Joey's funeral, she threatened to go have a little chat with you."

"So why didn't she?"

"Because I told her if she ever got within fifteen feet of you, I'd break her fucking neck." Just thinking about that bitch caused the tension in his jaw to ratchet up. He forced himself to breathe through it.

When it started to subside, he spoke to Liz. "I have a problem with my temper. It's one of the only things I inherited from my bastard of a father—that and my fondness for alcohol, but I've gotten a handle on both in the past year." He lowered his voice. "I'm afraid to think what I might've done if she'd gone near Katie, though."

Kate leaned against the window ledge, watching him.

"I can't blame Christa completely for my career tanking—god knows I did enough damage of my own—but things might've been different without her working against me. But I take responsibility for myself now. I've learned to live with my choices and my disappointments."

"What about the funeral?" Kate asked. "She left right behind you."

He shrugged. "Knowing her, she probably did that so you'd think we were together. I wouldn't put it past her."

"So for twenty years, this woman's been pining away for you?"

"Hardly. She's just an evil, vindictive bitch."

"I need to sit." Kate nearly folded in on herself as she slumped onto the couch, her arms wrapped tightly around her middle.

"Are you okay?" Liz asked.

Kate nodded, but she still looked lost. "Nobody else?"

He shook his head. "No one."

"But you kept me away," she said. "In all the years we were married, I never went on the road with you. I rarely went to gigs, even if you were local. I hardly ever met the musicians you played with. You had a million excuses for why I couldn't be there, and I bought all of them. Who were you trying to keep me away from, Billy?"

It was a difficult question to answer. "Me, I think. I love what I do, and there isn't anything else I'd want to do. I'm a musician. It's who I am. Regardless of what level you perform on—and I've been on the very top and the very bottom—the lifestyle is pretty much the same.

Only the degree of decadence is different. When we first met, I was playing in clubs and opening for people on their way up or on their way down. The drinks were free, and everybody had pot and pills or coke. And there were always women. You saw that for yourself, right?"

She nodded.

"Multiply that ten times over and then some, and that's what it's like on the road. Only now, whatever you want gets handed to you. Some chick catches your eye during a show, you just signal the tour manager and she's waiting for you backstage for as little or as long as you want. You see a few you like, no problem. And all the while, you're onstage, the fans are screaming and loving what you're doing, you're loving what you're doing, and you feel like you're on top of the world. You think you're a big fucking deal, and you want to be treated like that. And you are. Vendors line up before the show begging you to play their guitars, use their amps, their strings. To help convince you, they may have some of the finest Colombian weed or the purest white powder or the most beautiful women, just so maybe you'll give that new guitar a try at your next gig. When you're a rock star, every kid in the audience or buying your record or watching your YouTube video is gonna see you playing that guitar, and it's worth it to them to make you happy."

"So then I'd come home and there you were, you and the kids, and you were perfect—you were what really mattered. I didn't want you anywhere near that lifestyle. My upbringing was pretty ugly, Katie, but with you, my life was perfect. The little house, the two kids, the dog, even the vegetable garden in the back yard. Life with you was like living in paradise. I wanted to protect you from all the ugliness. The problem was I wasn't really living that perfect life with you. I was standing on the outside watching, like one of those living history museums, patting myself on the back for creating this diorama, totally unaware I wasn't even a part of it. I was so afraid of becoming either of my parents that I didn't become any type of parent at all. I left it all for you. Maybe it didn't always seem like that, but I had you on a pedestal to keep you away from all the bullshit, especially the stuff I was shoveling."

He tried to look as earnest as he could. "I was no angel, Katie. I'm the first to say that. When they were passing out the Jack and the coke or the weed, I was standing there with both hands out. But that's where it ended. No women. And when it was my band on the road and I was the boss, there were no women backstage and sure as hell none in my room. I made one terrible mistake twenty-two years ago, and I never repeated it. I lived with that guilt every single day, and I never came close ever again."

Their eyes were locked. It was as if they were alone. He knew Kate was weighing his words, trying to decide if she believed him. He couldn't look away, afraid she would take that to mean he was lying. He was afraid to even blink. He followed the rise and fall of her chest, the sadness in her eyes.

As long as she was looking at him and not through him, there was still hope.

CHAPTER FORTY-THREE

They'd been at it for over two hours. If he survived this without falling off the wagon, Billy figured he could survive anything.

"How are you feeling, Kate?" Liz asked.

She blinked several times. "Gutted."

"How are you feeling about what Billy's told you?"

"Not good, but I guess it could've been worse." Her lip quivered.

"What does that mean?" he asked, grasping at a granule of possibility.

"I don't know. I'm not sure. I think when you told me you cheated, I assumed it was lots of women over the years. Not that a tawdry backroom blow job is any easier to swallow."

Her eyes grew wide at the irony of what she'd said. Liz dipped her head to hide a tiny smile.

He didn't dare smile. No fucking way.

Kate's gaze dropped to the floor. When she shivered, he slipped off his jacket and draped it over her shoulders. She wrapped her arms around herself, pulling the edges close around her.

Billy had been talking for most of the session. He felt like a dried-up husk.

"Can I have a drink of water?" he asked Liz. "Something?"

"Certainly. Kate?"

"No, thanks."

"Are you okay?" he asked after Liz had left the room.

Kate's lips spread into a thin line. Was that a yes? A no?

"I'm sorry," he said. "You know I'm sorry, right?"

"Yeah."

That didn't mean she forgave him, though.

"Can I ask you something?"

Although hesitant, she nodded.

"After the shooting, you allowed me back into your life. We even made love a couple of times. If you were still so confused over us, why did you let that happen? Why let me come back at all?"

It was quiet for so long he thought she might not answer him.

"I've thought about that myself," she said finally. "I think there was so much else going on that I needed to compartmentalize. While I was hiding in that bathroom, all I could think about was that I might never see you again. After the police found me, I wanted them to call you. I needed you. I wasn't able to forgive you or even consider what you'd done, but I needed you." She shrugged. "I don't have a better answer than that. I'm sorry if it seemed I was jerking you around. I really didn't know what I was doing. I can't even say I was trying to survive. Maybe I was at first, but then . . . I don't know."

"I'm glad you wanted me. I wish I could've helped you."

Before she could answer, Liz returned and handed him a bottle of water. He took several long gulps and screwed the cap back on.

"I have a question," Kate said, "and you have to be honest with me."

"There can't be anything more difficult to say than what I've already told you."

"Maybe." She straightened up, as if preparing for another blow. "We've been separated for over ten months. For all you knew, I was never coming back." She pulled his jacket tighter around her. "Have you been seeing anyone since I've been gone? I mean, it would be hard to blame you, not to mention I'm well acquainted with your, er —how much you like sex." A pink flush rose from her neck to her cheeks.

"No. No one." He lowered his head to meet her eyes. "Because in my heart and in my head, it isn't over."

The stiffness left her body. Did that mean she was satisfied with his answer?

"How're we doing here?" Liz asked.

"I'm exhausted," Kate said.

"Me too."

"Do you want to end here and let some of this sink in? Kate? Are you okay with that?"

"Yeah. I'm drained right now."

"That's understandable. Normally, I'd ask that you put all of this away in some safe place until we can bring it out and talk about it again, but I don't think that's feasible. If you need or want to talk more, see what happens. If it dissolves into fighting and more hurt, give me a call and I'll try to squeeze you in. Otherwise, just try to process this as best you can, and give me a call in a day or two. Sooner, if need be."

Kate slipped off Billy's jacket, but he stopped her.

"Keep it."

She murmured her thanks and slipped her arms into the sleeves. Her slight form swam inside it.

"Would you mind if I spoke to Liz alone?" she asked. "Just for a moment."

"No problem." He shook Liz's hand. "That was hard, but thank you."

"DO you think he's telling the truth?" Kate asked after Billy had left her and Liz alone.

"That would be hard for me to assess fairly. What did you think?"

"I think he was, but he's lied before. I want to believe him, but that doesn't change the fact that he cheated in the first place."

Liz placed her hands on Kate's arms. "The night of your friend's funeral, he raped you, right?"

She shook her head insistently. "That was different. He didn't know what he was doing. I told you what he said."

"You did. And the night he cheated, what was different about that night?"

"It's not the same."

"No? Was he under the influence of drugs and alcohol?"

"When?"

"Both nights? Either night?"

"Yes."

"What I'm saying is that you forgave him for doing something horrible because he was under the influence of drugs and alcohol. If you're going to judge him for something he did more than twenty years ago, maybe you should use the same ruler."

She made it all sound so simple. Like Dorothy in *The Wizard of Oz*, all she had to do was click her heels three times and she could go home.

"You're saying I should forgive him?"

"No. All I'm saying is that you should apply the same rules. Is it unfair to excuse his behavior for one thing because he was on drugs but not for another? Think about what may be preventing you from applying the same logic to both incidents. Only you know what you're capable of forgiving and forgetting, and only you know if you love him enough to bother."

"I'm still so confused. I don't want to forgive him only because I'm lonely and—you know." She'd shared a lot with Liz over the past few months, but telling her she was horny wasn't something she was comfortable saying outright.

Liz seemed to understand perfectly. "I don't think you'll do that."

"Oh, no? You should have seen me Saturday night after a bottle of wine. He had to practically restrain me."

"He wouldn't sleep with you? Even though you clearly wanted to?"

"Nope. It was humiliating. He said he wouldn't until I made a commitment to him and to our marriage. He said it would be too difficult to be with me only to have me turn him away again."

"Sounds like he's either very controlling or he possesses a lot of character."

Controlling? Yes, he certainly could be, but not about something like that. Just what she needed: something else to think about.

THE SKY WAS gray and dreary when she emerged, but Kate still reached for her sunglasses.

Billy was leaning against the passenger side of the car. "Do you want me to drive?"

She nodded.

"You okay?"

Not really. "I'm tired, and I have a headache."

He opened the car door, and she slid inside.

"I'm sorry," he said after climbing into the driver's side.

"I know."

"Do you want to get something to eat? That should help your headache."

"Not really. Would you mind taking me home?"

"Home?" He looked so hopeful her heart hurt.

"I meant back to the house."

The ride wasn't long, but the silence was deafening. They pulled into the garage, but she made no move to get out of the car. Billy climbed out, came around, and opened her door. When he held out his hand, she took it. He helped her to her feet, and when she met his eyes, they were as sad as she imagined her own must be. Uncomfortable and tense, she lowered her head and made her way into the house.

"Do you want me to make you something to eat?"

He was being sweet and attentive, and she appreciated it, but it was all too much.

"If you don't mind, I'm going to take a couple of aspirin and lie down. I need to be alone for a bit." She felt like she was deserting him, but she needed some distance. And she really did need to lie down. "We'll talk later."

He looked lost. "Sure."

But before she could get very far, he reached for her and pulled her toward him, wrapping her in his arms. The scent of lemongrass enveloped her, and she breathed deep, feeling his heart beat steadily against her cheek. He pressed a soft kiss to the top of her head. When he let go, she bolted down the hall, immediately missing the warmth and comfort of his arms.

She turned down the covers and slipped between the sheets, too emotionally spent to get undressed. She closed her eyes and tried to empty her mind, hoping to dislodge the pain that had risen between her shoulders and her neck and shot into her temples. It was hopeless. Years of memories overwhelmed her: The way Billy's face would light up when he saw her after being on tour. The way he always found a way to touch her when she was nearby, from holding her hand to pressing the toe of his boot against her foot. How he'd tried to protect her and the kids from his mother's ridiculous threats by succumbing to blackmail. And maybe most revealing, the fact that she'd walked out on him nearly a year ago without even leaving him a note, yet the moment he'd learned where she was, he'd gotten on that damn motorcycle and ridden almost seven hours straight to find her.

She loved him. Of course she did. But her fears weren't about love. They were about forgiveness. About trust. About letting go.

What a mess they'd made of their lives.

She curled onto her side and had almost fallen asleep when she heard the rumble of the garage door below her, followed by the roar of the Harley.

That was another thing. Annoyance joined the jumble of emotions swirling around her head.

He knew she hated motorcycles.

CHAPTER FORTY-FOUR

Heavy rain beat down upon the roof. Kate opened her eyes in the darkened room. She stretched and rolled onto her back. The pounding in her head had given way to a dull ache, but her stomach growled, demanding to be fed.

Billy hadn't returned. Or she'd slept more soundly than usual and the motorcycle was parked in the garage. She pulled on a heavy pair of socks and a warmer sweater and after checking the garage and finding only the Saab, she shuffled into the living room.

Rain was coming down in sheets, bouncing off the pool cover and the patio. The tide was on its way out, but the water in the cove was alive with movement. A knot of anxiety twisted in her belly. It would be difficult to drive in this kind of downpour in a car; on a motorcycle, it would be impossible. Why the hell did he go out? He should've known it was going to rain.

She tried calling him, but the call went straight to voice mail. He was probably stuck somewhere, and judging by how hard it was raining, he'd be stuck for a while.

She set a large pot of water on the stove to boil and began chopping celery, carrots, and onions for chicken and dumplings. She browned the chicken, tossed it in the water with the vegetables, and set it to simmer for an hour.

With a fire blazing in the hearth downstairs, she tried to read, but the steady beat of the rain on the windows made it hard to focus. She needed something more distracting. She turned on the TV, popped *Legends of the Fall* into the DVD player, and curled up on the big leather sofa draped in her favorite quilt.

An hour later, the rain hadn't let up any and there was still no sign of Billy. Damn motorcycles. She paused the movie and returned to the kitchen, where she ripped the meat from the bones and chopped it a bit more aggressively than necessary. She dropped it back into the pot to simmer. Since there was no point in making the dumplings until he returned, she busied herself with putting together a salad.

When there was nothing left to distract her, she could no longer ignore the icy fingers creeping up her spine. Maybe he wasn't coming back. Maybe as abruptly as he'd come to Maine, he'd gone back to New Jersey. Could she blame him? He'd wanted to talk after the session with Liz, but she'd put him off. Again.

Or maybe he was drinking. Her stomach rolled. It was possible. It was after six, and he'd left hours ago. He could be halfway back to Jersey or wasted at some nearby bar. Or worse. He could have wrecked that stupid bike.

The deluge continued. Rain pelted the windows as if fire hoses had been trained at them.

She tried calling him again, and again it went straight to voice mail. She tucked the phone into her pocket and stood outside the guest room. What if his things were gone? Hesitating at first, she rested her hand on the knob, then opened the door slowly. The bed was made. His clothes were neatly folded on a chair in the corner. Relieved, she dropped to the edge of the bed, but her cruel mind wouldn't give in. None of that mattered. All of it was stuff he'd acquired since he arrived. There was nothing he needed to take if he had decided to leave.

She hugged his pillow to her chest. Would he leave without saying goodbye? No. That was her thing. That left two options: he was drunk, or he'd had an accident.

Given a choice, she'd rather him sitting in a bar somewhere—warm, safe, and drunk.

Damn it.

She turned off the stove, poured herself a glass of wine, and went back downstairs. She turned the movie back on, keeping the volume low.

The movie was almost over when she heard the rumble of the garage door.

Charlie shot up the stairs like a rocket. She wanted to follow, but she couldn't move.

What if he was drunk? And if he was, was it her fault for not talking to him earlier?

She climbed the stairs slowly. Would she be disappointed, angry? How should she handle it?

Prepared for the worst, she was surprised to find the kitchen and mudroom empty. She checked the bathroom and the guest room. Also empty. She was coming up the hall when she heard the door to the mudroom open and the click of Charlie's nails on the slate floor.

"Wait," Billy scolded. "You're going to track mud all through the house. Give me your paws so I can dry you off."

He didn't sound drunk, although he was only talking to the dog. A minute later, Charlie came bounding out of the mudroom, nearly knocking her over as he passed.

Billy tugged off his leather jacket. His hair was plastered to his scalp; long strands clung to his face and his neck. He dropped his jacket in front of the dryer with a heavy plop. Water pooled on the floor around him. He had begun to lift his wet sweater over his head when he caught sight of her in the doorway.

"Hey," he said before yanking the sweater off and dropping it on top of his jacket. "Feeling better?"

She nodded, watching as he toed off his boots.

"Headache gone?"

She couldn't find her voice, so she nodded again.

He leaned down and pulled off his socks. He unbuckled his belt and tugged it through the belt loops of his jeans. After dropping that in the growing pile, he reached into his pocket, pulled out his phone, and tossed it on top of the washer. "Pretty sure this is toast." He placed his keys and his wallet alongside the phone.

After unbuttoning his jeans, he stopped. "I need to get out of these clothes, and I know you don't want me to strip down in front of you, so if you don't mind . . ." He twirled his finger in a circle.

"I thought you might've left," she said, finally finding her voice. "I didn't think you were coming back."

"I wouldn't go without saying goodbye." His voice was a dull, flat monotone. Gooseflesh broke out over his wet skin, and he folded his arms across his chest. "And I would've called, but my phone was dead." The look he gave her made her feel as if she'd been the one left out in the rain. "Besides, I don't have your number."

She pulled a towel from the dryer and handed it to him, and then turned her back while he peeled away his pants. "Are you okay?" She hadn't smelled alcohol, and he'd seemed very steady for someone standing on one foot while trying to remove his boots and socks.

"I'm soaked, but other than that, I'm great."

His pants landed on the wet pile with a heavy thud.

"I'm decent."

It was hard to miss his frown. He was wet and bedraggled, but his eyes were clear and his speech wasn't slurred. A wave of relief passed over her.

"Where were you?"

"I went for a ride. Took a walk on the beach. I also needed a drink." His eyes remained fixed on hers. "So I tracked down a meeting in Portland, but it didn't start until five thirty, so I found this music store in Falmouth. I just hung out there and played for a while."

"Find anything you liked?"

He nodded. "I did, but it's not like I could take it with me." He grabbed a clean towel from the pile atop the dryer and rubbed it over his hair. "Then I went to my meeting, and here I am. I couldn't be any wetter if I'd swum to Portland and back."

"Are you hungry? I made chicken and dumplings. Why don't you take a shower, and I'll finish dinner."

"I just had a shower."

"A hot shower."

He scooped his things into the dryer and headed for the guest room, leaving wet prints on the hardwood floor, and not even looking at her as he passed.

CHAPTER FORTY-FIVE

Billy came into the kitchen wearing a black T-shirt Kate hadn't seen before and a dry pair of jeans. The quilt from the bed was draped over his shoulders, but he was still shivering.

She turned up the heat and suggested they eat downstairs where it was warmer.

"I hope you don't get sick," she said as they settled in front of the fire, bowls of chicken and dumplings in their laps.

He didn't look up. "I'm fine."

She deserved this. He'd been trying for days, and today, he'd put it all out there. It had hurt like hell to hear it all, but he was hurting too. Was that what she wanted? For him to suffer as well?

They ate in uncomfortable silence. When she spoke, he answered in a one- or two-word monotone, and he didn't initiate conversation. He didn't ask when they could talk. He didn't ask her to listen or work on their issues. He didn't ask what she was thinking. His silence spoke loudly: he was protecting his heart.

And it was killing her.

After dinner, she stoked the fire to a hearty blaze. "Do you want to watch a movie? I don't have much of a selection, but—"

"No, thanks." He rose from the couch, still not looking at her. "I think I'm just gonna head up to bed. I didn't sleep last night, and I'm kinda tired."

"Oh." She nodded. "Okay."

He picked up his empty dishes. "And, uh, Kate?"

Kate? How could the absence of one little vowel hurt so much?

"I'm heading out in the morning." He swallowed so hard it was as if his Adam's apple moved in slow motion. His eyes finally touched hers, and when they did, her bruised, beaten, and bandaged heart disintegrated.

Feeling as if her pockets were suddenly filled with lead weights, she struggled to stand. "You're leaving?"

"Yeah. I shouldn't have come. You were moving on with your life, and I'd found a way to stop destroying mine. All I've done is hurt you more. I need to go."

She should have said something, but her throat had closed up. All she could do was blink.

His eyes scraped over her face. "Guess that's it. G'night."

"Wait."

She took the dishes from him and put them on the coffee table.

"Sit, please. We need to talk." When he didn't move, she asked again. She wasn't beyond begging. "Please?"

With a loud sigh, he dropped back onto the sofa. "I don't know what else there is to say, but let me at least say this. All I ever wanted from almost the first moment I met you was to love you. Instead, I nearly destroyed us both. I think I've always known that, but it became a lot clearer today. Knowing that my lies and cheating contributed to your pain . . ." His face was etched with defeat and sadness. "We've been like two boats smashing ourselves against the rocks, neither of us wholly trusting the other. It was just so stupid."

The fire popped and crackled. The rain beat steadily on the windows. And the voices inside her head kept telling her she needed to fix this. *Now.*

She slipped off the sofa and perched on the edge of the coffee table. She tried to slide her knees between his. He resisted at first. Then, with a small sigh, he let her in, although he didn't look at her. She reached up and pulled the quilt tighter over his shoulders.

"I've been in some pretty intense therapy over the past several months, and it's taken awhile, but I think I finally understand that the damage done to us by our parents has affected how we respond to one another when we're at our worst. You know my mother didn't want me and would've had an abortion if my father hadn't talked her out of it."

"Katie." His voice was soft, soothing. "You don't have to—"

"Yes, I do." She scooted closer. "I thought when I shared this with you when we were first married that I'd dealt with it, but all I'd done was bury it. Even though you made me feel loved and wanted, the insecurity never left me. The feeling of not being good enough was still there. I just grew used to it. Something else I learned at an early age was to avoid conflict. I was good at escaping. Running away was my answer to everything that was difficult."

It hurt that he still wouldn't look at her, and for the first time she really understood she wasn't the only one who had suffered. She pushed forward.

"I didn't value myself, so I didn't expect you to value me either. And in that sense, I didn't demand the best from you. I enabled you, because I thought that would make you happy and you would keep loving me. For that, I'm sorry. When you began to depend more on alcohol and drugs, I refused to see it. I made excuses or looked the other way. And now I have this picture in my head of you shooting heroin into your arm, and it's almost as bad as the image of you and her." She choked back a sob. "I'm sorry I didn't try and get you to stop a long time ago."

His eyes flicked over her face. "That's not your fault. I made those mistakes all by myself."

She struggled to keep from crying. If she started, she might not stop.

"And you," he added, capturing her hands in his. "You are definitely worthy of love. And desirable? You have no idea how desirable you are."

The heat of the fire at her back felt warmer. There were things still left unsaid between them, but now it was his turn. She waited.

"My father was a mean drunk. He'd take a strap to me now and then." He shrugged. "Maybe I deserved it. I was a mouthy kid. But one day, he nearly killed me because I'd touched his fucking baseball. Up until then, I'd been a Little League pitching phenom. My size and my speed were almost unheard of for a kid my age. But after that day, I never touched another baseball. I always wanted to watch Devin play. He was a natural, and I was proud of him, but whenever I'd try to go, it made me physically ill. So I made excuses, or I made sure I wasn't home when he had a game. And if I had no choice, I self-medicated to get through it. I never saw my father after that day, but that didn't stop the fear of him returning, even as an adult. And by then, it wasn't just me I had to worry about. The thought that he might come anywhere near you . . ."

She squeezed his hands, unable to wipe away the tears streaming down her face. He brought his knees together, clamping hers between his own.

"You know that my mother took off after him. The police were looking for him, and the army after he went AWOL from Fort Kent, but I guess she tracked him down. She'd disappear for a while, then come back. My grandfather would send her packing. But after he died, my grandmother couldn't turn away her own daughter. My mother would hang around for a few weeks, try to be a mom, but then she'd get antsy and disappear. But not without helping herself to something of value. It wasn't till after she had taken all of Gram's jewelry, Pop's guns, and the Martin he gave me that my grandmother had enough. She hit every pawn shop in three counties looking for that guitar, and when she found it, she bought it back for five times what it was worth, just for me. After that, when my mother would show up, Gram would threaten to call the cops. Then she'd lock herself in her room and cry. It broke my heart, but Janet was still my mother, and I felt bad when Gram sent her away. You saw my mother. She was beautiful, but she's cunning. I don't know where it came from, because my grandparents were decent people, but my mother can be evil when she wants something."

He pulled his hands away and put some distance between them. "This is hard for me. I never wanted you to know what a shithole I came from."

He looked so broken and raw. She wanted to tell him to stop, that he didn't need to dredge up the past, but after burying her own for so long, wasn't this exactly what they needed?

She pressed her hands against the tops of his thighs, needing to keep the connection between them as strong as possible. "It doesn't matter where you came from. What matters is who you are."

His snort told her he didn't believe her. "One of the last times my mother was able to con my grandmother into letting her stay, she invited a couple of friends over. They were just like her—barflies looking for a good time. I was around fourteen. Gram went on a church retreat, and my mom, thinking she couldn't leave me alone or something, had her friends come over to party with her at the house. They were drinking and smoking pot. They even had some coke. Being the generous mother she was, she let me join them. She'd started partying long before her girlfriends arrived, so she passed out pretty early. Her one friend took off, which left me and Janelle."

She had a sick feeling she knew where this was going. "You don't have to finish," she croaked.

"I want to get this over with."

He stared at his hands as he spoke.

"Janelle was in her early thirties, I guess. Nice-looking. Anyway, she came on to me pretty heavy. And me? My brains were in my dick, what can I say? It wasn't just that night, either." He hesitated. "After that, I'd ride my bike over to her house and go in through the back door so no one would see me. It went on for a few months. At the time, I thought I was pretty freaking lucky. I know it was wrong, but for what it's worth, she taught me an awful lot."

"Lucky? It was rape."

"Probably. I was a willing participant, though."

"What if that had been our son?"

He shifted against the leather sofa. "I would've killed the bitch."

"Well," she said, trying to dispel some of the tension and sadness hanging over them, "my big sex revelation is that Digger Johnson squeezed my boob in the car after prom and then tried to slide his hand under my gown. I started crying, and he took me home."

"And for that alone, I wanna beat the shit out of him."

She knew he meant it. "Well, don't."

He smiled for the first time that day, but she wasn't convinced he wouldn't take a swing at Digger, given the chance.

"Go on if, there's more," she said. "Tell me."

"Over the years, because of what happened the night Devin was born . . ."

She tried not to react, but it was impossible. Invisible fingers wrapped around her heart and squeezed. Pain was her old friend, but now anger jockeyed for position. Instinctively, she tried to pull away, but Billy was quicker. He grasped her hands and held on tightly.

"I always felt guilty. Not a day went by I didn't think of that. For years, it haunted me. I tried to bury those feelings—drinking, drugs, anything to dull that ache. I can't say I wouldn't have touched any of that if that hadn't happened—my history goes way back—but I know it made it worse. Some days it felt as if that guilt might eat me alive."

Each tear that trickled down his beautiful face touched her heart and diluted her anger. They had both suffered; both been broken long before they'd even met. And those old wounds had caused them to hurt each other. But no more; it was long past time to heal.

She moved closer and touched the palm of her hand to his cheek. She brushed a tear away with her thumb. "Lie down and close your eyes."

He didn't resist. Tension and pain lined his face. She dusted his eyelids with the tips of her fingers. She traced the faded scar through his eyebrow, the one he'd gotten from his father, and then the one below his eye, the one from the fight with Pete, his old part-ner. With both hands, she reached behind his ears and gently rubbed the base of his skull and his neck. When she found the two-inch thread of raised scar tissue behind his ear, she focused on that, lightly stroking the reminder of a brutal beating at the hands of his father.

She held her right hand over his heart, absorbing the beat beneath her palm. Then she slid both hands over his chest and ribs, knowing some of those ribs had been broken. She pressed a kiss into the soft, pale skin at the crease of each arm, paying particular attention to a large blue vein, the one that had likely carried the poison he'd injected into his body. A tear of her own landed on that soft, vulnerable spot.

When she sat up, he was watching her. She ran her hands over his left leg, the one his father had caused him to break.

"What are you doing?"

"I'm not sure." Her voice was as soft as her touch. "I think I'm trying to take away your pain."

The clock on the mantel ticked. The fire crackled. Like a healer, she kept touching him, stroking his long-ago injuries until the rhythmic sound of his breathing told her he had relaxed into sleep. She covered him with the quilt and with the fire dying behind her, studied the face of the man she'd loved most of her life.

There was no reason to drag this out any longer. If her head had been clear all those months ago, she would have known it then. The answer had been with her all along.

She spread the embers in the fireplace, replaced the screen, and climbed the stairs. Despite her exhaustion, she stepped into the shower, hoping it would relieve not only the chill in her body, but her troubled mind. With her head resting on the wall of the shower and the hot water beating on her neck, she pictured the tension seeping out through her pores and running down the drain around her feet. She let the water wash away all of her thoughts until there was nothing but the sound of the water pounding in her ears—until the scrape of the shower curtain rings against the rod jarred her back to the present.

Her hands couldn't possibly cover all the parts of her that were exposed, but that didn't stop her from trying. "Billy! What are you doing?"

He blinked, his eyes swollen and sleepy. "I love you, Katie. I've loved you forever. Since the first time I saw you. And when I touched you, when I asked you to dance, I knew it was true. I knew it the same way I know that when that crazy grandfather clock chimes, it's chiming in the key of D. I knew before I met you that there would be one great love in my life. And there you were."

He stepped into the shower, the water soaking into his shirt and jeans.

"I've failed you miserably, and I'm sorry. If I could go back and fix it, I would. All the way back, back to the time you were that scared little girl in flannel nightgowns with dragons to fight. I would've stood next to your bed and fought my way into your dreams to keep them away. And when I saw how you were treated, that your parents didn't love you the way you deserved to be loved, I would've taken you away back then. Even if I was only nine or ten years old, I would've carried you away, and we would've lived in a treehouse if we had to. I loved you even then, before I knew you, and I would've protected you with my life."

She balled up her fist and pressed it against her mouth to keep the sob wedged in her throat from escaping.

His fingers dug into her shoulders. "So many of the horrible things you've been through, they're not your fault. They're mine. If I'd been honest with you in the beginning about my mother, she could never have blackmailed me, and I would never have given her all that money, and you would never have felt you needed to go to work. See, it's my fault you were at that meeting. I didn't protect you the way I'd promised. You didn't feel secure, and that's my fault. I know that now, and I don't want you to blame yourself. Let me take that burden from you." His grip tightened and his voice grew thick with emotion. "And what happened with Christa? That was one ugly, stupid, drunken mistake that I will regret all the days of my life. Let me love you. Let me make it right. I'm begging you to forgive me. Let me back into your heart. I promise I will never hurt you again. I've loved you forever, Katie, and I will always love you."

The water beat against his chest as the steam embraced them. The air was so heavy she couldn't seem to draw it into her lungs.

"I love you," she whispered.

His eyes softened. "But?"

"But nothing." She rested her hands on his chest. "I love you. Even when I should've hated you, I loved you."

A flicker of hope shot through the pain reflected in his blue-gray irises. "What're you saying, Katie?"

She gripped his wet T-shirt in her hands. "I'm saying you're my husband and I'm your wife, and that's the way I want it to stay. I'm saying I love you, Billy. I'm saying I want to be married to you, that I'm committed to you."

He touched his forehead to hers. "Say it again."

"I love you."

He trailed his nose over her temple and along the sweep of her jaw.

"No, not that."

"You're my husband?" Despite the hot water raining down upon them, goosebumps prickled her arms and over her bare chest.

"Unh-uh." He slid his teeth down the column of her neck, and her knees threatened to give way.

"I want to be your wife?"

He kissed his way along her collarbone. "Say it again."

"I want to be your wife."

He eased her against the wall of the shower as his lips ghosted over her throat, her neck, her chin.

"Say it again." He nibbled on her bottom lip.

"I want to be your wi—" She might have sighed. Or maybe she moaned. Whatever sound she had made was swallowed up when

Billy's mouth covered hers. His hand cradled the back of her head, while the other pulled her so close her breasts crushed against his chest and the tab of his zipper dug into her belly.

She lifted the hem of his sopping-wet shirt and unbuttoned his jeans, then tugged at the zipper.

"Wait," he said, breaking the kiss but still so close his breath caressed her lips. "So this is real? I need to know, Katie. I can't lose you again. Don't do this and then tell me you're not sure. Please. I'm begging you, be sure."

"I'm sure." She slipped her fingers around his neck. "I'm not going anywhere. No matter what."

He pulled away just long enough to reach back and tug his shirt over his head. It landed on the floor of the tub with a splat. It took a bit of effort, but he stripped off his jeans, turned off the shower, and wrapped a large towel around the two of them. Once she was caught up in his arms, he kissed her again. A flame ignited in her chest, flaring up and spreading warmth throughout her body, even as the towel cascaded down around their feet.

With his arms circling her waist, he lifted her up and carried her across the hall into her bedroom, where he gently lowered her onto the bed.

"I need to be inside you, Katie," he said, his eyes locked on hers. "I need to feel you tighten around me. I need to feel you melt into me until we're breathing the same air, until our hearts are beating to the same rhythm, until we are so entangled in one another there won't be anything strong enough to tear us apart again."

"I promise," she whispered, weaving her fingers through his hair. "Nothing will come between us again. Ever."

———

HOURS LATER, Kate felt Billy's weight settle on her in the dark. Warm, comfortable weight. His lips kissed a trail up her neck. She was too tired to open her eyes, but she yielded to the pure delicious-ness of having him back in her bed.

"Again?" she murmured against the shell of his ear.

"Again." His lips brushed her cheek. "And again." He breathed into her mouth. "And again." He kissed her deeply. "And again until we make up for all that we lost. And then again, because I never want to let you go. You are all I'll ever need. All I ever wanted."

CHAPTER FORTY-SIX

"Man, oh man." Billy stretched out the kinks in his back and a cramp in his right calf. "I am not twenty-five anymore."

It was disappointing to wake up alone, but the aroma of freshly brewed coffee and something equally as promising wafting in from the kitchen hurried him from Kate's warm bed. He slipped into a T-shirt and his last pair of dry jeans and headed for the kitchen, where he found Kate wearing his old chambray shirt and very likely nothing else. Canadian bacon sizzled while eggs poached in a shallow pan of boiling water. He leaned against the doorjamb and watched contentedly.

She saw him as she reached to take the English muffins from the toaster. "Good morning."

"Morning." His voice rumbled in his chest. "How're you feeling?"

She smiled wickedly. "Like an eighteen-year-old virgin holed up with a rock star in a cheap motel. You?"

"Like an aging rock star holed up with a hot eighteen-year-old."

He bent down and nibbled at her lips, his hand sliding under the hem of the shirt and running over her bare bottom.

"I thought so." He forced a frown. "Does the board of health know you cook bottomless?"

She batted her eyes. "How do you think I pass inspection?"

He gave her ass a quick squeeze. "I rolled over and reached for you, and you were gone."

"I was there the other three times, wasn't I?"

"You sure as hell were." He pulled a stool out and sat at the counter. "Is that what I think it is?"

"Eggs Benedict. I was going to serve you breakfast in bed, but maybe it's good you got up."

"I can go back." He gave her a look he hoped conveyed what would happen if they went back to bed.

She waved her spatula. "Too late. You want to eat before you do your karate thing or after?"

He chuckled. "Tai kwon do. And usually I eat after, but I won't make you wait."

She gave the hollandaise a final stir, arranged the eggs on two plates, and carried them to the dining room table.

"It's cold today," he said as he took a seat. "I was looking for my shirt, but I see you found it."

She smiled coyly and started to unbutton it. "You want it back?"

"Not if you want to eat your breakfast."

She dropped into her seat. "Looks like summer's finally over. It's in the low forties, and it's supposed to dip below freezing tonight." She pressed a bare leg against his. "We can go shopping later if you'd like and get you some warmer clothes."

"What's the point? We'll be heading home soon, right?"

Kate's fork froze in midair. She shook her head and his heart thudded to a stop.

"You said you were sure about us."

"I am." She set the fork down. "But I don't want to go back."

The blissful mood he'd awoken in disappeared along with his appetite. "I thought—"

"You can move here. Live here with me."

"I assumed you'd be coming home."

The look on her face made him afraid of what she might say next.

"You assumed wrong. I'm yours, Billy, but I'm not going back."

The knot in his belly began to loosen. "I guess I didn't think about not going home. But we can't live here. I'm guessing this is Tommy's house. The fact that he's let you stay this long is above and beyond, but I'm sure the money I've been giving him doesn't come anywhere near covering the expenses on this place."

"What are you talking about? What money?"

"C'mon, babe. How do you think you've been living all this time? I've been giving him money every month since you left."

Her eyes grew wide.

"He didn't want it, but I insisted, so he finally took it."

She sighed. "Oh, jeez."

"What?"

"Finish your breakfast. Then we'll talk."

He pushed his plate away. "I'm not hungry anymore."

She pushed it back. "It's okay. It'll just be easier when you don't have food in your mouth."

"That's reassuring."

"Trust me. Finish eating, and we'll talk."

As much as he loved eggs Benedict, they'd already formed a lump in his stomach. Trying to finish the rest wasn't helping. When he'd swallowed all he could choke down, she poured them each another cup of coffee and returned to her seat. She toyed with her spoon, looking several times as if she were about to speak, but would stop and stare out the window.

"Whatever it is, just say it, Katie. Nothing can be as bad as what we've already been through."

"It's not bad." She took a sip of her coffee, then set the cup down on the table and sat up straight. "The house? It's mine. The house, the car, the boats."

"Boats?"

"Not big boats. Little boats. You know, kayaks and stuff."

She was kidding, right? "Oh. Well. Little boats."

She met his sarcasm with a frown.

"I'm not following you."

"Let me start again." She faced him head on as if that might make what she was saying easier to understand. "Joey left me everything."

That made sense. "So this was Joey's house?"

"No, not really."

"Katie."

Her forehead puckered. "I'm not sure how it works, but the house is mine. Apparently, it always was mine, or maybe it belongs to some corporation I own."

His eyebrows might have just skimmed his hairline. "You own a corporation?"

She chewed her lower lip thoughtfully. "I guess. Tommy explained it to me, but it's confusing. A couple of years ago, Joey bought this house for me. He wanted me to have a place of my own."

Still sticking it to me from beyond the grave, huh, Joey? "So you owned a house in Maine and never mentioned it?"

"I didn't know until after he died, and I just couldn't process it at the time. Tom tried to tell me about Joey's will when I first came home from New York, but I didn't want to hear it. Not then. So he let it go. Then after I was in the hospital, I was so angry with Rhiannon —and with you."

Now he was angry with Rhiannon all over again. "I told you I didn't know you were even in the hospital, let alone that you'd been committed."

"I know that now, and I also understand it was the right thing to do. I was a real danger to myself. I wanted to die—"

He set the cup down so heavily the contents sloshed out onto the table. "Katie, please—"

She grabbed his hand and threaded their fingers together. "It's okay. I've been to the bottom. I won't let myself get that low again, I promise, but you have to understand it was bad. Rhiannon did the right thing. Even Tom tried to convince me of that."

She looked nervous and uncomfortable, and he was beginning to feel the same.

"Baby, whatever it is, it's okay. Just say it."

"Will you listen calmly to what I'm going to tell you?"

They had both faced so much pain already, the fact that she was preparing him for more was unsettling. He nodded anyway. "Yeah, sure."

She tucked a strand of hair behind her ear. "I had already decided how I wanted to die."

He tried not to react, but he found himself opening and closing one fist, although he had no idea who he wanted to hit.

"After I dropped you off that Sunday, I came home and I began drinking—a lot. I was trying to decide what I wanted to be buried in. I climbed up into the attic to get my wedding dress. Then I fell down the steps and nearly broke my neck." She paused. "At some point, I cut off all my hair, and I must've passed out sometime after that."

He was holding her hand so tightly it had to be hurting her.

"While I was out, I had a dream—or something. It was so real. I can still see the sunset, hear the birds." She stared out the window as if she could see the scene as she described it. "I was at the top of this cliff where Joey and I used to go hiking. That's where . . ." She cleared her throat. "Joey was there. He was so handsome. And just as sarcastic as ever. He told me it wasn't my time yet, and—oh!" She practically bounced in her chair and the sad smile she'd worn just a second ago blossomed into a grin. "He said you did a good job with the music for the funeral. It was perfect."

He thought his eyes might fall out of his head.

"Don't judge me," she said defiantly, her eyes flashing.

"I'm not. Go on."

"Joey reminded me there was money and a place for me to go. He made me promise to see a doctor." Her eyes locked on his. "I asked him about you, if you were cheating. He told me to listen to my heart, that it would tell me the truth. He was right. It just took me a bit longer to figure it out."

His throat felt thick. He was going to lose it over a fucking dream.

"He gave me a piece of sea glass. It was the most unusual thing I'd ever seen. It was pink and shaped like a heart. Then he reminded me how it had started out as just a piece of broken glass that had been scraped against the ocean floor and battered by the waves, and that's what made it beautiful and more prized than before. He said it was a little miracle from him to me."

Her hand curled open, and she stared down into her palm as if she could still see that piece of glass. "I told him I could feel him—and I could, just like I'm touching you now. He reminded me that he'd always be there for me and that I wasn't alone. He told me again that it wasn't my time. Then I heard Rhiannon calling me, and he was gone." She blinked once, twice. Then her eyes found his. "I woke up in the hospital sometime after that."

He pulled her to her feet and wrapped her in his arms, trying to shake off the memory of how close he'd come to losing her. The thought was still frightening, even with her safely tucked against him. Words failed him.

She rested her cheek against his chest, her arms snaking around his waist.

"It was Joey who convinced me not to do it." Her voice was little more than a whisper. "If he hadn't come to me like that, I might have followed through with my plans as soon as I got out of the hospital. Who knows?"

His arms tightened, and he kissed the top of her head. "Dream or vision, whatever it was, he saved you."

"And the only reason Tom agreed to help me was because I told him about the sea glass heart. Turns out he was with Joey when he found it. It was real. He said Joey was going to give it to me but had left it here. Tom and I looked everywhere, but we never found it."

It was all a little too fantastical for him. Was Joey was some kind of angel watching over Kate? He could live with that.

"I wish I'd been there for you," he said when he could trust his voice.

She placed her hands along the sides of his face. "I know. But we both had a lot of work to do this past year, and if everything we went through finally gives us our happily ever after, I'm okay with that."

"So where does that leave us?"

Her brows dipped. "Together, I hope."

"Absolutely. But you want to live here now?"

She nodded solemnly. "I'm whole again here. I can't go back home and drive past Eileen's house every day, or go to the grocery store and run into the husband or wife or child of someone who died at that meeting, or even drive past the municipal building anymore without being besieged by memories and guilt. If you're going to be on the road, the airport is twenty minutes from here—much better than Jersey. New York's not as close, but you can take a commuter flight. If you give it a chance, I think you'll love it as much as I do. Plus I told you I was working. Actually, I volunteer a few days a week at a soup kitchen. I feel connected here, Billy, like I belong. And I'm doing something to help others, which is important to me."

Her eyes sparkled as her excitement grew. "But I think what I really want is to help children. Kids who are struggling to find a better future, especially those who are being neglected or abused and who need a safe place. I'm not sure how I'll go about it yet, but it's something that really matters to me. I'll finally feel like I'm doing something important."

She told him about Sonja and her son and how she believed that shouting Billy's accomplishments at the fleeing mother had given the woman the courage to leave her husband and seek help.

"You chased a stranger down a dark alley?" That alone made him want to strap her onto the back of the bike and leave town immediately. But he was also proud of her.

"I did!" She was beaming. "And I wasn't scared. I did what I needed to do, and it might have saved someone. Isn't it wonderful?"

Her excitement was contagious. This was the girl he'd fallen in love with, the one who looked at the world as if it was filled with possibilities.

"Oh!" she cried. "If you're not convinced yet, I have to show you one more thing." She grabbed his hand and led him downstairs, where she dashed into the small den off the family room and re-emerged waving a key.

"Follow me." She led him to a locked room at the end of the hall. "Everything in this house was designed for me—except the master bedroom, of course, but we can change that—and I'd really like my four-poster bed. And this room here."

She spoke so fast he was having a hard time keeping up with her, but seeing her so much like her old self made it worthwhile.

"Ta-da!" She unlocked the door and flipped on the lights to reveal a large room, empty except for a box of CDs.

He stepped inside, unsure what he was looking at.

"It's doubly insulated." She pointed to the double wall. "It's meant to be a soundproof recording and rehearsal space."

The concept of the room, as well as its presence in a house created for her, slowly began to sink in. Even long departed from earth, the dude was still way ahead of him.

"Close your mouth," she said teasingly.

His confusion gelled into a full-on grin. "Seriously? Joey? But why?"

She nodded excitedly. "Yep! This room was built for you. For all he did to make you crazy, he understood how much I loved you and that you loved me, and he knew that even if I 'came to my senses . . .'" She wiggled her fingers to create air quotes. "He knew we'd always be together."

He was speechless. Stunned and speechless.

"It needs to be finished, of course. But that was left for you to decide how you wanted it."

He circled the room, already picturing his own recording studio. "I can't believe he'd do this. He hated me."

"No, Billy, I don't think he ever did," she said softly. "Maybe a little in the beginning, and I guess maybe after what you'd told him about Christa, but only because he didn't want me to get hurt."

He glanced over his shoulder and looked at this compassionate, beautiful woman—his wife—standing in the doorway. "Yet that's exactly what I did."

She covered the distance between them. "Yeah, but I hurt you too. I didn't mean to, and I don't believe you meant to hurt me either."

"No. Never."

"It's over. Today is the first day of the rest of our lives and all that happy horseshit." She was grinning again. "I love you, and I'll spend the rest of my life with you. If you really don't want to live here, then we can find another place. But I can't go back to Belleville."

He tried to speak, but she interrupted him again.

"Oh!" She waved her hands madly. "One more thing before you make up your mind. The loft in Tribeca? That's ours too, so when you need to be in the city, we have a home there as well. Tommy's staying there for now while he runs Joey's business—well, my business. God, what the hell was Joey thinking leaving that to me? I've done nothing, and every month I get this ridiculous stipend—which, knowing Tom, probably included the money you were giving him, even though I had no idea." She threw her arms around his neck. "And thank you for that. For still trying to take care of me after what I was putting you through."

It was like watching a tennis match, trying to follow her multiple trains of thought, but he didn't mind. Seeing her happy and excited? He didn't mind at all.

She rested her hands on her hips. "Well? What do you think?"

When he looked into her eyes, it was a wonder his heart didn't bust right out of his chest. He dipped his head and kissed the tip of her nose.

"Katie, I'd live in a shoebox with you. If this is where you want to live, then this is where we'll live." He scooped her up and tossed her over his shoulder, caveman style. Kate giggled and squealed.

"If this is our new home, it looks like we've got lots of rooms we need to break in. I say we start downstairs, and work our way up."

CHAPTER FORTY-SEVEN

Billy would have liked nothing more than to spend the day in bed with Kate making up for lost time, but she was scheduled to work at the resource center. Given the joy she'd expressed at her involvement there, he couldn't ask her to skip it.

While she was gone, he called his parole officer to let him know he was out of the state and to find out how to transfer the remaining fourteen months of his supervision to Cumberland County, Maine. He promised to return the following week for his regular monthly meeting.

With a few hours left to kill, he did his usual workout, took Charlie for a walk, and sketched out some ideas for the recording studio. When he couldn't find anything else to keep him occupied, he stretched out on the living room sofa and promptly fell asleep.

"Hey, Sleeping Beauty. Wake up." Kate stood near his feet, grinning.

He peeked up at her. "I have a better idea. Lie down and nap with me."

"Nope. Get up." Her grin grew wider, and he found himself smiling along with her.

"How was work?"

She nudged him with her knee. "Good. Sit up. I have a surprise for you."

It was then that he noticed her hands were behind her back. Grunting, he pulled himself up. She pivoted, revealing a very familiar silver-blue Thorn custom SoCal solid-body six-string.

He ran his hand along the maple neck. "What the hell?"

She was practically bouncing. "I know you have umpteen guitars, but you don't have any here. I went to that music store in Falmouth. The guy remembered you, of course, so I asked which guitar you liked best, and he said this one. So I bought it."

He whistled. "This isn't a cheap guitar."

"Yeah, but I've never been able to give you anything this special before. I know eventually you'll have all your stuff here, but you probably feel like you're missing an arm or something. There's an amp in the car."

"I feel like a kept man." It was a feeble attempt at a protest.

"You're in luck, then. Go unload that amp while I get changed. Then I'll take you to Freeport so I can buy you something pretty to keep you warm." She stopped bouncing. "Unless you'd rather stay here and play with your new toy."

He waggled his eyebrows. "How about I play with this now and play with you later? Shopping can wait until tomorrow."

THAT EVENING OVER DINNER, Billy told Kate about his plans to fly back to New Jersey on Monday, pack up some of his clothes and equipment, and drive back up Tuesday after meeting with his parole officer.

"I hate to leave you for even one day, let alone two. I don't suppose you'll come with me."

She visibly tensed. "Not yet."

"It's okay, but I'll miss you. I've been without you so long that it's hard to leave again. Going on tour is going to be tough. Maybe you can come with me?" he asked hopefully.

"I thought you didn't want me on tour with you." Her eyes sparkled. "Except for those booty calls."

"Oh, those were booty calls all right, but those were also the times I needed you the most. Those were the days I wanted to cash it in and come home. Seeing you helped me keep going."

"And the last few years, when I was working and couldn't drop what I was doing to fly all over the country?"

"It was hard. The drinking and the drugs got worse, obviously, but that's my fault. No more."

"So what will be different this time?"

"Me, for starters. I'm clean and sober for the first time since I was fourteen. It's my show, my tour, and I call the shots, which includes no drug use at all by anyone—not even pot, no alcohol at the show, and no unauthorized women backstage. It's in everyone's contract. C.J.'s put together a list of AA meetings in every city where we're playing so I can stay on track. I also have my workout and my martial arts training, which helps me control my temper. I think it's a pretty good start."

"It's a great start."

"I know you got your own thing going on here, but if you can come for a little bit, it would mean a lot to me."

"When are you going and where?"

It was hard to contain his smile. "The tour actually starts here in Portland on the twenty-fifth."

"You're kidding! How ironic."

"Not really. I remembered how much you said you loved Maine. When C.J. started planning the tour, I told him to book me here. I was hoping if you were here, maybe you would come."

"With no TV, no radio, no newspaper, I never would've known," she said sadly.

"I think somehow you would've known. If you believe that Joey came to you in a dream to save you, I believe you would've known I was here. And I would've known you were close. In my gut, I would've known."

She set her fork on her plate and linked her fingers with his. "I think you're right."

When she asked where he would be playing, he rattled off the cities he'd be touring over the next two months, playing up each and hoping she'd want to join him.

"Maybe I'll come to the first few gigs and see how it goes."

Before he could answer, the grandfather clock chimed several times. It was 6:52. The face she made was laughable.

"And first thing tomorrow, I'll call someone to come and fix that clock. I promise."

———

THEY SPENT the better part of Wednesday in downtown Freeport and then at the Maine Mall, where they dropped what Kate declared was an obscene amount of money. Considering she'd paid almost four grand for a guitar a day earlier, that was saying something.

With her help, Billy bought enough clothes, shoes, and outerwear that he wouldn't ever need to go back to the house in Jersey if he didn't want to. And he'd insisted on spending an equal amount on her. The first things they bought were pairs of large, dark glasses and a knitted slouch beanie for Billy. With his hair pulled back into a ponytail and tucked into the hat and the collar of his new jacket turned up, he wasn't quite so recognizable. As for Kate, no one would know or care who she was, but it was fun to play along. She draped a scarf over her head and around her neck like an Italian movie star. They held hands and kissed, and to her it felt the way it had when they first met. They could have been mistaken for newlyweds.

They were on the highway heading back to Cumberland when Billy's cell phone rang.

"Maine is hands-free only," she said. "You can't answer that and drive."

"It could be C.J. Would you check?"

She looked at the screen and shoved the phone at him almost as if it had bit her.

Rhiannon.

Billy signaled to pull over. "I haven't talked to her for almost two weeks. I have to take this."

He answered on the fourth ring. "Hey, baby girl. What's up?"

Her daughter's raised voice carried. She was worked up over something.

"I'm sorry. I should've told you I'd be away." He listened, his eyes widening. "I *am* in Maine. How'd you know that?"

Kate felt her own eyes doubling in size.

"Jeez," he continued. "I was just hanging out, jamming. I wouldn't have thought anyone would notice me. Guess I'll have to get better about watching for paparazzi."

He winked at her as she pantomimed, pointing to herself and mouthing questions, asking if Rhiannon knew he was with her. He shook his head.

"I had some things to deal with for the opening of the tour, so I just decided to head up. I've never been here before."

She chewed on a fingernail. He reached over, pulled her hand from her mouth, and held it.

"It was a long ride, but it was fine. I enjoyed it." He frowned. "Of course I wore my helmet." He pointed at Kate, probably blaming her for raising Rhiannon to be as nervous as she was.

"It's beautiful. The weather's turned colder, but it was almost eighty when I got here last week. . . . I'm sure you'd love it. In fact"— he squeezed Kate's hand—"I was thinking of finding a place up here for Thanksgiving. You and Doug can come up with the kids, and Devin. I have a few days off. We can spend some time together."

Panic bloomed in Kate's chest. What if she wasn't ready to face Rhiannon? There was too much at stake. What would she say?

Billy held up his hand. The look he gave her meant he was serious. This was happening. Rhiannon had lowered her voice since the frantic beginning of the call, so Kate could no longer hear her.

"I don't know. Maybe I'll cook." He rolled his eyes. Kate did as well. Then his face changed again. He listened quietly, running his thumb over Kate's hand as he did. "I know, sweetheart, but it'll be okay. Talk to Doug, see what he says. But this is important. I want you to make this happen." He rolled his eyes again and sighed. "I promise. No one expects you to cook. Maybe I'll just have it catered."

He brought Kate's hand to his lips. "I know. No one can cook like your mother. . . . It'll be fine. We'll all be together. It won't be that hard. I'm going to go ahead and make arrangements while I'm here. I'll call you next week and give you all the details. . . . No, I'll be home Monday, but just for a day. . . . Dinner Tuesday?"

When he looked at Kate, she nodded. "Sure. We'll talk then. . . . I love you too."

He ended the call. "She's dreading Thanksgiving."

"Me too."

He reached over the console and slipped an arm around her shoulders. "It'll be good. I promise."

"You're making lots of promises. I hope you can keep them all."

He tapped the end of her nose. "I can."

CHAPTER FORTY-EIGHT

"You know where you're going, right?"

"Yes. And if I get lost, I'll find my way. I'm a big boy."

They sat in front of the Portland Resource Center. It was raining again. Billy wanted to go to an AA meeting, and Kate had to work.

"Sorry. It's just that I got lost a lot when I first got here."

"Babe, you get lost everywhere," he reminded her. "I'll be fine. I'll be back around two."

She gave him a quick kiss, but as she reached for the door, he pulled her back and gave her a much better one, slipping his hand around to the back of her head, his tongue brushing hers. She blinked a few times and sighed when he let go.

"Wow. What was that for?"

"Because I love you, and I want you to remember how much."

"It's going to be hard to chop carrots and celery now."

He grinned, and she melted a little more. "Good."

She was still smiling when she entered the kitchen and humming as she peeled carrots for stew. Although she had no idea what she was doing, she clicked along with Miriam Makeba on the boom box

Samatar kept on the shelf above the stainless steel work surface. She swayed from side to side as she washed the pots in the deep industrial sink.

"Either you are on some very good drugs, or you won the lottery," Samatar said, backing through the kitchen door with a box of donated produce.

"Nope, just happy."

With narrowed eyes, he assessed her closely. "I have never seen you 'just happy.' I'm not sure I have ever seen you smile."

"Really?" She was surprised. "I never smile?"

He tilted his head, still watchful. "Not really. If you did, it didn't reach your eyes. That's not a real smile."

"Is this a real smile?" she asked, beaming.

His gap-toothed smile reached his eyes and then some. "Absolutely."

Returning to her dirty pots, she glanced at the clock over the door. It was almost two. With the colder weather, more people were showing up for hot meals, and lunch had run long again.

"Now you are frowning."

"Sorry. My husband is picking me up at two. I didn't realize it was so late." She reached for another pot.

"Husband?" He looked surprised. "I thought you were not married."

She held up her left hand.

"I knew you wore a ring. I just didn't know there was a husband still connected to it."

"There is."

"Leave the rest." He pointed to the remaining pots. "I will finish as soon as I bring in the other boxes."

"That's okay. I can do it. He won't mind."

"I insist. Do not let the reason you are smiling wait."

That smile grew. "What makes you think that's why I'm smiling?"

He touched his finger to his temple. "I am a smart man. Go. I will see you next week."

She pulled off her apron and blew him a kiss. "Thanks. See you Monday!"

She just needed to pop into Amy's office before she left.

"There you are!" Amy said, coming around the corner. "I was looking for you."

"I'm heading out. I wanted to remind you I'm not working the rest of the week, but I'll be in for the lunch shift Monday."

"That's fine." Amy leaned in and lowered her voice. "Why didn't you tell me Billy McDonald was stopping by?"

"I didn't know he was," she answered, surprised.

"I almost died when he walked in looking for you. I told him you were probably running behind, and he said he didn't mind waiting. The next thing I know, he's down in the activity room with some of the boys."

"Really? How long has he been here?"

"Half an hour, maybe longer. How in the world do you know Billy McDonald? Is he a friend of your husband's?"

"He is my husband."

She shot a happy grin at her astonished boss and slipped down the hall to the other side of the building. From the doorway, she could see Billy helping a boy of about sixteen form a chord on a beat-up Epiphone while several other teenagers watched.

"It's an A minor," Billy said. "Like this. Perfect. Now a G. Then A minor again, then G, and that's the lead in. Play it again."

Kate winced at the strangled chords eked from the overplayed nylon strings.

With his foot, Billy tapped out a beat. "That's right—A minor, G, A minor, G. Again. Good! Play that riff five times, and you have the intro." He spoke to another boy sitting next to him. "You ready to try, Keenan?"

The second boy nodded. The one with the guitar unhooked the strap and handed it to him.

"Sit back. That's it. Now relax your shoulders. Come on, don't be all hunched up. Girls like it when you sit up nice and tall."

A laugh bubbled up and Kate had to cover her mouth.

"I thought you had to go," Samatar said from behind her.

"So did I. If you didn't finish, I can run back there now."

"No, no, it's all done." He leaned in the doorway and saw Billy with the boys. "I think I see who is making you smile. What's he doing?"

"I think he's giving guitar lessons."

Billy spotted her, winked, and went back to the boy with the guitar. "Okay, Keenan. Run through the chords, and next time, I'll teach you and Jason the whole song. What do you say?"

Keenan nodded.

"Me too," said a younger boy.

"I want to be a singer," said one of several girls who had been watching the impromptu lesson.

"So do I," said another. "Like Beyoncé."

"Then you better learn to dance too," Billy said. "You guys practice, and I'll do my best to come back soon."

That got an enthusiastic response.

"Now, Keenan. What do we start with?"

"A minor?"

"Perfect. Go on."

Keenan thrummed out a tune similar to what the first boy had played, but Kate still had no clue what it was. They struggled through it a couple of times until Amy stepped in from the hallway and put a halt to the lessons.

"Mr. McDonald has to go, but I think we owe him a big thank-you for stopping by."

"It was my pleasure." Billy stood, towering over the teenagers gathered around him.

"Are you really coming back?" one of the girls asked.

Kate smiled. Of course it would be one of the girls.

"I'd like that. I'm going out on tour soon, but I'll see what my schedule is like."

"Thank you so much," Amy said as she walked Billy toward the door where Kate waited. "I've never seen them this excited."

"I enjoyed it just as much. I'd like to come back, if that's possible."

Amy seemed stunned. "We'd love that! You'd have to go through all the volunteer background checks, of course, but we'd be thrilled to have you."

He slipped his arm around Kate's shoulder. "That's fine."

"That was wonderful," Kate said when they stepped outside. "Those kids looked so excited. What were you trying to teach them?"

"*Somebody That I Used to Know* by Gotye."

"Seriously?" She laughed. "I would've never guessed."

"Give them time. If they want to learn, they'll get there. Although that guitar is a piece of shit."

"Yeah, even I could tell those strings were either very cheap or very old."

"Both."

"Did you mean what you said? About coming back?"

"Absolutely. Up until last month, I was teaching guitar at the Boys and Girls Club in Andrewsville. I loved it."

Volunteer work had never been his thing. Neither was dealing with people when he didn't have to, for that matter.

"Part of my sentence included a hundred hours of community service. I taught guitar a couple of hours a week. I liked it so much, I added a second day. I finished my hours a while ago, but I was still going when I could."

He folded himself into the car behind the wheel as she slid in on the other side. "Would it bother you if I volunteered? You know my background check is going to show jail time. Depending on how strict they are here, it shouldn't bar me from volunteering. They'll probably require someone from the center be present during the lessons, though. I don't want to do anything to embarrass you."

He looked so eager. How was it possible to love him more than she already did? Yet there it was. Her heart couldn't have been any fuller. She curled her fingers around his.

"Embarrass me? I couldn't be any prouder."

CHAPTER FORTY-NINE

K ate sent Billy off at the airport with the same amount of
emotion afforded someone going off to war—or at the very
least, somewhere longer than three days. After finally bidding him
farewell at the security checkpoint, she called Devin to tell him about
Thanksgiving.

"How's it going?" he asked, following up with a loud yawn.

"It's going well. I just dropped Daddy off at the airport. He's
flying back this morning. He's got an appointment with his parole
officer tomorrow, and he's having dinner at Rhiannon's tomorrow
night."

"Ugh," he murmured.

She smiled. Her daughter had many talents. Cooking wasn't one
of them.

"Is he going to tell her?" he asked.

"Not yet. Actually, he wants you all to come up for Thanksgiving. He told her he's renting a place for the holiday and it's important
that you all come."

"So more lying?"

"Devin." She tried not to sound like she was scolding. "It's easier for me this way. Rhiannon's not likely to get in the car and storm off if she's four hundred miles from home, is she?"

"What makes you think she'd do that, Mom? Don't you think she wants to see you?"

"In some ways, I'm sure she does. In others, she's probably still angry with me."

"Can you blame her?"

Kate fitted her keys into the ignition, leaned back, and closed her eyes. "No. I don't blame her. I don't blame any of you. I want to make this right. I don't need to tell you what this year has been like. We've already had that conversation."

He mumbled something that sounded like agreement. "How's it going with Dad?"

"I think we're going to be okay. It was hard saying goodbye this morning."

"He's coming back?"

"Yeah. He's—" She started to say he was making arrangements to move to Maine, but caught herself. She and Billy hadn't discussed how they would tell their children that they would be staying in Maine. They'd spent the past week reconnecting, and she didn't regret it. Besides, it would be best to tell Devin and Rhiannon at the same time—over Thanksgiving—when they could put up a united front.

Her hesitation wasn't at all about avoiding something potentially uncomfortable.

Yeah. Right.

"He's driving back up on Wednesday," she said.

"So you're coming home after Thanksgiving?"

"I might go with Dad for a bit." *Not a lie, right?*

"I was gonna spend Thanksgiving with Danielle."

"I'd say you're welcome to bring her, but I think it might be kind of stressful. She's welcome to come up on Friday, though."

"We'll see." He yawned again loudly. "What time is it, anyway?"

Thanks to Billy, the clock in the Saab now told the correct time.

"It's almost seven thirty."

Devin groaned. "Jeez, Mom. I didn't have to get up until ten."

"I'm sorry. I've been up since five."

"Yeah, well, you're old."

"Nice. Listen, Dad will tell Rhiannon to call you about Thanksgiving. Will you be coming up with them?"

"Yeah, sure. Why wouldn't I want to ride seven hours in a car with two three-year-olds and my five-foot-tall sister who refuses to sit in the back seat?"

"Be nice. I'm sure she'll let you sit in the front. And if that doesn't work—"

"Kiss up to Doug. I know the drill."

"I love you, sweetie. I have to go to work."

"I love you too. I have to go back to sleep."

She was still smiling fifteen minutes later as she made her way into the center.

"Kate," Amy called, launching herself out of her chair, seemingly prepared to follow Kate down the hall if need be.

"What's up?"

"I want to thank you and your husband for your very generous donation. The kids are going to be thrilled!"

Donation? Billy hadn't said anything about a donation.

"I'm sorry. I'm not following you."

Amy looked confused. "Oh dear. I just assumed it was from the two of you, especially after the other day."

"I don't know what you're talking about."

"Friday afternoon, four new guitars and stands, an electronic tuner, a few dozen sets of strings, a drum kit, and a laptop computer arrived. I assumed it was from you, or at least from your husband."

"It probably is," Kate said, "although he didn't mention it. He did tell me he filled out the volunteer application."

"Yes, yes, I have that. The kids don't know about the instruments yet. We thought it best if he gives everything to them himself.

They've been so diligent about practicing what he taught them, even just that little bit, but they keep asking when he's coming back."

"I just dropped him off at the airport. He'll be back late Wednesday. When I speak with him tonight, I'll find out when he can come back." The pride she was feeling in Billy almost overshadowed the importance of their anonymity, at least for now. "I do have one favor to ask. Could you please keep his coming here quiet? If he's performing, that's one thing, but when he's not . . ."

Amy waved her hands. "I didn't even tell my husband—although trust me, I was tempted."

Kate believed her, but she also had a feeling that Amy knew more about her personal life now than she had a few days ago. That article from the Boston paper was probably online: *The target of a madman's bullets* . . .

She shivered at the reminder as she made her way down the hall to the kitchen. She was safe, strong, and healthy, and she was loved very much. Her life was moving forward in a positive way, and other than a few loose, albeit important, threads, she was the happiest she'd been in a long time.

Life was good, and the past needed to stay where it belonged, in the past.

CHAPTER FIFTY

Billy came in through the mudroom after a grueling nine-hour drive and more than an hour stuck in traffic to find the kitchen transformed into a bakery. Apple pies cooled on the counter along with dozens of giant leaf-shaped cookies frosted in reds, golds, and greens.

Kate wore a dusting of flour on her cheek and a deer-in-the-headlights expression.

"How many people are coming for Thanksgiving?" he asked.

"Just us."

That's what he thought. Without asking, he knew she was stressing over facing Rhiannon, and that was still several weeks away.

"Does everyone get their own pie?"

She shook her head.

"Then what're you doing?"

She blinked.

"You're making yourself crazy, aren't you?" He winced as soon as the word left his mouth. "I didn't mean that the way it sounded."

Kate dragged her hands across the front of her apron, looking sheepish. "No. You're right. I already called Liz. We're seeing her Friday afternoon."

Relieved, he folded her into his arms. "Good idea. I think we should be going regularly—together."

She clung to him. "Thank you. I wanted to ask, but I didn't want you to take it the wrong way."

"Nope. I want to be sure we keep heading in the right direction together."

It was good to feel the tension draining from her body.

"I missed you," she said. "I know it was only a couple of days, and I've been on my own for so long now, but the house seemed empty without you."

He grabbed her ass and squeezed, then gave it a little pat before climbing onto a stool at the counter. Between the scent of all those pies and whatever was simmering on top of the stove, he was practically drooling. "I missed you too—and I missed your cooking. I'm starving."

Kate filled his plate with thick slices of pot roast, a mountain of mashed potatoes, and a heaping spoonful of carrots. His eyes rolled back in his head as he dug into the first decent meal he'd had since before he'd left.

"How'd it go last night?" she asked as she sponged flour off the counter.

"Good."

That wasn't exactly true. Dinner had been awful, meat loaf with no meat, as if there could be such a thing. It had been made from beans, and he'd had a stomach ache all night afterwards. Eating healthy was important, but damn. He had to wonder if Rhiannon created these monstrosities as a way to get out of cooking.

The other thing, which had been even harder to sit through, was their daughter's increasingly negative attitude about her mother. Rhiannon was hurt at her mother's abrupt disappearance. They all were. But he couldn't put all the blame on Kate. In fact, he put very little on her. She'd done what she needed to do, and it was the first time since he'd known her that she'd ever put herself first. Rhiannon had gone to family therapy to deal with some of her issues as well as the guilt of having her mother committed, but it seemed that the longer Kate remained gone, the angrier Rhiannon became.

Thanksgiving couldn't come soon enough.

"How was the meal?"

He chewed thoughtfully. "All I can say is Doug must really love her. I grabbed a burger afterward." He scooped up a forkful of potatoes and dragged it through gravy so thick and rich it could've made even Rhiannon's meat loaf palatable. "You have to wonder how those boys keep growing, not to mention why Doug isn't wasting away. I bet he stops at some fast food place on his way home from work every night."

He glanced up to see Kate staring into the sink at the pile of dirty dishes.

"Babe? What's wrong?"

She didn't look at him. "The twins probably have no idea who I am."

"That's not true." He knew this because he always showed them pictures of her on his phone. They might not recognize her with her shorter hair, but they knew who their Nonna was. "They'll know you, and they're going to be happy to see you."

A silent moment passed. "And Rhiannon?"

"It'll be fine." And it would. He would fix his family—whatever it took.

AFTER KATE WRAPPED her pies and cookies and stashed them in the freezer, she curled up next to Billy on the sofa downstairs and watched the fire while he sipped his coffee. Orange light flickered over his face, and the messy strands of hair that had escaped from his ponytail glowed almost red in the firelight. The tension that had filled her earlier, thinking about Thanksgiving, had faded. She was glad he was home.

"Do you have any idea how truly beautiful you are?" he said.

She pressed her fingers into his ribs and laughed. "I'm not even wearing makeup."

"You don't need makeup. You never did."

"Are you angling for something, Mr. Donaldson? Because if so, chances are you might be in luck."

He brushed his lips across her forehead. "I'm not, actually. But now that you mention it, there is something I've been wanting to talk to you about."

She tucked her legs under her and gave him her full attention.

"I want you to know I have some selfish reasons behind what I'm going to suggest. I just want to be up front about my intentions."

Her heart sank. "You don't want to live here."

"Why would you think that?"

"What's wrong, then?"

"Nothing. I'm just saying part of my suggestion is selfish, or at least a little selfish."

She waited.

"I know how important volunteering is to you, how you've always loved helping people. It's what makes you you. As for me, all this altruism is new, but I get it now. Helping kids, especially the ones with fucked up parents like ours—that's important. You want to help out by volunteering at the resource center, and that's great, but together, I think we can do more, especially where these kids are concerned."

She cupped his cheek. "I know about the guitars. Amy said the kids can't wait for you to come back. And I agree, we can do more. But with you on the road, that's going to be difficult."

"True, at least for the next few months. But that's my life. We both know that, right?"

A worm of apprehension began to grow inside her. He'd said

nothing to cause it, but she was so attuned to things going wrong, to disappointment, she couldn't stop it.

"I can teach a few lessons, even on the road. That's why I sent them the laptop, so we can Skype. But we can do more than that. You said there aren't enough programs for these kids or safe places for them to live if they need them, right?"

"Right."

"Why don't we focus on that?"

Now he'd lost her. Joey had left her a lot of money, but she felt guilty taking any more than she'd needed to survive. And of course, Billy wouldn't have a clue how much she had. Just like she still had no idea how much money they, as a couple, had.

"Can we really afford that?"

"No, not by ourselves, but we can get the ball rolling—in a big way."

"How?"

"I was talking with C.J. on the ride up. I have two concerts here in Portland. Both sold out almost immediately. It's a small venue, just under two thousand seats, but he thinks we could've easily sold out a third night or a much larger venue. So I asked him to find someplace where we can do another concert—Thanksgiving weekend. Something small. We'll charge more for the tickets, make it a little more personal to justify that, and we'll donate all the proceeds."

"I don't understand how any of this is selfish."

"It's selfish because I want you to come with me as much as possible."

"I said I'd come for the first few concerts."

He touched his forehead to hers. "I know, but I want more."

She pulled back, not liking the feeling that he was trying to manipulate her. "So you'll do this one concert if I give up volunteering?"

"No. Not exactly. I could do one or two concerts here a year easily, but no one wants a steady diet of me. What C.J. suggested is that he and I use our connections to get other artists to do the same thing. We could find a regular venue, rent it out, do it up right, and donate the proceeds."

"It sounds like a great idea, but I don't know what it has to do with me. How am I doing anything other than following you?"

"Like I said, C.J. and I would find the talent, but you'd be coordinating the rest of it. Find the venue, arrange for the tickets and sales, public relations, promotion, licenses, even food, if we decide to include that in the evening. It's a lot of work, but most of it can be done on the phone and by email once we have a location and vendors we can depend on. Plus C.J. will help us get it up and running."

That little worm or apprehension was threatening to grow into a full-blown panic attack. "You have an awful lot of faith in me. I'm still not even sure what I'm supposed to do with Joey's business. Tom's not going to want to run it forever."

Billy wrapped his hand around hers. "Be honest. Do you want to run Joey's business? If so, I'm behind you one hundred percent. Whatever you need, you'll have my support. But I want you to do what makes you happy. If that's it, great."

It was a hard question to answer. Not because she didn't know the answer, but because the answer wouldn't be what was expected of her. She shifted uncomfortably, chewed on lip, then let out a great sigh.

"No," she said, feeling relieved to say it out loud, especially when she'd barely acknowledged it to herself. "I don't have a clue what to do, and the thought terrifies me. But I can't let Joey down."

"Babe, do you think he really expected you to take over? Did he ever talk to you at any time over the years and tell you this was what he wanted if he was no longer here? Did he talk about grooming you to manage a stable of stylists, hire designers, operate boutiques? I believe you can do anything you put your mind to, Katie, and if this is what you want, and your heart's in it, there'll be no stopping you. But if it isn't, then you should do your best to find the right people to run it for you and find what makes you happy."

He locked his eyes on hers. "And that includes what I just

proposed. If the thought stresses you out too much, or if it isn't something that will make you happy, then just say no. I can still do one or two concerts here for the kids. C.J. can manage. And as far as coming on the road with me? Yeah, I want you there, but if you don't want to go, that's fine. Just as long as I know where to find you when I come home, I'm good."

This was a different Billy. Selfless, but sincere. The look on his face was intense, and she knew he meant every word. She didn't feel manipulated. She felt relief.

"You really think we can pull this off?" she asked, still concerned about what she'd have to do on her end.

"I do. The first concert we'll do by the seat of our pants, but we've already got a venue, some little art center that can seat up to two hundred people. We'll have a VIP reception after the concert. The record company's already agreed to pick up any costs not donated, and my band has offered to play for nothing. As for the cost of getting them here and putting them up, like I said, my label will cover that. We figure we can make at least twenty grand—and that's just one concert. If we do only five a year, that's a hundred grand, Katie. Think how many kids we could help with that kind of money."

The light in his eyes might have just been a reflection of the flames flickering in the fireplace, but she was pretty sure it was more. Excitement. Maybe even passion. And it was contagious.

"You sure you and C.J. just came up with this today?"

"You'd be amazed what you can accomplish on a nine-hour car ride when you put your mind to it." His thumb grazed her cheek. "Well? What do you think?"

She no longer felt panicked, but she was still a long way from confident. "I've never done anything like this. I wouldn't even know where to begin."

"Think about it. How many PTA fundraisers have you thrown over the years? School dances? Class trips? Boy Scouts, Girl Scouts, not to mention dealing with one hell of a temperamental pain in the ass for twenty-five years. You've been preparing all your life for something like this."

"Yeah, but—"

"And if you still want to volunteer at the resource center, that's your decision. I just don't want to overburden you. Maybe we start out with this one, see how it goes, and plan another for next summer. It's totally up to you."

This was it—a chance to make a real difference. She had no idea if she could pull it off, but if she could—if they could—the end result could be phenomenal.

"Okay. Let's start with this one and then we can decide where we can go from here."

He pulled her onto his lap and nuzzled her neck. "And I mean it, Katie, if it's too much for you, or if you just don't want to go traipsing around the country with me, it's okay. It's been about me for far too long."

"Yeah, but you're due. Your time has finally come."

"No, babe. Our time has finally come."

CHAPTER FIFTY-ONE

There was one condition tied to Kate agreeing to go on the road with Billy for the first couple of weeks: no one other than C.J. could know who she was. Even that made her uncomfortable, but there was no getting around it. The last thing they needed was for Rhiannon to find out she had resurfaced before she and Billy could speak to her face to face.

To keep her identity under wraps, she bought a red wig with a shaggy, layered cut and applied her makeup with a heavy hand. No one would recognize her. She hardly recognized herself.

"C'mon, Katie," Billy called from the front hall. "The limo just pulled up."

"I'm ready," she called, giving her wig one last tug to make sure it was secure before heading toward the foyer.

He groaned when he saw her.

"What? No good?"

"You look beautiful. You just don't look like you."

She poked him in the ribs. "That was the plan."

"That was *your* plan. I just wish I was going with *you*."

"You *are* going with me."

He held up her new fake leopard-print coat so she could slip her arms inside. "It's not the same."

He opened the front door just as C.J. was about to knock.

"Billy!" C.J.'s smile slipped into an odd quirk when he caught a glimpse of Kate standing beside him. He arched an eyebrow. "Reba." He didn't even try to hide the sarcasm.

"C.J., Kate's your date for this evening," Billy said.

"What?" they cried in unison.

Billy grabbed his keys off the table in the foyer. "Sorry, I don't want to be photographed with a strange redhead, and I don't want rumors circulating that I'm cheating on my estranged wife. So you're C.J.'s date."

C.J. plucked a short blond hair from the arm of his impeccably tailored charcoal gray overcoat and mad a face. "That might be a little unusual."

"Why?" Kate asked dryly. "You don't like gingers either?"

"Love them," he answered just as dryly. "Just not on women."

"Oh." How the hell had she not known C.J. was gay?

Billy laughed. "You don't have to make out or hold hands. You can be his assistant or his sister—I don't give a shit—but you can't be my date. Not until Thanksgiving, apparently."

C.J. frowned but appeared willing to do whatever his increasingly successful client asked. "So, assistant, how do I introduce you? I think Reba is a little too on the nose, don't you?"

"Ramona," Kate said. "Ramona Chinchilla Deville."

C.J. gaped at her. "Seriously?"

Billy chuckled and rolled his eyes.

Kate slipped on a pair of large, dark sunglasses.

"Seriously."

KATE WATCHED from a seat in the middle of the auditorium as Billy wore a groove between the massive speakers stacked on either side of the stage and the semicircle of monitors in front of his mic stand. Sound check had been completed earlier, but he'd insisted on running through everything again.

Pushing her cart through the produce section at SuperFresh was more exciting than this. She should've brought a book.

"Take a letter."

She startled at the voice behind her. "What?"

"You're my assistant," C.J. answered, climbing over the row of seats. "Take a letter."

He had to be kidding. "With what?"

"Don't know. This wasn't my idea, remember?" He sat down beside her. "How's it going?"

Kate watched Billy pace across the stage, stop, then call out to someone in the back of the house. "How many times is he gonna listen to every instrument and check every microphone?"

"Until he's satisfied that it's perfect, which it is. But this is a big deal for him."

"I know," she answered, feeling as if she'd just been scolded. "I never sat through this part of it. I never went on the road after the kids were born."

"Wise choice. It's not always the best environment to foster relationships. And as you can see, this part's pretty boring. Then it goes from zero to sixty once the crowd starts to filter in, and then it's fucking mind-blowing." He shifted uncomfortably. "Sorry."

With her index finger, she dragged the glasses down the bridge of her nose and leveled her gaze at him. "You think I never heard that word?"

"No," he laughed nervously. "It's just that Billy has you on this pedestal or something."

"I don't belong on any pedestal, trust me. Just be yourself. I'm sorry to make this weird for you, but until we can sit down and speak with our daughter—"

"It's fine," he said. "Let's just hope word doesn't get out that I was seen cavorting with a woman. I'd hate to give my father any false hope. Although . . ." He gave her another once-over. "Ramona Chin-chilla Deville. With that name, if you were a little taller, I might be able to pass you off as a drag queen."

Kate loved a good sense of sarcasm, and C.J. seemed well equipped in that department. She took his hand and shook it. "Mr. Davenport, I think you and I are gonna get along just fine."

An hour later, stumbling around backstage in her dark glasses, Kate wondered if she'd be mistaken for a drug addict, if not a drag queen, as she scanned the food setup for the dinner break. With Billy in his dressing room, the whole experience felt a little too much like the Bailey Swift video they had worked on not long after they'd first met.

Back then, it had been Billy who'd wanted to keep their relationship under wraps after Christa convinced him it would be bad for his career to have a girlfriend. This time, the secrecy was on her. She was starting to dislike it almost as much as she had the first time.

She was heaping green olives next to a salad of mixed greens, walnuts, and grilled chicken when a familiar voice whispered in her ear.

"Hey, Kate."

She spun around, nearly dropping her plate, to find Denny, Billy's drummer from the Viper days.

"Oh my god. How did you know it was me?"

He chuckled. "I didn't, but you're the only person I know who eats green olives like they're a side dish."

She set the plate down and hugged him. "I didn't know you were back with Billy."

"For a while now. He called me when he was getting ready to record the new album, and I jumped at the chance."

"I can't believe he didn't tell me."

"I'm guessing you two had more important things to talk about than who's banging the skins."

She collected her plate and stepped out of the buffet line. "True."

"Does he know you're here?"

"He knows."

"So it's all good. All is forgiven?" He gave her a tentative smile.

"We have some work to do, but yeah, this is what we both want."

"I'm glad, Kate. He's been lost without you. I knew something was different through these last few rehearsals. I was actually feeling kinda sad, because I thought he was moving on without you. I couldn't believe after all these years you guys were really finished." He looped an arm around her shoulders and pulled her in for a hug. "I'm glad you're not."

"Me too."

"So," he said, fingering a red curl near her cheek, "if he knows you're here, why the disguise? And why are you out here and not in his dressing room?"

She leaned in, cupping her hand to his ear, and explained why she was incognito.

"Ramona, is it?" Denny said loudly. "How'd you like to meet Billy?"

She gaped up at him.

"I'm sure C.J. wouldn't mind parting with you for a few minutes. He's pretty busy right now—last-minute details and all that. Let me introduce you to the boss."

He grabbed her elbow and steered her toward Billy's dressing room.

"What're you doing?" she whispered.

"He's a bundle of nerves about now, and I bet he would love to have his wife with him for moral support."

A giant in a black T-shirt with the word SECURITY emblazoned on the front stepped in their path. He looked as if his day job consisted of holding up suspension bridges.

"No unauthorized women," he barked, glaring at Kate.

Billy sure as hell meant business.

Denny held up the all-access pass hanging around Kate's neck and waved it at the behemoth. "This is C.J.'s assistant. Billy needs to dictate a letter."

Her neck hurt from looking up at him. He was six foot seven if he was an inch.

"She don't look like an assistant." He sized her up, from the top of her bright red head to the tip of her platform heels. He probably also noticed she was holding a salad, piled high with olives, and not a clipboard.

"This is rock 'n' roll, dude. What'd you expect C.J.'s assistant to look like? Besides, it's something to do with payroll." Denny dropped his voice. "I dunno about you, man, but I need my paycheck."

The security guard mulled Denny's words and stepped aside, allowing him to knock.

When Billy opened the door, Denny pulled Kate in front of him. "C.J. asked me to bring Ramona back so you can dictate that letter."

The muscles in Billy's face relaxed into a smile.

Denny stuck out his hand. "Well, Ramona, it was nice meeting you. I'm gonna finish up dinner." He slapped Billy on the shoulder. "See you out there, buddy."

Billy closed the door and locked it behind her. He pulled off her sunglasses and tugged at the wig.

"What're you doing?" She grabbed a fistful of synthetic hair and struggled to keep it in place while olives rained off the plate onto the floor.

"Please take that off," he begged. "You can put it back on when we're done."

"Done with what?"

One final tug, and the wig slipped from her head. He tossed it onto the sofa and ran his fingers through her flat, matted hair. Then he kissed her while pushing her jacket off over her shoulders.

"I'm supposed to be taking a letter," she mumbled into his mouth.

His low chuckle shimmied down her spine, setting off a fire even lower.

"Don't even . . ." She gasped as his teeth sunk into the soft spot between her neck and shoulder.

"I don't drink anymore," he breathed between kisses, his fingers tweaking a nipple as they ran over her breasts. "I don't do drugs." The words tumbled out like a love song. "You are my only addiction." He held her close with one hand while the other fumbled for her zipper. "I need you," he whispered desperately. "I mean it, Katie. I *need* you."

"We're getting too old for this," she said as his hand urgently tugged down his zipper and then traced up her thigh and under her skirt.

"No, we're not." He sighed into her ear as his fingers found their target. "We'll never be too old for this."

KATE TUCKED the last strands of dark hair under the wig while Billy paced small circles around the dressing room. She watched his reflection in the mirror. He was unusually pale, maybe even on the verge of turning green.

"I thought that was supposed to help," she said as he absentmindedly zipped her back into her dress.

"It did. I was worse."

She'd never seen him this nervous before a gig, probably because he'd never been completely sober. She grabbed him by the wrist and led him to the chair in front of the mirror.

"Sit." She picked up his brush and began running it though his hair. "You are so incredibly talented, and all of those people out there came to see you." She smoothed each stroke with the palm of her hand. "You've earned this, and I'm so blessed to be here with you."

She put the brush down, ran her fingers under the thick mane of gold, and gently massaged his scalp and neck, moving to the knotted muscles along the broad expanse of his shoulders. "Ponytail or loose?"

"Loose."

"I agree." She smiled at his reflection "Although you're a heartbreaker either way. I pity those women in the front row who'll be wishing they could take you home tonight."

He snickered. "I think those days are long past."

"No, they're not. Just remember, I'm the only one."

He captured her wrists in his hands. "You've always been the only one." He gave her a slow smile, the sparkle in his eyes returning. "You and the dark-haired woman I'm married to."

There was a knock followed by a rattle of the doorknob.

"Billy?" It was C.J. "Open up."

When Kate opened the door he frowned, then stepped inside quickly and closed it behind him. "If you're gonna make me date her, then you can't steal her from me too." He gave Billy a sour look. "My fucking ego is fragile enough as it is."

After going over some last-minute details with Billy, C.J. addressed Kate. "Come on. I'll show you where you can stand."

"Can you give us a minute?" she asked.

"What the hell?" He glared at her. "Another reason I don't date women. Thirty seconds. Tops!"

After the door closed, she reached up and pulled Billy's face close to hers. "Ignore the hair. Just look into my eyes."

After all his years of standing on a stage, she was surprised to see the tension in Billy's jaw and if not fear, then something close to it, in his eyes.

"You're gonna be great and later, we'll toast your success with sparkling cider." She made her voice extra breathy. "I even bought strawberries."

"Jesus, Kate. How am I supposed to sing, thinking about you and strawberries?"

She gave him a sly look. "Use it to your advantage. I bet you'll sell even more CDs."

CHAPTER FIFTY-TWO

The theater was mostly dark except for a soft blue spot that pooled onto the floor in front of Billy's mic stand. Denny was already at the drums, and the rhythm, bass, and second leads were in place. The buzz of the crowd was palpable.

Kate could feel the electricity. If Billy was nervous, then she was downright petrified. Her heart was thumping so loudly she was certain people in the first few rows could hear it. Her elbow burned with the squeeze he'd given her as he passed, and she covered the spot with her other hand to hold it there.

Standing several feet outside the spotlight, ghostlike, Billy played the first few bars on his acoustic and began to sing. She strained to hear him over the drumming of her heart and prayed her legs wouldn't give out. After a few more bars, the second lead and rhythm guitars joined in, and then the background vocals, softly at first, as Denny kept time on the rim of his snare. Billy swung around, and an almost-invisible roadie seamlessly removed the Martin and strapped his new Thorn into place. Billy completed the circle just as center stage exploded with light and sound.

Kate squealed with excitement. She bounced on the balls of her feet, her fist pressed against her mouth, until the song ended.

"What do you think?" C.J. was beaming.

"He's wonderful," she gushed. "This should've happened years ago."

"I agree," C.J. shouted. "I don't think I've ever worked with anyone more talented, both as a songwriter and as a musician."

She dabbed at her eyes. Thank god for waterproof mascara.

C.J. took her by the elbow. "Come on, I'm going to move you out front."

She pulled back. "What if someone recognizes me?"

"No one will recognize you," he scoffed. "Not in that getup. I'll sit you next to the soundman. No one will pay any attention to you."

Since she was dying to see the concert from the theater like everyone else, she reluctantly agreed.

"Jason." C.J. tapped the sound engineer on the shoulder. "This is Ramona. She's my date. I want her to sit here with you for a while."

Kate pressed her lips together when she saw the look Jason gave C.J. at the word "date." She slipped as quickly as she could into the seat between the two sound engineers in the boxed-in area at the back of the auditorium.

Billy played two more songs before moving to the grand piano that had been wheeled out onstage. He looked out at the crowd and smiled, then took a sip from a bottle of water that had appeared out of nowhere. He scanned the crowd again, and when his gaze settled on the sound booth, Kate knew her seat there wasn't C.J.'s idea.

"Oh, man," Billy drawled. "This is awesome."

The crowd laughed as if he'd said something funny. Some cheered. He played a familiar string of notes, then repeated it.

"As you may know, this is a special night for me." He played the riff again. "This is the beginning of my first solo tour since I began my career some"—he ran his palm over his mouth—"*mmphmm* years ago." He grinned when the audience cheered. "It's been a long time coming."

He spoke slowly, punctuating each silence with the familiar riff. "Sometimes it takes a long time to get it right. I'm living proof of that. Sometimes you need to lose it all before you realize what you had was what you needed, was all you ever wanted, and if you're blessed—like me—you'll realize that before it's too late."

He played more of the riff and added a few more notes.

"I'm going to do something tonight I never do and I'm unlikely to do again, but since you guys are my first . . ." The smile that made her melt was having a similar effect on most of the women in the audience, and they shrieked appreciatively. " . . . my very first . . ." More screams and cheering; much more grinning. " . . . my very first solo concert."

The place was going crazy now. Kate's fingernails were practically embedded into her palms.

"I've been known to screw up over the years—a lot."

A voice from the balcony shouted, "No way, baby!"

Billy laughed. "Oh yeah, big time. And it took me a long time—years, actually—to finally get it right. I want you to remember . . ." He played the familiar refrain. "It's never too late to fix yourself. And if you're really lucky, the people who love you might give you a second, or in my case, a third or a fourth chance. They might be waiting for you when you're done being an ass. And if you're really, really lucky, the woman or the man you love might just be willing to take your sorry ass back." The crowd was going crazy. "That's if you're really lucky."

He played the riff again and launched into the lead of his platinum single, "Without You."

"Katie," he said softly into the mic, his eyes on her, "baby, this one's for you."

The cheers almost drowned him out at first, but the crowd settled down as he began to sing. Eyes glued to his face, Kate could barely breathe. He'd played the song before for her on the guitar, and it was beautiful. But on the piano, in this concert hall, in front of two thousand people, it was mesmerizing. Throughout the theater, people were singing along with the chorus. It was a moment she didn't think she would ever forget.

By the end of the song, there was only one thing left on her mind. As dubious as she'd been about coming with Billy on the road, she wanted nothing more than to toss her red wig into the crowd, march onto that stage, and show him exactly how much she loved him.

CHAPTER FIFTY-THREE

The tour was off to a great start. Billy had already played concerts in Maine, Massachusetts, and Connecticut as well as upstate New York. After that night's gig in the city, they'd be heading to Jersey. From there, Kate couldn't remember where they were going.

The concerts were getting better each night, if that were even possible, and tonight's was no exception. The atmosphere was electric. Kate was standing in her usual spot backstage when she spotted a small group of fashionably clad people in the wings. Record execs, probably, but one of them, a woman, looked disturbingly familiar.

"You've got to be kidding me," she muttered as she recognized the tiny blonde.

She ducked into the shadows and made a beeline for Billy's dressing room. She tore off her red wig and did her best to fluff her flat hair and fix her makeup. When she was satisfied, she returned to her spot backstage and watched Christa Dunphy watch her husband.

When Christa had wandered far enough downstage from her companions, Kate made her move.

"Hello, Christa." Her heart ricocheted against her rib cage. The name was bitter on her tongue, but the unpleasantness strengthened her.

The woman's automatic smile faded, and for a split second, she seemed about to lose some of her self-control. Her response confirmed exactly what Kate suspected—this appearance was not business-related.

Kate smiled warmly, although there was a part of her that wanted to scratch the bitch's eyes out.

"Kate," Christa said, regaining some of her composure. "What a surprise seeing you here."

"Really? I'm actually surprised to see *you* here."

"Don't be ridiculous—Billy and I go way back," Christa purred, at least as much as she was able to over the sound of a rock band shaking the rafters just twenty feet away.

Kate recognized an evil smile when she saw one. She had grown up with one. "So I've heard."

Christa's eyebrows arched and she chuckled. "Oh, I doubt that."

"No, really." Kate rested her hand on Christa's arm, pleased at how clearly unnerved she'd become. Kate leaned closer. "I do. I know all of it. What I don't know is why you keep torturing yourself. It's quite sad, actually."

Christa's eyes narrowed. In case she still didn't believe her, Kate continued.

"My husband has his faults. He made a terrible mistake a long time ago, one he's regretted ever since. He's not perfect—none of us are. But he loves me, and he always has. You want what we have? I suggest you stop chasing other women's husbands and find one of your own. Maybe one closer to your own age."

It was bitchy, but that last comment hit a nerve.

Emboldened, Kate continued. "If you can find a man to love you half as much as my husband loves me, then you'll be a lucky woman. Let it go already. You can't hurt him, and you can't hurt me."

Christa was glowering, but then her lips curled into a wicked smile. She crossed her arms and attempted to stare Kate down. "You expect me to believe he told you about us?"

Kate laughed. "Us? There was never any 'us.' And if you're referring to what happened in a drunken, drugged-out stupor twenty-some years ago, that's not at all what I meant. The mistake I was referring to was ever getting involved with you in the first place. The other thing? That was just stupidity on his part. And as far as you're concerned, well, it was just kinda slutty."

Christa's mouth fell. She struggled for a retort, but Kate didn't give her a chance.

"I think we're done here. It was nice to see you again, Christa, and I do mean that. It gave me the opportunity to get that off my chest, and it feels great. And if I'm being totally honest, I have to add that I hope this is the last time we run into each other. Enjoy the rest of the concert." She gave Christa's arm a little squeeze. "He's just wonderful."

Praying her shaking knees wouldn't give her away, Kate walked to the spot where she knew Billy would exit the stage, while Christa returned to the small cluster of men she had arrived with.

When Billy stepped backstage a short time later, he headed straight toward her. He looked surprised to see her in the area where reporters and those with backstage passes would be congregating.

"Katie! What're you doing out here? Where's Red?"

She gripped a handful of his damp T-shirt. "Kiss me."

"I'm dripping wet," he warned her over the sound of thunderous applause.

"I don't care. Kiss me like you mean it."

"You asked for it."

Grinning, he wrapped his arms around her and bent her over backward as if they were posing for the cover of a romance novel. He kissed her so hard and so long that she staggered when he set her back on her feet.

"How was that?" he asked, his eyes blazing.

"Not bad."

"Not bad?" he growled.

She squealed as he grabbed her again. Dipping her back, he kissed her until she was sure she'd forgotten her own name.

"Everything okay?" he asked after he'd finally come up for air.

"Absolutely."

Holding her against him, he nuzzled her neck. "I love you."

"I know."

While Kate and Billy had been tongue wrestling, it seemed Christa had made her exit. The audience, waiting for an encore, stomped and cheered, and Kate couldn't help imagining they were cheering for her.

This slaying dragons thing? Piece of cake.

BILLY SIGNED his last autograph and ducked into his dressing room for a quick shower.

"Where's Katie?" he asked C.J. as he tugged his shirt over his head.

"Last time I saw her, she was with Denny."

"Everything set for tonight?"

"All ready to go. The key card is in your wallet, and my niece is taking care of everything else."

"Great. Thanks."

C.J. turned to go, but Billy stopped him. "What was Christa Dunphy doing here?"

C.J. raised his hands in resignation. "Look, I'm sorry. I had no idea. She was a plus one for a backstage pass with Tony Steel. I was as surprised to see her as you were."

"Somehow, I doubt that." He stripped off his shirt and tossed it in the corner. "Did Katie see her?"

C.J. nodded, and Billy wanted to punch something. "Sonofabitch."

"Kate disappeared for a few minutes, and the next thing I knew, she had taken off her wig and was standing next to Christa. I saw them talking for a few minutes, and then Kate went and waited for you."

"Did she say anything to you?"

C.J. shook his head. "Honestly? She didn't even seem fazed. Christa was the one who seemed unnerved. She and Tony left before your encore. I thought it was odd, especially since he'd gone to the trouble of getting backstage passes in the first place."

It was odd, since it was so unlike Christa to miss an opportunity to take a shot at him. She must be fuming now that he was finally having some success despite her best efforts to destroy him.

"Go shower. I'll find Kate and send her back."

"Thanks. And C.J.?"

"Yeah?"

"I don't want to see that bitch anywhere near me or Katie again. Understood?"

"I'm sorry."

"I know, but if she shows up as someone else's guest in the future, I want her ass escorted out immediately. And if she won't go willingly, you have security throw her out. You got that?"

"Consider it done."

CHAPTER FIFTY-FOUR

"Where are we?" Kate asked with a yawn, stretching in the back seat of the rented SUV. Billy glanced in the rearview mirror and hoped the buildings whizzing by wouldn't tip her off to their whereabouts.

"We've got a little ways yet. Go back to sleep. I'll wake you when we get there."

She yawned loudly. "I'm okay."

He chuckled. "I can tell."

She unbuckled her seat belt.

"What're you doing?"

"I was going to come up and keep you company. If I'm tired, you must be exhausted."

"I'm fine. I had a cup of coffee during the last interview. I'm wide awake. I promise. Go back to sleep."

"You sure?" She yawned again.

"I am." He reached behind the seat and gave her leg a squeeze. "Trust me."

"All right," she said, her voice disappearing into the pillow she took wherever they went. "Wake me if you want me to drive."

A half hour later, he pulled into a parking lot past the blinking neon sign, past a long row of pickups and economy cars, and parked. He had one moment of self-doubt, then assured himself that regardless of what the place looked like, she would love it. He climbed out and opened the back door. Kate lay with her coat draped over her, snoring softly.

He shook her gently. "Babe? We're here. Wake up."

She lifted her head, straining to focus. "What time is it?"

"Funny how you never wear a watch, but you always want to know what time it is." He helped her sit up. "It's a little after two."

"Where are we? A motel?" She slid out of the back seat and braced herself against the car.

"You seem a little shaky." He closed the door and locked it, then scooped her up in his arms.

"What are you doing? I can walk. You're going to hurt yourself."

"Shh! It's late. People are sleeping."

"Billy!" she whispered loudly. "Put me down!" He kept walking, and when he started for the stairs, she began squirming. "I mean it! You're getting too old for this."

He halted. "You tell me I'm too old again, and I will drop you. On purpose."

"You're probably gonna drop me anyway. Please put me down. I can walk. You're gonna get a hernia."

"Seriously. Be quiet."

He picked his way up the outdoor stairs and turned down a long walkway.

"Where are we?" she asked again, craning her neck.

At the last door, he squatted low enough to slip the key card into the lock. He pushed the door open and stepped inside.

She was silent as she scanned the room. He waited for her reaction. True, the place had changed, but the layout was the same. She looked at the bed, covered with rose petals, then the bathroom, and then at him. There was a champagne bucket on a stand and in it, a bottle was chilling. On the bedside table was a crystal bowl of strawberries, and in the corner, his Martin guitar rested on its stand. She blinked several times, trying to take it all in.

"Well, Chatty Katie, cat got your tongue?"

"This isn't . . . Is it?"

"Is it what?" A smile spread over his face.

"It can't be."

"Can't be what?" he asked, playing dumb.

"Put me down." She wiggled so much that he had to put her down to keep from dropping her. As soon as her feet touched the floor, she darted out onto the balcony and peered down at the parking lot.

"Are we in Bound Brook?"

"Twenty-five years ago tonight, I fell in love with you right in this room." He pressed a soft kiss on her lips. "Happy anniversary."

She kissed him back, then tugged him to the end of the balcony. "Look over there." She pointed. "Just beyond that silver Mercury."

"What about it?"

"That's where I fell in love with you. Lying in a snow bank." She threw her arms around his neck.

"If I could have filled the parking lot with snow, I would have done it."

She snuggled up against him. "And I believe you."

"It's pretty cold," he said, watching his breath curl into the night. "Maybe it will snow after all."

"Wouldn't that be something?"

He led her back into the room.

"Thirsty?" he asked, opening the bottle of sparkling cider.

She nodded. "How'd you do this? You already had the key."

"C.J. helped. This place—it's still a rat trap, so he got all new bedding. And his niece lives nearby. She took care of the finishing touches."

Kate sat down on the edge of the bed, wide awake now, and bounced up and down. "Might be the same mattress."

"I don't care. I wanted to be here with you. In a way, it's like a fresh start. I can't erase any of the bad things, but I can promise to do my best to see that there aren't any more."

He handed her a glass of cider and touched the rim with his own.

"Here's to new beginnings."

BILLY SNATCHED his keys off the dresser and patted his coat pocket. The small box was still there, just as it had been the last two times he'd checked.

They'd slept until well past noon, and after a leisurely breakfast at the Somerset Diner, they spent the rest of the afternoon retracing their steps around the Rutgers campus before heading back to the motel to get ready for dinner.

"Where are we going?" Kate asked as he helped her into her jacket.

"Where do you think?"

She gave him a playful smile. "Pub burger and a wedge salad?"

"Anything for you, babe."

Kildare's Pub had changed over the last twenty-five years. The layout was different, and the section where they sat all those years ago was gone. They took a seat by the stage, which was empty on a Monday night. The jukebox played in the background, but not nearly as loudly as it had the night they'd met.

They were waiting for their burgers, splitting an appetizer of onion rings and sipping unsweetened ice teas, when Christina Perri's "A Thousand Years" came on the jukebox.

"Dance with me," Billy said, holding out his hand.

The restaurant was quiet, the dance floor empty as he lead Kate out onto the floor. They'd danced a thousand times since the night they'd met, but the memories of that first dance were as strong as if it had been just last week. He pulled her close, slipping his fingers beneath the hem of her blouse and trailing them in lazy circles against her lower back. When the song ended, he kissed her as if they were the only two people in the room.

The waitress arrived with their dinner as they returned to their table.

"Perfect timing," Kate said, scooting closer to the table and dropping her napkin into her lap.

As she reached for her burger, he took her hand.

"Do you remember coming here that Sunday night before I brought you back to your dorm?"

"Of course I do. You were flirting with the waitress."

He gave her a sly smile and shook his head. "No, she was flirting with me. Anyway, I asked where you wanted to go eat, and when we decided to come here, you said something about returning to the scene of the crime."

She gave him an apologetic shrug. "I don't really remember."

"Doesn't matter. I thought since we were returning to the scene of the crime—again—it would be a good place to give you this." He pulled the small red leather box out of his pocket and slid it across the table.

She eyed him suspiciously. "What's this?"

"Open it." No matter how hard he struggled to appear nonchalant, he couldn't control the grin spreading across his face.

She flipped open the lid and gasped.

Either somebody had upped the bass on the jukebox, or his heart was beating loud enough for him to hear. "Like it?"

Kate would have never picked out anything like this for herself, but he couldn't help it. Set in platinum, a two-carat diamond nestled between two halos of smaller round diamonds. Two rectangular baguettes sat on either side, surrounded by smaller round diamonds, which encircled the rest of the ring. It had cost him a small fortune, but he didn't care.

"Oh my god." Her voice was barely audible.

"Katie."

She gaped at him. "Oh my god."

"You said that."

"Is it real?"

He laughed and the tightness in his chest began to subside. "Of course it's real. I know it's over the top, but I wanted something to show you and anyone who saw it how much you mean to me, how much I love you."

Her hands were shaking so hard he felt sure she would drop it. He took the box and removed the ring. She held out her left hand, stretching her fingers, and allowed him to slip it into place.

"Oh my god."

He was grinning like a fool, but he couldn't help it. "Since I can't get anything else out of you, I'll assume you like it."

Her eyes were the size of quarters. She lifted her hand and wiggled her fingers, watching the light dance on the multifaceted stones.

"I probably should've waited until you'd finished your hamburger." He took a massive bite of his own. "It's going to get cold."

She nodded in agreement but continued to stare at the ring. When she finally looked up, her eyes glistening.

"This is the most beautiful ring I've ever seen." She leaned across the table and kissed him. She pressed her hand against her heart. "I love it, and I love you."

He watched as she plunked back into her seat and dove into her burger with relish, pausing every now and then to gaze at her finger and flash him a smile.

"When you're done, I'd like to head back to the motel," she said, leaving little more than a couple of bites of her burger and a few lettuce leaves. "Unless, of course, you had something else planned."

"Whatever you want. We can go back to the motel."

She gave him a sly smile. "Good. I'd love to see how this looks on me naked." She gave him a coy smile and batted her eyes.

They couldn't get back to the motel soon enough, as far as he was concerned. "Check, please."

He helped her slip into her coat.

"You know, it's not fair," she said. "I don't have anything for you."

He brushed his lips against her ear. "Weren't you planning on thanking me later?"

She giggled. "Multiple times."

He pulled a hundred-dollar bill from his wallet and tossed it onto the table.

"Then the hell with the check. Let's go."

CHAPTER FIFTY-FIVE

T he flight was vv other than dealing with the overabundance of
luggage Rhiannon had insisted they bring, which was why
Doug had wanted to drive. As usual, he'd been overruled.

"You've been awfully quiet," he said, glancing at his wife as they
sailed up the Maine Turnpike from Portland. "What's wrong?"

Rhiannon looked up from her phone. "What do you mean what's
wrong? These first holidays without someone are always the hardest."
She'd meant to be snarky, but he could hear the underlying pain in
her voice. He also knew her well enough to know she was trying not
to cry.

"She's not dead, you know."

"Might as well be." She turned her head and stared out the
window.

He reached across the console, picked up her hand and squeezed
it. There wasn't much more to say that he hadn't said in the past year.
None of it mattered now. He could say whatever he wanted; he
couldn't fix it.

She let out a long sigh. "I think I know why my dad wants us all together. I think Devin knows something too, although he wouldn't tell me anything."

"What makes you think that?"

"When he called to tell me he was driving up yesterday, he said something like 'Whatever happens, don't freak out.' I asked him what the hell that was supposed to mean. He skirted the question, then said he wasn't sure but he figured Dad wanted us to come up for some reason."

"Maybe your dad just wants to spend the holiday together as a family."

She glared at him as if he were an idiot. It was his turn to sigh. He forged ahead nevertheless.

"You're reading too much into it. It's probably just that it's the holiday and he's got that benefit Saturday, and he wanted his family with him. Nothing more."

"I think . . ."

He could hear the hitch in her breath as she struggled to continue.

"I think he's found someone else."

Shocked, he glanced over in time to see a fat tear roll out from behind her sunglasses. She swiped at it angrily.

"Why would you think that?" He felt almost as disjointed as she seemed.

"C'mon, Doug. It's been a year. Is he supposed to wait forever? Obviously she's moved on. Or worse."

"What do you mean, worse?"

"Worse, like she can't get better. Like there's no helping her. That's possible, you know. Didn't you ever think that? Maybe she's gotten worse and Tom hasn't told us. Who knows? Maybe he's told my dad, and that's what he wants to tell us, that my mother is so out of it she doesn't even know who we are anymore. Or maybe he's found someone new, and he's ready to move on."

She dropped her phone into her Louis Vuitton tote. "Oh god!"

she squeaked. "What if she's there? What if he wants us to meet his new girlfriend?"

New girlfriend? No way. Despite Kate being gone for almost a year, he couldn't imagine Billy giving up. For one thing, he was the most stubborn man Doug had ever known.

"Your father has never been my idea of the perfect husband, but when it comes to your mother . . . I know it's a long time. I guess I've just pictured the two of them on hold somehow."

"Well, people don't stay on hold forever. What would you do?" She twisted in her seat. "If I decided one day I couldn't take it anymore and just disappeared, how long would you wait for me to decide if I wanted to come back?"

To be honest, it wasn't the first time he'd thought about that over the past year.

They had just exited the Maine Turnpike. He drove through the toll booth, then eased the car onto the shoulder and shifted into park. He gently removed her sunglasses and looked into her red-rimmed pale blue eyes. "Forever. I'd wait for you forever, because I love you. And I wouldn't expect any less of your father."

Her face crumpled in on itself. He unbuckled his seat belt and jumped out of the car. Racing around to the other side, he opened Rhiannon's door, reached in, and held her while she cried. He prayed the twins wouldn't wake. When their mother cried, they usually cried as well, and he didn't think he could manage all three of them in tears right now.

But he meant what he'd said. He'd often caught Billy showing the twins Kate's picture and telling them stories about their Nonna, telling them how much she loved them. No way had that man given up.

But still, a year was a long time.

He rocked Rhiannon until the little gasps had faded away.

"You okay now?"

She dug in her purse for a tissue. "I guess I'm as good as I'm gonna be."

"That's pretty amazing, as far as I'm concerned."

She laughed and gave him a gentle shove. "All right, let's not push it."

He climbed back in on his side and buckled up. "We should be there in a few minutes. Are you ready, or do you want me to drive around a little?"

"Nah, let's just get it over with."

CHAPTER FIFTY-SIX

Billy paced in front of the dining room window. His nerves were getting the best of him. It could all go to shit today. Then what?

Devin sat at the table, his long legs stretched out in front of him. Kate was already waiting at Harold's with Charlie.

"It's Rhiannon, Dad," Devin said calmly. "She's gonna freak, but then she'll get over it."

Billy frowned. "I don't want her to freak out at all."

"Yeah, well, good luck with that."

A black minivan made its way to the end of the street and turned into the driveway. Billy gave himself a few seconds to calm his nerves, then he plastered on a smile and followed Devin outside to greet them.

"Daddy, this is beautiful," Rhiannon said as she hopped out of the car and surveyed the expansive lawn rolling down to the ocean. "How'd you find this place?"

"Like it?" He ignored the question and reached into the back seat to unbuckle Dayton. Or Dalton. He still couldn't tell one from the other.

"I love it. Doesn't look very big, though. Is there enough room for all of us?"

"It's a lot bigger than it looks. We're going to put you downstairs. You'll see."

Her head snapped toward him. "We?"

"Devin and I have rooms upstairs, and you, Doug, and the boys can have the whole downstairs." He amped up his smile. "There's a big-screen TV down there."

"Nice save," Devin said, taking the sleeping child from his arms.

"Shut up," he mumbled under his breath, shooting his son a warning glance.

Rhiannon paused halfway up the steps, her head cocked. "Listen to that. Somebody's dog is freaking out. I can hear him all the way over here."

"Just wait," Devin assured her. "You think that's freaking out. You have no idea."

Billy had never been one to discipline the kids. That had been Kate's job, but one more word out of Devin, and he'd make up for lost time. Hopefully, the look he gave his son conveyed that message.

After Rhiannon had changed the boys and put them down to finish their naps in the rented cribs downstairs, Billy gave them an abbreviated tour, excluding the room he and Kate were using, the master bedroom, and the unfinished music room. He finished by leading them into the kitchen and stirring up a Manhattan for Doug and a Cosmo for Rhiannon.

"Daddy," she scolded, "you shouldn't have alcohol in the house. You didn't need to do this for us." In spite of her objections, she downed a healthy swallow.

"Thanks," Doug said, sinking into the leather armchair. "Just what the doctor ordered."

Maybe he should mix up a pitcher of each, just in case.

Rhiannon curled up on the love seat near the fireplace. "I can't get over how nice this is for a rental. It's just spectacular. Look at that view, Doug. Can you imagine getting up every morning and looking at that?"

"The sunrise is pretty amazing," Billy assured her, looking out over the cove.

"When did you get here, Daddy?"

"I was on the road until Sunday," he answered truthfully. Before she could ask anything else, he added, "I'm flying to New Mexico Tuesday morning."

From the dining room, Devin gave him a nod. Kate was on her way.

"I have some cheese and stuff," he said. "Let me get it."

"I'll help you," Rhiannon offered, setting down her drink.

"No!" Billy and Devin cried out at the same time.

"Jeez!" She sat back, startled.

Billy waved her off. "You must be tired, sweetheart. Devin, you keep everyone entertained while I get the snacks."

"Sure." Devin pulled a chair over from the dining room. "So. A priest, a rabbi, and a Native American walk into a bar . . ."

Billy was too nervous to get annoyed. He patted his son on the shoulder and left the room. From the kitchen window, he could see Kate trudging across the lawn. When he opened the front door, she looked pale, and her eyes were wide and fearful.

"Breathe," he whispered.

She sucked in a lungful of air, then slowly exhaled.

He had no idea how this was going to go, but it was too late to rethink it now. He was almost afraid to look at her for fear that if she saw him getting emotional, she'd be right behind him.

"C'mon. It'll be okay." He pressed his lips to the top of her head, then led her through the kitchen and into the dining room, where they stood quietly, his arm around her shoulder.

It was Doug who saw her first. "Oh my god." He leaned forward and set his drink on the coffee table. Then he stood.

Devin stood as well and gave his mother a thumbs-up. Rhiannon had her back to them as she looked over the collection of books in one of the enclosed bookcases.

"Rhiannon," Doug said, softly. "Honey."

She turned toward him, her eyebrows raised. When she saw her mother, she froze. Her mouth opened, but nothing came out. She closed it and looked at Doug again.

Sensing her distress, he moved across the room and put his arm around her. "Look, babe."

Rhiannon blinked several times. Her eyes traveled to Devin, and when she realized that he didn't seem as shocked as she and Doug were, something snapped into place.

"You knew!"

Devin leaned back as if she'd struck him.

"You knew!" Rhiannon cried, louder.

"So!"

Billy cringed. That was clearly not the right thing to say.

"Oh my god!" She whirled toward Doug. "Did you know?"

He looked stunned. "Of course not!"

"Did you all think this would be funny?"

"Jesus Christ, Ree," Devin said. "Nobody was trying to pull anything over on you."

"Easy for you to say, Golden Boy."

"Rhiannon," Billy began.

She jabbed a finger at him. "You're the last one who should say anything. Next to her, of course!" She pointed at Kate.

"Sweetheart," Kate begged.

"Don't, Mom!" she cried, holding her palms toward her mother. "Just don't."

Rhiannon stalked out of the room and down the stairs. A few moments later, they heard the door leading to the side yard slam.

"I'll go," Kate said, moving as if through molasses.

"No, I will." Billy grabbed his jacket. "Devin, look after your mother."

The slamming door had woken the twins, who were now crying.

"I'll go," Doug said, pausing as he headed for the stairs. "It'll be okay, Kate. Just give her a little time."

Devin flopped backward into a chair. "Well, that went about as well as expected."

Billy sighed. "When did you develop such a sharp tongue?"

"C'mon, Dad. I've been biting it for so long I've honed it into a nice, sharp point."

CHAPTER FIFTY-SEVEN

Billy found his daughter standing on the dock. The sun had slipped behind the trees, and the chilled air blowing off the water made it downright cold. He stepped down onto the dock, and it swayed under his weight. Rhiannon lifted her head and, seeing him, frowned. Other than into the water, she had nowhere to go, although she appeared to be weighing her options. So damn headstrong. He wouldn't put anything past her.

He stood beside her, his hands thrust into the pockets of his jeans, and watched a hawk soar above the cove. He could be stubborn too, and if he had to wait her out, he would. And he did, for a little while at least.

"We thought it best to tell you in person," he said finally. "We probably shouldn't have waited this long, but I had to let this happen on your mother's terms. Just the shock of seeing me and dealing with our shit was a lot for your mother to focus on at first."

"What do you mean, 'shock'? Did you just appear out of thin air?"

"Kind of. Devin told me she where she was. And as soon as he did, I came."

"And how did he know?" The familiar tones of sibling rivalry came through loud and clear, only this time, the stakes were much more painful.

"She called him." He could see she was trying not to cry. "Near the end of August."

"August?" She gaped up at him. "You've known since August?"

"No. He came to see her before he went back to school, but she made him promise not to tell anyone. She also promised him she would contact you as soon as she could face you, so don't be mad at him. He was just doing what she asked." He spoke faster, hoping to stem any tantrum or meltdown that might be brewing. "I know you're mad at your mother—and I'm sure me too—but she's been afraid to face you. She's afraid you won't forgive her."

He moved closer. The look she threw him warned him to stay back.

"Your mother loves you, Rhiannon. Believe that or not, she does. I shouldn't have to remind you that she's been through hell. But she's fought her way back. More than anyone, you know how close we came to losing her."

He stared at a leaf floating on the calm surface of the water until he could trust his voice not to break. "She did what she had to do to survive, baby. We can't fault her for that. She believed the only way she could get better was to go away. She meant to leave me permanently, but that was never her intention as far as you and Devin were concerned."

"Why did Devin tell you if he promised not to?"

"I'm not sure. I think he believed we were ready to face each other. I blew up at him for not telling me sooner, but I apologized. I'm still mending fences, baby girl. I hope I don't have to start mending them with you too."

Judging by the set of her jaw, he just might.

"You found out last month, right? When you came up on the bike."

"Yep. As soon as Devin told me, I came. I didn't even pack."

"I guess it worked out. You're still here."

"Yeah, but we've been working hard. I wasn't always a good husband, Rhiannon. I love your mother, but I never deserved her, probably never will. I've just been lucky that she loves me as much as she does and that she's willing to forgive me."

"Forgive you?" She rolled her eyes. "For what? You didn't do anything. She ran off and left you—left all of us. I don't think you're the one who needs to be forgiven."

He looped an arm around her and drew her closer. "You know, baby girl, you have me on a pedestal I don't deserve. You want to know what a good husband looks like? He's up there"—he pointed toward the house—"taking care of his boys and loving his wife. Eating her cooking with hardly a complaint. And honestly, sweetheart, if that isn't love, I don't know what is."

A glimmer of a smile appeared in her eyes, but the frown remained.

"He works his ass off," Billy continued, "and he's patient. He thinks of you and the boys above everything else. You're a lucky young woman. I hope you realize that."

"And you're a great dad," she said, leaning in and wrapping her arms around his waist.

"I'm flattered, but you're wrong." He kissed the top of her head. "But maybe someday. I'm working on it."

KATE WATCHED them from the shore, praying for the right words to find their way to her lips. This was the moment she had looked forward to and dreaded for weeks. Rhiannon's voice had risen a few times as Kate had picked her way down the hill, but now that she was closer, she could no longer make out she and Billy were saying.

Billy spotted her standing just beyond the ramp and winked. He leaned down, said something to Rhiannon, and led her to a pair of Adirondack chairs near the boathouse that had yet to be stowed for the winter. Rhiannon dropped into the first chair, folded her arms tightly across her chest, crossed her legs, and angled herself toward the water and away from Kate.

Kate walked resolutely down to the boathouse. Billy ran his hand along her arm and gave her a lingering squeeze as he passed, then headed up the path, leaving them alone. She gave herself a few seconds to gather her courage and sat in the chair beside her daughter.

The silence was colder than the breeze off the water.

"Are you cold?" A lame question, given everything unsaid between them, but a legitimate one.

"No."

Kate shivered, not sure if it was from the air or her daughter's sharp retort. Other than the lapping of the water and the occasional cry of a seagull, the shoreline was quiet—peaceful even, if not for the tension and anger hanging in the air.

After she summoned every ounce of strength she possessed, she spoke again. "Thank you."

Rhiannon didn't respond, but the frantic back-and-forth swing of her leg slowed.

"You saved my life."

The swinging stopped.

"I didn't understand that at first, but you did. If you hadn't found me and called 911 . . . I don't think I'd be here."

Still refusing to look at her, Rhiannon stared out over the water, her body tense, bristling with nervous energy. Kate pushed on.

"I'm sorry I left the way I did. But it was the only thing that made sense at the time. Running away was the only way I knew to survive."

Obviously, Rhiannon could hear her, but was she even listening?

"It was selfish, and I'm sorry for hurting you all, but I had to do it. I needed to focus on myself. I knew you'd be okay. I just didn't realize it would take me so long to recover—I'm still recovering, actually. But you helped me take the first step. You and Joey."

Rhiannon glanced at her. "Joey?"

Kate peeled a strip of chipped paint off her chair. "He came to me in a dream—or maybe it was a drunken stupor. This is hard for me to say, and it might be hard for you to hear, but I believed I had no right to live when so many people had died. I believed the shooting was my fault. In that state of mind, I had it all planned out . . ."

This was ridiculous. How could she tell her own child that she wanted to die?

The grimace that crossed Rhiannon's lovely features told Kate she already knew.

"Joey told me it wasn't my time and it wasn't my fault," she said.

Rhiannon twisted her multi-carat diamond engagement and wedding rings on her perfectly manicured finger.

"Then he gave me—" No, that wasn't right. It was a dream. Joey hadn't really given her anything, no matter how real it had seemed. "Anyway, the next thing I knew, I heard you calling. I guess that's when you found me."

"I guess."

She touched Rhiannon's arm but pulled back when she flinched. It hurt as much as if Rhiannon had slapped her. "I'm sorry you had to find me that way, but I'm not sorry you found me."

It took a little while for Rhiannon to speak, but when she did, she didn't hold back.

"Why'd you cut me off? You wouldn't even let me visit at the hospital. Do you know how embarrassing that was to show up the next day and be told you wouldn't see me?" The hurt in her voice shifted into anger. "How would you've felt if your mother had done that to you? Just cut you off as if you didn't matter?"

Kate's mouth went dry. The thought that she might have hurt her children as much as her mother had hurt her was staggering.

"Yeah, I didn't think so." Rhiannon pushed herself from the chair and glared down at Kate. "And then to make it worse, after all this time, you still can't be bothered with me. You called Devin. Okay, I get it. He was always the favorite. But a couple of days, a week or two later, you still couldn't be bothered to tell me you were even alive.

Here you and Dad are shacking up, and fuck me, I'm still wondering if my mother's sitting in some institution drooling all over herself. I guess it didn't occur to either of you to bother telling me, as long as Golden Boy knew. That's all that matters!"

Kate shook her head. "I thought it would be easier this way."

"For who?" Rhiannon yelled. "You? It sure as hell wasn't easier for me!"

Rhiannon started toward the path. Kate jumped up and reached for her, but Rhiannon stepped aside before she could touch her.

"Don't!" She raised her hands. "Leave me alone. You're good at that. Just keep doing what you've been doing."

She disappeared up the path toward the house.

Kate slumped into the chair. Up the hill, a door slammed. She heard shouting. Rhiannon and Devin, most likely. She should go after her, but she couldn't bring herself to stand up. The sun had dropped, leaving her completely in the shadows. Where she should have stayed.

A squirrel chattered angrily and darted over the roof of the boathouse. The crack of dead branches signaled someone coming down the path. Billy dropped into the empty chair beside her.

"I'm sorry." She wiped a tear from her cheek with the back of her hand. "We should've told her sooner."

"No." He held out his hand. "We needed to work on us first. That was most important. Those two up there . . ." He pointed overhead toward the house, where loud voices could still be heard. "They're adults. They'll survive, and they'll forgive us—eventually. You and me, we're the priority here. We did what we needed to do. I'm not sorry."

Kate clasped his hand. "I expect to hear glass breaking any second."

"That's fine. I know where we keep the broom."

CHAPTER FIFTY-EIGHT

"No," Doug said, trying to remain calm. He followed his wife into the guest room.

"Excuse me?" Rhiannon asked, looking incredulous that after what she'd just been through with her mother and then her brother, he would dare refuse her.

"I said no. We're not leaving. You're going to stay here and work this out with your family."

"I am not! I'm leaving. If you want to stay, then you can damn well stay, but I'm going."

"No, you're not. You're staying."

"Who the fuck do you think you're talking to?"

"I'm talking to you, Rhiannon, and don't use that tone with me or that language." His voice remained low, but he meant every word. "I'm your husband. I deserve to be treated with the same respect I give you."

Her mouth opened and he was certain a sharp retort hung on the tip of her tongue, but at the last second, she snapped it shut. She returned to the suitcase sitting open on the bed and began emptying the drawers she'd filled less than an hour ago.

There was a sharp rap on the door. Doug pulled it open.

"Dinner's ready," Devin said. "The boys are already eating, if you want to go up and join them."

Doug looked at Rhiannon, who kept her back to both of them, and tilted his head in her direction: *What about her?*

"Rhiannon," Devin said. When she looked up, he tossed her jacket to her. "You have five minutes to get ready, then you and I are going out to eat."

She glared at him as if he'd lost his mind. Doug wondered if maybe she was right.

"I'm not going anywhere with you. I'm going home."

Devin leaned against the doorjamb, his arms folded. "You can go home if you want, but not until you listen to what I have to say. Bring your suitcase. I'll even drive you to the airport. But not until we talk."

"Fine." She angrily tossed the rest of her things into her designer luggage, then zipped it shut. She glared as she pushed past him, but not before giving Doug a look just as evil. "I need to get my things from the bathroom."

When she was gone, Doug sank down onto the bed.

"You really think you can make her listen?"

"Dunno. She's stubborn and pigheaded, but I'm gonna try."

"Yeah, well, good luck with that. She had a meltdown on the way here because she was convinced your dad was going to tell us he'd found someone else, so now she flips out because the exact opposite has happened."

Doug toyed with the strap on Rhiannon's suitcase. "She's my wife, and I love her, but god knows if I'll ever understand her."

RHIANNON FINISHED PACKING. Doug had gone up to dinner, and Devin was nowhere to be found. Figures. She lugged the heavy suitcases up the stairs, grunting loudly. Hours at the gym each week more than enabled her to carry her bags, but the fact that no one bothered to help her pissed her off. She dropped the bags in the foyer with a crash and crossed through the kitchen to kiss the twins good-bye, ignoring her parents and her husband. Traitorous bastard.

Devin stood at the window, looking out into the soft dusk that had fallen since she had stormed inside. The horizon was stained with pink, purple, and indigo, and if she weren't in such a hurry to leave, she might have wanted to slow down to appreciate it. No matter. She was leaving, and if having to listen to Devin for an hour before he would take her to the airport was the price she had to pay, then so be it. And if he thought she was paying for dinner, he was in for a rude awakening. The aroma of vegetarian chili made her mouth water. She was starving. Squares of cornbread beckoned from a covered basket on the table, but she wouldn't give her mother the satisfaction of taking one, knowing she'd probably made them because they were one of Rhiannon's favorites.

She dropped kisses on the two little blond heads. "Mommy's got to go, but you be good for Daddy, okay?"

"Look, Mommy," Dayton pointed a chubby finger in her mother's direction. "It's Nonna."

She cupped his cheek. "Yes, sweetie. You be good for Nonna and Poppy too. Okay?" Her voice cracked. Damn it. With a bit of effort, she pulled herself together and addressed her brother.

"I'm ready. Let's go."

Devin didn't budge. The bastard just raised his eyebrows as if pointing out that she wasn't done.

She pursed her lips and stood her ground. As far as she was concerned, there was no one else she needed to speak to. And if he still didn't believe that, she stalked out of the dining room and into the foyer, where she struggled excessively with her luggage.

Devin grabbed his jacket and followed.

"Don't wait up," he called over his shoulder, pissing her off even more. "This might take a while."

CHAPTER FIFTY-NINE

They drove in silence to a little tavern in Freeport. Devin ordered a Shipyard ale for himself and a cosmopolitan for Rhiannon.

"I'll have the beer," she snapped. She'd be damned if he would order for her. She wasn't really a fan of beer, but it was the first thing that popped into her head.

The waitress gave her a quick smile, then hastily retreated.

"Well?" She folded her arms and pressed herself into the back of the wooden booth. "Start talking. When we're done, you're taking me to the airport. I have a plane to catch."

He lay the salt shaker on its side and gave it a spin. "You don't even know if there's a plane heading back to Jersey tonight."

"I don't care. I'll sit in the airport all night if I have to."

He shook his head and kept spinning the salt shaker. She snatched it up and slammed it next to its counterpart, then gave him a look to let him know she wasn't in the mood for his childishness, in case he was too dense to have figured that out.

The waitress brought their drinks. Rhiannon grabbed hers and took a cautious sip. Not bad, for beer. When Devin ordered appetizers of mussels in garlic, shallots, and white wine, and two steamed lobsters, she didn't argue. She was in Maine; might as well eat a lobster while she was here, especially since it would be her only chance.

Thanks to the beer on an empty stomach, she began to unclench. Devin ordered a second round, and she kept her mouth shut. When the mussels arrived, she tore off a hunk of crusty bread and dipped it into the garlicky broth. Fuck carbs.

She took a bite and groaned. God, this was good. She closed her eyes and swallowed. She really needed to learn how to cook.

Devin grinned, the fucker. He was probably thinking he'd somehow won. It made her angry all over again.

"You better start talking." She tapped on the face of the David Yurman watch Doug had given her last month for her birthday.

"You better start listening." He sucked the meat from a mussel, tossed the shell into an empty bowl, picked up another mussel, and launched into his lecture. "When Evelyn found out she was pregnant with Mom, she wanted an abortion, but Arthur stopped her."

Rhiannon stopped chewing. How odd it was to refer to their grandparents by their first names. They hadn't really known either of them. She had been two when Arthur died. She'd seen her grandmother a handful of times after that, but there was no particular memory that stuck with her. Evelyn had died a few years after he did. As for her father's parents, she knew nothing.

"Who told you that?" She pushed a soggy mass of bread to one side of her mouth, afraid to swallow for fear it would get caught in her throat.

"Dad did, a few months ago. Sometimes I think he needed to talk about Mom, to keep her close. Other times, I think he wanted me to understand some of the reasons she might have left."

A small snort escaped.

The look he gave her was positively ugly. "Why don't you reserve your judgment until I finish talking, okay?"

She was about to snap back, but she realized she had no idea where they were, and she still needed a ride to the airport. She picked up her beer. "I'm listening."

He took a long swallow of his own beer. "Not too long after they met, Mom came across one of her mother's journals. In it, Evelyn had written that she didn't want to be pregnant and had never wanted a child. Arthur talked her out of the abortion, which was illegal at the time, and promised if she still didn't want the baby after it was born, he would agree to put it up for adoption. Good old Grandma never changed her mind but was too concerned about how it would look to give her own child up for adoption, so they kept her. But she never forgave Arthur, from what Dad says. He says Mom grew up feeling unloved and unwanted, believing it was her fault, that she just wasn't good enough."

A random image of her mother popped into her head; singing at top of her lungs, curlers in her hair, driving a vanload of cheerleaders to Cherry Hill for a competition at five o'clock in the morning.

"She'd only known Dad a few weeks when she found that journal, but she still called him. He came and got her that night. The rest, as they say, is history."

"Did she ever confront her mother?"

It was Devin's turn to snort. "No, but she did take the journal. She showed it to Dad right before you were born. He told me he tossed it in the incinerator. That night, they went to a tattoo parlor."

Her dad was covered in tattoos—his back, his chest, his arms. As a little girl, she'd sit on his lap and point, and he would tell her the story behind each one. But there was one in particular on his rib cage he'd told her was his favorite.

She recited it as if she were reading it off his body. "'My precious Katie. Always wanted. Always loved. Always adored. Always forever.'"

That lousy lump of bread had turned into a rock in her stomach.

Devin nodded. "Eat." He motioned to the mussels. "They get chewy if you let them get cold."

But she couldn't. Her mother's face swam before her—the expression she'd had right after Rhiannon had demanded how she would feel if her mother had turned her back on her; how her mother hadn't been able to answer.

She slid out of the booth. "Excuse me. I'll be right back."

In the bathroom, she leaned against the wall, willing the nausea to pass. When she felt she could manage, she stood before the mirror. Blond and blue-eyed like her father, with the same temperament, it had been her mother who'd raised them. Her father was gone for weeks at a time, but her mother had always been there, hovering, a helicopter parent before her time. It had driven Rhiannon crazy.

Had she been that way because her own parents hadn't cared at all? The nausea threatened to return.

She slowly made her way back to the table.

"You okay?" Devin asked.

"I guess." She finished her beer and frowned at the empty glass. "Maybe I need something stronger."

Admonishing her not to mix her drinks—as if she didn't know—he signaled for the waitress and ordered another round.

"I don't know why Mom called me. Maybe she just thought it would be easiest to start with me."

Of course he was right, but it didn't make her feel any better.

"She was still pretty frail-looking when I got here. But she looked a hell of a lot better than the last time we saw her. She told me she'd been having one of those recurring dreams with some kind of monster. She thought some part of it was her mother and the other part was Sedge Stevens, the guy who shot all those—"

Her head snapped up. "I know who Sedge Stevens is, Dev. Give me a little credit, will you?"

"I'm just saying. Chill." He took a swig from the freshly filled mug.

"The night she called me, she said she woke up feeling like she'd won. She might not have called if she hadn't had that dream or hadn't been half asleep. Who knows?"

"Why didn't she call Dad?"

Devin fidgeted with his napkin, tearing it into long strips. Then he crumpled them all into a wad and tossed it into the center of the table.

"Because, Ree, I know you don't want to hear this, but Dad cheated on Mom. She was hurt, and as far as she was concerned, it was over."

"You're right. I don't believe it." She jutted out her chin, but his words were like a punch to the gut.

Devin shrugged. "Ask him. When he told me he thought that might be part of the reason Mom left, I hated him for it. He swears it was just once. Turns out it was the night I was born, the night he won his Grammy." He reached for the balled-up paper napkin and pinched it between his fingers. "Did you know Mom almost died that night? Both of us, actually. They were cutting me out of her before she was even under anesthesia."

"Oh god," she whispered.

"He also told me he refused to have any more kids after that. Mom wanted a big family, but Dad refused. He had a vasectomy without even telling her. When she found out, he said she didn't talk to him for a week, but he didn't care. He refused to risk losing her with another pregnancy."

It all sounded so dire. Living without her mother this past year had been difficult, but she couldn't imagine having to grow up without her: No one to make doll clothes or play dress-up. No one to drive her to ballet, voice, and cheerleading practice or sit in the audience or the stands at every performance, every game. No one to lead her Girl Scout troop. No one to bake two hundred cookies to hand out to her classmates when she ran for student council president or homecoming queen. No one to cry when she walked out of the dressing room in her wedding gown and tell her she would be the most beautiful bride in the world.

No one to pick up off the floor unconscious in her own wedding gown, her beautiful hair lying in handfuls on the bathroom floor.

Tears pricked the backs of her eyes, but she refused to let them fall.

Devin kept talking. "And while Mom had it bad growing up, Dad had it a lot worse, I think. Maybe someday he'll tell you about it. He's shared a lot of things with me over the past few months. It hasn't been easy to hear, trust me, but it's helped me understand him and, eventually, forgive him."

He drained the rest of his beer and motioned for the waitress.

"I gotta tell you, Ree. It's amazing either of them turned out as good as they did, because their childhoods sucked. Despite that, look at us. We turned out just fine. You may think Dad was the best, but he wasn't, and if you really think about it, you have to agree. He was never around, and he left everything to Mom. She was a mother and a father to both of us. Now that I know Dad better, I can forgive him. Yeah, this past year sucked, but you need to remember what Mom did for us and move on. You need to forgive her."

The waitress finally showed up with the lobsters and two more glasses of beer.

"Why didn't anyone bother to tell me anything?" she croaked. Her throat was dry, despite the half gallon of beer she'd downed. "How come you know all this?"

He toyed with the red lobster cracker next to his plate. "Dunno. I asked? I listened? I didn't judge? I don't really know. What I do know is that she left us in order to survive. Give her a chance. You'll see that not only did she survive, she's stronger. So is Dad. They're different—new and improved. There's something about the both of them you'll have to see yourself. If you leave now, you're only going to be mad at yourself in the end. And you'll hurt Mom."

She rolled her eyes. "Hmph."

He waved her off. "I know she's hurt you. She hurt all of us, but she didn't mean to. And hasn't she been hurt enough? Uncle Joey's death was the worst thing she'd ever been through, and then a few weeks later, her world got completely ripped apart. All this on top of finding out that the one person she could count on other than Uncle

Joey had betrayed her. Who wouldn't shut down? She tried to hang in there—you know that. But she couldn't. So she did what she had to. It's as simple as that."

He cracked open a claw, so she did the same. Forgetting all the drama for just one moment, she pulled a piece of tender white meat from her lobster, dipped it in the butter, and popped it into her mouth. She closed her eyes and savored it, remembering just how good butter tasted.

When she opened her eyes, her brother was watching her.

She swirled another piece of lobster in the butter-filled ramekin. "I'll try. But I'm still hurt."

"So am I. But we can move past this. I promise."

IT WAS past midnight when Rhiannon climbed into bed next to Doug. She was drunk, but she managed to keep quiet right up until the moment she stubbed her toe on the corner of the nightstand. She muttered a curse, then clapped her hand over her mouth. The twins snored softly, but Doug was silent.

She slipped under the covers, and he looped his arm around her waist and pulled her against his chest.

"Welcome back," he whispered into her hair.

She grunted her acknowledgment.

"You okay?"

"I'm drunk." She muffled a burp. "I'm not sure if I'm okay or not."

"You're here. That's a start."

RHIANNON WOKE to an empty bed and two empty cribs. Footsteps pounded overhead. Small ones, running, and loud ones, chasing, followed by the sweet sounds of her boys' laughter. If her head hadn't been throbbing so badly, she might have smiled. She rolled over and buried her head beneath her pillow. Ugh, she hated hangovers.

What the hell had she been thinking? Four beers? Six hundred calories. And then all that butter. How the hell was she going to eat turkey and stuffing? She dragged herself upright. Maybe she should go for a run. The little silver clock on the nightstand said 1:17.

Holy shit! How the hell had she slept so late?

She threw off the covers and searched for her watch: 10:08. She squinted at the clock; the second hand wasn't moving. *Jeez, Mom.* Her mother and clocks were like oil and water.

She dug through her suitcase until she found her Lululemon running tights and jacket and got dressed. She laced up her sneakers, praying there was coffee and aspirin readily available.

With more effort than normally required, she hoisted herself up the stairs and followed the aroma of roasting turkey. She rarely ate meat. Today she would make an exception.

She found her mother in the kitchen rinsing cranberries.

"Morning," Rhiannon mumbled.

"Morning. How did you sleep?"

"Good." It was an honest answer, despite waking up with a hangover. "Is there coffee?"

"I can make a fresh pot if you'd like, or you can use the Keurig if you don't want to wait."

"Keurig."

"There's aspirin in the cabinet next to the refrigerator, and there's a mug for you by the sugar bowl."

Rhiannon slipped a K-cup into the Keurig and set the mug in place. She cleared her throat. "Is there anything you'd like me to do before I go run?"

The smile her mother gave her was tentative but genuine. "No, we're all set. Devin's in his room. I think he wants to go for a run, but he's waiting for you. Daddy took Doug and the twins to show them the boats in the marina."

Rhiannon reached for the half and half. Why not? Her diet was shot to hell anyway. She watched her mother bustle around the kitchen. Other than the sound of soft jazz coming from the other room, the house was quiet. Too quiet.

"Mom?" she asked hesitantly. "Did Charlie die?"

"Charlie? Oh, no. He's with Daddy and the boys. He was over at the neighbors' yesterday until everyone could get settled."

"So has he calmed down any?"

Her mother laughed, but the sound was thin, tenuous. "Hardly. Although he is better behaved when your father's around."

Rhiannon felt a pang of guilt. Her mother seemed so nervous, as if she were weighing every word before she spoke. She was trying, but it was hard. If Devin hadn't gotten her drunk last night and told her all of their parents' deep, dark secrets, she'd be home by now. Home, and probably feeling guilty.

Her mother pulled her hands from the sink, and a sparkle caught Rhiannon's eye. "Holy shit!" She launched herself across the kitchen and grabbed her mother's hand. "Wow!"

A smile spread across her mother's face—a real one, this time. "Do you like it? Daddy gave it to me a couple of weeks ago. He took me back to the motel where we—kind of where we, um. It was our anniversary. Sort of."

Rhiannon laughed. Some of the tension from earlier eased. "I was born five months after you got married. I figured out a long time ago you weren't a virgin."

Her mother was actually blushing. "No, not really."

"It's beautiful." As her mother continued to beam at the ring, she felt her heart give a little.

"Your father was afraid I wouldn't like it, since it's so over the top, but I love it."

"You know me," she gushed. "Big fan of over the top. I guess I get that from him."

Her mother wiped her hands on a dish towel. "Do you want some breakfast?"

Rhiannon shook her head. "I'm still full from last night. I ate a whole lobster and about a pound of butter. I need to go run it off or I won't be able to eat dinner."

Devin strolled in, pulling on a knit cap and gloves. "About time you got up. You ready?"

"I need coffee first."

"I've been waiting an hour and a half. You can have coffee when you get back. There are no bathrooms where we're going, so no coffee."

"Devin," she growled.

"Now! Let's go."

With a longing glance at her unfilled mug, she followed him into the foyer.

He opened the door and looked back at their mother. "Be back in a bit."

She wasn't positive, but she was pretty sure the brat winked.

CHAPTER SIXTY

Thanksgiving dinner went well, Kate thought, happy to have been able to use the dining room table and the extensions. Ten months ago, she had believed she would never have that opportunity again. The twins were downstairs watching Nick Jr. Billy was stoking the fire in the living room, while Doug savored a glass of fine port and Kate sipped decaf. Devin and Rhiannon, still fighting the remnants of a hangover, continued to rehydrate with water.

Billy perched on the arm of the leather chair beside her and slipped his arm around her shoulders. Despite the underlying tension between Rhiannon and just about everyone, especially Kate, there were things that needed to be said.

She cleared her throat. "Since we're all here, there are a few things your father and I need to discuss with you." The weight of Billy's hand on her back was comforting. While there was only one thing really to be nervous about, it helped to know he had her back —literally.

"When Uncle Joey died, he left me everything: the business, his property, his bank accounts, all of it. I knew he was successful, but I didn't have a clue as to how successful." She glanced up at Billy. "Maybe I should back up a bit."

He nodded.

"About two years before he died, Joey bought this house and had it renovated and decorated for me, right down to the books on the shelves. It was a gift he wanted me to have, but since he knew I would refuse it, he was a bit secretive about it. Seems I have a bad habit of signing what people tell me to sign without reading the fine print—or any of the print, actually. Joey said Tommy had papers for me to sign with regard to the business, which we all know I had some stock in. I signed what he gave me without a second thought."

Tom or Joey would never have handed her anything that would have brought her harm, but that didn't stop Doug from looking ready to comment. She cut him off before he could say a word. "This is my house. It's paid for, and the taxes and maintenance are covered under some type of trust that's too legal and boring for anyone but Doug." She smiled at her son-in-law. "And before you ask, I have a copy of the documents for you to dissect to your heart's content. I promise."

Doug's expression gave away nothing, but she knew he'd want to look sooner rather than later.

"After Joey died, Tommy tried to tell me about the house and the will, but I wasn't interested in any of it, and he didn't push me. He's been taking care of everything, even though he was hurting as much as I was. More, actually."

"So this house is yours?" Devin asked. "Free and clear?"

"Yes. It wasn't left to me in the will. It was already mine."

"What are you going to do with it?" Rhiannon asked.

"We're going to live in it," Billy answered. "We've discussed it, and this is where we want to live."

The tick of the grandfather clock echoed in the dining room, and the sound of the twins' laughter downstairs seemed loud in the awkward silence.

"What? Why?" Devin lurched forward. "I thought you'd be coming home now."

Rhiannon didn't say anything. She sat quietly, looking gobsmacked.

"I know this is a lot all at once, especially for Rhiannon, and I'm sorry," Kate said. "But I can't go back to Belleville. I have a lot of wonderful memories there. Unfortunately, there are bad memories too. It's too much for me. Please try to understand."

"I get it." Rhiannon addressed Devin. "Think about it. Do you ever walk into the music room without imagining Daddy on the floor? I can't go upstairs without picturing—" She glanced at Kate. "I get it."

"What are you going to do with the house?" Devin asked.

"Sell it, I guess," Kate said, looking at Billy. "We don't have to do it right away, though. Not until you're finished with grad school."

She slid to the edge of her seat. "Which brings me to the rest of our little family meeting."

She focused on the anxious faces of her children.

"Although Joey left everything to me, Tommy has shared with me some suggestions on how Joey wanted things managed. Surprise, surprise."

She smiled. Though Joey might be gone, no one had forgotten his larger-than-life personality or the way he loved to take charge.

"Devin, Joey knew how much you enjoyed working with children, especially troubled kids. He wanted you to have enough money to finish grad school and even get your PhD in child psychology if you want. Tom tells me that would've been your graduation gift. The money is there for you if you want it."

Devin seemed too shocked to say anything, but she was almost certain he would go for a doctorate once he'd thought it over. She hoped he would.

"Rhiannon, what Joey wanted for you might be a bit more difficult, but it's doable, providing you get the support you need at home."

Rhiannon looked at Doug, then back at her mother.

"He always hoped that someday you'd work with him. We all know he didn't hide those feelings when you announced you were getting married while you were still in school."

Rhiannon laughed. "No, he did not."

"It's not too late," Kate said. "He hoped you'd go back to school eventually—well, not just to school, but to FIT for a master's in fashion management. You'll have to go to work with Tom for a couple of years before you can get into the program, but eventually, if all goes well, Joey believed—and your father, Tommy, and I believe as well—that one day you might be able to run the business."

Rhiannon's eyes were wide as saucers. "Me?"

"Yes, you."

"Holy shit," Devin muttered under his breath, which earned him dirty looks from his mother, father, and sister.

Doug, however, seemed to concur with Devin's assessment. "How?"

"We have the loft in Tribeca," Kate said. "She could use that when she wanted to stay in the city instead of commuting. I'm not suggesting that Rhiannon live there and Doug live at home—I'm not suggesting that at all—but there are ways to make it work if you want to. It's a lot to think about, and you don't need to make a decision right away. Tommy's running the day-to-day operations. He knows what he's doing, and I trust him to do it. Neither of us wants to see Joey's legacy fail, and I'm certainly not equipped to manage it. I'll do what's required of me, but there are other things I need to do as well."

She laced her fingers with Billy's.

"Give it some thought. You and Doug talk. Figure out what you want to do. You don't have to go back to school right away. You can go to work with Tommy and maybe in a few years, after the boys start kindergarten . . . Whatever you decide, we'll make it work."

CHAPTER SIXTY-ONE

Early Saturday evening, Kate ran through her mental checklist for the benefit. Again. Billy and C.J. had handled the performance and everything related to it, but the reception and meet and greet were all on her.

The gallery where the reception would be held looked beautiful. An exhibit of watercolor and pastel seascapes by a collective of Maine artists hung on the walls. After Billy had negotiated the purchase of one of her favorites, the gallery owner had donated the use of the space for the concert. High bar tables draped in autumn hues had been rented to accommodate the guests, and trays of hors d'oeuvres would be passed by resource center workers who had volunteered to serve as waiters.

Almost all of the food had been donated or sold to them at cost. Samatar had taken over the small kitchen at the gallery and was thrilled at the chance to flex his culinary muscles. He spent the better part of the day preparing fresh shrimp to be served on shaved ice, lobster thermidor in puff pastry cups, mini quiches, tiny flatbread pizzas with roasted garlic jam and blue cheese, small cups of butternut squash soup, and as a concession to the young people who would be attending, hamburger sliders with homemade pickles and ketchup. A cheese board anchored the center of the room near an enormous cornucopia Kate had decorated with fruits, nuts, gourds, and pumpkins.

"Wow."

Billy stood before her, looking pretty "wow" himself. Her heart did a little dance. He wore a black suit with a black button-down shirt, and his hair hung loose over his shoulders. He was still the most beautiful man she had ever seen.

"You look great," she said.

"You're not so bad yourself."

"You think?" She rested her hand on her hip, then did a full three-sixty. Her black velvet dress was short and formfitting, with ruched sides and a crisscross of satin ribbon over an inset of black and silver lace. The squared bodice was cut into a deep V in the center and stiffened to stand up. She gave it a tug. "Is it too low? I don't want to fall out."

Billy peeked into her décolleté and raised his hands. "No offense —and you know I adore your breasts, I worship them—but you'd need a little more than that to be in any danger of falling out of your dress."

She gave him a swat. "Yeah, but still."

"So are you ready?"

"Me? Are you ready?"

"I'm always ready."

She made a face. "Wait. What are we talking about?"

"Get your mind out of the gutter."

She slapped him again, playfully, although her face turned pink. "That's not what I meant—although . . ." She slipped her hands around his waist, tilted her face up, and rested her chin against his chest.

He brushed his lips over her forehead. "This is all you, you know. All this here tonight, it's all because of you."

"It was your idea."

"Because of you. You helped me see past the tip of my nose, Katie. You helped me see beyond myself."

She swallowed, afraid if she tried to speak, she'd end up crying.

"You okay?"

"I am." She smiled gamely. "How're the kids doing?"

Billy's music students from the resource center were scheduled to perform one of the songs he had taught them.

"They'll be fine. I gave them the 'picture everybody naked' speech. They liked that."

She rolled her eyes and laughed, but the tops of her ears were beginning to warm from the way he was looking at her. "You're picturing me naked, aren't you?"

He ran his teeth along the curve of her neck.

"Always."

CHAPTER SIXTY-TWO

The house lights dropped. When they came up again, her father stood center stage, bathed in a single blue light. It only took a few seconds for the boys to recognize him, but when they did, the house was quiet enough that when Dalton yelled "Poppy," everyone, including her father, heard him.

He leaned into the mic. "Hey, buddy!"

A general titter ran through the crowd. Some people applauded. Doug grimaced.

"No talking!" Rhiannon whispered into her son's ear. "You have to be quiet or we'll have to go home."

He nodded solemnly and settled on her lap. For the better part of the concert, he mirrored his brother's enthralled expression. When the audience applauded and cheered, the twins did too, with gusto.

As the concert wound down, her father switched out his Stratocaster for an acoustic guitar. After strapping it on, he stood in front of the mic and gazed out over the appreciative audience.

"The people you're going to meet next are part of the reason we're putting on this performance. I only met them about seven or eight weeks ago, and in that time, they've learned to play some instruments and sing, and it makes me really happy to show them off tonight. I'm going to give them a little bit of help, but it's mostly them."

Nine young teenagers filed onto the stage to thunderous applause. Some walked with a cocky swagger. Some were prodded on by the kid behind them. They looked nervous, but by the time the audience settled down, the smiles on their faces couldn't have been any wider. They performed a song by Gotye, with her father singing the lead opposite a teen decked out like a younger version of Janelle Monáe. Three other girls were singing backup, two boys played guitar, another one bass, one on keyboard, and another girl on drums. It was far from the best version she'd ever heard, but it wasn't bad. Not bad at all. The audience must have agreed. When the song ended, the response was enthusiastic. It was a good feeling, not only for the kids' sake, but for her parents' as well.

Grinning and waving, the young musicians took their bows and dispersed, leaving her father alone on the empty stage. He waited for the hall to quiet down before he began to speak.

"There are a lot of folks to thank tonight: everyone at the Portland Resource Center, all of the individuals and businesses that donated food and drinks, my band—who did not get paid—and my record label, which covered all of their expenses and then some." He beamed out at the audience. "And all of you for coming. It means a lot to me. It also means a lot to someone I want you to meet. She's the impetus behind all of this. She has the biggest heart of anyone I've ever known, although she's kind of a thief. She stole my heart twenty-five years ago, and she never gave it back. Ladies and gentlemen, my wife, Katie."

Dayton and Dalton clapped their pudgy hands and cheered. Rhiannon let loose an ear-splitting whistle, silencing her boys as well as her brother and her husband, who gaped at her. Guess she surprised them. She whooped and pumped her fist in the air as her mother made her way onto the stage. Her father met her halfway, dropped a kiss on her forehead, and together they walked to the mic.

For all her anger, resentment, and hurt, seeing them together on stage, so obviously in love, made her heart melt, along with what remained of the pain of the past year. And when her father called her mother "the love of my life," she was pretty much a puddle.

"We have one more song tonight, but before I get the band back out here, I want to tell you a little something about why what we're doing here tonight is so important." He looked at her mother. "You okay?" He spoke quietly, but his voice carried over the audio. She nodded, although she looked nervous.

"My dad was a huge baseball fan," he began. "So was I. In fact, I was a regular little Pedro Martinez."

Scattered cheers erupted at the name of the former Red Sox All-Star. Rhiannon stole a look at her brother. He looked as shell-shocked as she felt. It was the first time she'd ever heard their father mention his own father—and in front of several hundred strangers, no less.

"My father's prized possession was a Babe Ruth autographed baseball he kept in a plastic box. He never took that ball out of the box. I wasn't allowed to touch it, of course, and I didn't—until one day, when I was ten and trying to impress some new buddies, I brought it outside. Long story short, the ball ended up in a puddle, and the Babe's signature got smeared."

A chorus of groans echoed through the auditorium.

Through her dad's story, Rhiannon couldn't take her eyes off her brother. Devin had loved baseball. Not once could she recall their father going to one of his games, let alone playing a game of catch with him. The fact that he had been a Little League all-star yet shared none of that with his own son had to sting. Poor Devin. This had to hurt.

"It took about a week for my father to notice," her dad continued, "or at least a week before he let me know he noticed."

Other than the clearing of a throat or the creak of a chair, it was eerily silent.

"My father beat me that day. He beat me so badly I almost died."

A low murmur rippled through the hall. Her father waited for the audience to quiet, then looked down at her mother. She nodded.

"I had more than a dozen broken bones and a punctured lung, and I temporarily lost hearing in one ear. I can't even remember how many stitches I had. I spent several weeks in the hospital. I never saw my father again. My grandfather ran him off, told him never to come back. He took that baseball and my mother, who decided she loved a man who beat us both more than she loved me."

Dalton squirmed in Rhiannon's arms and knocked his heel against her shin.

"Ow!" he cried.

She hadn't realized how tightly she was holding him. She pressed a soft kiss against his cheek. "I'm sorry, sweetheart," she murmured. Neither of her children were angels, far from it, but to strike them? The fennel and goat cheese salad she'd enjoyed for dinner was threatening a repeat performance.

Doug shifted Dayton to one knee and settled Dalton on the other.

She leaned toward her brother and whispered, "Are you okay?"

His eyes looked wet. "No. You?"

She shook her head as her fingers curled around her brother's arm.

"After that, I was raised by my grandparents," he continued. "They thought I hung the moon, and I was lucky to have them. The thing is, abuse isn't only physical. There are children who suffer emotional or psychological abuse, which is harder to see because the scars are invisible. And it's even harder to stop because we don't always know it's happening."

He pulled her mother closer. "This woman—this beautiful, sensitive, kind, talented, funny, loving, wonderful woman—was emotionally abused for the first eighteen years of her life. She was belittled, degraded, punished, humiliated, criticized, yet both of her parents were long-standing, respected members of their community. She grew up believing that she was flawed somehow, that there was something wrong with her. It wasn't until she went away to college that she understood not everyone's parents treat their children like that."

Tears streamed down Rhiannon's face. People nearby were sniffling and dabbing at their eyes.

"Katie and I were ashamed of the lives we came from, so much so that not only did neither of us seek help, but we kept most of our pasts hidden from each other. Neither of us believed we were worthy of love. Neither of us believed that someone else could love us unconditionally."

His hand traveled up and down her mother's arm as he spoke. She'd never seen her father standing on a stage looking this uncomfortable. And no wonder. She had grown up knowing nothing about his childhood. She'd never even seen a picture. Yet here he stood, painting an image more vivid than any camera could have captured.

"The only real love Katie had growing up was from her best friend, Joey, but his life was no picnic either. He lost his mother when he was seven, and his father, an alcoholic, threw him out of the house as a teenager when he learned Joey was gay. But unlike Katie or me, Joey's confidence and ambition grew, and he went on to become a huge success. You might even have heard of him. Joey Buccacino. He was a stylist to some of the biggest names in Hollywood and New York, and he also owned several high-end boutiques and salons. He even designed his own line of accessories."

His voice softened. "Joey was shot during a robbery last year. He died a few hours later."

A ripple of gasps and murmurs moved through the hall.

"I'm not trying to win your sympathy," he said to the now somber audience. "In fact, I don't like telling these stories at all. But Katie and I decided to come forward so that you can understand how committed we are to this cause.

"At first, our goal was to raise some money to help purchase instruments and some other things for the kids from the resource center, like the ones you heard here tonight. But we think we can do more. We're hoping not only to partner with the resource center but also to create our own identity with a focus on kids like us.

"Tonight is the first step. I want to thank you for coming and helping us get this off the ground. It's our goal to continue special concerts like this one with other artists—I'm not naming names, but I think it's going to be pretty exciting. We're already grateful for your support, but if after hearing our story, you're moved to contribute a little more to the cause, we sure as hell won't turn you down. You can do so afterward at the reception, where I'm looking forward to meeting each and every one of you."

The applause began before he finished speaking.

Her mother, looking relieved her part was over, gave a wave and called out a loud "Thank you!" Then she blew a kiss toward her and Devin. Rhiannon wanted to reach up and grab it, like she'd done when she was a little girl, but she was still too stunned to move. Between everything she'd seen and heard the last few days, she felt as if she'd stepped onto an emotional landmine.

As her mother tried to head off the stage, her father tugged her back. A huge grin stretched across his face. "Not so fast. I have another confession to make."

Her mother laughed uncomfortably. "I think that's enough for one night."

"Just one more."

He adjusted the strap on his acoustic. "When I met Katie, she was an eighteen-year-old freshman at Rutgers hanging out in a bar with her roommate, both of them with fake IDs."

"Billy!" She swatted at him.

"To be fair, it was the first time she'd ever done anything like that."

The hall rumbled as the audience chuckled their disbelief.

"No, it's true. Her roommate got the IDs and then dragged her out on a Friday night. She had planned to stay in and finish reading *Beowulf,* right?"

Her mother rolled her eyes.

"Like I said, that night she stole my heart, but I swept her off her feet. She left school and ran off with me—and that, I'm not proud of, but I wouldn't change a thing. Until we started our family, I'd bring her to gigs with me. Because she was so young, there were times we knew a fake ID wouldn't fly, so"—he motioned to someone offstage —"she had to make like she was in the band to get in . . ."

Denny trotted onstage with a tambourine and handed it to her mother. The rest of the band followed, returning to their places on stage.

"And she did a pretty admirable job. She was my first backup singer too."

Rhiannon laughed. The idea of her mother as a backup singer was almost impossible to imagine, although looking at her right now, it seemed the most natural thing in the world.

"We're gonna end with a song I think is appropriate for this evening and one that fills me with hope. It was written by my friend John Rzeznik, and it's been sung many times to express hope in our future and the possibility for change. I don't think he'll mind that we're sharing it here tonight."

KATE'S HANDS WERE SHAKING, and for a second, she thought she might throw up. Yes, she'd done this in the past, but sadly, it had always been with some kind of drug or alcohol in her system. It had also been a long, long time ago.

At the back of the room, Rhiannon and Devin were already on their feet. Rhiannon whistled, and Devin flashed her the thumbs-up. Her eyes grew teary and the audience grew fuzzy—probably not a bad thing, since she was so nervous her knees had to be banging together.

Denny counted out the rhythm. The piano followed. With a nod from Billy, she tapped the tambourine against her palm, and he began to sing.

And you ask me what I want this year
And I try to make this kind and clear
Just a chance that maybe we'll find better days
'Cause I don't need boxes wrapped in strings
And designer love and empty things
Just a chance that maybe we'll find better days
So take these words
And sing out loud
'Cause everyone is forgiven now
'Cause tonight's the night the world begins again
I need someplace simple where we could live
And something only you can give
And that's faith and trust and peace while we're alive
And the one poor child who saved this world
And there's ten million more who probably could
If we all just stopped and said a prayer for them

Kate hadn't stood this close to Billy on a stage since she was eighteen, and she was loving the view. Strands of damp, golden hair curled over the collar of his black shirt. A fine sheen of sweat glistened on his face. His lips, which could drive her crazy in so many ways, pressed against the mic as he sang. Here was her heart, all six feet, four inches of him. Her soulmate. She couldn't love him more if she tried.

Billy tilted his head, smiled, and leaned away from the mic.

"C'mon, babe, last verse. Sing it with me."

The audience was on its feet, ready to join in the final chorus of the Goo Goo Dolls hit. She caught sight of her family rushing the stage, led by Rhiannon and flanked by security staffers, arms raised and cheering. Within moments, they were all up there beside her and Billy, even Doug and the twins, singing loudly and clapping to the final chorus.

So take these words

And sing out loud
'Cause everyone is forgiven now
'Cause tonight's the night the world begins again

The applause was thunderous. Kate reached for Billy as he swung his guitar to his side and grabbed her around the waist. In front of all those people, he bent her backward and kissed her.

"Better days, babe!" he yelled as the crowd's cheering surged. "Better days."

CHAPTER SIXTY-THREE

It hardly seemed possible, but hours after the concert, Kate was still running on adrenaline.

"I can't believe you're still awake." Billy yawned as he handed her a cup of herbal tea.

"I know." She savored the warmth of the mug in her hands, inhaling the soothing floral scent. The chill coursing through her might be more from exhaustion than the actual temperature, but her mind refused to wind down.

Billy sat beside her with a cup of his own, put his arm around her, and pulled her close. She snuggled into him.

"We should get a gas fireplace," he said. "Then we could just flip a switch and have a roaring fire."

He yawned again.

"True, but a wood fire smells so nice."

He kissed the top of her head. They stared at the empty hearth, too excited to go to bed yet too exhausted to do anything else. The room was dark, other than the flicker of a candle in the center of the coffee table—her concession to the effort of making an actual fire.

"Mom? Daddy?" Rhiannon had come up the stairs so quietly Kate hadn't heard her.

"Hey, baby," Billy said. "How come you're still awake? Everything okay?"

"Yeah. I couldn't sleep." She sat on the sofa across from them.

"You want some tea?" he asked.

She shook her head. "I just wanted to tell you both how proud I am." She fidgeted with the sash of her robe. "I had no idea. What you did tonight, sharing your stories . . . You put yourselves out there. I think the response will be tremendous."

"Thank you, sweetie," Kate said. "It wasn't easy, but if it helps other kids, it was worth it."

"I think it will. I think tonight was a great start, and if you can do that a couple of times a year, I think you'll realize your dream in a very short time."

This new warmth from her daughter melted some of Kate's chilliness. "I hope so."

Rhiannon reached into the pocket of her robe and pulled out a slip of paper, which she handed to Kate. "In the meantime, here's a check from Doug and me."

She was dumbfounded. "Five thousand dollars?"

"Baby girl, that's too much," Billy said.

Rhiannon waved them off. "No, it's not. I've dropped more than that on a handbag."

"Rhiannon!" She shouldn't have been shocked by that revelation, but she was.

"I know, but hey—I may be a style maven some day, right? I have to look good."

A surge of hope rushed through her. "You've decided, then?"

"Not yet. Uncle Joey and I had talked about it a few times, you know . . . Before. So it's always been in the back of my mind. I just figured after he was gone, it was no longer an option." She shrugged. "And I guess I always thought he was just being nice."

Kate laughed. "When was Joey ever just being nice?"

"When he was dealing with me?" Billy said, but he was laughing too.

"Oh, stop." Kate poked him playfully. "He liked you. He just had a hard time accepting that you were good enough for me. He would've hated anyone."

He pressed his lips against her temple. "He was right. I'll never be good enough for you, but I'll keep trying."

"Well," Rhiannon said gruffly, "before you two start making out . . ."

"Sorry," Billy said. "Is there something else?"

She nodded. "Doug spoke with his dad. The firm will also be making a donation—a substantial one—to . . . whatever you call your foundation."

Kate hadn't thought that far ahead. "I guess we should come up with a name, shouldn't we?"

Billy looked surprised. "Really? I thought this was a no-brainer."

No-brainer? They hadn't even discussed it. "Why? What do you want to call it?"

"Joey's Place. What else?"

It was perfect. So perfect she couldn't form the words to say so.

"That's a great idea," Rhiannon cried, echoing what she would have said if she could have found her tongue.

Since her hand already rested on Billy's thigh, Kate gave it a squeeze.

"Doug and I have also been talking about something else," Rhiannon continued. "We'd like to host Christmas this year."

Kate and Billy exchanged glances.

"I mean it. You've got a lot going on, and we wouldn't want to take the boys away for the holiday. I want us to be together, and you know Devin will want to see Danielle, so coming up here again would be hard for him."

"That sounds terrific," Billy said. "But who's doing the cooking? I'm not eating anything made out of beans."

Rhiannon looked hopeful. "Mom?"

She smiled. "I'll be happy to cook—but I'm not cleaning up."

"I'll help, I promise. I need to learn how to cook something edible anyway. The boys can clean up."

"Dayton and Dalton?" Billy asked, teasing.

She waggled her eyebrows at him. "The bigger boys: you, Devin, and Doug."

"I can live with that."

"Me too," said Kate.

Rhiannon rocked back and tucked a long, blond strand of hair behind her ear. "Daddy, would you mind if I talked with Mom alone?"

He squeezed Kate's leg as he stood. "I was just heading to bed." He leaned over and kissed her. "In case I'm asleep when you come in."

He kissed the top of Rhiannon's head as he passed. When he was gone, she moved next to Kate on the sofa.

"I'm sorry, Mom."

Her beautiful girl. "Sweetheart, for what?"

"Everything. For years of stuff, I guess." She was looking up at the ceiling as if collecting her thoughts. "Somewhere along the way, I built Daddy up in my mind as some kind of hero, and I just saw you as someone who got in the way. All little girls fall in love with their dads, I guess, but I worshiped him. I was wrong. I realized that this past year. I love him, don't get me wrong. But he was never the hero. It took me awhile to realize that was your job. I just didn't realize it until you were gone."

Kate settled her hands on Rhiannon's shoulders. "Oh baby, I'm nobody's hero."

"You are, Mom. Tonight reconfirmed it. You're amazing. You always have been. I stopped seeing it at some point, and I'm sorry about that."

"If you want to think of me as some type of hero, I'm flattered. Unworthy, but flattered."

"You're my hero. I also want to apologize for getting so angry with you when we arrived. I was shocked and embarrassed that everyone knew except me, but I get it now. Obviously you knew how I would react, so you were right to wait and tell me the way you did. I'm sorry it's taken me this long to apologize. I mean, I was in tears half the way up here because I was convinced Daddy was going to tell us that he'd found someone new, and then here you were, and I flew off into a huff." She ducked her head. "I was just thinking about myself. I'm sorry."

Too overcome with emotion to speak, she squeezed Rhiannon's hand.

"But even though I'm sorry about having you committed last year, I'm not sorry I did it. I may not have handled it the right way, and I should've told Daddy immediately . . . I'm sure he already told you about that."

"You did what you thought was right, and like I told you, you saved my life. You and Uncle Joey."

Rhiannon nodded. "Oh! That reminds me."

She reached into the pocket of her robe.

"I found this earlier today. It's the strangest thing. It was tucked behind a book I pulled out. I meant to give it to you this afternoon, but I forgot about it."

She dropped something into Kate's hand.

Before she could see it, Kate could feel it. Cool and solid. Her fingers closed around the roughly polished edges, remembering exactly how its weight had felt when Joey had pressed it into her palm. She squeezed harder, afraid if she opened her hand, it might disappear again.

Her mind reeled with a million thoughts and images, but now she held them all in her hand—a sea glass heart, picked up by her dearest friend and destined for her.

"Where . . ." Kate's throat had gone dry. "Where did you find this?"

"On the shelf over there." Rhiannon walked to the bookshelf in the far corner of the room and switched on the lamp.

Kate blinked at the sudden rush of light.

Rhiannon pulled a book from the shelf. "Here it is: *Romeo and Juliet*."

She handed the book to Kate. It was an expensive edition, red leather with gold embossing.

"There's a message inside." She kissed Kate's cheek. "I love you, Mom. I'll see you in the morning."

"I love you too, and thank you. For everything."

Kate stared at her closed fist, feeling the hard edges of the glass bite into her palm. She opened her hand slowly. It was exactly how she remembered. A frosted piece of sea glass shaped like a heart. It was pale pink, exactly like the one Joey had given her in her dream. Her heart stuttered as she closed her fingers around it again. How could it be?

With the heart clenched in her fist, she opened *Romeo and Juliet*. Written on the inside was an inscription in a handwriting as familiar as her own. It was dated May 16, 2012.

MY DEAREST KATE,

Chances are if you're reading this, I'm no longer with you. Losing my mother suddenly at such a young age, I've always been aware of my own mortality, and it made me realize it could happen to me just as easily. I never wanted to leave without being able to say goodbye.

So this house? Something else, am I right? I hope you love it as much as I think you will. Some of my most treasured memories were made with you in Maine when we were children, so that's why I bought you this house. As I write this, I'm hoping we'll have decades of new memories to make right here.

So why Romeo and Juliet? *First of all, I know you love this book and will pick it up to read again. Second, it's a love story, duh! And third, it's a tragedy. Now, you might be getting annoyed with me at this point, but let me finish. I don't mean to say your love story is a tragedy. Quite the contrary. You and the rock star are perfect for each other. Although it was one of my greatest joys in life to give him a hard time, I know you love him and I know he loves you—worships you, which is as it should be. Please tell him I said so and that I hope he forgives me for all the little digs at his expense over the years. He would always turn such a delicious shade of red when he got mad. I just couldn't help myself.*

If I'm not there to tell you myself, I pray that the rest of your lives will be long and happy and filled with love.

And even though you might not see me, I'm here. I won't ever be far away. Listen for my laughter in the tinkle of the wind chimes. When you feel a breeze lifting off the ocean, close your eyes and imagine my kiss on your cheek. When you look up to the night sky, imagine the stars are millions of tiny holes I've poked in the earth's canopy to shine heaven down upon you.

If you forget my smile, turn to page 245, where I've enclosed a photograph. (In this case, there are no substitutions!)

I hope I made you smile, and maybe shed a tear or two as well, just because. Always remember me, Kate, and remember how much I love you. You were the best thing that ever happened to me. And when the time comes, I'll be waiting on the other side.

Until then . . .

Joey

THE BOOK SHOOK in her trembling hands as she turned to page 245, which was marked with a silk ribbon. Sure enough, there they were: her and Joey in Central Park, smiling, their heads close together, her arms flung around his neck. She was looking at Joey, and his eyes were fixed on the camera, filled with devilish merriment. She remembered the day Billy had snapped that photo, but she'd never seen it before.

Her finger gently caressed her best friend's face as her other hand tightened around the piece of glass. She closed the book, slipped it back into its spot on the shelf, and stood at the window looking out into the velvet night.

The moon was barely a sliver, hanging in a sky studded with a million stars. Was he looking down at her right now?

"Everything okay?"

Billy stood behind her, half asleep. Her heart thudded with joy, and a welcome sense of peace washed over her.

She stretched out her hand and nodded.

"Then why the tears?" he asked, wiping them away with his thumbs.

"Happy tears."

"Good."

"Dance with me."

"There's no music," he said as he gathered her in his arms, still warm from their bed, and slowly rocked her to and fro.

"Sure there is," she said. "There's always music."

She closed her eyes, and as they danced, the wind chimes outside the window tinkled.

Like laughter on a breeze.

THE END

THANK you for reading *ALL I EVER WANTED*! I hope you've loved Kate and Billy's story, but guess what? It isn't over yet! *The Of Love and Madness* Series continues in *BETTER MAN*!

Whoever said *change is good* should have their head examined.

As far as Billy McDonald is concerned, he's changed enough for one lifetime. Life should be easier now. Smooth sailing. No surprises, right?

Not so fast. Katie wants him to become a father—again.

As the saying goes, been there, done that. He sucked the first time around, and as far as he's concerned, you don't get a do-over.

After everything they've been through and all they've fought to overcome, could this be the one thing they can't get past?

One-click BETTER MAN now!

NOTE TO READERS

Reviews are important to independent authors. If you decide to leave a review after you've read this book, please email me a link to your review at authorkarencimms@gmail.com, and I'll send you a bookmark as a thank you.

You can find the playlist for *ALL I EVER WANTED* here: https://spoti.fi/3zZmcks

You can find the Pinterest board for *ALL I EVER WANTED* here: https://bit.ly/3frnvzi

ACKNOWLEDGMENTS

I think the most difficult part of writing these acknowledgements is knowing that Billy and Kate's story is just about over. I have lived with them, and Joey, just about every waking moment—and some non-waking moments—since the summer of 2013. I don't know that I'll ever create two characters that I love as much as Billy and Kate, which is probably the main reason they get one more chapter in the form of a Christmas novella.

I hope their story touched you as well.

Over the course of the past few years there have been many people who have helped me get to this point. For some, saying "thank you" hardly seems like enough, but believe me when I say it is said with much love. I hope I don't miss anyone. Here goes.

Thank you to my critique group whose input can be felt on every page of this book. We were randomly connected, but like soulmates, it was meant to be. We've been through sickness, health, tears, and laughter. David L. Williams, Gretchen Anthony, and Laura Broullire, you three have carved a special place in my heart.

To my beta readers for all three books: Patty Morgan, Diane Lane Stone, Ace Leccese, Beth Yaroszeufski, Amber McKenney, Allison Hart, Dena Williams, Sally McGarry, and Rhonda Donaldson. Thank you.

A very special thanks to Tyra Hattersley, Ann Travis, and Lydia Fasteland for your detailed feedback and suggestions.

Lori Ryser, you are amazing. I have to keep wondering what I did to deserve you. I'm not sure I can ever truly express my gratitude for your input and your exceptional proofreading skills, but I'll keep trying.

Garrett Cimms, thanks for another amazing cover design, and Olka Cimms, thanks for being our cover model. Sorry we had to edit out Stickman. And Jade Eby, thank you for another awesome interior design.

Karla Sorensen and Kerry Palumbo, you don't even know each other, but as far as I'm concerned, you two are the dynamic duo of back-cover blurbs. Thank you.

Whitney Barbetti, you are not only one of my favorite authors, you are a wonderful, kind, generous person. You have helped me in so many ways. I don't know that I can ever truly thank you enough. If it weren't for you, I'm not sure very many people would even know about my books. You are forever in my heart.

To my family in Maine, especially Amy and Bob. Thank you for giving me and Kate a second home. You know my heart is always there. And Sally, thanks for sharing Ramona.

Nancy Blaha, thank you for helping me believe in myself. You might hear your words on some of these pages. It's not a coincidence.

Liz Vigue, thank you for your ongoing encouragement and support, and for telling me about Pedro Martinez.

Sue Johnston, thanks for sharing your beautiful photo with me. You're an amazing photographer.

Jena Camp, thanks for your amazing teasers and for getting the word out about all my books.

Nick Denmon, thanks for allowing me to share your perfect words for my epigraph. Your work speaks to me.

Thank you John Rzeznik of the Goo Goo Dolls for "Better Days." If I didn't know better, I'd think you wrote it for *All I Ever Wanted*.

To my children: Karen, Margaux, Garrett, and Amanda, thank you for being you and for allowing me to be me. I love you.

And all my love and gratitude to my husband and favorite lead guitarist, Jim. Without your love and support, I would still be thinking how much I'd like to write a book someday. I couldn't do this without you.

Thank you to the bloggers who have read my books, posted reviews, and shared my work. You guys are the best.

And to the readers. I'm truly honored every time you pick up one of my books. Thank you for making my dreams come true.

TURN THE PAGE FOR AN EXCLUSIVE
SNEAK PEEK OF:

BETTER MAN

Book four in Karen Cimms'
Of Love and Madness series

CHAPTER 1

"No more!" Kate cried, raising the Veuve Clicquot to her lips. "If I didn't know better, I'd say you were trying to get me drunk."

Billy grinned and brandished the bottle in a triumphant toast. They didn't normally keep alcohol in the house, but his magnificent wife deserved to be feted. The ribbon-cutting had included light fare, but he was determined that her efforts deserved the best, even if she'd all but given up drinking in solidarity with his sobriety.

"C'mon, Mom," Devin said. "You earned it."

Kate scrunched her shoulders and gave a little shiver, clearly embarrassed by the attention.

Billy slipped his arm around her slim waist and drew her closer. She'd done it—she'd turned the old storefront they'd purchased in downtown Portland into a counseling and after-school center for disadvantaged youths and temporary shelter for runaways. If there was any way he could be more proud of her at this moment, he didn't know how. What she'd accomplished in a year was astonishing.

"Because of you,"—Devin tipped his glass in Billy's direction —"and Dad, kids in Portland have a shot at getting help." He slipped

Charlie a piece of cheddar from the tray on the coffee table and gave the yellow Lab a scratch behind the ears. "You know, when you guys came up with this idea and held that first benefit concert last Thanksgiving, I never thought you'd be able to make it happen so quickly. I'm proud of you—both of you."

Billy set down the champagne and raised his glass of sparkling cider. The others followed his lead: Devin, Rhiannon, and Doug, as well as Tom, and Billy's manager, C.J. It was a salute to the love of his life, the woman who'd not only made him a better man but brought opportunities to kids struggling to overcome the same kind of crappy start in life that he himself had once moved past.

"To my wife," he said, "who sows seeds of love in everything she does. May the young people who come to Joey's Place be nurtured and encouraged, and may they blossom and grow under the warmest, brightest sunshine—my Katie."

Kate's cheeks pinked from the smattering of applause, cheers, and shouts of "Bravo" and "Speech!" or perhaps from the champagne. Didn't matter what caused it. It was as adorable as when they'd first met more than twenty-five years ago.

"Go ahead, babe, say something," he said.

After a fortifying gulp of champagne, she tucked a strand of dark, shoulder-length hair behind her ear and braced herself. "Okay, but only because I want to thank all of you again. Without your help, we couldn't have made this happen. Being able to create a safe place for these kids and get them the help they need is a dream come true for me, and for that, and for helping keep Joey's memory alive, I'm so very grateful."

She lifted her glass before continuing. "And to Joey, who I love as much today as I did before he left us. I'd give anything for him to be standing here with us tonight, but in my heart, in this house, I can feel him the same as always. So please join me in raising your glasses and toasting our dear fried, Joey Bucca-CHEEE-no!"

A loud chorus of *Bucca-CHEEE-no* rang out, followed by peals of laughter. Joey would've loved it.

Her eyes filled and damn it, so did Billy's. Joey's Place had become a dream of his too. While he'd begun by facilitating a somewhat steady revenue stream for the burgeoning center by hosting concerts and calling on friends in the music industry to join him, working beside her on the project had become almost cathartic. How could he not think about the past? The thought of any kid suffering at the hands of one of their parents made him want to hurt someone. No amount of counseling or anger management classes would ever change that.

But thanks to Katie, kids who were abused, neglected, abandoned, or disowned by the people who were supposed to love them would get the support they needed. It was a miracle his pride hadn't sent the buttons of his shirt flying, his chest had puffed out so far.

Pressing an open palm to her heart, she continued. "Rhiannon and Doug, you guys have been beyond generous with your donations, and Ree, the fashion show helped us not only meet our goal but exceed it. Without that extra boost, it would've been another six months before we opened."

She turned to Tommy, and Billy gave her a little pat of encouragement as tears spilled over her smile at her late friend's lover.

"And Tommy, I know this testament to Joey means as much to you as it does to us, so while I understand you're not interested in or expecting any thanks, I'm saying it anyway. Thank you. If we'd had to pay an attorney for the billable hours you've dedicated, we wouldn't be open yet."

She next set her sights on C.J. "And Gavin McManus? Really?" Pressing the back of her hand to her forehead, she faked a swoon.

Billy pretended to push her away in disgust. "Okay, okay, we know you love Rogue." Kate was a devoted fan of the Irish rock icon.

She wrapped her arms around his waist but focused on his manager. "I'm still pinching myself that you convinced the lead singer from one of my favorite bands to come to Portland for a benefit concert for Joey's Place. You are the absolute best."

C.J. lapped up the accolades. "Eh, I'm friends with Rogue's

manager. They were coming to Boston—it was worth a shot. As soon as Gavin heard all the proceeds would benefit the kids, he was eager to help. I think if we'd had a bigger venue, he would've brought the whole band."

Billy groaned. "Awww, C.J., don't tell her that. If she thinks she might get to meet Conor Quinn too—well, there's no telling what she might do." He smiled down at Katie. "She claims I'm her favorite lead guitarist, but I'm pretty sure it's Quinn."

"Pretty sure?"

He clutched his chest. "Baby, why you gotta be so cold?"

"I can only deal with one lead-guitarist-sized ego in my life." She gave him a consoling pat on the chest. "You're it for me, babe."

"Well, thank god for that."

"And on that note," Tom said, setting his glass on the coffee table, "I think C.J. and I should be heading back to our hotel. It's late, and we have an early flight in the morning. We'll see you in New York next month, right?"

Billy raised his eyebrows. "New York?"

"I forgot to tell you," Kate said. "Tom's having a cocktail party at the loft in Tribeca the Sunday before Christmas. Since we're already heading to Rhiannon and Doug's, I figured we'd spend a night in the city, go to Rockefeller Plaza and see the tree. Do some last-minute shopping."

"We're going too," Rhiannon said. "The party's mainly for execs and a few others from Pizzazz."

"C.J.'s coming," Tom added.

C.J. snatched up Tom's discarded flute. "Um, right. We should be going." He carried the glasses into the kitchen.

C.J. was usually a regular ballbuster, sarcastic as hell. This was the first time Billy had seen him flustered. He glanced at Kate, who arched an eyebrow as she pulled their coats from the hall closet. Clearly, he wasn't the only one who'd noticed.

Kate gave Tom a long hug while Billy shook C.J.'s hand.

"Look, I have some things I need to firm up, but I should have some news on new tour dates by the end of the next week," C.J. said, leaning in and lowering his voice. "I know you weren't planning on anything until next summer, but Rogue's interested in having you join their tour starting in late April. If this pans out, you might want to give me a raise."

"Doubtful," Billy said. But opening for Rogue's world tour? Yeah, C.J. would definitely deserve a raise, not that he was willing to admit it.

C.J. winked. "We'll see."

Billy slapped him on the back, returned Tom's side hug, and waved as they bolted down the sidewalk toward their rental car, hurrying to escape the wintry blast blowing off the ocean. He closed the door to find Rhiannon in the doorway to the kitchen, arms folded over her chest, her eyes narrowed.

"Is it just me," she said, "or is anyone else suspicious that something's going on between those two?"

"Suspicious how?" Doug asked.

"I'm not sure *suspicious* is the word I'd use." Kate blew past carrying a picked-over tray of sliced fruit.

Billy grabbed a grape on her way by. "I'm with Rhiannon. I think C.J. actually blushed when Tom said they needed to get back to their hotel."

"Yep," Rhiannon replied, loudly popping the *p*. "And during the reception, they went off by themselves, heads bent together, all whispery and stuff."

Doug chuckled. "Whispery and stuff? What does that even mean?"

"It means they're sharing secrets. Or something."

"Or something," Billy repeated. "I didn't want to come out and ask, at least not tonight with everyone around, but I got the same vibe."

"Well, if you ask me, it's about time." Kate bustled past with the rest of the glasses and the empty bottle of Veuve. "Tom deserves to be happy, and if that person is C.J., I'm all for it."

Devin snickered. "Don't you think you're getting a little ahead of yourselves? They've become friends through you and Dad. They both live in New York. They flew up together, shared a rental car, and stayed in the same hotel. That says convenience, not relationship."

"Maybe. But wouldn't it be wonderful?" Kate answered. "C'mon, Billy. In all the time that C.J. has worked for you, has he ever been in a relationship that would result in him introducing us to someone?"

"Other than the infamous Ramona Chinchilla Deville?" He laughed at the memory of Kate in a red wig, posing as C.J.'s date at Billy's first concert in Portland last year. "He *still* hasn't introduced us to anyone."

"Maybe the timing's not right." She propped her hip against the counter and tapped a finger against her lips. "We should invite them up for a long weekend after the holidays. We could go skiing up at Sunday River."

"You're all projecting," Devin said. "Except Doug, of course."

Doug fist-bumped Devin. "Thank you. I try to be the voice of reason whenever I can."

"Ditto, brother."

Rhiannon frowned at her husband, so he planted a quick kiss on the top of her head.

"And on that note, if I know what's good for me, I'm heading off to bed," Doug said. "The twins are sure to give us an early start. I'll see you all in the morning. You coming, babe?"

Rhiannon kissed her parents and gave her brother a tender pop on the shoulder. "Right behind you."

Once Doug and Rhiannon retired downstairs and Devin headed for the guest room, only the two of them remained. Billy stifled a yawn. Kate had to be exhausted after a week getting ready for the ribbon-cutting. To save money, she'd prepared most of the refreshments herself, with a little help from her friend Samatar.

Yet despite all that, she was glowing. Beautiful. And strong. She was still his Katie, but fiercer. During their time apart, she'd faced down the fears foisted upon her by Joey's death and a mass shooting. It was hard to admit, but maybe their time apart had been well spent. She'd tackled her demons, and he'd faced down his own—the drugs and alcohol, the anger, all his weaknesses. It had been hard work, but they'd done it. They were stronger than ever.

And Katie? Katie was his fucking hero.

She wiped her hands on a dish towel and flipped off the kitchen light, then sidled up to him. Reaching up on her tiptoes, she kissed his chin. "What about you, rock star? You too tired?"

He gripped her hips and pulled her closer, close enough for her to know he wasn't that tired after all. Having Katie in his arms gave him a second wind—and he planned to show her, too.

"Rock star? Not tonight, baby." He planted the first of many more kisses on her forehead. "After all you've done for those kids and all they'll gain in the future, the only rock star I see is you."

One-click BETTER MAN now!

ABOUT THE AUTHOR

Karen Cimms is a writer, editor, and music lover. She was born and raised in New Jersey and still thinks of the Garden State as home. She began her career at an early age rewriting the endings to her favorite books. It was a mostly unsuccessful endeavor, but she likes to think she invented fanfiction.

Karen is a lifelong Jersey corn enthusiast, and is obsessed with (in no particular order) books, shoes, dishes, and Brad Pitt. In her spare time she likes to quilt, decorate, and entertain. Just kidding–she has no spare time.

Although she loves pigeons, she is terrified of pet birds, scary movies, and Mr. Peanut.

Karen is married to her favorite lead guitar player. Her children enjoy tormenting her with countless mean-spirited pranks because they love her. She currently lives in Northeast Pennsylvania, although her heart is usually in Maine.

MORE BOOKS BY KAREN CIMMS

Of Love and Madness Series

At This Moment
We All Fall Down
Better Man
You're All I Want for Christmas (a holiday novella)

Calendar Girl Duet
Miss February
Mrs. February

Standalone Books
Love, Lies, and Lattes (formerly Broadway Beans)

www.karencimms.com

Made in the USA
Middletown, DE
09 May 2022